A visit . . .

He smiled. 'I'm not really meant to be nere.'

Covering her mouth to hide the cheeky grin, she said, 'I know that. A man should never enter a woman's bedroom without permission.'

'I thought you'd be asleep.'

'Did you come to harm me?' Her tone dropped to a hushed whisper.

'No, no. Don't be afraid. I'm visiting, from the future.'

'The future?' She laughed and picked up her brush, pretended to smack him. 'Naughty boy, that's the best excuse I've ever heard.'

'I should go.'

'Oh, please, don't go, not yet.' She whirled round to face him. 'Stay awhile and talk with me. The party was such fun and I'm still buzzing from all the excitement. I shall never sleep, you know.'

'Was it a Christmas party?'

'Of course. Daddy throws the best parties ever.' She sighed. 'Why didn't you come? Didn't you get an invitation?'

He shook his head. 'Another time, maybe.'

'Next year,' she promised, then frowned and pouted. 'You will visit, in-between, won't you?'

'I don't think that will be possible. I really do come from your future...'

And danger . . .

'Jake, did you leave your front door open?'

'What?' Talbot swung round and stared at the front door. He'd shut it, locked it, and now it was half-open. Shit. 'Stay put,' he ordered, leapt out of the car and ran across the garden.

Ducking down under the hall window, he reached round, pressed his fingertips against the door and eased it open a fraction wider. A sound from inside, a flicker of torch light shimmering up the wall, searching. His heart lurched. Wrong move. He swallowed hard, crouched down and pressed his back against the wall. Running was the only option. Not yet. Listen. A boot scrunched on broken glass. It stopped, shifted in the dark. One person? Two? The narrow beam of light drifted out as far as the front door step. Talbot held his breath. A voice, low, masculine, whispering. Time to run.

He did no more than lift his head and the shot whizzed past.

VISITING LILLY

TONI ALLEN

Booktrope Editions
Seattle WA 2014

Cover Design by Greg Simanson
Edited by C J Wyckoff

This is a work of fiction. Names, characters, places, brands, media, and incidents are either the product of the author's imagination or are used fictitiously. Any resemblance to similarly named places or to persons living or deceased is unintentional.

Print ISBN 978-1-62015-399-4
EPUB ISBN 978-1-62015-409-0

Library of Congress Control Number: 2014916571

The wipers swung from side to side, clearing the windscreen, then chasing back after the rain drops before they covered the glass. Just like detective work, one minute there was clarity, and the next it was peppered with confusion again.

Time didn't exist, time went one way and then another, depending on which way round the world one flew. One could travel backwards in time. Hayward's spirit travelled backwards in time. Lilly grew old. Time collided, met itself coming the other way.

1

FRANKIE STOOD IN THE RAIN. It had started out mild, but a driving wind had kicked up, and now he was freezing cold. He stared at the building, looked up and across the windows, wondering which room she was in. He'd rehearsed what to say a hundred times over, but that had been in his head, in his imagination. The nursing home had been built in the sixties, straight lined, pebble-dashed—no character. In the rain the building looked grim. The idea of going inside was daunting, and for the past hour his courage had failed him. He dug his hands into his pockets. He'd bought new clothes especially for the occasion, a pair of black jeans, a chestnut brown sweater, and some leather shoes, not trainers. He knew she'd like the shoes, polished and smart; but they didn't look smart anymore. It was silly standing there getting wet with no umbrella and his waterproof left in the car. He was supposed to go straight in, only it wasn't happening as he'd planned. His nerve had failed him.

He walked round the block a couple of times, and at the end of his third lap strode up to the front door of Mellow Acres Residential Home for the Elderly and pushing it open, stepped inside.

A young woman in a white blouse sat behind a long curved desk, the open magazine apparently of more interest than the red light flashing on the switchboard. Waterlogged, the sleeves on his sweater stretched down over his hands, and she stared at them as she spoke.

'Yes?'

He approached the desk. 'I've come to visit Lilly.' His jaw quivered. From the cold? From fear? He clamped it shut.

'Lilly who?' She adjusted a computer screen and hovered painted finger nails over a keyboard, ready to type.

'Mrs Lillian Charteris.'

'And your name is?'

'I'm her grandson.'

The young woman looked him in the eye. 'I asked your name.'

This was the moment that Frankie had dreaded. Her irritation, the slight flare of her nostrils, the need for a name.

'Francis.' He attempted a smile.

'Francis who?'

'Charteris.' Swallowing down the lie, he held his breath and counted.

She tapped the keys, read the screen, and frowned. 'Your name isn't here.'

'Well, I'm sure she'd be pleased to see me.' He kept very still, dripped water into the deep pile of the carpet.

'I'm sorry, I can't let you see her.' She gave a small, sympathetic shrug. 'Mr Charteris has insisted that we only let in named visitors. Apparently there was some issue at her previous home. I'm sure that if you speak to him your name can be added.'

Frankie nodded and hoped she would go away for a minute. If she would go and fix her make-up or something, then he could quickly glance at the screen and see who was on her list. If only. She was smiling at him, waiting, because he was the one who was supposed to leave. From the far end of the vestibule the sound of feet hurrying down a stone staircase attracted her attention. Frankie glanced instead towards the front door. A prickly sixth sense told him his exit was going to be swift. He started off moving slowly, but when the man who burst out from the bottom of the stairwell instantly recognised him and yelled, 'Hey, you!' Frankie ran, yanked the door open, and nearly collided with a man in a wheelchair.

'Sorry,' he shouted out, more for not holding the door open than for bumping into the invalid, and took off down the street.

'Hey, you!'

There he was again, right behind him, running, hardly out of breath at all. 'I've warned you to stay away!'

The man's voice chased him for a mile through puddles and across busy roads, down alleyways and up narrow side streets. Relentless, but then Peter Charteris had always pursued him with vigour. 'I'll get you!' were the last words Frankie heard him shout before a lorry thundered past, churning a tidal wave up over the kerb and soaking him through.

Frankie assumed that he'd lost him; that Peter Charteris had given up and decided to go back and get out of the rain. Assumptions were demons, they tricked the mind into false realities that suited one's desires. For half an hour he walked around in the rain, looking, hunting, sensing the hairs on his neck twitch as if someone were watching him.

In the end he went home.

THE VICTORIAN TOWN HOUSE in Farnham had been left to him by his grandmother. She had loved him; she had understood him. The only thing he'd had to pay for was a garage he'd bought up around the corner, somewhere to keep his car off the road so that it didn't lose its sparkle. He didn't mind the short walk to his house, or the six concrete steps that led up to the front door. In fact he rather liked them—they gave the place a feeling of grandeur; and since he'd painted the front door burgundy and replaced the number eleven with shiny brass fittings, he thought it looked traditional and splendid.

Seeing it lifted his spirits a little after his failed attempt at visiting Lilly, but the hall felt damp and smelt musty, and he knew the central heating had packed up again. Damn, why did it always go wrong in winter? Kicking off his shoes he padded along the corridor and into the kitchen, where he stripped off all of his clothes, including his boxers, and threw them in the bin. They were soaked, ruined, and to see them again would only remind him of today's bitter fiasco. He wanted to cry. Straight from the packet, the white boxers had smelt fresh and made his pulse race with anticipation. They would never have got that far, he knew that, but he had to dream… or there was nothing.

Before going upstairs to dry his hair and find a robe, he flicked the kettle on to make a warm drink. Goosebumps were erupting on his skin, and a course wind was howling under the back door and rattling the cat flap, making him shiver. His feet were frozen. Tomorrow he would get a new wind stop, one of those ones with brushes on the bottom, and a couple of new magnets for Millie's cat flap. Yes, he would do that, concentrate on practical issues.

Millie was curled up on his bed, a purring ball of tortoiseshell fluff who felt so soft as he lifted her up to his naked body. To have the warmth of something alive next to his skin was what he craved. If only it were Lilly. He'd chosen Millie because of her ginger markings, those two front paws, and the impressionist splashes across the black on her back. They were the colour of Lilly's hair, auburn, not ginger at all.

'Do you really see her—all of this—in colour?' Dr Weissman had asked.

'Of course.'

Dr Weissman had smiled, clicked his teeth, written something down, and told Frankie it was time to finish the session. There had been no true desire to discuss the important issues, such as when could he go and visit Lilly.

Holding the cat close, Frankie murmured, 'You love me, don't you, my sweetheart.' She purred her response, and licked his face, her tongue so rough it tickled and made him laugh. 'Come on, Daddy Frankie must get dry, and then he can find you some dinner.'

The act of feeding her and fussing over her always made him feel better, gave him someone outside himself to care about. He knew it was cupboard love, the rattle of a box of biscuits guaranteed to have an instant response, but it made him feel needed.

The house was too cold for just a robe, so he put on jeans and a woollen sweater instead, and fished out his halogen heater, an emergency measure until he could get the leaking radiator and boiler looked at. Too depressed to cook, he warmed up a ready meal in the oven, then ate it sitting in front of his computer, only half concentrating on the insipid food while he wrote his blog entry for the day. 'Failure' was the first word he typed, and then thought for over half an hour of what to say next. Rain lashed against the French windows, the sudden swirling drum roll making him spin round to see what was going on.

'I'm all on edge,' he said to Millie, and got up to draw the curtains. For a moment he stared into the darkness, then looked harder as he made out an ethereal shape moving around in the garden. He shivered. Lilly was going to die before he ever got to touch her, he just knew she would.

Determined not to cry, he went into the kitchen to make some tea, and as the clock on the wall clicked round to half past eight, the doorbell rang. He'd been watching the clock, counting the minutes off until the tea was brewed. Bugger, he wouldn't get to drink it now. He poured it anyway, took it to the front door, sipping it as he walked, knowing who would be on the other side.

'Good evening. Mr Francis Hayward?' The police officer who spoke looked him up and down. There were two of them, both men, the angle of the outside light making the rain drops sparkle on their uniforms before soaking in.

Frankie nodded.

'Can we have a word with you, sir?'

'Yes, of course.' Frankie sipped his tea, leant against the doorframe, made himself comfortable. When he'd opened the door they'd retreated to the step below him, so now they were looking up, the spokesman blinking as water dripped off the guttering and hit his eyes. To have regained the top step would have crowded Frankie, made it look like police intimidation. They were stuffed.

'Would you mind if we come in, sir?'

'Yes, I would.'

The younger PC to Frankie's right scowled and flicked up his collar. 'We need to ask you a few questions about your movements today.'

Frankie blinked, and frowned, but didn't respond.

The spokesman referred to his pocket book. 'Your vehicle was seen today parked in Bright's car park in Guildford.'

'Is that a crime? I paid for a ticket.' Frankie wanted to fold his arms but he'd have to finish his tea first or he'd spill it.

'No, sir, only a man fitting your description was seen at Mellow Acres Residential Home, attempting to visit one of the residents there, one Mrs Lillian Charteris.'

Frankie shrugged. 'I don't follow.'

'Was that you, sir?'

'No, it wasn't. I don't know anyone by that name.'

The PC nodded, scribbled something down. 'What were you doing in the vicinity, sir?'

'I beg your pardon?' Frankie swigged back his tea and placed the mug on the jardinière beside the door. Now he could fold his arms. 'The vicinity of what? The car park?'

'No, the nursing home.'

'I can't answer that, I'm not even sure which one you're referring to, there are so many about.'

'I see.' The PC scribbled something else down, making sure he shielded the paper with the notebook's cover. Already the pages were crinkling up in protestation at getting wet. 'So, what was your business in town?'

'My business was business.' Frankie's heart began beating far too fast, and he felt like getting cocky with them. Against the cops one never won, but he couldn't help saying, 'Why are you asking me all of these questions? What has it got to do with you, or anyone else come to that, what I do with myself?'

'We're just trying to establish if you were the young man who attempted to visit Mrs Charteris today.'

'Well, I've said I wasn't, isn't that good enough?'

The PC snapped his notebook shut. 'Don't try it again, son.' The finger he jabbed was spiteful, a nasty warning that Frankie was in trouble, the force of it making his gut churn. The PC motioned that his colleague should follow and together they sauntered down the steps.

'Old people shouldn't be kept prisoner!' Frankie shouted after them, and slammed the door.

2

DETECTIVE INSPECTOR JAKE TALBOT couldn't help but overhear the conversation erupting into warfare over at the front desk. He was snooping around, trying to find out who'd nicked his favourite mug, when a man burst in from the street demanding to know why a certain someone hadn't been arrested. Apart from the raised voice there was one word that made Jake Talbot stop and listen. Pervert. Hmm, he was always interested in smut; he'd built his name and reputation on it. Perching on one of the desks, just out of view, he tried to piece the fragments that he could hear into coherent sentences.

'... the man wanted to visit my grandmother... nutter... perv...'

Now to Jake's mind a nutter and a perv were two completely different animals, so which were they dealing with here? A perv was inclined to proceed towards sex or masturbation, while a nutter—well, that all depended on precisely how nuts they were. It was tempting to go and get involved, but the man sounded far too irate for reasonable conversation. Currently, Talbot couldn't be doing with unreasonableness; his last interview, a final questioning of a suspect on the Lasseter case, had seen to that.

By the time the angry man agreed to go away, all of the circulation had been cut off down Talbot's left leg, resulting in pins and needles when he peeled himself away from the table. Damn, at forty-three he was getting to that stupid age where you had to start looking after yourself a bit better. Swearing under his breath, he limped up to the desk sergeant.

'What was all that about?'

'The guy's a nutcase, sir.' The desk sergeant shook his head. 'I don't see his problem, I really don't.'

'And his problem is?' Talbot peered over his shoulder, impatient to read his notes. 'So why does a twenty-seven-year-old man wish to visit Mrs... what name is that?'

'Charteris.'

'I take it that is *the* Mr Peter Charteris we are talking of here?'

'Dunno.'

Talbot picked up the notes and scanned them. 'Peter Charteris isn't even thirty, and already owns a golf course over at Woking, and a couple of posh hotels—and all his money can buy is a grotty room at Mellow Acres for his beloved grandmother to live out her final days. Tight git.' Without asking, Talbot folded the notes into four and tucked the square of paper into his jacket pocket.

'You taking that with you then? Sir?' The desk sergeant held out a pen anticipating a signature.

'Looks like it.' Talbot smiled and patted his colleague's shoulder, and went off to find the two officers who had questioned the suspect.

They had conflicting opinions. PC Oliver described him as sullen, while the younger PC, Reynolds, described him as surly.

'Unhelpful,' Oliver said for the umpteenth time. 'Didn't even want to give us the time of day.'

'He kept us outside, in the rain,' Reynolds complained.

'He's not obliged to let you into his property.' Talbot was irritated by Reynolds's surly nature; yes, he was the surly one, hardly likely to inspire confidence even in the innocent. 'But he did answer your questions,' Talbot went on. 'He did comply.'

'His place stunk,' Oliver threw in, as if that were sure to make the man guilty.

'And the man himself? This Francis Hayward, was he clean and tidy? Dirty?'

'Suppose so,' Oliver said.

'Was that "suppose so" relating to clean or dirty?' Talbot leant against the table and, by changing his view, caught a glimpse of green china, and closed the case on who'd stolen his mug.

'Clean, I guess.'

'And you think he was obstructive?'

'Well, let's just say he wasn't particularly co-operative.' Oliver's voice rose as he took a confrontational step forward, intent on driving his point home.

Talbot knew Oliver's type, and didn't much like it.

'And this Peter Charteris, the complainant, did you speak with him?'

'On the phone,' Oliver said. 'He was polite.'

'Yes, but what was his grievance?' Talbot picked up Oliver's note book again and flicked through it. 'Well, what was his problem?'

Reynolds sprang to Oliver's defence. 'Why would this Hayward guy want to go and perv on someone's grandma?' He grimaced, the idea repugnant.

'If you had your way you'd have everyone under forty who volunteers to visit the sick or elderly locked up.' Talbot jabbed his finger down hard onto Oliver's note book. 'Type it up, every word; I want it on my desk in thirty minutes.'

WAS THERE A LAW AGAINST IT? Talbot leant back in his chair and twiddled his pen round and round. He'd spent all the previous evening pondering the question, put pins in a map showing everyone's location. Charteris lived near Woking, the nursing home was in Guildford, yet he had chosen to report the incident to Farnham police, the town where Hayward resided. Which proved, if nothing else, that Charteris already knew where Hayward lived.

Talbot had walked into work this morning feeling confident enough to request the Super's okay on pursuing further enquiries.

'Not sure you're going to come up with much, Jake,' Super-intendent John Bailey had said with accustomed circumspection, never being one to show too much enthusiasm. 'Check it out for a week or so. It'll do you good to have something less—you know— for this time of year, than the Lasseter case.'

'Less what, sir?' Talbot met his gaze, challenged him to use the word he had used throughout their entire investigation. Sinister.

'Stressful.'

Ah well, at least it began with an 's'. Only it was the wrong 's' and Talbot knew they were playing games. Bailey never liked coming straight out with it and ordering him to take some leave, which he eventually ended up doing every Christmas anyway. No doubt Bailey viewed this Charteris enquiry as relaxing, an easy couple of weeks pootling about over nothing, Bailey's premise probably being that if he could push Talbot through one Christmas without taking leave, the next year would be easier. Talbot knew it was a ploy to help him begin to put the traumas of this season behind him.

'Thank you,' was all he could find to say, and hoped that perhaps he *would* be able to get all the way through to the new year without falling to pieces.

Across the room Detective Sergeant Gary Yates was staring into space, day-dreaming most likely, which he'd been doing a lot of recently, since meeting the love of his life. So far he'd refused to name her, but Talbot suspected she was one of the girls who worked down in archives, the only evidence he had to prove his case so far being Yates's eagerness to go and enquire about records. Unless, of course, he'd suddenly taken an interest in criminal history. Still, it was no bad thing, as long as she was kinder to Yates than Claire had been to him.

Yates was fiddling around on his computer, his face changing colour in time to the shifting patterns on the screen. He didn't look old enough to be a copper, his full cheeks making him appear more seventeen than thirty-two, but right now that baby-face might be rather useful.

'What do you think, Yates?'

'Sir?'

'This Hayward kid wanting to see Grandma: is there a law against it?'

Yates pushed his keyboard away and shrugged. 'I guess it could be classed as harassment.'

Talbot laughed, stood up and slipped his coat on. 'Yes, but it's Peter Charteris who's feeling harassed, not his grandmother; the old lady and Francis Hayward have never met.'

Yates sprang up and grabbed his raincoat, shrugged himself into it, and opened the door. 'Have you checked that out, sir?'

Stopping in the doorway Talbot looked him in the eye. 'No. Perhaps we should get onto it, have your friend in archives look into them both.'

'Both?' Yates sounded shocked.

'Yes, why not.'

OUT OF A NEED to know the problem, Talbot decided to pay a call on Peter Charteris first, because it was raining again, and a wealthy man with a gripe was less likely to keep them hanging around on the doorstep.

'Of course, in some respects, Francis Hayward is being harassed by Charteris,' Talbot said as they stopped the car outside a pair of huge wrought-iron gates.

'Well, there must be a reason. I mean, he wouldn't just go picking on "random bloke", would he?' Yates sighed on seeing the intercom, three yards away, fixed to a wall, and way beyond reach.

'Unless he has some motive for intimidating him away from his grandmother.'

Unbuckling his seat belt, Yates threw open the car door and made a dash for it, letting in a blast of freezing cold air and a torrent of rain. He stood with his hands on his hips for a full two minutes, shouting into the intercom, before the black gates started to inch open. Throwing himself down in his seat, he shook water off his hands, had a quick look in the mirror to shove back his hair, and flicked on the wipers.

'I guess I should have phoned ahead,' Talbot said.

'You got his number?'

'Uh-huh.'

'You bastard.'

The driveway went on forever, through wide fields with distant woodland, and past ornamental gardens. In spring it would look pretty, but right now Talbot thought it was bleak and unwelcoming.

'Shit, does he really own all of this?' Yates asked as they parked in front of a fine example of Queen Anne architecture.

'Apparently so,' Talbot said, and wrinkled up his nose, already finding the smell of Peter Charteris's money distasteful.

A young woman dressed in jeans and a turquoise sweatshirt answered the door, her perfume so strong Talbot sniffed back a sneeze. How was anyone supposed to get close to her through that invisible barbed wire? She was slim, fair-haired, and not unattractive in a pointy kind of way.

'Detective Inspector Talbot,' he said, and flipped open his warrant card. 'And this is Detective Sergeant Yates. Is Mr Charteris at home?'

'Peter? Yes, I'll see if he's free.' She half turned, and from the gloom at the end of the hallway a man called out, 'For Christ's sake, Melanie, let them in.'

She stood back and motioned to a hat stand where they could hang their wet coats. The man at the end of the hallway raised his hand, half in salutation and half to halt their progress while he spoke into a mobile phone.

'I'll call you back.... Yes.... Yes.' He slipped the phone into his pocket and strode towards them, emerging out of the shadows looking athletic in jeans and a rugby shirt. 'Detective Inspector, did you say? Well, too bloody right. About time they put some clout behind this.'

He strode into a side room, politeness and invitation ignored, used to his minions following.

'Well, have you arrested him?' Charteris demanded as soon as Talbot was through the door.

'No, sir.' Talbot paused meaningfully, enough time for Charteris to wait and for him to assess his surroundings. It was gloomy, no overhead or sidelight switched on, grey light filtering in from outside. Expensive deep pile rugs covered the floor, changing colour where it was divided into two sitting areas, one either side of the door. All of the furniture was wooden, antique period pieces in keeping with the house, the sofas reupholstered, firm, uncomfortable, never sat on. Across the length of the room were tall sash windows, sheet after sheet of glass, rain lashing against them giving the room a hollow sound. Curtains matched the sofas, pink damask, Charteris out of place beside them as he emptied the last of what looked like Scotch from a decanter set on a round table in front of the centre window. He swigged half back, stared into the finely cut glass tumbler, his grip enough to crush it.

'At present we don't have anything to arrest him for.'

There went the tumbler. 'Damn!' Charteris dropped the shattered glass, and it bounced around on the carpet before tilting over. He whipped a handkerchief out of his pocket and dabbed away at his hand, quickly hiding any blood; then turned to the light and dabbed at his rugby shirt. 'Damn!'

'We'll wait… if you need to go and clean up, sir.' Talbot offered his most sympathetic tone of voice.

'Just tell me why you haven't arrested that… that…' Charteris looked straight at him, blue eyes bright with hostility under a shock of dark hair. Talbot thought the man would be classed as handsome, if one went in for that kind of thing.

'Mr Hayward hasn't committed any crime, sir.'

'He's bothering my grandmother.' Charteris pointed an accusing finger. 'He's done it before, you know. Made her ill, so ill and… and afraid—yes, so afraid that we had to move her.'

'Did he, sir?' Talbot glanced across to check that Yates was making notes. 'When and where was this?'

'Kent, two years ago.' Suddenly Charteris strode over and barged past them, stuck his head into the hallway and yelled, 'Melanie! Bring more whisky!'

'What happened, in Kent?' Talbot asked.

'He tried to get in to see her, and my grandmother became ill, very ill. She isn't a well woman, you know.' He strode back to the window, placed his cut palm on the glass, and stared out at the pouring rain. 'Hayward's a weirdo. Schizophrenic, a dangerous madman that this society has permitted to run free under the guise of care in the community!'

'And he told you this?'

'What?'

'Did Mr Hayward share this medical information with you?'

'No, of course he bloody well didn't.' Charteris yelled out, 'Melanie! Whisky!' He tugged down the bottom of his rugby shirt. 'I've never spoken to the man.'

'Then how exactly do you know—'

'I make it my business to know,' he said with surly contempt.

He might have said more, but the clinking of glass made him stop and look around with interest. Melanie struggled in, carrying a heavy tray laden with bottles and glasses. Yates put his hands out to take it from her, but was shrugged away, and she dumped it on the nearest coffee table, scowling and moving the glasses apart to stop the vibration.

'I thought everyone might like a drink,' she said, pouring a large whisky.

'Not on duty, thank you, Mrs Charteris, but tea would be very nice,' Talbot said.

'You people know nothing,' Charteris said vehemently. 'Melanie's my sister. If you can't get that fact right, no wonder you haven't fished up enough evidence to arrest the little shit.'

'Mr Charteris,' Talbot said, thrusting his hands into his trouser pockets, 'at present we have no reason to arrest Mr Hayward. First we must prove a crime. For that we require evidence, and we need facts, so it would be best if you calm down and tell us the facts, as you see them.'

Melanie shot a glance from her brother to Talbot and back again. 'Tea.' She nodded and retreated out of a door at the far end of the room.

'The fact is,' Charteris said, knocking back his whisky, 'that I've had to move my grandmother, uproot her, upset her routine, so that she is nearer to me, so that I can be on hand, to look after her.'

'And what are your parents' thoughts on the situation?'

'Go and do your bloody homework.' Charteris poured more Scotch, splashing it in without care for the antique table. 'My parents died in a light aircraft crash four years ago.'

'I'm terribly sorry to hear that, sir.' Talbot took his hands out of his pockets and motioned with a discreet sweep of his index finger for Yates to fetch his overcoat. 'We'll make enquiries,' he said. 'What was the name of the home in Kent?'

'Maidstone, Tall Trees.'

'Nice place?'

'It was a very expensive home, the best.' Charteris bared his teeth. 'I thought a cheaper home would put him off her scent.' He shook his head. 'Bastard.'

3

'WE COULD HAVE GOT more information out of him, sir,' Yates said, as he swung the car out through the wrought-iron gates and back towards the heart of Woking.

'He was right, we need to do some homework.' Talbot chuckled. 'Oh yes, we need to go digging. Not once did he give us a direct answer as to why he wants to keep Francis Hayward away from his grandmother. What is he hiding?'

'Sounds like he's simply trying to keep the old girl safe.'

'But from what?' Talbot took out his notebook to check the addresses. 'Let's visit Grandma first, see what she has to say.'

Yates stopped at a red traffic light and looked across, frowning. 'The beat officers didn't mention that these people had collided before.'

'No. Well, they haven't, have they? From what I can make out, Charteris has never met Hayward, and Hayward has never met Grandma. Bloody peculiar if you ask me.'

They pulled away, and Talbot watched as the wipers swung from side to side, clearing the windscreen, then chasing back after the rain drops before they covered the glass. Just like detective work, one minute there was clarity, and the next it was peppered with confusion again. He was going to speak, but Yates was concentrating on the traffic, nudging his way carefully through snarl-ups. He'd leave him to drive, jot down notes they could discuss later.

Not yet 11.30 and Charteris had already been hitting the whisky, hard. He'd cut his hand when he'd bust that tumbler, definitely cut it; there had been smears of red on his handkerchief. It must have hurt or he wouldn't have placed it on the cool window to soothe away the pain. Yes, that's what he'd done, tried to hide it from them; but whether from pride or deceit was the question.

On the straight stretch out towards Guildford, Yates said, 'I can't believe his excuse for moving her to somewhere cheaper.'

'Or closer,' Talbot agreed. 'It may be nearer than Kent, but it's hardly on his doorstep.'

When they neared Mellow Acres, Talbot motioned for Yates to pull over and park a hundred yards away from the building.

'Right, I want you to go in and ask to see Lillian Charteris,' Talbot said.

'Aren't you coming as well?' Hands clasped tight on the steering wheel, Yates peered out at the pouring rain.

'No, I'm going to sit here and keep nice and warm, while you, a young man, go in and ask to visit. Don't let on that you're a copper. Phone me now and keep your phone on in your top pocket, so that I can hear every word.'

Laughing, Yates did as he was told. 'A change from your usual routine, sir. No "grow some stubble and try and look old enough to be a grown-up", today then.'

The *Dambusters* theme erupted from Talbot's phone; and he took a moment or two to listen to the music before answering and switching it to speaker mode.

'Today it's good that you look younger.' Reluctantly Yates stepped out into the sheeting rain. Talbot watched him hurry towards the building and disappear inside.

He just wanted to hear their reaction, get an idea of how Hayward had been treated. Coldly, by the sound of what he heard down his phone. He smoked a cigarette, the first of the five he allowed himself each day. He'd quit; it was a compromise. So, Mellow Acres had a list of acceptables, and he bet only two names were on that, Peter and Melanie Charteris. He'd go in tomorrow, show his ID, get to speak to the old girl. There was Yates coming out now, dodging puddles, dancing around them rather than hurrying back. The car had lost its warmth and the windows were fogged up, his hands wet from playing at internal windscreen wipers. He wanted a hot drink and a bite to eat, but first there was the Hayward question. Two weeks was never enough.

Yates, yanking open the driver's door, startled him, brought in a chill of discontent along with a dripping coat.

'Huh, you think it's cold in here,' Yates said, firing up the engine and blowing on his hands. 'It's freezing in that place.'

'Perhaps he wants the old girl dead,' Talbot said.

'Nah, he'd have to sue the home for malpractice or some such. Wouldn't be personally liable, would he, sir?'

'No, he wouldn't,' Talbot agreed, and folded his arms.

He counted the minutes to Hayward's house in Farnham, so that he could judge an average journey time. Thirty-two, but the roads had been busy. Maybe twenty-five on a good run. Once they'd located the property, up a hill in a secluded backwater, Yates drove round and round for another ten minutes, hunting for a parking space. Frustration oozed from every pore, but the young DS maintained an unflustered exterior. Talbot knew that he would have sworn and shouted, griped about everything.

'Buggered on doing this every day,' he said as they trudged up the road in the rain, water worming its way down inside his collar. 'Give me a house with off-road parking any day.'

Hayward had enough room to create a parking space large enough for an average saloon if he knocked out one side of the front brick wall and put in some hard standing, as many had done up and down the street. Talbot could understand why Hayward had chosen not to do that here. It would have spoilt the elegance of the building, marred its symmetry.

For a moment Talbot stood in the rain and listened. High Park Road was a very quiet street, Farnham's hustle and bustle far away below them; this privileged row of detached town houses backed onto the serenity of Farnham Park. This property was probably valued at a little less than three-quarters of a mill, so it couldn't have been Hayward's financial circumstances that Charteris objected to. A white van was parked astride the kerb, half blocking the pavement, Yates busily scribbling down the registration. Looking up the short flight of steps to Hayward's front door, Talbot noticed it was ajar, and guessed he was the one who had the plumbers in.

'Leave it,' he said to Yates and pointed to the open door. 'They're only going about their business. Let's go find some grub and come back around knocking off time.'

'Too soft, you are, sir.' Yates saved his response until they were sitting outside a café under a covered walkway, tucking into egg and chips. 'You'd never have got past that van in a wheelchair.'

'Thankfully, today, I was not in a wheelchair, Yates.' Talbot sucked ketchup off a chip, wondered if they'd vinegared it down. 'Maybe Grandma's in a wheelchair. Christ, we don't even know what age the old girl is. Seventy, and she could be walking and talking; ninety, she might be decrepit, on her last legs.'

'Why did we get this case, sir?' Yates grinned. 'Did the Old Bailey match it with your love of antiques and decide it was a goer?'

'Very funny.'

Yates was on a roll, his weird humour snapping in quicker than the MC at the Comedy Club. 'Then it must have been your keen interest in family history.' Sweeping his hands out as if flying, he cried, 'This is a case for Inspector Genealogist… da, da la, laaa…'

'Oh, do shut up, you're turning the vinegar sour.' Talbot scowled at him.

Yates laughed and stabbed his egg with a chip. 'Still, it makes a change from the likes of the Lasseter case and his nasty DVD collection.'

'Yeah, that was the general idea when the Super gave it to us.' Talbot sipped his tea, pleased with the flavour of good old builder's brew. It did no harm if Yates believed they'd been allocated the case rather than him having begged for it. He stared out across the street, lost for a moment in the beauty of coloured lights reflecting in darkening puddles, as shops and cars alike decided that evening had already arrived, even though it was barely one o'clock. That's what winter, and only having twenty-three shopping days left until Christmas, did to people: made them aware of the dark.

A small boy caught his attention, the hand he gripped white, whereas his own was black. The picture nudged him into ideas, got him thinking about how often it was difficult to make a family connection, because on first sight it wasn't obvious.

'Maybe Hayward's related.' He lit his second cigarette, and asked the girl clearing the next table to bring another mug of tea. 'Maybe he was born the wrong side of the sheets, to Daddy or Granny.'

'Surely he'd stake his claim.' Yates leant back away from the smoke. 'If he's got documents, then I'd understand Charteris crapping himself.'

'Yes, lot of money at stake.' A siren whined and Talbot instinctively looked up, hunting for the blue lights. Gone up behind them by the sound of it, round the one way system—yep, there they were, racing out of town. The car's engine changed beat, and Talbot stood up in time to see its rear end disappear up a side street, the one they'd walked down from Hayward's house. 'Lawyers,' he said tossing a coin onto the table for the tea he hadn't had. 'If Hayward was illegitimate and going after inheritance, Charteris would have lawyers onto it, not cops.' He buttoned his raincoat and flicked up the collar. 'Let's go.'

'Didn't think we were in a hurry, sir,' Yates said, gulping down the last of his coffee.

'Well, we are now.' Talbot pointed to a second stream of blue light bouncing around the sheeting rain, and urged Yates to step it up as the siren faded into the distance.

Two yards from the corner of High Park Road, and Talbot could clearly make out words amidst raised voices hammering into the rain.

'Leave her alone… pervert…'

Shit, that was Charteris. He broke into a run. Up, round the corner, Yates keeping pace. Ahead, white van, two police cars, four officers, the whole street ablaze with blue, the lights going round and round, hypnotic, Charteris standing near the kerb shouting to the rhythm. Workman, blue boiler suit, open-palmed, protesting.

Youngster in maroon fleece, being manhandled, trying to get an officer to let go of his arm. He was pointing over towards the house, but Talbot couldn't work out why. Slight, thin, weedy, the young man was soaked, dark hair plastered down around his ears, quiet, not shouting. Hayward?

People were stopping, standing, even in the rain, gaping, a clutch of umbrellas swarming on the opposite pavement. Talbot's stomach lurched, and he sprinted the last few yards.

He drove straight past Charteris and into the fray, halting to face the PC who was gripping Maroon Fleece's arm. The eyes that met his were filled with aggression, the sneer on his lips a shame to the uniform. It was PC Oliver.

'Unhand him,' Talbot hissed through gritted teeth, and stared down at the bruising fingers.

'I'm arresting this man,' Oliver responded, and refused to let go.

'On what charge?' Talbot demanded, dug inside his coat, pulled out his warrant card and flicked it up at Maroon Fleece's face, saying, 'Detective Inspector Talbot. I outrank this officer. I would like you to tell me what has gone on here please, sir.'

The voice that replied was almost a whisper. 'That man over there.' He pointed at Charteris. 'He threw a brick at my window and broke it.'

Talbot followed the line of his finger, and now he saw it: the shattered glass, the gaping hole letting in water.

'Charteris was wound up,' PC Oliver said vehemently. 'This is Francis Hayward, and he's been round upsetting Charteris's grandmother again.'

'I beg your pardon.' Talbot took one step closer, placed his hand firmly around Oliver's forearm and squeezed; added pressure bit by bit. Oliver frowned, then winced, then bared his teeth and released his grip on Hayward. 'Go inside,' Talbot barked at Hayward, before he could even raise a hand to soothe his arm. Dragging Oliver aside, he shoved him down into the gutter, gave him nowhere to go except over the bonnet of the patrol car. He would have been tempted to hit him, if not for the clutch of umbrellas across the street, and the outstretched arms with clever recording devices in the guise of mobile phones. They'd be on bloody YouTube before the six o'clock news.

'You are well out of order,' Talbot said in a seething, lowered tone. 'No man has a right to take the law into his own hands, and that includes you. Now turn these lights off and go and arrest Charteris for criminal damage, do you hear me?'

'Yes… sir.' Oliver stood up straight, waiting for Talbot to back off, his eyes bright with hostility. 'I'll leave it up to you to get the witness statements then, sir.'

'You do that,' Talbot agreed, and walked away to speak with the man in the boiler suit.

Up close he could read the logo on the front of the man's garment. *'Ready Fix: If You Need It Fixed, We'll Fix It Quick.'*

'I'm just doing a job, guv,' the man said as soon as he saw the warrant card and heard the word 'inspector'. Talbot nodded. White, fortyish, slightly overweight, bit thin on top; typical working class, 'knock a bit off for cash, mate'. The officer guarding him was PC

Reynolds, his face pinched from the cold or bitterness, it was hard to tell. 'And this is Mr?' he directed at Reynolds.

'Stevens, sir, was here fixing Mr Hayward's central heating system.'

'Right, then perhaps you'd like to step inside, Mr Stevens, and ask Mr Hayward to put the kettle on, so that we can talk this through in the warm over a nice cup of tea.'

'Ain't that warm,' Stevens said, shaking his head and scowling across towards Charteris. 'I'd have had it sorted by five, if not for this riot.'

'We'll discuss the details inside, sir.' Talbot motioned him onwards. 'I'll be with you shortly.'

The second he'd half-turned, Mr Fix-it raised his hands in victory and drew a resounding cheer from the crowd. 'Fixer fixed up by the cops.' It would make YouTube's top one hundred by midnight. Talbot closed his eyes for a moment, drew in a deep breath, and strode towards Charteris.

Yates was holding him at bay, by words rather than force, Oliver standing next to him, a foot in each camp, glaring at the two unoccupied officers as if they were surplus to requirements and ought to be on their way.

'Don't leave yet,' Talbot said to the nearest one, then went right up to Charteris and sniffed. 'Well, Mr Charteris, twice in one day. And how did you get here, sir?'

'Don't be so fucking stupid,' Charteris spat at him.

'No swearing, please, sir.' He leant very close, smiled, and whispered, 'Not only is it an offence to swear at a police officer going about his duty, but we wouldn't want you shown in a bad light, now would we.' Talbot gave a cursory wave to the crowd. 'YouTube, Facebook, Twitter... we'll be nettified within the hour, if we haven't been already.' He grinned at Charteris. 'So, how did you get here, sir?'

'I drove my car.' Charteris sucked in his lips and folded his arms.

'Then I suggest you hand the keys to Detective Sergeant Yates. That way we won't need to arrest you for driving under the influence.'

'Don't be absurd.' Blue eyes locked onto his with stony precision, and something startling shot through Talbot's veins. He swallowed and adjusted his collar, made a cold stream of water run down around his neck.

'I'll speak with you at the station, when I've finished here,' Talbot said, and started to walk away.

Charteris yelled after him, 'That pervert was round again! He should be locked up!'

Talbot spun to face him, the 'oooh' of the crowd pushing him back, the 'ahhhh' of the crowd halting him directly in front of Charteris, palm open, demanding his car keys.

'Hayward went nowhere near your grandmother today,' Talbot said, snapping his fingers shut around the key fob. 'If you ask for a full description, you'll find that it better fits Detective Sergeant Yates.' Talbot pointed at one of the officers, 'Get him in a car, get him out of here. And get that crowd dispersed.'

'You've fitted me up!' Charteris shouted as his head was being pushed down so that he didn't crack it wide open getting into the car.

'It was your choice to throw the brick,' Talbot muttered on passing, and knew there would be hell to pay.

4

IT WAS POLITE TO KNOCK, and Talbot was just about to do so, only somehow Yates had already wormed his way inside. He could hear him talking in another room. Talbot closed the front door behind him, shut out the sound of rain and excited chatter from the crowd across the street as they started to disperse. The hallway smelt rank, damp and unlived-in. Without a light on, it was nearly grey, the only illumination coming from a half-open door at the end of the passage. The carpet squelched under his feet; and a short distance ahead lay a dark, box-like shape.

'Watch for the tools,' a voice called out, and a silhouette appeared and flicked on an overhead light.

So this was Francis Hayward. This slight, dark-haired, dark-eyed man was what all the fuss was about. He didn't look too bad, now that he'd changed into blue jeans and a dry sweater, a chunky Aran knit that gave him a healthy nautical look. He was smiling, so Talbot smiled back, reached out and accepted the hand that was offered.

'Francis Hayward,' the young man said. 'I know why you're here. I'm sure you weren't merely passing, but thank you for stepping in to help.'

Talbot nodded. 'How's the arm?'

The question made Hayward rub his lips and look away; nervous, embarrassed, a reaction Talbot couldn't work out.

Hayward eased the heavy tool-box aside with his foot. 'The radiator pipe broke,' he said apologetically. 'Flooded the carpet.'

'Be an insurance job then.' Talbot tilted his head to one side and smiled, caught himself doing it and pulled himself up straight. This wasn't a child, even though he came across as young for his age.

'I'm rather fond of the carpet, be nice if I could save it.' Hayward sighed and gestured towards the kitchen. 'Tea first, Inspector, or would you prefer to admire my broken window?'

'Perhaps my sergeant could bring the tea out to me.'

While Hayward headed towards the kitchen, Talbot went to assess the damage. He let out a low whistle; it was heart-breaking. The brick had embedded itself in a glass-fronted display cabinet, Psyche au Bain clutching a pink towel to cover her shame at the horror. Capo Di Monte circa 1901-1920, worth a bob or two if she'd survived undamaged. The old man mending watches hadn't fared so well, and his severed head lay on a pile of shattered glass, as if he'd stepped on thin ice and was drowning fast. It would all need to be photographed. In the centre of the room was a fireplace, open hearth, no fire. Up the far end, in what should have been a dining room, was a computer and other office equipment, a chair facing the screen in the corner, anyone sitting there having their back to the French windows. It was tempting to go and snoop around, other people's PCs always being far more interesting than one's own. His coat was dripping puddles onto the carpet, and he was bound to leave a watery trail of indiscretion, so best left alone.

Footsteps approached along the hallway and Talbot turned to the broken window, studied how spoiled the sofa underneath was from an hour of being rained on. A keen wind whipped in, bringing flurries of water. No net curtains to slow down the missile, maximum damage. To Charteris it was a brick through a window, to Hayward the loss was personal and painful, the consequences time-consuming. It made Talbot want to spit in the rich bastard's eye. Unexpectedly, it wasn't Yates who brought the tea through, but the plumber.

'I've got a mate who could fix that, at least get it boarded up for the night,' he said, handing over the tea.

Talbot nodded. 'Yes, give him a call, if that's alright by Mr Hayward.'

'He was needing your okay on it, sir.' If they'd been born a hundred years earlier, Mr Stevens, the fix-it man, was the type who would have doffed his cap and slunk off to cut a deal with his mate for obtaining him gainful employ. It was what made the world go round. The mobile was halfway to Steven's ear, a quick response having him say, 'Hang on, mate,' as Talbot spoke over him saying, 'Don't touch anything,' and left him to go and speak with Hayward.

Yates was leaning against the sink unit, notebook in hand, listening attentively to Hayward, who was standing in the centre of the kitchen with his arms folded, saying how worried he was about his cat.

'I haven't seen her since this happened,' he was repeating over and over, his eyes twitching to the cat flap every time a gust of wind rattled it.

Clearing his throat to announce his presence, Talbot smiled and said, 'I need my sergeant to photograph all of the damage, before it's tidied up.'

'Yes, of course.' Hayward gestured to a chair next to a small table covered with a square of pale green wipeable fabric. 'I'm sorry it's so cold. I'll make some more tea.'

'Any chance of Mr Stevens working a bit late?' Talbot motioned for Yates to go and take the photos, make good use of that top-of-the-range point-and-shoot he'd claimed on expenses.

'I guess he might, for a price.'

Hayward emptied a teapot into the sink and swilled it round with hot water. Tea leaves, too. Oh my, Talbot hadn't seen this kind of ritual for years. Maybe it was the old-fashioned kitchen that encouraged the ancient craft, or maybe Hayward styled his furnishings around his habits. There were tea bags too, Talbot could see them loitering in a glass jar, so perhaps he was being treated as a special guest, the new friend invited home for tea. Once it was laid on the table, Hayward sat opposite, lifted the lid and stirred the pot, a spiral of steam rising up like a genie.

'What will happen now?'

'We'll need a statement and for you to lodge a formal complaint. We'll allocate a crime reference number.' Talbot wriggled out of his raincoat and discreetly pressed the record button on a mini Dictaphone he kept in his inside pocket. Totally inadmissible as evidence, but always a fascinating listen afterwards.

'I suppose I'll have to, or the insurers won't pay up.' Hayward rubbed a finger under his nose, and sniffed, holding back his upset.

'The china was my grandmother's. She collected it, loved it.' He looked Talbot in the eye. 'It's all ruined, isn't it?'

Talbot shrugged, unwilling to admit that he'd noticed precious little that was intact.

'Speaking of grandmothers, what has Peter Charteris got against you visiting his grandmother?'

'I don't know.' He sniffed again, then poured the tea, his hand trembling as he held the tea strainer. 'I didn't go anywhere near her today.'

'But you did the other day, didn't you?'

Hayward peered into the jug. 'I'll get some more milk.'

'You haven't answered my question.' Talbot kept his tone mild, watched and waited as Hayward moved around, soft-footed, like a wily cat.

The fridge door swung open and the internal light bathed Hayward's face a cool yellow. 'I haven't done anything wrong,' he said quietly. 'I… I just want to see Lilly.'

Talbot kept very still, not minding that his quarry hid behind the fridge door while he spoke.

'Why do you want to see her?'

'Because I've never met her, and I… I'd like to see her before she dies.'

'Why her, Mr Hayward?'

He closed the fridge door, held a pint of milk in both hands and counted his steps back to his chair.

'You won't believe me,' he said. 'So there's little point in mentioning it.'

'Try me.'

Hayward shook his head. 'I'm not mad, and I'm not a schizophrenic, and… and… well, you're a policeman, go and read all of the lies they've written about me.' Tears welled up in the corners of his eyes. 'I'll never get to see her, will I?'

'I don't see why not.' Talbot frowned, wondering who had already written things about him and what there was to read. 'You just want to see her?'

'To hold her hand would be nice.'

'Any more than that?'

Hayward shook his head. 'No, to hold her hand would be enough.'

'Honestly?' Talbot sipped his tea, sat back and thought to go for his cigarettes.

'I don't mind if you smoke.'

'How did you know?'

'You… well, you smell like a smoker.' Hayward bounced up and fetched an ashtray. 'Was it Sergeant Yates who visited Lilly today?'

'Yes, only he wasn't allowed in.' He offered over his packet and was surprised when Hayward accepted one and joined in. 'But I'm sure we will get to see her, and then…'

Hayward's face lit up, his smile genuine and glorious. 'Ask if she'd like Frankie to visit? Just ask her for me, please.'

'So you prefer Frankie to Francis?'

'Oh yes, she doesn't know me as Francis.'

'I see.' Talbot smiled and drew heavily on his cigarette. 'So you two do know each other?'

'Sort of,' he admitted. 'We've… er… sort of been pen pals, of a kind, you know; know of each other but never met… in person.'

'And Mr Charteris is aware of this… correspondence?'

'There aren't any letters.' Hayward stared into his tea and frowned. 'Perhaps she's mentioned me.' He looked up. 'Do you think that might be his problem? That she's mentioned me to him?'

'Possibly.' Talbot paused. 'How have you communicated with Lilly?'

'When two people love each other there are subtle ways to communicate that go beyond the physical world, which many people don't understand.'

'Do you mean telepathy?' Talbot hadn't intended scepticism to barb his words.

'Not quite…'

A loud knock on the front door broke the stillness, made them both flinch and look towards the hallway. A deep voice greeted a deep voice, and Yates mentioned the word kitchen. Damn, that was the guy come to fix the window.

Hayward leapt to the door as if to go and give instructions, but halted and turned towards Talbot.

'I'd best leave you to it,' Talbot said, stood up and put on his coat, its wetness disgusting after his being free of it for a while. 'You won't mind me calling again, will you, Frankie?'

'Will you betray me?' he asked, and pressed his back against the door so that no one could burst in. 'Will you come on all friendly and Frankie and then lock me up for doing nothing?'

Shocked, Talbot took a moment to gather his thoughts. 'That's not my style,' he said at length. 'If you commit a crime, then I will arrest you. If you don't commit a crime, then I won't.'

'But will you help me visit Lilly?'

'That's not my job.'

'Then make it your job,' he begged. 'Make it your business to get Charteris off my back. There must be rules, human rights or something that say you can't lock an old person up and keep her a prisoner away from people who wish to see her. That must be a crime, against humanity.'

'I'll speak with my colleagues in social services.'

The door shifted a fraction and Yates hollered from the other side, 'You in there, sir?'

Hayward moved aside and folded his arms. 'You're the same as everyone else.'

'I don't think so.' Talbot braced his shoulder against the door to keep Yates out. 'You tell me the truth, the absolute truth, and I'll help you visit Lilly.'

Hayward smiled. 'Then we have a deal, Detective Inspector Talbot,' and offered his hand to shake on it.

5

PRECISELY WHAT KIND OF a deal he was getting himself into concerned Talbot. Shit, that had been rash; Hayward barring his path like that, so unpredictable. Had he shaken hands on the deal just so the kid would let him go? A false promise so that he could get out safely? No, no, this kid wasn't going to harm him. Lasseter would have done, but not Hayward: surely he was just an obsessive nutter. But why the obsession? That was what worried him the most, especially as Hayward had mentioned the word love, which Talbot knew induced people to act in many peculiar ways.

They had all parted amicably, Mr Fix-it and his mate agreeing to stay on late and get the place sorted in exchange for a few extra quid and a takeaway thrown in. Maybe that was the key: Hayward was a bit odd, but a likeable kind of chap. The effect he had on people was strange, as if he were a child who needed taking care of. Perhaps he had Asperger's or some other indefinable condition. Maybe, but he was a bright bugger, shrewd too, and had a way of rubbing people like PC Oliver up the wrong way, almost deliberately.

The rain was still falling, his coat damp all the way through, renewed body heat making it sticky and uncomfortable; and Yates trying to side-step puddles so that his shoes didn't get too wet—a thorough irritation.

'I'll walk back to the station,' he said as Yates unlocked the car.

Yates looked across the top of the vehicle and frowned. 'You alright, sir? You've been terribly quiet.'

'I'm thinking.' He tossed Charteris's car keys over. 'Before you start dealing with him, get onto your friend in archives, see what she's managed to fish up on them.'

'Are we looking for anything in particular, sir?'

'Anything and everything.' He didn't wait to see him off but went straight back to the café, ordered some tea, and phoned Helen, a not-quite friend, more of an acquaintance he knew in social services.

She answered promptly and he said all the right words through the preamble of 'lovely to hear from you', and 'well done on Lasseter', yes, yes, not gone to court yet, blah, blah, 'you can't help but win'.

'Okay, Jake, so this isn't a social call,' she said at length. 'I can feel you bursting to jump in with something.'

Talbot laughed. 'I know you'll tell me that you can't divulge client information, but I need to know if you've ever had any dealings with a young man named Francis Hayward.'

'So why are you asking after young Frankie Hayward?' There was a grin in her voice. 'What's he been up to now?'

'Ah, so you do know of him.' Talbot clenched his fist and jabbed it in victory.

'Along with thousands of other faithful followers.' She paused, played cat and mouse, wanting him to chase for the answer.

'I'm sure you'd prefer to tell me over a pint and a sandwich, which is probably all I'll have time for this evening.'

'It's easy pickings,' she said, 'but I'll accept anyway.' Unexpectedly, she gasped. 'Is he in trouble, Jake?' Her tone had become deadly serious. 'Has Lilly's grandson really got the police involved? Oh my God, I thought he was making that up.'

How the fuck did she know about Lilly? There was a loop and he was out of it, and it made him feel foolish. 'We'll speak later,' he said, ground his dog-end into the pavement, and didn't bother to finish his tea. 'Say eight o'clock, somewhere out of town… that new place up near me in Wrecclesham.'

'I'll be there,' she agreed, and on his way back to the station, Talbot went into the first newsagents and bought two packets of cigarettes.

BAILEY WAS IN FULL RANT.

Even when he wasn't, there was something about Superintendent Bailey's office that always made Talbot cringe. The distasteful sensation started creeping up his spine as soon as he clapped eyes on the cold cast bronze statue of Justice, a replica of the one standing on the Old Bailey, her arms spread wide, scales in her left hand, the sword in her right piercing through a leaf on Bailey's giant cheese plant. Bailey claimed policing was his destiny, that he'd seen that statue as a child and knew that justice was calling him to uphold law and order. There was a hint of the frustrated barrister about the room, a photograph of the Old Bailey hanging behind his desk, slanting light from a table lamp bouncing off the glass so that you couldn't see the image unless there was daylight.

Talbot stood very still, breathed in a lungful of scented polish and looked straight into Bailey's eyes, refusing to break the dead lock and look away.

'A man like Charteris will have tough lawyers, and they'll squash this is in a matter of seconds,' Bailey was saying. 'You can't go around arresting someone like Charteris without enough evidence to make it stick.'

'I have evidence, sir. And witnesses.'

'I've let him go, told him that no formal charges will be brought against him.' Bailey stepped over to the window, pushed down a slat on the blinds and stared out.

'That isn't your choice to make, sir. Mr Hayward's property was damaged…'

'A window,' Bailey said and tapped the one in front of him. 'A few quid.'

'There's also a cabinet full of antique china…'

'Antiques!' Bailey spun round, his jaw quivering with rage. 'Trust you to bring bloody antiques into it.'

Talbot stood up a little straighter. Now which officer had been chatting to Charteris? Reynolds? Oliver? One of them had obviously omitted to inform Bailey of all the details.

'Mr Hayward's antiques were broken when the brick Mr Charteris threw through his window smashed into his display cabinet… I would imagine it amounts to several thousand pounds worth of damage.'

'You what!'

'And there is water damage to a very expensive sofa… sir.'

Bailey clenched his fist. 'Then they'll settle it privately…. Charteris will send him a cheque.'

'I can't imagine that…'

'I am not, I repeat, not, having an upstanding member of society shamed because you decided to break the rules and incited malicious actions.' Bailey was nodding his head. 'Oh yes, you can do it with the likes of Lasseter, but not with someone like Charteris, it doesn't wash, Jake, simply doesn't wash.'

'And what precisely…'

'You know damn well what you did!' Bailey's fist crashed down onto the table upsetting a cube of pens. 'You sent Yates in alone to visit Granny, set it up to look like Hayward.'

Talbot shook his head. 'I was right behind him.' He paused, created a dreadful silence. 'There is absolutely no justification for Charteris's actions. He'd been drinking, heavily, then drove to Farnham, under the influence, and trashed Hayward's belongings.'

'I've heard this from Charteris.' Bailey jabbed a finger at him. 'Taking his car keys, accusing him of drink-driving. Outrageous.' The finger jabbed again. 'Don't you go bringing your personal issues into this.'

'I spoke with Mr Charteris earlier this morning, sir, and witnessed him down two large whiskies, before mid-day.'

'They will settle the matter privately.' Bailey sat down and started picking up the spilt pens and placing them back in their container. 'Lawyer to lawyer, if needs be.'

'And put Hayward to a lot of unnecessary expense?' Talbot sighed and drove his hands into his pockets. 'I'll phone him through the crime reference number, so that his insurers can deal with it.'

'You've already let this situation get out of control,' Bailey said. 'Simple enquiries, that was all it was meant to be; and in less than twenty-four hours you've invoked bedlam.' He stood and moved towards the door, implying the interview was over. 'Keep it calm, eh? Warn Hayward off Charteris's grandmother and put it to bed, quietly.'

'I'll see that justice is maintained, sir,' Talbot said firmly, opened the door and went to find Yates.

Talbot didn't have words inside his head to describe how he felt; oh no, the words were stuck in his gut as heaving fury. Incensed, yes, that's what he was, the injustice of Bailey's attitude an assault on all that was righteous. Oh, he knew that Bailey had made a political decision, it was the same everywhere; and at times it made him wonder why the hell he bothered to try and do a proper job. A light was on in his office and a flutter of female vocals drifted down the corridor, prompting him to do a U-turn and slip outside for a fag before interrupting Yates and his tête-à-tête with her from archives. The smoke tasted good, and the rain drumming on car roofs tried hard to blot out the words screaming in his head, but his gut still churned and his neck muscles cramped until he released his jaw. Perhaps he should give up being in the police, but there were those who thought he should have packed it in years ago, and damned if he was going to prove them right.

'VERY INTERESTING, SIR,' Yates said as soon as he saw him. 'This is Trudy, she'll tell you the score.'

'Good to meet you at last, Detective Inspector Talbot.' The girl who spoke was one of those fresh-faced, outdoorsy-looking types, with a mass of rebellious dark hair pulled back into a ponytail, and big brown eyes. Talbot thoroughly understood Yates's fascination and hoped she wasn't just a pretty face as well as a distraction.

They were sitting side by side, huddled close to peer at the same computer screen, and made no attempt to move apart.

'Your man Hayward is an intriguing character,' she said. 'Come and look at this, sir.'

Talbot moved round and joined the huddle. There was what appeared to be an old photograph of Hayward, taken when he was late teens or early twenties. It stated his name and underneath was a message saying, 'Apply for Permissions.'

'What does that mean?' he asked.

"We need special authority to access any information that's on file regarding Hayward." Yates swung round and looked up at him, grinning. 'It means that someone is very interested in our boy.'

'And who might that someone be?' Talbot moved back and perched on the desk behind them.

'The MOD most likely,' Trudy said, lifting her shoulders in a slight shrug. 'I've done a few for psychiatric cases, but mostly it's the Ministry of Defence.'

"Really?" He couldn't imagine the MOD bothering to place restrictions on nutters wanting to visit little old ladies in nursing homes. It piqued his curiosity even more. 'Then we'd best get on and apply for those Permissions.'

'I can do that for you, sir,' Trudy said, turned to face him and added, 'it does mean that you'll need to make me privy to the case, sir. The Permissions forms are overly complicated and if I get any facts wrong they'll only throw it back and we'll have to start again.'

'Yates can fill you in on the detail.' He laughed and shook his head. 'You do know all about the case, don't you, Yates?'

'Oh yes, sir, nutter versus nutter.'

'That would be the one.'

Trudy frowned and Yates murmured, 'I'll explain later.'

'Has Charteris got a Permissions notice as well?' Talbot asked, glancing at his watch to see if he had time to rush home and change before meeting Helen.

'No, sir,' Trudy said. 'But he does have form.'

'Oh, really?'

'Yes, sir, assault, but charges were dropped.'

'Don't tell me, assault on one Francis Hayward, in Kent, about two years ago.'

'Why, yes, sir.' She sounded amazed that he knew. Referring back to her computer screen, she said, 'He was done for drunk driving four years ago. I dug into his parents for you as well. Did you know there was an enquiry into the light aircraft crash that killed them, that there were claims the aircraft had been tampered with?'

Talbot rubbed his face. 'I bet Granny was supposed to be on that flight with them.'

'Sir!' Trudy spun round and gaped at him. How on earth did you know that?'

'Please, call me Talbot or Jake in my own office,' he said, sprang off the table, sauntered over to the door and before leaving asked, 'So, why didn't she travel?'

Yates burst out laughing. 'You need Permissions, sir. Lillian Charteris is also a closed book.'

'Bloody hell, two invisible people.' He pulled out his cigarettes and stuck one in his mouth. 'Well, Lilly can't be the MOD, surely?

Yates, speak with Bailey, get Trudy allocated to our team as a research assistant. I think we're going to need all the help we can get.'

THE PUB HE'D CHOSEN to meet Helen in was old and quaint and had an open fire, which was exactly what was needed on a wet night like tonight. It smelt of woody smoke and real ale, and the mellow heat took the ache from his limbs. He'd driven home feeling damp to the core, his feet complaining at having been bundled up in sodden leather for hours, and his shirt collar still moist all the way down the back of his neck. A quick shower, hot cup of tea, comfy jeans and a fleecy top made him feel less like he was carrying the weight of the day with him; and now the real fire eased out the last shreds of stress and mayhem.

He chose a quiet corner to sit in, and after a few minutes Helen walked in, stopping in the doorway to look around for him. She was, he guessed, somewhere in her mid-fifties, the calf length skirts she always wore a throwback to the eighties, as if she'd bought a job lot at the time. Tonight it was a two-tone green one with a mushy floral design, along with a matching jacket and plain green blouse, the whole ensemble making her appear youthful and her short grey hair a fashion statement.

'There you are,' she said, pouncing on him as if he hadn't spotted her.

They swapped perfunctory kisses on either cheek, ordered food quickly before the chef stopped cooking, and exchanged niceties while they waited to be served.

'I hear you've split up with Claire,' she said as a plate of chicken salad was set down in front of her.

'We're taking some space.' Talbot shook salt over his pasta, aware that the barter of exchange had begun.

'So, do you think you'll get back together?' She looked at him over the top of her glass of red wine, her lips resting on the rim.

'Probably not.' He smiled, to make out that it didn't hurt, to show that he had accepted being abandoned. At the time it had been a shock, the hollowness when he walked in the front door, to be greeted by that sense of knowing that something was different, and wrong. And him a detective, too. It had taken him well over half an hour to realise that one of her paintings was missing from the hall, and that her things were gone from the bathroom.

The note: well, it must have been an hour before he found that, propped up against the bread bin. 'Are you really so unaware of your surroundings?' That's what he would have asked in an enquiry, bluntly, squarely, swinging a full punch. Stupid. He'd made every excuse under the sun to himself. He was tired, he'd been working late, night after night, and that's why she'd left him.

'Sorry, found someone else', was all she'd bothered to write. He'd read it twice, then burnt it, publicly announced they were taking some space, and buried the dreams of her bearing his children—something they had spoken of only a few days before. Utter betrayal. How stupid could stupid get?

'Love's a strange thing, isn't it?' Helen said softly, and gave him a wistful smile.

'Yates is in love.' He laughed and sipped his apple juice. 'They're at that secretive, "nobody really knows and will never guess even though we're breathing life through the same straw" phase.'

'Do you think Frankie Hayward is capable of love?'

Now there was an odd question. He frowned. Wasn't everyone capable of love? 'I don't see why not.'

Raising a finger for silence Helen took out her mobile, flicked a few buttons, and before passing it across, said, 'It's all on his website, www.visitinglilly.com. Frankie is in love with Lilly.' She met his gaze, Talbot sensing her shock mingled in with deep emotion. 'It's real, isn't it, Jake? I always thought he had an amazingly vivid imagination, but you wouldn't be involved if it wasn't real, would you?'

Talbot didn't answer. Right now he had no idea what was real and what was not, except that he existed, anything else being supposition. Helen was several steps ahead, and he hated lagging behind. He took the phone and started to read.

6

It was more a blog than a website; daily entries that built into a personal journal. Under each post there was opportunity for readers to comment, and Hayward was one hell of a popular guy, some commentaries being far longer than the original entry. They had an opinion. They were outraged, or pleased, or crying with him, for him, wanting to hug him.

Talbot smiled. Hayward was an honest bugger. His write-up of the brick through the window was as accurate and impartial as any man's could be. Sure, he mentioned his emotions, but the facts were straight, no elaboration to sway the crowd.

'How long's he been writing this?' His eyes ached with the strain of reading off such a small screen.

'Seven years.'

'You're kidding!' Talbot sat back and stretched. 'That's something like two and a half thousand entries.'

Helen laughed and sipped her wine. 'It doesn't seem like that much if you read it every day.'

A waiter came over and asked if they'd enjoyed their meal, cleared their plates, and offered coffee. Talbot hesitated. What he really wanted was to rush home, jump on the net, and give himself a headache reading millions of words.

'Yes, please, we'll both have a coffee,' Helen said, teased her phone from his fingers, leant close and whispered, 'How about I fill you in a little? That way you can enjoy your coffee and stop twitching.'

'I'll read it anyway, for the detail.'

'Sure, but it'll take you weeks.'

They took their coffees outside and sat under a giant umbrella, huddling next to a patio heater so that Talbot could smoke while Helen darted around through Hayward's history.

'He's in love with Lilly,' she was saying. 'He never mentions her surname, or anyone else's name or surname, but he does use his own real name.'

'How did you know it was his real name?'

'If you keep interrupting…'

Talbot opened his arms, pleading innocence. He'd only interrupted once and it was a question he wanted answered.

'Right at the beginning Hayward claims that he first met Lilly while astral travelling—'

'He what?'

'Shush, Jake.' She smacked his hand. 'I know you may know otherwise but this is what it says, and this is why people read it and why it's so gripping and—well, it's terribly romantic. It's a story of unrequited love, deep yearning, and passion.'

Passion. Now, love he could imagine Hayward experiencing, but never passion.

'Frankie says he met Lilly in a different time, that he met her in the past when she was young and beautiful. By all accounts she was drop-dead gorgeous.' She smiled wistfully. 'Because of this time shift he couldn't touch her, and she experienced him as a spirit, or ghost.'

Talbot drew heavily on his cigarette. Frankie had said he only wanted to hold her hand. It gave him the shivers.

Helen stole one of his cigarettes, but didn't light it, preferring to use it as a baton, orchestrating her words and building them into a story.

'For a while Frankie visited her like this, every day, and they fell in love; only she lived in one world, while he lived in another. The more he visited her, the more he found out about her; and then one day he realised that now she would be older and that she could still be alive. So he set about finding her. He started writing the blog when he began looking for her, to share his hunt for true love with others. Then he found her, five years ago, but she was like a princess locked away in a tower by an evil grandson, and every move he made was dogged by that awful man, who is determined that he and Lilly shall never meet.' She paused, and the pause went on, so Talbot decided it was safe to speak.

'Does he still visit Lilly? Through this astral whatsit?'

'Oh yes, every day; but he can only visit her in the past.'

Talbot stirred his coffee, watched the vortex he created as the liquid spun round and round. If he jumped in, it would drag him down.

'The romantic tale's become a nasty reality, hasn't it?' Helen said, obviously upset. 'I assumed he was making it up.'

'Who's to say he isn't?' Talbot exclaimed, keen to keep sharp and avoid being sucked into some hazy make-believe world. 'How did you first find out about him—his website, the story?'

'There's a buzz.' She shrugged. 'Someone emailed me, said, "Hey, have you seen this website?"'

'As if. Well, I'm not buying any of that.' Talbot flicked his lighter, hoping she'd smoke the cigarette rather than just playing with it. She refused and handed it back, impregnated with her subtle perfume. 'You know a damned sight more about this than you're letting on.'

'Just leave it at that, Jake.' She stood as if to go.

'Come on, Helen.' He leapt up and placed his hands gently on her shoulders, looked her in the eye. 'You knew it was his real name. How did you know that?'

'I can't answer that, you know I can't. He's a good man, Jake, please don't harm him, don't crush him; and don't let that grandson crush him either.' Lifting his hand off her shoulder, she gently kissed his fingers, stirring his interest in all the right places.

'Look, why don't we go back to mine and drink more coffee, or open a bottle of wine?'

'Not tonight, another time maybe.'

He stepped aside. 'Has he ever been under a psychiatrist?'

'Jake! Stop it, you know I can't—'

'Okay, okay.' He motioned that he would walk her to her car. 'Grandson says he has,' Talbot offered, as she climbed in and buckled her seat belt.

It was dark and the rain had faded to watery mist, but he glimpsed the shock in her eyes, the utter disbelief.

She thumped the steering wheel with her fist. 'You're making that up.'

'I wish I were.' He crouched down to be on eye level. 'Grandson has money and influence.'

'Well, who is he then?'

He rubbed his thumb across his mouth, then shook his head. 'You know I can't divulge that.'

'Bastard.'

He laughed and raced round the car, jumped in the passenger side. 'Get out your clever phone, and go onto YouTube. Search for something like "police Farnham".'

She closed the door on her side and the interior light went out, plunged them into darkness. It was eerie, a different world, the windscreen spangled with orange haloes, the silence an ominous hush, the rain an occasional breath trying to get in. Helen's fingers skimmed the buttons, and he admired the fine line of her nose and lips. In the dim light cast by the phone her face appeared ethereal, almost ghostly. Was that how Lilly experienced Frankie? Did they speak in this other world? Did they feel each other's emotions? Talbot's feet were cold, and he wondered if they could feel each other's body heat, as he could feel Helen's now. She fidgeted, perhaps sensing his gaze, not unhappy with it, almost smiling, her eyes flicking from side to side as she concentrated and read.

Bloody hell, being close to Helen was sucking him into this absurd fantasy, making him analyse life as if astral travel were really possible.

'This is it!' She twisted so that he could see the video on the screen, and then snatched it back and stuck her face down over the phone. 'Shit, that's Peter Charteris.'

'You know him?'

'I went to a conference once in one of his hotels.' She sighed, switched the phone off and fired the engine up. 'We need a bigger screen. Yours or mine?'

'I'll lead the way.'

IT HAD BEEN A LONG time since Talbot had invited a woman home, let alone a female colleague. Okay, so she was a friend, not a conquest, but it made him anxious about whether the place might be seen as tidy or untidy, mannish, or void of warmth because his live-in partner had stripped the place of all things feminine. Eight months, and it still felt like a hollow shell. There was food in the fridge, and no washing up in the sink, and loads of wine; well, there would be—that was always Claire's tipple and he'd never much liked the stuff.

Opening the front door he realised how stark the hallway wall was, that he really should have found something else to fill that gaping space, that empty space, that spiteful reminder that she had painted that picture especially for him, and then reclaimed it as her own. Now it hung on *his* wall, whoever *he* was. Thief. She should have taken the bloody wine.

Helen was trailing after him, looking, scanning, chatting about how nice it was, being polite; he imagined her breathing in the atmosphere of who he was, noting the damp coat over the banister, feeling the chill in the air.

He was pleased when she opted for coffee: avoided the awkwardness of asking for wine and her getting tiddly and him not letting her drive home. Bed or sofa: share a bed, or sit up all night? She was nice, and he might have been up for it, but after Claire, he wasn't sure he was ready for anything like that yet. Shit, Helen might be married, her husband might phone just as they were having it away, and she'd end up having to lie and say she was working late. Didn't bear thinking about.

They sat side by side on the sofa, the laptop on the coffee table in front of them, but to get a clear view they had to sit close, and he could feel his body tense up as soon as her shoulder nudged his sleeve.

'I don't bite,' she said with a hint of seduction. 'And it's years since I jumped a guy.'

'So glad I'm safe in my own home,' he said, and laughed; but pulled his feet up and sat cross-legged, placing the ashtray in his lap, ready for the main feature.

Most of it he'd seen first-hand in real time, but it was fascinating to watch again, see the action from a different viewpoint.

'So Charteris is the grandson,' Helen said thoughtfully, and once the clip had finished, opened a fresh browser window and logged onto Hayward's blog. She took ages finding the entry she was hunting for, and Talbot waited patiently, studying his sitting room with fresh eyes, and noticing the dust on the TV and the dying houseplant he hadn't bothered to water. It had been Claire's, and part of him wanted it to die, give him an excuse to throw it away.

For a man who collected antiques, his sitting room was devoid of anything ancient. Pathetic, letting a woman take over and rule his life, move all of his treasures up to the spare room because she didn't like anything old. New, new, new, and he had pandered to her every whim. Huh, he hadn't even brought them back down once she had gone, made the effort to re-stake his claim, but then he had been busy — that was the excuse he was sticking to.

Helen tapped his arm, startled him out of his thoughts. 'Here, read this.'

He skimmed the page, then reread it. Hayward had written:

> *I've cried non-stop since I read the newspaper this morning. Lilly, my love, I can't believe that you're gone. I can't bear it! I've never wanted to change the past, but can I?*

> *I'm going to try and change what happened yesterday. My yesterday is Lilly's tomorrow, so there must be a chance to change things. I cannot live with this grief, and if I can't bring about a new future, I shall kill myself. I am going to speak with Lilly and tell her not to get on that plane with her son and his wife. I know the date. I know the time. I am going to warn her!*

A tingle went up and down Talbot's spine. He shivered, reached for a cigarette; found that his fingers shook as he pulled one from the packet. The tingle felt cold and sinister and tangled his insides, made his stomach lurch.

'Me, too,' Helen said, and stole his cigarette. 'Do you think anyone else will put these two items together? The video and the blog?'

'I hope not,' Talbot said. 'Shit.' No wonder Hayward and Granny needed Permissions. Someone, maybe the MOD, was definitely putting the pieces together, and for whatever reason, wasn't going to permit just anyone to access vital details. 'You're not to divulge this information,' he warned. 'This is a police enquiry and not to be interfered with.'

Putting the unlit cigarette on the table, Helen said, 'I think I'll have that wine now.'

'Mine's a beer, it's in the cupboard.'

'And your last slave died of?' She laughed, the sound of it breaking the tension, and he made to get up, but she shushed him down. He watched the video again while she went to fetch the drinks.

There was a second clip, too, this guy having arrived before the police turned up, Charteris yelling at him to 'turn that fucking thing off!' Hayward didn't open the front door, no, that had already been open, and it was Mr Fix-it who ran out to see if he could catch the yob who'd thrown the brick, yelling 'Oi! You!' Charteris responding with, 'Where's that pervert?' Confrontation—blimey, Charteris smacked him one. Well, that was news. A voice. Hayward on the steps, calling Mr Fix-it back inside, begging him not to get involved. Mr Fix-it running back, standing in front of Hayward, protecting him as Charteris tried to rush the steps. A tussle, Charteris losing his footing, stumbling backwards, shouting accusations. Police sirens, cars screeching to a halt, PC Oliver taking Charteris aside. Words. What words? Damn, he couldn't make them out.

'I want that video,' he said, took the glass of beer Helen handed him and smiled. Without a second thought he picked up his mobile and called Yates.

'Sir, do you know what time it is?' Yates said sleepily.

'Just gone 11.30. Fire your PC up, there's a clip on YouTube. I want you to track down the guy who posted it and obtain the original.'

'What, now... sir?'

'Yes, now.'

Talbot flicked his phone on to speaker and Helen giggled at the sound of Yates climbing out of bed and grumbling as he dragged on a gown and pattered around.

'Sir? Have you got a woman with you, sir?'

'Yes, thank you, Yates. Have you got a woman with you?'

'No, sir.'

'Then that is why you get to make the enquiries, and I get to sit here and drink my beer.'

After emailing a link over and getting Yates onto the right clip, Talbot left him to it. To his surprise Helen had brought the bottle of wine through and was busy pouring a second glass, a very large glass.

'I feel the need to get drunk,' she admitted. 'You won't mind if I get ratted and crash on your sofa, will you?'

He shook his head.

'You need to speak with a man named Dr Weissman, Dr Michael Weissman. He's a psychiatrist based in Guildford. But you didn't hear that from me, do you understand?'

Talbot nodded. 'Is he Frankie's psychiatrist?'

'I can't answer that, you know I can't.'

'Is he?'

As soon as he pushed for more, he saw her face change. Within seconds she completely clammed up, downed two more glasses of wine in quick succession, then went to fetch another bottle. Beating a hasty retreat was his best option.

'I think I'll…' He jerked a thumb in the general direction of the stairs. 'You sure you wouldn't prefer the bed?'

'No, that's very sweet, but I need to be on my own.'

'Another time, perhaps,' he said, not wishing to break the illusion by explaining that he had meant on her own; then kissed her cheek, and on his way up to bed, cranked up the heating to save the awkwardness of having to fetch her down a blanket.

So WHAT ABOUT KENT, where Charteris assaulted Hayward? Talbot tapped his pencil over and over until the lead broke. Permissions, it had to be. This thing had the lid shut down so tight that the right hand didn't know what the left was doing. Everyone had stopped communicating, and Hayward was getting away with whatever he wanted. Like changing the past.

Idiot. Of course he wasn't.

But Hayward was writing a fucking blog. Telling the world what he was up to. Telling everyone that he *was* changing the past. Only he wasn't telling the truth, he *couldn't* be, and someone, up there, in the highest seats of power, had warned him not to spill the beans, and that way everyone rubbed along nicely together. Astral bloody travel. Impossible.

Shit. The MOD wouldn't be involved unless something dodgy was going on, now would they? Communications, that would be it: Hayward had to be secretly playing around with some fancy telecommunications gimmick. They'd want to shut him up about that, keep it under wraps. Only, Talbot couldn't see where Lilly would slot into that. Why the infatuation with her when she was so old?

He spent most of the night reading Frankie's blog in his bedroom, the soft glow from a table lamp enough to scribble down some notes, the bed behind him unused, and his eyes aching from staring at the machine. For comfort he'd stripped off and put on his dressing gown, made himself as relaxed as the tension in his neck would allow. It must have been gone three when the door swung open, the sound of Helen creeping in making him turn, the sight of her mussed-up hair where she'd tried to sleep startling him into thinking she was a ghost. His pulses raced. Christ, this is what Frankie's blog did for you, got you so involved in his crazy world that suddenly his reality became your own.

'You okay?' he whispered.

'No,' she said, sounding maudlin. She slumped down onto the bottom of the bed and burst into tears, a half-empty bottle of wine cradled in her lap.

'Hey, hey,' he said softly, and placed an arm around her shoulders, drawing her close.

'I... I'm so... confused,' she managed to say between great, heaving, alcohol-fuelled sobs. 'Everyone's lied to me, haven't they?'

Not knowing what everyone had said, Talbot chose the middle line, 'Not lied, Helen.'

'What then?'

'It's a cover up, for something.' He kissed her forehead.

'He's meant to be crazy,' she said angrily. 'Frankie is supposed to be a harmless schizophrenic, with a wild imagination, who lives in his own bizarre dream world... and... and writes a love story about someone who isn't real called Lilly.' She looked up at him, tears sparkling on her cheeks. 'Now it's all sinister, Jake, all creepy and bad — and bloody scary.'

'Yes, but —' He cajoled her to stand and led her round to lie on the bed. Putting the pieces together, he started to understand why Charteris might want to keep Frankie away from his grandmother, so that the world didn't put two and two together when Frankie eventually named the real people involved. He would, Talbot was certain of that. Permissions.

'What?' Helen asked as he prised the wine bottle from her fingers.

He crouched by the side of the bed and drew the cover over her. 'Permissions. Frankie's file needs special permission to access it. Whoever slapped that notice on it... well, they haven't issued a court order for Frankie to keep away from Lilly; they don't appear to have inhibited him.'

'I don't understand.'

'They want it to run its course,' he whispered. 'Try and get some sleep.' He kissed her cheek and stroked her hair, smelt her delicate perfume amidst the heat of red wine. 'Stay here tomorrow, I'll phone you in sick.'

As he made to move away, she grabbed his hand. 'You've got to let me see this through. Please, Jake, you've got to let me stay in the loop.'

'As much as I can,' he promised, and wondered what would explode in their faces if Hayward was simply allowed to see Lilly.

On his way to work, Talbot took a drive past Hayward's to check that his window had been fixed and that Charteris had shifted his vehicle. The key he'd confiscated had been from a dark BMW. The only visible cars matching that description were tucked away on hard standings, bright rays of hopeful sunshine bouncing off their polished paint work. Hayward's house looked secure, and Talbot wondered if his cat had come home — a good point of human compassion to open their next conversation.

Farnham police station looked grim as ever. Talbot speculated whether anyone had ever found the pigs allegedly hidden away in the rural bas-reliefs decorating the exterior. He'd often looked for them, wondering if the myth held any truth. People wanted to be part of the same tribe, see what others saw, point and say, 'there are the pigs'.

So who was pointing at astral travel and visiting people in the past? Who was believing in that?

As soon as he walked into the office, Yates glanced up and grinned. 'You look like you've been up all night, sir.'

'And you look far too chipper.' Talbot stifled a yawn and flicked the kettle on. 'Any joy with the YouTube clip?'

'Easy-peasy. The guy who recorded it's one of Hayward's neighbours, and only too eager to let us have a copy if it stops all of that rough stuff in his neighbourhood.'

'Did he have an opinion on Hayward?' Talbot plonked a coffee down in front of Yates, pleased to notice dark shadows under his eyes and a hint of puffiness in those chubby cheeks.

'Only that he's a good neighbour and generally keeps himself to himself.'

'Good, then call him and ask him, very nicely, to remove this video from YouTube, tell him it's a very sensitive case, threaten legal action if needs be. Do the same with the other guy who's put a recording on there.'

Yates frowned. 'Has Peter Charteris been tightening the thumb screws?'

'No, it's a direct order—from me.'

'Then I'd best crack on.'

The video was already installed on a laptop and Talbot watched it while drinking his tea, pausing it, replaying it, and rubbing his eyes as if that might help him see what he thought was going on. The sound quality was poor, a million raindrops beating the voices into submission, the visuals blurry if you looked too close. Bribery was the word that kept tripping through his mind, but that would be impossible to prove with something as indistinct as this. While Yates finished his calls, he looked up Dr Weissman, easily found his number, and stored it in his mobile. There was no rush to call him. He'd prefer to read the other half of Hayward's blog first, get inside his head some more, sift the fact from fiction… then approach the shrink.

7

LILLY CHARTERIS LOOKED OUT of the window. It was raining again, grey and grim and nothing but rooftops to sit and stare at. No fields, no green, no lights, and only on the luckiest of days did she get to see the odd pigeon perched on that chimney pot over there. Occasionally she kept some crumbs back from breakfast, her mind brimming with the fantasy that she might, one day, have the strength to undo the window, to break the lock, and encourage the birds to come and feed. She'd turned the chair to face the window, and positioned it so that she could just about see over the window ledge, even though it was high. She got a better view if she stood, but her legs didn't like standing for very long, not any more, not since she'd stopped walking to the shops and spending hours dancing through the fields on ripe summer days. Lazy they'd called her, and senile too, because she preferred life to cleaning and cooking.

So now she stared, and waited. It was cold and there was nothing else to do. No television, no radio, no magazines, and no conversation. It was almost as if the staff had been told not to speak to her. She knew who would have done that: her grandson, who always smelt of whisky, and said she was daft. Her companions were a bed and a chair, and one of those tables that had legs going under the bed and a tray on top, for when she was fed. The bed was uncomfortable, the chair old and threadbare around the arms. The cardigan she was wearing wasn't her own, she was sure it wasn't. She'd never have bought a green one, not green; no, she never wore green.

Her husband had always led her to believe that he had done well, that they had scrimped and planned for old age, and that come their twilight years they would bask in luxury. Often she tried to work out how he might have spent it all, how he had lost it all just before he died. One minute rich, the next minute poor; so strange.

So she sat, and waited, and stared. She stared into the past and spoke with Frankie; such a comfort. Seeing his dark eyes made her go all a-quiver. Such a smouldering gaze, it had stolen her heart, right from the very first time. She sighed, smiling at the thought, remembering how his dark hair was so thick and fell in slight curls around his ears and across his forehead. A touch of the gypsy about him—so romantic.

She hadn't seen him for years, and he had explained that there might be a time in the future when he wouldn't be around, but he had promised to visit, in person; so she sat, and waited. Memories of him were always so fresh, so renewed, new thoughts and words coming to her all of the time, as if it were yesterday. She smiled and lifted her fingers to touch her lips. One kiss—yes, she would like one kiss before she died.

She turned her head at the sound of the door opening.

'Frankie?' she whispered and felt her heart flutter.

'No, Mrs Charteris, just me,' the girl said, kicking the door shut behind her as she balanced a tray.

It was a new girl, one she hadn't seen before, a fresh young thing with a smile and words tripping from her lips. No other girl had ever spoken to her, not even to say hello.

'Would you like to eat there, in your chair, or in bed?'

Choices. The girl made her feel that at long last she could have a say in her own life.

'Here. I'd like to eat here.' Lilly replied, and smiled as the girl's eyes met hers. Lilly lifted the metal cover off the food, her hand trembling, her heart thumping with anxiety. A new girl. Oh my God, she was going to risk it. 'I'd like to write some Christmas cards.'

'I could pop across the road and buy some for you.' The girl sniffed the food and turned her nose up at the ghastly smell. 'I'd best get you a chocolate bar, too, or something.'

'This stuff's disgusting,' Lilly agreed. 'They think that old people have lost all sense of taste and smell.'

The girl laughed, softly, quietly, afraid in case anyone heard. 'It'll be like a dorm feast,' she whispered. 'Lots of illegal snacks. Crisps, and sandwiches, and sweets for later.'

'And a pen and a telephone directory.' Lilly held her breath, terrified of refusal.

'Oh, you haven't even got your address book here?' The girl stuck her hands on her hips and gazed around the room. 'Stamps, you'll need stamps.'

'Oh, yes please!'

SUCCESS MADE LILLY'S HAND SHAKE as she pressed the pen firmly against the paper and formed the words.

> *Dear Frankie,*
>
> *If you are the right Francis Hayward, my address is Mellow Acres, Guildford. I am so looking forward to seeing you, my mystical gypsy.*
>
> *Love from Lilly   x*

She'd hesitated before placing that *x* after her name, felt a moment of uncertainty about sending him a kiss.

She wrote seventeen in all, one to every F. Hayward in the telephone directory. To avoid suspicion she wrote ten more addressed to random people, so that a few different names would be spotted if anyone flicked through. Hope was such a strange feeling. She knew that if a letter got through to her Frankie, he would visit. After all, he had promised to visit, to sit and hold her hand. He wouldn't let her down.

But she doubted they would get posted. There had been no response at all from the last batch of letters she'd sent out, or the ones before, and she often suspected that they had never got as far as the post box. Hope. She would take them herself, but she wasn't allowed out. Hope. If one of these was her Frankie, he would visit, she just knew he would. The girl had smiled when she came back and took them away, a smile of promise and conspiracy, the sweets she pressed into Lilly's hand already opened so she didn't have to struggle with the packaging.

It had been so long since Lilly had had a sweet treat. She sucked the fruit jelly—lemon, so tart and wonderful, the flavour bursting onto her tongue, her mouth tingling with the pleasure of it.

Suddenly life was exciting, the grey clouds had lifted, and the sun was shining.

Such short-lived joy, the girl's piercing scream startling her so much that she flinched and looked back towards the door. Fear slashed through her happiness, the cold hail of envelopes falling down around her face sharp enough to cut her cheek. Peter was skimming them at her, his face tight with rage, his focus entirely on her, oblivious of the terrified girl he was dragging back into the room by her wrist like a sack of potatoes.

Lashing out, the girl shouted, 'Let me go! Let me go!'

Lilly's heart raced and she tried to raise herself out of the chair. She was nearly standing when he lunged towards her, pulling the screaming girl along as he shook his fist. Lilly cried out, half shielded her face, and slumped back down.

'Stay put, you silly bitch.'

Tears pricked her eyes and she started to shake.

'You bastard!' the girl yelled, kicking and thumping and twisting herself away. Peter held fast, her wrist reddening under his grip.

'Peter! Let her go!' Lilly demanded, but her quavering words possessed no authority.

The girl was being flung around, jerked this way and that with bruising fingers, her hair scattering across her forehead and her pretty face creasing with pain. Lilly caught the stench of whisky, good malt and plenty of it. She spat at him, but he didn't seem to notice.

'I've told them not to let you write letters.' Peter hurled another envelope at her and it whizzed past her cheek, buzzing like a terrible insect. Pulling the girl in close so that they were face to face, he snarled and said, 'She's unwell. She's gaga, lives in a fantasy world, always has; don't you idiots understand anything?'

'Let me go,' the girl begged, sobbing and buckling to her knees as he pushed her down.

'This is it,' he said, discarding her so unexpectedly that she sprawled across the floor. 'I'm taking my grandmother away, and this is the last you, or anyone else, will ever see of her.'

Scrabbling to her feet, the girl rushed to the door.

'Don't phone the police,' Lilly called after her. 'It's not worth getting involved.' She could hear sobs echoing down the corridor, steps moving away, terror quickening the pace. How dare he treat the poor girl so roughly? Anger rose. She looked him in the eyes, braced herself against his wrath. 'Well, Peter, what are you going to do with me *this* time?'

ON HEARING HELEN'S FLUSTERED TONE, Talbot smiled and raised a finger for Yates to stop walking. He'd answered his mobile on the hoof and now wanted to listen and pay full attention to her embarrassed apology.

'Jake, I am so very sorry,' she was saying, her voice breathy with anxiety. 'Whatever must you think of me?'

'It's okay, really, don't worry about it.'

'It's just so… you know… I mean, I woke up in your bed, and I can't remember how I got there.'

'Oh, I think three bottles of red had something to do with it.' He suppressed a snort of laughter and flicked his hand at Yates, who was grinning and trying to listen in. 'Go away,' he mouthed. 'How's the head?'

'Head's fine, mouth tastes like a sewer.'

'Nice.'

There was a pause. He guessed he'd overstepped the mark and prepared to jump in with an apology.

'Look, would you mind terribly if I leave my car at yours and collect it tomorrow?'

It was his turn to hesitate, the idea of her phoning from his house making him feel uncomfortable and violated. Somehow he'd imagined she would wake up and leave as quickly as possible, but it was already two in the afternoon. She'd slept right through until now. Under the circumstances he would have done the same.

'Sure, no problem.'

'Oh, you are a sweetie,' she said. Perhaps she was too hung over to notice his reluctance. 'We'll speak soon on the case. I haven't got a brain in right now.'

'Sure,' he said, and hung up, a stab of resentment upsetting his gut at her calling it 'the case' as if she were Frankie's caseworker.

That was the problem with women, they never read him right, always took things for granted. Claire had done that, all of the time; and right now Helen's attitude was reminding him of her and pushing all the wrong buttons. Yates had picked up his intonation, seen the look on his face, taken the hint, and was leaning against a wall a few yards away, pretending he wasn't there. He'd known when the fun was over and things had turned sour.

'Everything all right, sir?' Yates asked as he joined him.

'Probably.'

They walked on in silence, the pebble-dash of Mellow Acres drawing closer and looking no more welcoming for being bathed in warm winter sunshine. Today they had a game plan, go in together and show their warrant cards, follow procedure. Talbot hadn't explained all of last night's findings to Yates yet, thinking it better to take him back to his place later for coffee, so that his exclamations of disbelief didn't create an uproar in the station. They were nearly at the path leading up to the front entrance when a car screeched to a halt and blasted its horn, barely missing a young woman who dashed across the road right in front of it.

'Steady!' Yates called out, but she ran past and straight into Mellow Acres. 'Idiot.'

'Late back to Colditz is probably a punishable offence,' Talbot said dryly.

'I've got a get-out-of-jail-free card,' Yates said. 'It's called a warrant card.'

'We have to break in first.' Talbot grinned and opened the door for Yates.

Yates laughed. 'Cannon fodder, sir?' He was just about to step into the firing line, when the woman who'd run across the road hurried straight past him, avoiding his gaze, her stride purposeful.

'Thanks,' she mumbled, then spun round and said loudly, 'I should take your relatives out of there, if I were you.'

'Why's that?' Yates asked.

'I'm going to make an official complaint, have the dump closed down.' Standing there, feet slightly apart, black overcoat pulled in by a beige bag slung across her chest, she gave Talbot the impression she was a student or hippy type. Early thirty-something at a guess. Her hair was bundled up under a colourful knitted hat, but he could see dark wisps escaping across her forehead, and could feel the rage seething behind those dark eyes. She must be staff. Why else would a young woman like this wear flat shoes and tights when he'd expect to see jeans? He slid his finger slyly towards Yates, indicating that he should get round behind her, instinct warning him that this was a skittish quarry.

'Perhaps we can help.' He took measured steps towards her as he pulled out his ID. 'Detective Inspector Jake Talbot, and this is Detective Sergeant Yates.'

'She said she didn't want the police.' The woman glanced towards Yates, moved backwards.

'Whoa.' Talbot raised his hands for a truce, afraid that she would step back straight into the road. 'We'd just like a word, like to know what's happened to upset you so much.'

'I couldn't do anything to stop him.' Her eyes darted all over the place, searching for escape. 'I didn't do anything.'

'Look, this isn't a good place to talk—'

'I'm not going to the police station; I haven't done anything wrong.' She folded her arms.

Talbot smiled and pointed up the street. 'Cup of tea, coffee, get warm and chat, eh?'

She stared ahead, frozen like a rabbit in the headlights. A sure sign of shock or fear.

'I'm Gary and he's Jake,' Yates said. 'What's your name?'

'Why are you here?' She looked at Yates, someone closer to her own age.

'We came to visit somebody, but that can wait.'

'Well, I hope they aren't being treated as badly as Lilly was.' Her face crumpled and she tossed her head back, taking in a deep breath to stifle the tears.

'Lillian Charteris?'

She gasped and covered her mouth. 'Lilly's gone,' she cried and burst into tears. 'He's taken her away, and I think he's going to kill her.'

8

WHILE SERVING HIM, the man at the counter looked over Talbot's shoulder with interest to where Yates and the woman were sitting, obviously concerned that two men had come in with a young woman crying her eyes out.

'A sudden bereavement,' Talbot said, and hoped it was enough to satisfy the man's curiosity.

Passing the hot drinks round, he was happy to take a back seat if it meant the woman would talk. Yates was leaning close and trying to calm her down, repeating soothing words while she sobbed and clutched the clean hankie he'd given her. It was stuffy in the café, overly hot after the biting cold outside, yet she refused to take her coat off, or her hat.

Unconsciously, Talbot pulled out his cigarettes as soon as he sat down, then shrugged and put the packet away again. The woman sniffed and smiled.

Talbot understood that look in her eye. 'You prefer to sit outside and have a fag?' Without waiting for a reply, he picked up both of their cups and made for the door. She was prompt to follow, Yates flustering around to catch up.

It was almost dark, the light filtering out through the café window enough for Talbot to glimpse what he thought were red pressure marks on her wrist as she leant forward to light up from the cupped flame he offered. Her coat sleeve had ridden up, exposing the shadowy shape on her skin, and alerting him to treat this particular frightened rabbit with caution, just as you would with any wounded animal. There were tables and chairs, but he decided to stand, make it feel as if they weren't settling down and that everything could be over and done with quickly.

'If we're lucky, Gary'll go in and fetch us out another cuppa,' he said, downing his tea.

Yates frowned and glanced from one to the other, clearly wondering why Talbot wanted shot of him, then did as he was told.

'How was Lilly when you saw her?' Talbot asked, looking out across the street and traffic as if casually making chit-chat.

'I… I hadn't worked there long,' she replied, puffing away on her cigarette in short spurts, as if she were afraid of inhaling the smoke. 'I… I didn't know there were special instructions for her. The poor old dear had nothing.' She faltered and reached for her tea. 'Her room was so barren. I felt really sorry for her.' She looked up at Talbot, and he turned and smiled, made eye contact. 'She wanted to write some Christmas cards, so I bought her some.' Her face crumpled and she started to sob again. 'Her grandson came in.' She shoved back her coat sleeve and thrust her sore wrist up. 'Look what he did to me.'

Bloody hell: that was worse than he'd thought. 'Was his name Peter Charteris?'

'Yes. How do you know that?' She pulled her sleeve down and shifted from foot to foot. 'He threw the cards he snatched off me right into Lilly's face, cut her cheek.'

Talbot nodded, assured her that he was listening.

'And I fell to the floor when he let go of my wrist, bruised my knee. He…' a sobbing, panicky breath, '… he said that no one would ever see her again. I ran from the room, and I…' She wiped at her tears with Yates's damp handkerchief. 'I was collecting my things when I heard him down in the lobby, shouting that he was taking his grandmother away.'

'Have you any idea where to?' Talbot saw Yates on the other side of the glass door, struggling to open it with his hands full, and discreetly signalled for him to stay put.

'No, no idea.'

'It was Lilly we were going to visit,' Talbot said, perched on the table so that he was at eye level, and added gently, 'It would be really useful to our enquiries if you made a formal statement.'

'Can I do him for assault?' She folded her arms, pursed her lips.

'You can certainly make an official allegation. We'll need to have a doctor check you over.'

'Is it worth it?' She swung her bag round and started hunting in it, pulling out a packet of cigarettes. 'Can I win?'

'No guarantees, but you're in with a good chance.' He went and opened the door for Yates, gave her a few seconds to think it through.

On taking the mug from Yates, her hand shook violently, and she spilt it all over their fingers. 'Look what he's done to me,' she said, her face crumpling. 'This isn't me, this isn't me. I'm not like this, such a pathetic—'

'No, I'm sure you're not....' Talbot paused and smiled, tilting his head slightly in the hope that she'd say her name.

'Kate.' She slumped down into one of the chairs, covered her face with her hands and burst into tears again.

Leaning close to Yates, Talbot whispered, 'Call uniform, make sure there's a female officer attending. Charteris assaulted her.'

'Yes, sir,' Yates said with astonishment and strode away a few feet to make the call.

'You're going to be okay, Kate,' Talbot said, pulling a chair round and sitting down close to her. 'Some officers are on their way and they'll take you to the station to make a full statement. They'll look after you.' He felt like patting her hand to offer reassurance, but that wasn't permitted, so he lit a cigarette, showed they were part of the same tribe. She smiled, nodded, and he gave her one of his business cards. 'My number's on there. Call me any time.'

For a moment she studied it. 'Will I get into trouble if I tell the whole truth?'

'That all depends.' He grinned, and added teasingly, 'On how naughty you've been.'

'I went back,' she admitted, mischievous lights dancing in her eyes. 'I went back and picked up Lilly's Christmas cards. I posted them for her.'

Talbot swallowed hard and felt a tingle rush up his spine. Bloody hell, she never mentioned that Lilly had actually written the cards. That was why Kate had been dicing with death rushing across the road, back from the post box on the other side of the street.

'Did you happen to notice who they were addressed to?'

Kate shook her head. 'I was frightened. As soon as he'd taken Lilly away, I rushed back in and grabbed them.'

Blue lights swirled across their faces, and Talbot patted her hand—to hell with the rules. 'We'll speak again,' he promised, and stood to discuss details with uniform before handing her over.

'Come on, Helen, you've got to help me out here.' Talbot slammed the kettle down and flicked the switch. Yates was safely ensconced in the sitting room skimming through Hayward's blog, hopefully engrossed enough not to want to eavesdrop on a private phone conversation. So far Talbot had received a flat rebuttal from Helen, and his temper was rising. 'You're a social worker,' he repeated. 'Lilly has been taken away, surely you can make enquiries to find out where to, and ensure that she's safe.'

'That really isn't my job,' Helen stated, her tone dry and matter of fact. 'She isn't my case.'

Lowering his voice, he hissed down the phone, 'Look, you wanted to be included in *my* case, and now I'm asking for assistance.'

'Begging won't help, Jake. It's out of my district, and way beyond my powers to go marching in and make accusations, and demands, purely because her family…' she emphasised the word family, '…have decided to look after her elsewhere. It isn't a crime, you know, to be nurtured by your loved ones.'

'Well, fuck you too!' he shouted, but he'd already killed the call. Snatching up the mug that stank of her lipstick he smashed it down into the sink. 'Arghh!'

'Everything alright, sir?' Yates called out.

'The ex!' Talbot yelled back, left the shattered china and banged about searching for where he'd filed the stack of junk mail from local takeaways. Begging! How dare she? His phone started ringing, pulsing out 'Friends' by Queen, and he wished he could find some more appropriate tune for those people one simply knew; acquaintances, like Helen, who right now could bloody well piss off. He waited the full chorus until it went to voicemail then switched it onto silent.

From the sitting room Yates called out, 'I thought you'd relegated Claire to "I Will Survive" by Gloria Gaynor.'

It was best not to answer that one. Helen's car was still filling his drive and Yates wasn't a detective for nothing.

'Indian or Chinese?' he yelled back. Greeted by silence, he strode into the sitting room, armed with a handful of colourful flyers enticing one to get a coronary from pizzas, burgers, or any other exotic cuisine.

On seeing him, Yates frantically waved a hand to make sure he didn't speak, while he nodded into his mobile phone.

'Yes, sir,' he said, 'I'll hand over the phone immediately, sir.' He winced as he passed it across, sticking his arms out to impersonate Justice.

Shit, that was Bailey. What did he want at this hour of the evening?

'Yes, sir,' Talbot said, eyes up to heaven as Bailey ranted about him switching his phone off. 'Must have left it in the car, sir. Didn't hear it.'

'You're a bloody liar and you know it,' Bailey hissed down the line. 'Now what is going on, Jake? And don't even consider lying to me on this one.'

'Which one?' Talbot braced himself.

'You and this one-man, single-handed, personal vendetta against Peter Charteris.' Bailey lowered his tone and said pointedly, 'I was called away from a very respectable drinks party. I was called into the station to sort out your mess. Assault! You're so bloody determined to pin something on him, aren't you? Honestly, Jake, what are you playing at?'

'I'm playing detective, sir, and I detected that Mr Charteris had…'

'Don't give me that old chestnut. Where did you fish her up from, eh? Did you pay her to make this accusation?'

Talbot swallowed a lump in his throat, followed by a very sour taste.

'I shall pretend I did not hear you say that, sir.' He beckoned Yates over and motioned that he wanted the phone switched to speaker. He felt the need to have a witness to this particular conversation. 'The young lady alleges that she was…'

'I know what she alleges!' Talbot heard Bailey thump his desk at the other end. 'It stinks of being a bloody setup, Jake! Charteris claims he's never seen the girl, Mellow Acres claim they never employed her…'

'Don't you think it might be Mr Charteris who's paying the piper, sir?' Talbot crushed the bundle of flyers in his hand.

'Well, one of you must be throwing the readies around… or everyone's lying!'

Dropping the flyers to the floor Talbot kicked them, scattering them around. 'Perhaps we should discuss this in the morning, sir, when you're a little calmer.'

'Oh no, this was a simple enquiry. You butted your nose in, and now it's turning into a full-scale fiasco. Charteris has threatened an official complaint: police harassment. He'll take you down, Jake, mark my word, he will if you don't back off.'

'With all due respect, sir…'

'Enough! I don't want to hear any of your excuses.' Bailey paused. 'Wind this up, get Hayward to leave Granny alone, and take some time off.'

'I attempted to speak with Mrs Charteris today so that I could do precisely that, sir.' Talbot paused, waited for his reaction.

'Why the hell did you want to talk to her? She's senile.'

'Not from what I have heard, sir; and I needed to validate that point. On the supposition that she is *compos mentis*, Mrs Charteris is a person in her own right, and surely it is up to her whether or not she sees Hayward.'

Bailey sighed, long and hard, ensuring it could be heard down the phone. 'Go on; tell me, what did she say?'

'I didn't get to speak with her, sir. Mr Charteris had removed her from Mellow Acres.'

'Don't be absurd.'

'The young woman who alleges assault witnessed him taking her away.'

'Well, so she says, but Charteris says otherwise.'

'Then he won't mind if I pop along tomorrow and visit her, will he?'

'We'll go one better than that, Jake.' Bailey fiddled with the pens on his desk, the rattle making a dreadful scraping noise down the phone. 'We'll go tonight. I'll come and pick you up in forty-five minutes.'

'Will you be informing Mr Charteris, sir?'

'I don't think so. Do you?'

Rushing food never suited Talbot, and he could feel his stomach knotting as huge pockets of gassy air crashed around inside. In a minute he would burp, and it would stink of spicy food and onions, and Yates would take the piss. Or maybe not, as Bailey was sitting in the back, commanding which way to turn the wheel, as if Yates had never driven to the place before. Now he had two cars stacked in his driveway, and anxiety was creating dreadful scenarios of Bailey colliding with Helen and more questions being asked. Bugger, he couldn't even smoke with Bailey on board.

It took several buzzes on the intercom before they gained entry, the woman who opened the door insisting on seeing everyone's ID before letting them in. Correct procedure, but now his toes were frozen, and his hands numb, even though he'd had them shoved in his pockets.

'Mrs Charteris left today,' the woman said, folding her arms. 'Mr Charteris has decided to look after her at home, with a private nurse.'

'Well, there you are,' Bailey said, as soon as they were back in the car. 'He's got the money and he's paying for the best.'

Leaving his seat belt off Talbot swung right round to look at him. Sulphur street lights threw an orange cast across Bailey's face, and he creased his lips, appearing smug and self-satisfied.

'He lied to you.' Talbot pointed a finger straight at him. 'He's twisted the facts to suit himself, made out the poor girl he assaulted is the liar—and you swallowed it. Sir.'

Bailey leant forward, ducked away from the lights and plunged his face into darkness. Talbot could smell the wine on his Super's breath as he drew close and whispered, 'Jake, it's only a few bruises. Just let it rest.' He turned his head, as if he knew that his eyes would appear wide and stern, then said loudly, 'Warn Hayward off, that's all you have to do. Then take a month off. You're overworked and stressed, overreacting to every minor situation.'

Clenching his hand into a tight fist, Talbot shifted round. He was being forced to be the bad guy, the one who was to tell Hayward that neither he nor Lilly had any rights. He was to be the one to tell young Kate that he had been wrong, and that she could never win against a man like Charteris; and worst of all he was being forced to go against his principles, and he really couldn't tolerate that. He buckled his seat belt and gestured for Yates to drive on. His mouth was dry and his insides shaking, only this time it wasn't indigestion. Beside him Yates looked ahead, his mouth pinched, his lips quivering as if he was bursting to say something. Talbot pressed play on the stereo, cranked up the volume, and lit a cigarette.

9

UNDER ORDERS FROM BAILEY, he'd turned his phone off silent; otherwise, he would never have noticed the text from Helen. All it said was that she'd come and collect her car tomorrow, which was fine by him, as he'd be at work and wouldn't have to see her. She'd rubbed him up the wrong way by outstaying her welcome, and he didn't want to seem ungrateful for her help by presenting as tetchy; and he knew he would. It was the kind of damned awkward situation he'd been trying to avoid, having a colleague in a drunken stupor wake up in his bed, questioning whether they'd done the deed or not.

'I'll go and visit Hayward tomorrow, tell him the bad news,' Talbot said as he saw Yates off. 'You get onto Trudy and see if she can hurry along those Permissions. Oh, and find out that girl Kate's details for me, surname and contact number.'

'Jake! Bailey told you to cool it.' Yates climbed back out of the car and looked across the top of the door at him. 'You can't be serious.'

'And while you're at it…' Talbot ushered him back in, 'find out where Bailey was partying tonight. I'll put a fiver on it being at the 3Gs golf course in Woking.'

'Charteris's place?'

Standing back, Talbot smiled and waved, ignoring Yates as he wound down the window and raised his voice above the engine noise to shout, 'You're treading on thin ice, Jake.'

Sure, he thought as he turned and walked indoors, only I won't be the one falling in. Charteris will be the one going under.

RIGHT FROM THE BEGINNING of the day, Talbot felt under pressure, and he hated getting off to a bad start. When Helen had said that she'd

come round to fetch her car, she hadn't mentioned that it would be
7.30 in the morning, and that she'd ring the doorbell, and phone, and
bash on the door, and try and force him to speak with her. Of course
she would know he was home, his car was sitting in the drive beside
hers; but sheer cussedness made him ignore her and pretend he wasn't
there. Hiding behind the curtains, he peered out of the window and
glimpsed the taxi that she'd arrived in pulling off down the road. If
he craned his neck, he could just about see her when she stood back
from the door and looked up. She was frowning, most likely because
it was dark and she was getting wet, a fine drizzle moistening the
pavement. In the distance his phone rang and he guessed he'd been
spotted, so he retreated to the kitchen and made tea. By eight o'clock
she gave up, shoving a note through the door as she left.

'I've checked up on Lilly, she's fine. I know where she is. H'

Bollocks. This is what came of playing the idiot. It was too late to
flag her down; the only glimpse he caught of her car as he rushed
outside being a brief flash of orange lights as she braked for the
corner. Dashing back inside, he texted her.

'Thanks. Where is she?'

It took a full five minutes for her to respond.

'In a very nice nursing home.'

Talbot read the words twice before their true meaning sunk in.
He knew she wouldn't tell him, but he texted back, 'Which one?'

'I can't tell you that.' He could hear the smugness in her message.

'I'd like to speak with her. Can you arrange that?'

'Probably not. I'll try.'

'Thanks.'

From there, he'd taken too long to shower, thoughts slowing his
hands down as he washed his hair, and more thoughts making him
pace up and down rather than getting on with the job of getting
dressed. Where was Lilly? First she was at Charteris's, then she was
in a nursing home, everyone taking what they were told at face
value. Had anyone seen her since she was removed from Mellow
Acres? Was she still alive? He shivered, blamed it on the cold and
slipped a lightweight V-neck sweater over his shirt. It was already
gone nine, so he called Yates, got Kate's details off him, said that he
was going straight up to see Hayward, then cooked a full breakfast
and ate it while reading Hayward's blog.

Common sense had warned him to keep off fried foods after last night's curry, but he never listened, and ended up feeling bloated, even though the bacon and eggs had tasted great. Never work while you eat; it was a recipe for an ulcer. He and Yates had discussed Hayward's blog while they'd shovelled down the Indian takeaway, Yates reckoning it was all fiction with a peppering of fact thrown in for realism; and Talbot brewing to show him the entry concerning the plane crash, but never getting round to it before Bailey turned up. Now he was reading it again, the same rush of adrenaline twisting his gut, and his insides complaining.

He Googled astral travel and tried to get his head round the concept of his alleged soul leaving his body. This was entering the realm of heebie-jeebie and verging on bonkers, a total headfuck. Perhaps Hayward used drugs to hallucinate, or to induce a near-death experience. There were certainly enough entries mentioning spontaneous out-of-body experiences during an operation. People believed in it, that was the sad part, or the twisted part, or the outright absurd part, but whichever, he filed it firmly in the box marked 'delusional'. Leaning back he shoved his plate away and lit a cigarette. There was something that didn't quite click, and he simply couldn't put his finger on it. What wasn't he seeing?

Driving up to Hayward's, he got caught in a stationary queue of traffic, the guy in front's full-width brake light shining straight into his eyes and making him squint every time the driver ahead nudged the pedal. Why the hell had everything ground to a halt? He drummed his fingers on the steering wheel, flicked the wipers on and off to clear the smatterings of rain, and smoked. It was all taking so much time. There was so much to read, so much research to do before he understood, and here he was, waiting. Everyone crept forwards a pace, and then he spied the obstacle: two men and a hole and a guy in a fluorescent bib twisting a stop-go sign round. It was going to take all day if he only let one through at a time. Talbot smacked his hand on the wheel. Yes! That was it. Time. Not one of those websites he'd read through had mentioned astral travel taking you anywhere but somewhere else in the here and now. Float above your bed. Step outside the door. Whisper in your lover's ear. Not one had suggested travelling backwards, or forwards, in time.

No, no, Hayward had to be lying, making it all up; using some clever web coding to make it look as if he'd placed an entry before or after an event. Yes, Hayward was a fraud, his mental illness presenting as a weird fixation. Ah yes, now he was beginning to see Peter Charteris's point of view, understand how his nerves had been frayed by being dogged by a nutter year in, year out. But there was no just cause. Hayward never mentioned names on his blog… bloody hell, just thinking about it was tiring. With only 'Mr I-have-strip-brake-lights' to go before the lollipop swung round and let him through, Talbot phoned Yates.

'Hey, Gary, dig up all you can on the plane crash that Charteris's folks died in. If it has Permissions, then apply, and go fishing in every news item possible, newspapers, TV, video clips, internet. I want it all.'

'We must be desperate.' Yates chuckled. 'You called me Gary.'

Talbot grinned. 'And while you're at it, source me a really good local psychic who can tell me all about astral travel.'

'Has Bailey given us more manpower… Jake?'

The car behind tooted and Talbot glanced up at the green 'go' sign, the guy holding it sweeping his arm. 'It'll give you and Trudy more time together,' he said, threw the phone onto the passenger seat, and drove through just as the sign was spun back to 'stop'.

HAYWARD DIDN'T HAVE MUCH of a reaction when he opened the door and saw Talbot, simply stepped aside and said, 'You'd better come in.'

Today his house was roastie-toastie, Mr Fix-it having done a cracking job of mending the heating system, and now that the place had dried out, it smelt warm and inviting. Slinging his coat over the end of the banister, Talbot noticed that there was a door the other side of the stairs, which of course there would be if you considered the shape of the front of the house, and he wondered if Hayward ever used that room. It was a large house for one man: what, four, maybe five bedrooms?

'You own this place?' Talbot asked, following him into the kitchen.

'Yes, my grandmother left it to me.' He filled the kettle and started to make tea.

Talbot nodded, noticed the half-empty dish of cat food on the floor. 'Came home safe did she? Your cat?'

'Yes, thank you.' Hayward turned to face him, leant against the sink, folded his arms and said, 'How do you know it's a she?'

'You said you were worried about *her* the other day.'

'Don't miss a trick, do you, Mr Talbot.'

He shook his head and smiled, then watched as Hayward set out a tray and made the tea, which he carried through to the sitting room. In jeans, T-shirt, and an unzipped fleece, Hayward presented as normal, the only thing odd about him his old-fashioned habits, like making sure coasters were down so the mugs didn't mark the wooden coffee table. The cabinet that Charteris had smashed was gone, the sofa from under the window now positioned in front of a radiator. Two armchairs at a slight angle to each other filled the space it had vacated, the coffee table in front of them.

'Have you got your Permissions through yet?' Hayward asked as he passed Talbot's tea over.

The look on Talbot's face must have said how shocked he was, because Hayward smiled and gestured that he should sit down and take the tea.

'Now you're wondering how I know, aren't you?' Hayward's eyes were locked on him, unnerving in their persistence.

'Uh-huh.'

Laughing, Hayward picked up his mug and sat back in his chair. 'I've been told not to speak with you,' he said. 'Warned off.'

'I beg your pardon.' Talbot fished out his cigarettes and offered one over.

Rather than leaning forwards, Hayward held out his hand so he could be thrown one. He caught it in mid-air. Impressive.

'I'm a police officer.' Talbot lit his own before chucking the lighter over. 'Who has the authority to instruct you not to speak with me?'

'You'll find out... if they give you your Permissions.' Hayward lit his cigarette and leant forwards to flick ash that wasn't there yet into the ashtray. Neat, obsessively neat. 'I'm a man of honour,' he said, looking down as if ashamed. 'But I'd much rather be free, and able to try and see Lilly, than locked up. I'm sorry.'

'Hold it, hold it. Locked up. Are you serious?'

'Never more so.'

Sipping his tea, Talbot stared at Hayward, tried to judge whether he was lying. Being blocked by someone stronger and more important than him made his pulses race and nerves jangle. He wasn't used to being trodden on from invisible heights.

'Tell me, Frankie… can I call you Frankie?'

Frankie shook his head. 'We're not friends. It would mar the line, wouldn't it?'

'Sure.' Talbot saw his point: it would cross a boundary, and Hayward wasn't ready for that yet.

'Well, tell me, if you speak to me, about Lilly and what is important, how would they ever know?'

Hayward shrugged. 'They'd know.' He drew heavily on his cigarette and smiled. 'You'd become involved. You'd ask different questions. You'd tread on their toes.'

'Will my being here get you into trouble?'

'Not if we stick to the weather.' They both burst out laughing, threw silly quips at each other about how wet it was for the time of year, and then suddenly stopped, Talbot feeling the bubble burst, the fun over.

'Mr Hayward.' He leant forwards. 'We have a huge dilemma. You see, I need to speak with you, and this… issue… is going to make it a very one-sided conversation.'

'Perhaps you'll get your Permissions. Meanwhile all you need to do is protect me from Peter Charteris's rage. Some pressure for him to pay up for the damage wouldn't go amiss, either.'

'I'll have a word.' Talbot looked to the empty space where the cabinet had been. 'And Lilly?'

'Oh, I will still try and see her.'

'That,' Talbot said, stubbing his cigarette out, 'will be difficult. You, me, and the rest of the world need to find out where she is first.' He felt Hayward fall very still. 'He's moved her, and I don't know where she is right now.'

Stunned, Hayward stared into space, then pulled his legs up onto the chair, and curled himself into a fetal position.

'I'm sorry.' Talbot tried to smile. He was worried sick about the old girl and it was impossible to hide it. 'You see, I've been ordered to instruct you to back off and leave the Charteris family alone.' He shrugged. 'I've been ordered to back off, too.'

'I see.' Hayward rubbed a hand around his face, swept his hair aside and stood up. 'I… I have to find her.'

He paced the room, walked up and down with his arms folded, watching his feet, counting the steps. Sudden squalls of rain hit the window, and Talbot listened to the silence in-between the rat-a-tat of the raindrops, heard the emptiness in Hayward's heart as it filled with despair. An unseen clock ticked and a car pulled up outside, the people getting out slamming the doors behind them with unnecessary force. Voices accompanied footsteps up the front steps, and Talbot half stood to see who was coming to the door. A middle-aged woman dressed in a faux fur coat, a man of about thirty trying to hold an umbrella over her head, and trailing behind, a sulky looking twenty-something woman with bright pink hair.

The doorbell rang and Hayward froze. He'd seen them too.

'Quick,' he said, and hid out of sight behind the sitting room door, so that he couldn't be seen from the window. 'Quick, over here.'

Keeping low, Talbot joined him. 'Who are we hiding from?' he whispered.

'The family. That's my mother, brother Joe, and sister Kirsty.'

'And we don't want to make them tea?'

'Certainly not.' Hayward met his gaze. 'My mother will rant, Kirsty's a born kleptomaniac, as in, if it isn't bolted down she'll lift it, and Joe, uh, he's just a "yes" person.'

Whoever had their finger pressed on the buzzer kept it there, the house filling with the angry vibration until they momentarily stopped and yelled out, 'I know you're in there, Frankie!'

'Mother,' Hayward said, as if Talbot wouldn't have guessed it was the older woman.

'Why don't I go and tell them to leave?' Talbot suggested. The racket was doing his head in and he didn't like the idea of hiding behind doors. He'd already done enough of that for one day.

'They'll barge past.'

It was Hayward's house and Hayward's choice, so Talbot trenched in and sat on the floor, back against the doorframe, hands over his ears, one eye on the window. Suddenly a face appeared at it and he flinched, the sight of brother Joe peering in such a surprise, because he didn't think anyone could reach it where the ground outside fell away so steeply.

'What the hell's he standing on?' Talbot hissed.

'They bring a small step-ladder.' Hayward was matter-of-fact.

Getting to his feet, Talbot brushed himself down. 'How often do they hold you to siege?'

Hayward shrugged, which Talbot read as frequently.

Striding to the front door, Talbot yanked it open and glared at the woman whose finger was still on the doorbell.

'Who the fuck are you?' she demanded, let go the bell, and put her hand out, intending to push him aside.

Talbot stood his ground, flicked his warrant card into her face and said, 'I wouldn't try that.'

'Huh, so the cops are involved again.' Opening her painted lips wide, she yelled out, 'I always said they'd catch up with you, Frankie! You murdering bastard!'

'Does this mean we get the house at last?' sister Kirsty asked, leaning against the handrail and lighting a cigarette.

'Well, are you arresting him for Keith's murder or not?' Mother Hayward folded her arms, two cold blue eyes mocking Talbot, the wicked smile creasing her lips challenging him to admit that he didn't know what on earth she was going on about.

10

Brother Joe had climbed down from his step-ladder and come to stand behind Mother, shorter than her where he stood on the step below, but backing her up by making his presence felt. Smartly dressed, trousers, not jeans, and an expensive raincoat that fell down past his knees, he strained to reach high enough with the umbrella to protect his mother's head from the rain. Kirsty was still leaning against the handrail, hands driven into the pockets of a white hoodie: a modern-day stick-insect with black jeans sprayed onto matchstick legs, her fluorescent pink hair soaked and unkempt. Mother's lips were much the same colour, the fur coat grey to match her hair, low lights of chocolate brown giving her a crazy witch-like appearance. Blimey, Hayward was related to the Addams Family.

Taking out one of his cards Talbot handed it over. 'Call me,' he said. 'Frankie and I are busy right now, but I'm sure you'd like to speak to me some other time.'

'Oh, I'll do that all right.' She snatched the card and handed it backwards for Joe to take care of. Lowering her voice, she added, 'It's wrong that he's got away with it for so long, isn't it, Inspector? You know that, and I know that.' A supercilious smile crept across her lips. 'You know you can rely on me, that I'll do all I can to help, to ensure that justice is done.'

No doubt, especially if it meant stealing Hayward's house out from under him.

'You give me a call,' Talbot said, and started to close the door.

Being armed with an inroad to success was enough to satisfy, so she gathered up her entourage and strode down the steps holding court, speaking of how well they would fit in with the neighbours.

Closing the door, Talbot leant against it and looked Hayward in the eye. He was standing just inside the kitchen, cowering, ready to leap for cover if they broke in. The space between them was icy, Talbot sensing Hayward's fear shutting him down and locking him away. Now he'd need a pick-axe to break through the barriers.

'Are you allowed to talk about Keith?' he asked, pushing away from the door and walking slowly towards him.

'No, but I didn't kill him, I swear I didn't.'

'Why would anyone think you had?' Talbot smiled as he went past, filled the kettle, and popped tea bags into fresh mugs.

'He was my best friend. He went missing. We... we went out together and I lost him... He never came back.' He stared at the ground. 'I was questioned at the time.'

'How long ago was that?'

'About ten years.' Hayward eased him aside and took control of making the tea, pouring boiling water carefully into each mug. 'That's all I can say, and that's probably too much.'

'What's Keith's surname?'

'Ask my mother.' He rested his palms on the work surface, facing the wall as he spoke. 'She'll give you facts amidst the lies. Best it comes from her, not me.'

Standing next to him, Talbot picked up a spoon and squeezed the teabags, making sure the tea was a good colour. 'I dare say Keith's got Permissions as well, hasn't he?'

'Probably.'

'Why the secrecy, Frankie?' Talbot flicked the teabag into the sink with a splat. 'I've read your blog, and there's nothing wrong with a bit of astral travel, surely?'

Wide-eyed Hayward faced him. 'Read between the lines, *Mr* Talbot. Use your detective mind and work it out for yourself.'

FROM HABIT ALONE, Talbot popped into the station before heading home. Trudy was sitting at a computer studying the screen and Yates was nowhere in sight, which instantly made him feel awkward entering his own space. Most peculiar, because he hadn't felt at all uncomfortable in Hayward's house. They'd ended up chatting about nothing in particular, mainly Hayward elaborating on character profiles of his family; and then explaining that his cabinet had been deemed a write-off by his insurers, so he'd sent it away to be repaired at his own expense. There was, from what Talbot gathered, no father on the scene, Hayward never mentioning him or explaining his absence.

Trudy glanced up, eager to catch his eye. 'No joy with the Permissions yet, sir. We might hear something one way or the other by Monday, or Tuesday.'

'They most likely don't work over the weekend.' He perched on his desk and picked up a pile of papers that appeared to require attention. 'Where's Yates?'

'Gone to fetch sandwiches. He's been doing really well gathering material about that plane crash.'

'Excellent.' What he really wanted to do was to phone Kate, but he didn't want to do it with Trudy sitting there being all enthusiastic and interested. 'Get him to call me when he gets back. I'm going home.' Trudy frowned judgementally. Laughing, he waggled a finger at her. 'I'm not skiving. I'm going to work from home.' He didn't need to justify himself to her, but he felt he should.

'Yes, sir. Gary says you never stop.'

Well, tomorrow he would stop working and go to the antiques fair at Farnham Maltings, something he'd promised to himself weeks ago when he'd first noticed it advertised in the local paper. Seeing that blank space on the hallway wall had fired him with enthusiasm, set him on a mission to find something half-decent to cover the emptiness. A mirror or a painting, he didn't mind which. Twice he tried to phone Kate, but she didn't answer, and on the second put-through to voicemail he left a message, simply asking her to call him back. A twinge of suspicion made him imagine she'd already entered his number into her phone and was refusing his calls. After all, he had let her down.

When Yates phoned, he yapped on about collating information regarding the plane crash, and said he'd have it in some kind of coherent order by Monday.

'Is Trudy a permanent fixture in my office now?' Damn, his question had come out far too blunt and accusatory.

'She's quite well trained; you only have to ask her to shift and she will,' Yates retaliated, with understandable defensiveness.

'Point taken.' He could have asked him to trawl through missing persons for some lad named Keith who disappeared ten years ago, but he didn't, and as he whiled away the evening eating Chinese and reading Hayward's blog, he wondered why he was keeping it secret. Yes, if he was honest, he was being secretive, hogging information. He'd never done that before on a case, always kept his sergeant up to speed. Only there was no case here, was there? Except an old accusation of murder. They'd never found Keith, so no body, no murder, no crime. Merely a missing person. Frankie had given him a hint, mentioned that they'd left together, but he'd lost him… what, in a crowd? And Keith had never returned. Someone going out and never returning doesn't always make for murder; but where had they gone that day, and why had Hayward been accused of killing him? According to Hayward, the answers were in front of him, in his blog, between the lines, but by three in the morning, Talbot still hadn't found them.

Bright winter sunshine dazzled as it bounced off puddles. Using his space at the station saved on parking. Talbot smiled. The Maltings was only a spit away and sunshine meant there would be more stalls outside and rich pickings. Unfortunately it also meant there would be more punters, but that was okay, he knew what he was looking for and most of them were casual browsers. Only sometimes the idiots beat him to a gem, so he'd learnt to perfect that disinterested look, and that sneer, and that knack of putting rivals off the scent of a bargain. Mostly he collected nothing in particular, just anything that took his fancy, from china, to Bakelite, to definitely not silver—all those hallmarks and tarnish putting him off. Junk, Claire had called it, but if it fascinated him, who cared? These days the halls were peppered with modern stuff, too: silk paintings, arty photographs, and occasionally the work of some new local artist.

There was one today, up on the stage at the back of the hall, the canvases large and inviting, the semi-abstract landscapes of woodland scenes done with daubs of bright colours. A fresh vista of bluebells with sunshine filtering down through a lime-green leafy wood caught his attention. It was tempting. Yes, he quite liked that; it definitely had a certain something. People kept getting in his way as he tried to stand back and get a feel for what it might look like in his hallway. They were browsing, only half interested, standing too close to truly appreciate the design. Damn, would the same happen in his hall?

Moving on, he went upstairs to visit a man he knew sold mirrors. Well, he was never one to buy something without judging the competition, yet anxiety riddled him with impatience in case someone beat him to that painting. Perhaps he should go back and buy it before it went. Halfway down the stairs he collided with Hayward going in the opposite direction.

'Wouldn't expect to see you here,' Hayward said, instinctively holding out his hand for Talbot to shake.

Talbot shook it, as gentlemen did when they met. 'On a mission to buy a painting before someone snaps it up.'

'Mind if I have a look?'

'Not at all. What brings you here?'

Hayward about-turned, fell into step beside him, and together they pushed through the crowd.

'Someone told me there's a dealer here who's an expert on Capo Di Monte figurines. I need to arrange a valuation for the insurers.'

'They were worth at least two grand.' Talbot halted by the steps that went up to the stage. 'I can let you have copies of all the photos we took.'

'That would be useful, thank you.' Hayward stepped back and let people through as they barged past. 'You know about antiques, don't you, Mr Talbot?'

'A little.' Starting with a vibration in his pocket Talbot's mobile burst into 'Broken Wings' by Mr Mister, giving him the clue it was a victim of crime. 'Excuse me,' he said to Hayward, read the name, and hurried to answer it before every head turned to locate the outburst of rock music. 'Kate, thanks for calling me back.'

'Are you stalking me?'

Taken aback, he hesitated. 'No, I was wanting to speak with you.'

'So, just because I didn't get back to you immediately, you decided to track me down and upset my work.' She made an infuriated grunting noise down the phone. 'Well, I can't talk to you now. I don't want to discuss details of my private life in public.'

'Kate, Kate, I'm off duty, at Farnham Maltings...'

'I know where you bloody well are! I can see you from here.'

You can? Looking up the length of the great hall, Talbot tried to recognise her amidst the clamour of stalls and punters. What would she be wearing? She'd look different without her coat and hat. Nope. Slowly he pivoted round three hundred and… ah, that would be her, standing up on the stage, in front of the painting he wanted to buy. Yep, that was her alright, glaring down at him, not even bothering to wave.

'What are you selling?' he asked, and smiled up at her, his heart sinking before he'd even heard the answer.

'My paintings.'

'Then I'll leave you to it.' He was going to hang up and walk away, but she rushed towards the railings at the edge of the stage and peered down at him, saying, 'Were you really just walking around?'

He nodded. She was almost loud enough not to need to the phone, her words carrying down across the babble of voices bartering below. Frankie was following his gaze, tracking it up to where she stood, the painting a glorious backdrop to her shock of dark hair. It really was not a good idea for the two of them to meet, for them to get stuck in awkward conversation, until one of them eventually blurted out the name Charteris or Lilly. Shit. He imagined them comparing notes, ganging up to ensure Charteris was nicked. In public that could be highly combustible. No doubt Bailey would string him up by way of reward for gross incompetence.

'Phone me at your convenience,' he said, and cut the call. Nudging Hayward's arm, he leant close and said, 'Let's go find your china expert.'

'What about your painting?' Hayward stood still, tilted his head, and stared up at Kate with deep curiosity. Her arms were draped languidly over the railing, the phone clasped lightly between her fingers, the cream crepe pressure sock on her right arm fully visible. Conscious of her scrutiny, Talbot's skin prickled.

'It's a good painting,' Hayward said. 'You should buy it.'

'Too bold.' Talbot shrugged his dismissal and Hayward laughed, took a final glance up at Kate, and started back down the hall. 'You're a dreadful liar.'

'Glad to hear it.'

'Who is she?'

'A client.'

'A client?' Hayward stopped in the corridor leading onto the stairs. 'Oh, I see. Suspect or victim? No, you can't answer that.' He raised a silencing hand. 'Let me see, bandaged arm… she must be the victim.'

'Hayward, leave the detective work up to me, okay?'

'Of course.' At the top of the stairs Hayward stopped again. 'I've got it. She's the artist, isn't she? I could go and buy it for you, if you're not allowed to patronise… clients.'

'No. Thank you.' Talbot stuck his hands in his pockets and wished Hayward would shut up about it. With such a persistent bugger he could foresee having to stay beside him all day to make sure he didn't go doing something stupid and make contact with Kate. 'The china guy's usually second stall on the left.'

Smiling, Hayward led the way, engaged the seller in efficient conversation, and arranged for him to call round during the week. His companion's confidence intrigued Talbot, and it made him wonder how much of Hayward's behaviour was merely a reaction to his overbearing family, and not wholly inbred, after all. Out in the world, doing business, Hayward presented as normal.

Fiddling with some of the pieces on display, Talbot noticed the seller's prices were sky high and hoped he'd assess Hayward's damage with equal enthusiasm. Charteris was never going to pay up, but at least his insurers might if the valuation had room for negotiation.

Afterwards they meandered downstairs again, and on Hayward's invitation, Talbot joined him for lunch. Despite the cold they sat outside in the sunshine, so that they could smoke with their coffee once they'd finished. Even in the bright light, Talbot thought Hayward had a dark-haired gypsy-like mystery, and noticed that several young women took a second glance on passing. He was pretty sure they weren't admiring a non-descript, middle-aged guy.

'Ever had a girlfriend?' he asked, downing the last of his extra-strong coffee.

'Only Lilly.'

No surprises there, then. 'How old were you when you first met her?'

Hayward shook his head. 'I'm not supposed to speak to you about Lilly.'

The song 'Friends' erupted from Talbot's pocket and on seeing it was Helen, thought he'd best answer it and briefly make his peace.

'I can't speak…'

'Lilly isn't there.' Helen cut across him, shrill and impatient. 'I used a bit of leverage and went to the home I was told she was in—Jesus Christ, Jake! Charteris lied…'

'Keep your voice down.' Talbot glanced at Hayward; convinced he could hear every word.

'I'll get more coffee,' Hayward mouthed, picked up the empties and took them inside.

'Look, Helen, perhaps we should meet up. I've bumped into Hayward, and it isn't good to discuss this right now.'

'Not tonight, I've got friends round for dinner.' She sighed. 'Look, Jake, there isn't much more to it really. Charteris said he'd put her in Tree Tops up North Farnham way, but honest to God, the people there have never heard of Lilly.'

'Then let's hope he's looking after her at home.'

For a moment Helen went quiet. 'Jake… Jake, do you think he's done away with her?'

'For fuck's sake, Helen, you're the social worker, get onto it, demand to see her or something!' Turning his back on Hayward returning with the coffees he hissed, 'My hands are tied. I can't go looking for a missing person, because someone needs to report her missing, and Charteris isn't going to be doing that, now, is he?'

'Okay, okay, don't shout at me, I'm doing my best.'

'I wasn't—' He slammed the phone down onto the table. How dare she hang up on him like that? She didn't even give him a chance to explain.

Beside him, Hayward was staring blankly into space, his eyes glistening with unspilt tears. 'You really don't know where Lilly is, do you?' His voice came out thin and hoarse with emotion. 'If you don't get your Permissions… within a week… I'll tell you everything.' He squeezed the corners of his eyes. 'But you must promise to uphold our bargain. You must promise to help me see Lilly before she dies. I… I have to see her.'

'I'll do what I can.' Talbot lit a cigarette and offered the packet over. 'There may be plenty of time…'

'For once time is not on my side.' Hayward's spoon click-clicked against the mug as he stirred his coffee. 'Lilly is ninety. Not many people live past four score and ten; do they, Mr Talbot?'

11

SOMEHOW SUNDAYS NEVER ENDED up as a day of rest, but Talbot hadn't expected the mayhem to start quite so early. It was barely gone 7.30 when his phone started playing Aker Bilk's 'Stranger on the Shore', and he rolled over in bed and patted the side table, searching for the bastard caller who deemed it civil to phone at this unearthly hour on a Sunday.

'Talbot.'

'Detective Inspector Talbot.' Abrupt and female and undoubtedly Hayward's mother.

He suppressed a groan.

'It's Dorothy Hayward, I'm glad I've caught you. What progress have you made regarding Frankie?'

'Mmm.' Heaving himself up on one elbow, he rubbed his eyes and tried to focus on the conversation.

'Come for brunch.' It was a command, not an invitation. 'Joe and I always eat at eleven, sharp.'

Why, when you get up so fucking early! Why not eat now, like civilised human beings, and then do lunch?

'Mrs Hayward…'

'Dorothy.'

'Dorothy, it isn't appropriate for me to come and…' What the hell did you call it? 'Brunch with you, to involve myself with your family. It would be much better if I interview you at the station.'

'Certainly not! I'm not the criminal, Francis is, and you saw perfectly fit to speak with him in the comfort of his own home.'

'Expect two,' he said firmly, flicked on the bedside lamp, and scribbled down her address. 'I shall be bringing Detective Sergeant Yates with me.'

'Someone of higher rank would be preferable.' Her tone stank of disdain and disappointment. 'Superintendent Bailey would be most welcome.'

'Meanwhile you will make my sergeant welcome.' He cut the call, rolled onto his back and covered his face with his hands. 'Why me?' he murmured, and let the groan escape.

Yates was equally disgruntled, although it did sound as if he were already up and about. 'You have got to be kidding?'

'Nope. Come and pick me up at ten. I'll fill you in before we leave.'

'Murder!' Yates exclaimed, watching him force down the last piece of toast before they set off. 'So now we have Charteris tampering with wires and bumping off Ma and Pa; along with the odd pilot, and Hayward doing away with his childhood chum.'

'You got it.' Talbot pushed a finger into the crease of his mouth to shift vagrant food, dumped the dirty plate in the sink, and switched on the kettle.

'I thought we were going?'

'Fag and tea.'

'We'll be late, sir.'

'Oh, dear.'

Laughing, Yates sat down and started fiddling with the salt cellar. 'You didn't get to speak with Kate, then?'

'Not with Hayward there.' Images of the painting flooded his mind, and he bit back the desire to sigh over lost pleasure. 'I thought the two of them getting together might have been a tad combustible.'

'What? You thought they might gang up on Charteris?' Yates frowned. 'I wonder why Mr Fix-it never made an allegation against him, for that whack in the face.'

'Hayward probably warned him off, told him it would be useless.' Talbot removed the salt cellar before Yates spilt any more, plonked a mug of tea down in front of him, and added, 'But you've got a good point. Follow it through, have a word with Mr Fix-it.'

'Yes, sir,' Yates said wearily and glanced up at the clock for the umpteenth time.

THEY ARRIVED AT PRECISELY eleven fifteen, Talbot having insisted that Yates drive round for a while so he could get a feel for the neighbourhood. Nice. Frensham, horsey, rural, narrow lanes, mainly old houses with bundles of character and far too many zeroes on the price tag. Land, that's mostly what people paid for out here, as well as the peace and quiet. No neighbours opposite, just a hedgerow and a copse and the sound of bird song. He wondered if Hayward had been born and bred in the mini manor house Yates pulled up in front of. The drive arced round, not quite completing a circle, and the front lawns were interspersed with lozenges of roses: pathetic sticks now, but they'd make a fine display in summer.

Getting out of the car, Talbot stretched and breathed in the scent of damp grass and oodles of fresh air. It was one of those muzzy grey days that made him feel as if he were walking through a cloud, not quite mist, not quite rain, the house looming out of it and perfectly fitting the ring tune he'd assigned to Hayward's family.

'*The Addams Family*,' he murmured.

Yates tittered and pursed his lips for him to shush.

It was Joe who answered the door, immaculately dressed in slacks and a white-and-blue-checked ski sweater that appeared to have started life in a sixties film, but Talbot guessed they were back in fashion.

Keeping to a whisper, Joe said, 'You're late, and Mother is very upset.'

Ah, a conspirator, letting them know the lie of the land before they entered the fray. Talbot smiled and nodded, introduced Yates, and lingered to look at this and that as they were led through to a vast conservatory. Antiques, reproductions, all fairly mediocre; the carpets nylon, not wool; and one or two paintings: old, but not valuable.

By contrast the conservatory was ancient, but well preserved. A veritable triumph of Victorian architecture, the soft light streaming in, mellowing Dorothy Hayward's harsh expression. As yet there was no food in sight, but Talbot assumed that this was where they were going to eat.

'Sorry to hold you up,' he said, not offering his hand, as she didn't bother to get up and offer hers. Sitting there behind a huge round wicker table, a purple mohair shawl draped over her shoulders, she reminded him of an ageing film idol; one of those child stars whose lights had quickly faded. She enjoyed her drama, did Dorothy; he'd noted that with the performance for her son's neighbours when leaving on the Friday. He added cheerily, 'Got called away to a crime scene; couldn't be helped.'

She raised her eyes to the ceiling as if it were all too much, paid little attention to Yates being introduced, flicked her hand towards the wicker chair opposite that he was to sit on, and then pointed a finger at the one next to her for Talbot. He obliged, pulling it right out and positioning it further afield so that he might look at her and not sit on top of her. Joe was given her opposite flank, and once everyone was settled she rang a small bell.

'The girl will serve us,' she stated, and they all sat in awkward silence while a middle-aged woman in a black dress placed several covered dishes in the centre of the table. Yates was staring up at a giant plant hanging overhead, which Talbot recognised as an antler fern; but only because Claire had bitched about wanting one for her birthday, and that particular year he couldn't find one anywhere. Life kept spitting her back at him everywhere he went.

Like a fawning slave, Joe served his mother kedgeree, grilled tomatoes and two slices of toast. The kedgeree smelt like it had been swamped in salt, Yates slyly sniffing it to gauge how much to dollop on his plate, and scowling at Talbot as he went for a boiled egg, tomatoes and toast. Well, what did Yates expect? Talbot had taught him to always eat before dining at someone else's house, warned him that there was no telling what trash they might serve up. There was no fruit juice; and the maid didn't return with tea until after they had eaten. No napkins either, Talbot noted, no jam or marmalade for the toast; and definitely a poor show of fine breeding.

'Francis has always been… difficult,' Dorothy Hayward said, leaping in with the character assassination. 'Even as a small boy he would stand and stare and refuse to join in with normal games.'

'He never played cards with us, did he, Mother? He always said he preferred being on his own; but it was such a simple thing to ask, to play cards together.'

'He said…' Dorothy shook her head and sighed. 'He said he didn't like being competitive; it made him anxious, you see.'

Talbot nodded.

'He never slept. He was always so awake, so alert. His anxiety was infectious. The nanny couldn't cope; we had to let her go. There was no help to be had, no one would stay. I gave up my amateur dramatics, my exciting career, dedicated my life to my child.' She clasped her hands. 'I sacrificed everything for that boy.'

Talbot nodded sympathetically. 'You would have made an excellent actress. You still have so much talent for theatre and showmanship.'

'I try. I'm still hoping Kirsty will follow in my footsteps and take to the stage.' She let out a little sigh. 'Francis has never got along with women, you know; ignored his sister from the start, so terribly distressing for her. He snubbed her affection.' Dorothy dipped her head and raised her eyes, anticipating a response.

'Where is Kirsty today?'

'Out, somewhere,' Joe snapped. 'She uses this place like a hotel. Never eats with us, always over at…'

'Joe, Joe…' Dorothy placed a restraining hand across her son's, a sure signal that he was to shut up. 'We're here to discuss Francis, not Kirsty.'

'Of course, Mother.'

Testing his luck, Talbot took out his cigarettes, said, 'Do you mind?' and lit one before anyone could object. 'Perhaps you could let me know the ages of your children, Dorothy, so that I get a clearer picture of where Francis fits in the family.'

'Joe's the eldest at twenty-nine, then Francis is twenty-seven, and Kirsty, twenty-four.'

'And your husband?' Yates enquired.

'We divorced.'

'And how long ago might that have been?'

Folding her arms she glared at him. 'What has that got to do with anything?'

'It would give us an idea whether Francis was adversely affected by a family breakdown.' Yates gave her his best puppy-dog smile, but it backfired.

'Don't be absurd! Frankie was mad from the start. We had him under a shrink when he was three; awkward little bugger.' She leant right across the table, nearly spitting in Yates's face as she blurted out, 'He would stand and stare at us, with utter contempt, as if we were the shit on his heel. Read, all he ever did was bloody well read. Speak? He didn't speak until he was five. Counting, counting, numbers and sums… the bloody shrink said he was a genius! We spent thousands on that kid, and all we got was, "He's far too bright!" Bright my arse. Stupid.' She paused for breath, briefly. 'Oh, his father doted on him, sent him up to his grandmother's every weekend, without fail, "to get him away from me", he said.' She sat back and folded her arms. 'Well, I put the blame firmly at his father's door.'

'For what?' Talbot interjected.

'Everything! Encouraging him with that nerdy twerp Keith; for a start.'

Raising both hands like a prima donna, she stood, demanding they keep silent while she paced and continued her diatribe.

'It was an unnatural relationship. I warned him, you know; told my husband there was funny business going on between those two boys; but oh, he wouldn't listen, not to me, oh no.' She directed an accusing finger at Talbot, the venom in that fingertip making him flinch and drop ash onto the floor. 'He said there was no harm in it, down in the basement 'til God knows what hour, Frankie staying on into the week, never coming home. They pushed my son away from me! Him and his dreadful mother. Then he left me, the bastard. As soon as the trouble started, he scarpered!' She threw her head back and roared with laughter. 'Ran away, couldn't face up to it. Didn't like to think that his precious Frankie had done away with his best friend. Couldn't accept it.' She nodded, lips curled down in a disdainful grimace. 'I got the psychiatrist straight back onto the boy. Got them to look at their notes. They were forced to reconsider their fucking expert opinion. Years they took from me, stole from me, with their wrong diagnosis. Bright! No chance. He's a paranoid schizophrenic, rubber-stamped in black and white.'

Talbot caught Yates's expression out of the corner of his eye. Poor kid looked dumbfounded.

'What was Keith's surname?' Talbot asked.

'McKenzie. They used to live next door, at number 9.'

'Uh-huh, and your husband's name?' He slid a finger towards Yates, directing him to write some notes.

'George.' She strode up to the table and placed both hands firmly round the tea pot, then yelled at the maid to fill it up again.

It was a painful shriek and Talbot tried not to wince.

'Then there was Lilly,' she said with utter exasperation. 'Lilly this, Lilly that, and his grandmother playing up to his delusions, claiming he was in love, and there was no harm in a little tenderness. Silly cow.' She gave Talbot a smug grin. 'Oh, I know all about Lilly Charteris, how he's become obsessed with the woman, and is so deranged that he thinks she's the same Lilly he fell in love with. Make one up, then go and find someone to latch onto to make it all seem real. It isn't acceptable. In fact, it's downright immoral.'

'Tell me more about what went on between Frankie and Keith.' Talbot shifted aside to let the maid have room to swap the teapots over.

'They used to... play... together, down in the basement.'

Joe cringed and crossed his legs.

'Play at what?' Talbot asked, preferring facts to innuendo.

'All they would say is that they were experimenting with love.' She shuddered. 'Disgusting.'

'Do you really think they were?' Yates asked. 'You know.'

'Well, two boys, puberty, locked away for hours on end. They were so bloody secretive and evasive. Never a straight answer from either of them.'

Talbot lit another cigarette, wished the maid would clear away the sodden fag-end he'd left floating in a saucer of slops. 'What about Keith's parents?'

'Oh, they moved away, after the enquiry.' With a toss of her head she dismissed them. Her lips turned down at the corners as she added, 'The enquiry in which my son was proclaimed completely innocent! Well, they couldn't stay around, could they?'

Sucking his pencil, Yates asked, 'Where did they move to?'

She shrugged and thumped down into her chair, the weight of the issue appearing to make her entire body heavy. 'Up north, somewhere.'

Permissions, Talbot thought, or assigned new identities, like witness protection. If a child of his went missing, he wouldn't move away; he'd stay rooted to the spot in the vain hope that one day the child would walk right through that door, and would know where home was.

He motioned for Yates to pour more tea, into the dirty cup. Yates looked scathingly at the drowned dog-end in the saucer, but obliged.

'What, precisely, happened on the day Keith went missing?' Talbot met Dorothy's gaze, hoping to get a straight answer.

'How should I know? The police questioned Frankie with a psychiatrist present, said that he would be the appropriate adult.' She sniffed back what might have been a genuine tear. 'They stole my rights, questioned him without me.'

'So, Keith was reported missing by his parents?' Talbot sipped his fresh cup of tea.

'No.' She glared at him. 'Frankie walked into the police station and reported it himself.'

The tea refused to go down, and Talbot choked, and coughed, and spluttered. He'd reported it himself! Now why the hell would he want to go doing that?

12

IT WASN'T MUCH OF a day for being shown around the gardens, but Talbot asked Joe to go out anyway, on the excuse that he could see that his smoke was upsetting Dorothy, so he'd take his filthy habit outside.

'You owe me,' Yates mouthed as Talbot smiled and abandoned him to finish prising what sense he could out of Hayward's mother.

Turning his collar up, Talbot strolled down the sloping lawn towards a small orchard at the bottom of the garden, Joe steering him in that direction rather than offering to show him the panoramic view. The fruit trees were fenced off in their own corral, a wooden gate the divider between formal garden and rural farming. A few paces in and the air was dank with rotting leaves and the smell of fermenting fruit, mostly fallen apples, the harvest wasted. In the hazy grey of mist, Talbot thought it felt sad and abandoned, the quiet unwelcoming rather than peaceful.

'Would you mind?' Joe asked, as soon as he saw Talbot take out his cigarettes. 'Mother doesn't approve.' He sniffed along the length of the cigarette before lighting it, as if it were a cigar and something to be savoured.

He was fuller in the face than Frankie—not plump, simply not so gaunt; and his dark hair was cut neat and business-like. Even with similar dark eyes, Talbot would never have instantly labelled them as brothers, although he did sense that Joe worked hard at appearing conventional, and that it probably wasn't something that came naturally. His mother and Kirsty flaunted weird hair and a dramatic dress style: they both made a statement. Joe? He was between here and there, that sweater an attempt at being conservative, but not outrageous enough to make a personal statement.

There was no doubt in Talbot's mind that they were hiding in the orchard, Joe grabbing the opportunity to slope off and have a sly fag.

'Do you have much to do with your brother?' Talbot asked.

'Not really.' Joe laughed and stopped by a brook that ran along the edge of the orchard to gaze down into the water. 'I live with Mother; therefore I'm in the enemy's camp.' He drew heavily on his cigarette. 'If I did go and visit Frankie, Mother would pump me for information as soon as I got home; it wouldn't be worth it.'

'So you stay where your bread is buttered.'

'No, no, I do the buttering, Inspector Talbot.' He smiled and lowered his head, a small bashful motion that Talbot recognised from Frankie. 'When my parents divorced, Father let Mother live in this house. He still owns it. He only gave her financial support until Kirsty was eighteen, so I followed in my father's footsteps and went to work in the city, as a broker. It pays the bills.'

'And Frankie got Granny's house.'

'Oh, she left him everything. The house, her money, her valuable antiques.' He looked up at the bare branches overhead and sniffed. 'She only lasted a year after everything blew up over Keith. Frankie was devastated, poor chap, he was devoted to her. Mother was livid over the inheritance, but she was so harsh on Frankie. I reckon Gran changed her will at the last, not to spite Mother, but to offer Frankie some protection in life.' He threw his dog-end into the brook and walked on a pace, his hands searching for jacket pockets where there weren't any.

'Do you think that Frankie killed Keith?'

Joe shrugged. 'I was excluded. Old enough to start making money, but not old enough to be included in adult conversation.' He halted, looked Talbot in the eye and said emphatically, 'I can't see it myself. Frankie was too fond of Keith, probably in love with him. It would need to have been one hell of a lover's tiff, wouldn't it?'

Talbot nodded and flashed the ash again, keen to keep Joe outside and talking.

'What about Lilly?' he asked, lighting Joe's cigarette for him.

'As you know, Frankie is obsessed with Lillian Charteris. But why her? I, for one, have no idea.' Joe held the lit cigarette up in front of his eyes and studied it. 'Judas Iscariot took thirty pieces of silver in exchange for betrayal. Two cigarettes is an unworthy sum…'

'I don't offer bribes.' Talbot swallowed hard; his mouth was uncommonly dry.

'I wasn't wanting one, merely assessing my own moral standards.' Joe smoked and walked on again. 'If I tell you certain things, then you must ensure that Mother never finds out who told you.'

'Of course.'

Joe stood very still, took in a deep breath and exhaled a white cloud before saying, 'Mother is in cahoots with Peter Charteris. They discuss Frankie all of the time. On the phone mostly, although sometimes she goes and meets him for lunch.'

Now there was a surprise. 'I see,' Talbot said, and nodded his appreciation.

'Charteris has some kind of deal going with Mother.' Bitterness drew his mouth down. 'If he gives her money for information, then she certainly never tells me, never offers to contribute.'

'Does she ever take you to speak with Charteris?'

'Don't be silly.' Looking back up towards the house through the lines of trees, Joe motioned that they should join the others again. 'See that big house over there?' He held the gate open for Talbot and pointed. 'That's where my father lives, next door, and that is where Kirsty is right now, eating lunch with the git and rooting around by his boots for crumbs off his table.'

'You never speak with him?'

'Not if I can help it.' He slammed the gate. 'Precious Frankie was always his darling. So fascinating and misunderstood, so persecuted for being exceptional. I was the shadow on the wall, invisible when the light was switched on.' Smoothing his sweater down, he pulled his shoulders back, then strode towards the house. 'I expect you'd like a warm drink before you leave, Inspector. The girl makes excellent coffee.'

LYING BACK ON THE SOFA, Talbot muted the sound on the TV, and gave up trying to concentrate on the late-afternoon film. Somehow, leaving the picture on made him feel less alone, and less tired; and at any moment he might regain interest in the moving wallpaper.

It was no good. Thinking about Hayward was useful, but writing it down would be better. Moving seemed like an enormous effort, so he used his foot to flick the notebook closer, then swore as the pen worked loose from the spiral binding and did a nose dive onto the floor. Sod it, thinking would have to do.

Nutter, schizophrenic, genius. Shy, bashful, polite. Murderer, stalker, fanatic. Mostly brought up by Granny, creating a respect and liking for older women. Mother resentful; hated all that extra work and the social embarrassment of having a difficult child. She never understood him, therefore... hated him? Father... ah yes, must pay a visit to Father. Granny was Father's mother, and that appeared to be where the family's money came from. This put Dorothy Hayward in a lose-lose situation. Divorced, no money, family money going to Frankie. Assume her family has none. Mother loathed Frankie from the start... now why did he keep returning to that?

On the drive back Yates had mentioned how much Mother banged on about Frankie as a child. Difficult, awkward, unsocial, didn't fit, didn't watch TV... uh-huh, she was correct there, that was the one thing that was missing from Frankie's living room; but hey, it was a big house, he might have created a TV room elsewhere. Brother Joe was bitter, understandably so, as all of the attention had been poured into Frankie. Attention, not because he was especially loved, but because he was different, exceptional. Closing his eyes, Talbot drew pictures in his mind of them all playing down in the orchard on a sunny summer's day. Kirsty would have traipsed along with the boys, disinterested in climbing trees, mindful of getting her new shoes muddy. Joe would have wanted to run and play, and Frankie, well, he would have counted his steps down to the little brook, and frustrated even the simplest of games. Nope, it would never have happened like that; Joe probably went on his own to escape the atmosphere at home, became the invisible man.

A few more seconds and he would have been asleep, but the phone rang, jolting him out of his dreams, and for a moment he thought he'd rolled onto the remote and knocked the TV off mute. Who the hell had he given the ring tone 'Run Rabbit Run'? Ah yes, Kate, only she hadn't looked much like a frightened rabbit when he'd seen her languishing over those railings yesterday.

'Talbot,' he said, suppressing a yawn.

'I'm sorry, have I woken you up?'

'Not really.'

She laughed. 'I was going to ask if you wanted that chat, but...'

'No, no, I'm awake.' He pushed himself upright and rubbed his forehead. The clock was lying. It said seven o'clock; perhaps he had fallen asleep after all. 'I wanted to say that I'm sorry we can't take things any further regarding the assault.'

'I knew I'd never win, but you were so persuasive...'

'I hope you don't feel let down.' Without warning he yawned.

'Look, I'll leave you to sleep...'

'No, no, give me an hour to shake out the cobwebs. Perhaps we could meet up and speak in person. Grab a bite to eat.'

She hesitated, but he knew she would. 'I... I can't afford to eat out, if that's what you had in mind.'

'Then dinner's on me.'

He chose an inexpensive Chinese restaurant, so that she wouldn't feel awkward at not paying her way, and she arrived promptly, either because she truly was the starving artist, or because she was considerate and efficient. It was busy for a Sunday, the place full of noise and chatter, and the waiter hurrying to clear a table for them. Talbot helped her off with her coat, her injured arm making the simple task complicated in a confined space, and up close he briefly smelt her scent, a subtle mixture of lavender and linseed oil. It was raw and earthy and not unpleasant, giving him the sense that underneath the jeans and sweater was a real person without any artifice.

'I don't know what more I can add,' she said, choosing a beer when the waiter came round hassling for drinks while they studied menus, and never questioning that he chose sparkling water. 'Charteris was brutal, and his behaviour towards his grandmother was atrocious.'

'In what way?'

'He threw the letters at her, and one clipped her in the face.' Unconsciously she rubbed her bandaged arm. 'I saw blood.'

'Did you mention this when you were interviewed?'

'Yes, of course I did.' Her voice rose with indignation.

He nodded and leant back as the waiter brought their drinks. 'I'll pass your statement on to a friend of mine in social services.'

'You're worried about Lilly, aren't you?' Kate's manner softened to the level he imagined a counsellor would use when speaking with a troubled client.

'To be honest,' he said, 'we don't know where she is.'

'If any information I can give might help you find her…'

'Thank you.' He sipped his sparkling mineral water. 'How's the arm?'

'Bruised, swollen, torn ligaments, painful…' She chewed her lip and shrugged. 'It stops me working.'

'And Charteris said it was your word against his, no witnesses—' Talbot smacked the table. 'Except Lilly. By Christ, we can call her in as a witness.'

'Nice idea, but honestly, Inspector Talbot, he'll claim she's senile, make out she doesn't know what she's saying.'

'Maybe, but it's worth a go.' He leant across the table and whispered, 'Call me Jake; using the word "inspector" will get people watching us in a restaurant.'

She laughed and flicked hair away from her face. 'If I call you Jake I'll forget that you're a policeman.'

'Now *that* word really will frighten the natives.'

The waiter smiled to see them laughing and enjoying themselves, placed several dishes of exotic-smelling food in the centre of the table, and made Kate blush crimson when he wished her and her husband a pleasant meal.

'Now that *is* a word that frightens the natives.' She stabbed a sweet and sour prawn ball as if it had insulted her.

'Don't worry, I'm off the market,' he muttered, and her eyes flicked open with curiosity. 'Licking my wounds.'

'For long?'

'There are those who say I should be over it—by now.' Filling his plate with food, he felt her gaze upon him, questioning, sympathising, and no doubt, guessing that he had been the one who was dumped. 'So, you're an artist, and supplement your income with a bit of care work?'

'Well put, much better than those who say I'm a care worker who dabbles.' She raised her glass in salute.

'You're a very good artist. In fact…' He hesitated, conscious of how she might misconstrue what he was about to say and think he was offering charity. 'You had a painting the other day that I wanted to buy, the bluebell wood.'

She plonked her knife and fork down and stared at him, her eyelids closing slightly as she studied his face. 'You're making that up.'

Smiling, he shook his head. 'Is it still for sale?'

'You, Jake Talbot, are a rogue.' She picked up her fork and pointed it at him. 'You had an ulterior motive for inviting me for dinner.'

'Uh-huh.'

IT WAS MONDAY MORNING, it was raining again, but Talbot didn't mind; his spirits were up, and there was an edge of excitement and anticipation in his life that he hadn't experienced for a long while. Kate had promised to bring round the painting and let him look at it *in situ*, hang it in the hall for a week or so to see if it really suited, before deciding anything definite. Now how good could that be? There was a swagger in his step as he strolled along the corridor to his office, and a renewed determination to give up smoking. He didn't need the fags when he was happy. Pushing his office door open he started to chuckle.

'Well, you can wipe that silly grin off your face.' Superintendent Bailey's words startled him, his presence in *his* office unheard of, the sight of him sitting behind Talbot's desk a shock to the system.

'Morning, sir.' Talbot closed the door and leant on it, waiting for his superior officer to explain himself.

'I'm not happy with the situation, Jake.' Bailey tapped a pen up and down on the desk, unconsciously creating a myriad of tiny ink spots. 'You were seen having lunch with Francis Hayward on Saturday. It isn't on, Jake, not when he's a suspect in an ongoing investigation.'

'I bumped into him, sir, and —'

'I don't want your excuses.' Bailey set the pen aside, clasped his hands in front of his chin and stared at Talbot over the top of his thumbs. 'Have you warned Hayward off?'

Before he could reply, his mobile erupted with the *Time Team* theme tune. Bugger, that was Hayward's ring tone.

'Leave it,' Bailey barked, as he went to answer it. 'You and your damned silly games.' He stood and marched across to the window, looked out across the car park. 'Is there any mileage in what you're doing, Jake?'

'Sir?' Shit, that was Hayward phoning again. Why didn't he just leave a message?

'Dig, dig, dig, you'll have a trench as long as one of Phil Harding's and no findings.' Bailey spun round. 'Well, Jake, is there anything in your bloody trench?'

'Yes, sir.' Talbot eased away from the door and took his coat off, slung it over the back of Yates's chair. 'Only it's a broken artefact and I'm still putting the pieces together to see exactly what it is.' His phone jingle-jangled, letting him know he'd received a text message.

'Write the case up. I want a full report. Get Yates to write it up as well, you're supposed to be collaborating, working together.' Bailey drummed his fingers on the window ledge. 'I'm not happy, Jake. I'm not happy with your conduct, and… well, I'm not happy with Charteris's conduct either. He's up to something, they both are.' The *Time Team* theme rang out again. 'Who the hell is that?'

'Hayward, sir.'

Bailey frowned. 'There's a method behind your silly tunes…' He shook his head, unable to work it out. 'Write it all up, in as much detail as possible, as soon as possible.' Turning around, he spotted the ink marks on the desk, and attempted to rub them away. 'I'm not supposed to let you know,' he said, as if speaking to the desk. 'You've applied for some Permissions, and what you write in that report could have a very large bearing on whether or not you're given access to certain files.'

Talbot's heart skipped a beat. Did knowing too much or too little unlock the treasure chest? Too little and they might refuse, too much and he might just get a Permissions notice slapped on himself as well.

13

By the time Talbot got a moment alone with his phone there was one frantic voicemail from Hayward and an equally frantic text.

'Jake, Jake, I *must* see you, today, as soon as possible.'

Bloody hell, he was calling him Jake, reeling in friendship to generate an immediate response.

'I'll be with you by lunch time,' he texted back, wondered why Yates wasn't in, and called Helen.

'I don't know if that's enough for us to use,' she said thoughtfully after listening to how Kate had witnessed Charteris throw something at Lilly and cut her.

'When my sergeant gets here I'll have Kate's statement emailed over immediately.'

'Would you prefer to pass it over in person, perhaps do dinner?' There was a purr of seduction running through her words.

It was a pity to disappoint. 'Sorry, I'm going to a private view of a painting this evening.'

'Just the one?'

'Yep.'

'Then it must be very special.'

The conversation ended on a note of intrigue, bringing a wry smile to his lips as it crossed his mind that Helen might fancy him, just a little bit.

Next he called Yates, only it was Trudy's dulcet tones that greeted him with, 'Morning, sir.'

'What have you done with Yates?'

She laughed, which wasn't the response he was looking for. It wasn't friendly laughter, and the derogatory sound made him resent her lingering perfume in his office and want to fight for his territory like an angry dog. If she'd flipped back with a witty quip, he would have laughed along with her.

'Well, where is he?' Talbot demanded.

'He's driving, sir.' There was still an irritating giggle in her voice. 'We're going to interview Mr Fix-it.'

'Well, tell Yates to drive right back and interview him on the phone.'

'He's finding somewhere to pull over, sir.'

'No, no, just put the phone on speaker, so that I can communicate with him.'

Mumblings and mutterings were followed by Trudy exclaiming, 'Found it,' followed by a surround sound audio of the car's interior, the distinctive click-click of the indicator going, and both of them shifting in their seats.

'Sir.' Even in the one word he could perceive Yates's frustration.

'I need you back here. Bailey wants a full and comprehensive report on all of our findings. Every tiny detail.'

'Is there a rush for it, sir?'

Talbot knew that tone: slightly sarcastic and designed to make one feel a fool for suggesting urgency.

'Yes, five o'clock tomorrow, at the latest.' It did no harm to give him a deadline, and he certainly wasn't going to tread on Bailey's toes by mentioning the Permissions.

'I can easily get it done by then, sir.'

No doubt Yates had copious amounts of notes, the efficient bastard. Huh, he most likely had Trudy playing secretary and speed-typing dictation.

'Did you find me a number for a specialist in astral travel?'

'Yes, sir, it's on a Post-it note on the monitor.'

Spinning round, Talbot spied the yellow square of paper. 'I need a copy of Kate's statement.'

'In your in-tray, sir.' There was a pause, and he heard Trudy stifle a giggle. 'And before you ask, station gossip has it that Bailey was out at a friend's drinks party the other night, nothing to do with Charteris.'

'Excellent; then you'd best get on and interview Mr Fix-it.' He was about to hang up, but Trudy obviously didn't know which button to press on Yates's phone because her voice lingered on, encouraging him to listen.

'He's in a dreadful strop,' Trudy said.

'Yeah, and for no good reason. Bailey told us to drop the case, but Jake's still storming ahead into nothing.' Yates sounded exasperated. 'I daresay Bailey wants the report so that he can see what we've been wasting our time on.'

'I thought you mentioned a murder?'

'Missing person. No body, no crime. The kid probably came home one day and no one thought to inform freaky Mother Hayward, so she's still banging on about it.' He spoke as if it were a fact.

'Is he always so stressed?' Trudy sounded judgmental.

'It's the time of year that does it to him. But he coped better before the Lasseter case; and Claire up and leaving didn't help.'

'I thought that was months ago.'

'Nearly a year. He arrived home one day to find that she'd stripped the place bare.'

'Not *everything*.' Trudy giggled, and a knot tightened in Talbot's gut. No, not everything, Trudy, she left me a roomful of antiques, the kitchen appliances, a bed, a sofa and some stale bread. He felt like shouting at her to mind her own business, but he should have known better than to eavesdrop, because it was always painful hearing what other people had to say about you in your absence.

Deciding to hang up, in a minute, he snatched the Post-it note off the monitor. That's when he heard Trudy say, 'He's a bit washed up really, isn't he.'

'Yep. He can't cope with Christmas. He shouldn't be working at all. And that's why Bailey's letting him fiddle around with this pile of crap.'

Talbot hung up. A painful stab tightened his chest as his solar plexus took the full force of the blow. For a moment he stood very still, staring into the aching space that had become his life. One very nasty criminal was up for trial. A job well done, worthy of national news coverage. Is that what had cost him his relationship with Claire? She had been his sticky plaster, and as soon as she abandoned him, the old wound had opened up with a vengeance. The pain of Christmas alone, with all of its haunting memories, threatened to overwhelm him. He perched on the back of Yates's chair and blinked several times, trying to focus on the number scrawled across the Post-it note.

Damn Trudy. What did she know? He didn't have to explain himself to them, to tell them he had chosen the Hayward case, that he had seen something sinister lurking in the shadows, and that he was the one who was bloody well going to find out what it was. Oh Christ, he needed a fag.

Opting for the warmth of the office instead of the cold and nicotine, he made a mug of tea before phoning John the psychic, the expert in astral travel. Keep going, he told himself, keep motivated, Kate would be coming round this evening with the painting, and that was something personal and exciting to look forward to. No, he wasn't sad, or washed-up; he was mending, in his own way. In his own time.

Twice he dialled John the psychic, and twice it went through to voicemail. There was little point in leaving a message, so he hunted down Kate's statement and sent it over to Helen's office. Ah, so Kate was thirty-five, and a miss. To his mind she hadn't emphasised the point enough about Charteris having cut Lilly. The officer writing it down should have used stronger words. It was all they had, so it would have to do. A third attempt with John the psychic proved fruitful, but the guy didn't seem to want to give a straight answer and preferred to go on and on about his personal out of body experiences.

'John, do you have enough knowledge and expertise to answer my question or not?' Talbot asked, prepared to hang up if he waffled on any more.

'I don't quite understand what you're asking,' John admitted.

Neither did Talbot. The very idea of separating yourself in two, of your consciousness leaving your body, voluntarily, pressed all the wrong buttons in him; yet here he was asking stupid questions because he was trying to do his job. He sucked in a long breath and once again said, 'John, during astral travel, can you go backwards in time?'

There was a pause while John pondered, and Talbot could hear the cogs whirring. 'I don't see why not.'

'Have you experienced it, or known of it, in any case study?' Knuckle him down to specifics, Talbot thought.

'Well… no, but I imagine it's possible. The human psyche is very complex, and when one travels through the astral plane, all manner of phenomena may manifest. Many people have accessed information regarding the past and future.'

'Ah, so it can be done.' At last.

'Of course!' His tone was indignant.

'So, someone can astral travel back in time and interact with someone in the past.'

John's voice turned pompous. 'I spoke with a man once who witnessed Nero burning Rome...'

'Did he speak with him? Did they have a conversation?'

'Your questions imply that you've been experiencing etheric projection, and not true astral travel at all.'

'You didn't answer my question.' Talbot unclenched his fingers; they were aching. He hadn't realised how much force he was putting into his fist. Perhaps psychic John could feel the energy of him hitting him square on the chin through the astral plane; he certainly hoped so.

'It sounds like you require a full consultation, a private sitting, Mr Talbot, to help process the phenomena you have been encountering.'

'No thanks.'

He sighed as if Talbot were a lost soul. 'Where shall I send the bill for today's session?'

'Surrey Constabulary, accounts department, and put it for the attention of Detective Inspector Talbot; you've been helping the police with their enquiries.'

Driving up to see Hayward he tried to focus on the positive in his life, to see the good and not the crumbling rubble falling all around. Kate was going to come round later with her painting... yes, yes, that is what had been keeping him buoyant all day, the thought of seeing her and spending more time with her. Not his usual type, no, she was rounder, and dark haired, but compassionate, and warm hearted, and he needed, yes, needed, to be in the company of someone who had sincere human emotions.

'Don't be such a baby,' Claire had said, her voice harsh and uncompromising the evening he'd arrived home late from work, slumped in the kitchen chair, and wept. 'You shouldn't be a copper if you can't stand what you see.'

'I am allowed to process my revulsion and abhorrence.' He knew his voice had sounded pathetic and weak, the sneer on her lips belittling him even further.

'You should snap out of it and go and catch the bastard.' The plate of food she'd slammed down on the table was cold, the chicken already congealed with grease.

He remembered looking up at the clock, seeing the second hand click round and the minute hand settle on 11.15, precisely. Snap, snap. Yes, everything had snapped and clicked into place, his tired brain snapping into overdrive, his imagination clicking vivid pictures of a clock, up on the wall in the background, and the time-date data on the jpegs.

'He's tampered with the bloody things,' he said, shoved the food away, ran for the door and jumped back into the car. Lasseter had been there, and his own degenerate photographs proved it. Oh, very clever. Get us concentrating on the camera's metadata and we'll avert our gaze from the sordid image, close our eyes to anything beyond the suffering. It had been six more sleepless months before he got anywhere close to validating his point. Claire had gone by then, taking her hard heart with her and bestowing its brittle affection on another poor unsuspecting sod.

Arriving at Hayward's, he wondered if the bizarre love the young man felt for Lilly would have survived the real world if they had ever shared a meal together, or been home late, or become confused over unsatisfactory sex.

Like a puppy dog bounding to the door to greet his master, Hayward opened the front door before Talbot's finger had even touched the buzzer.

'I thought you were never going to turn up,' he exclaimed, with all the excitement of a child before Christmas. 'Come in, come in.'

Hayward's happiness was infectious, and Talbot couldn't help but feel it. He let himself be led into the sitting room, where Hayward stood and beamed, his grin broad and ecstatic. His hair was tousled as if he'd run his hand through it over and over again, giving him a wayward, impish appearance.

'She's written to me.' Hayward's voice breathed out the secret in a hushed whisper. 'Jake, Lilly has sent me a Christmas card.' Tears brimmed in Hayward's eyes, all of his love gathering in those sparkling pools.

Momentarily Talbot hesitated, his mind somersaulting, his heart racing, his nerves rattling as the penny dropped. Bloody hell, it had to be one Kate had posted for Lilly. It must have been a full minute before he spoke, his mind trying to take in the enormity of the event.

'May I see it, please?'

Reverently the card was placed in Talbot's hand. A lump of emotion stuck in his throat as he read:

Dear Frankie,

If you are the right Francis Hayward, my address is Mellow Acres, Guildford. I am so looking forward to seeing you, my mystical gypsy.

Love from Lilly   x

The picture on the front was sweet, a pretty winter scene with snow and a rural church in the distance, and a robin sitting on a branch in the foreground. Had the pack all been the same picture, or had it been a bumper box of assorted scenes? He'd never thought to ask Kate, hadn't thought it important at the time. The writing was clear but shaky, the script old-fashioned, with loops and proper punctuation. If she'd had any, he was convinced she would have added scent. It wasn't a desperate note, yet it held desire, and she'd placed a kiss firmly after her name.

'Jake, Lilly's been looking for me, hasn't she?' Without shame Hayward let the tears fall.

Talbot nodded.

'Surely I can see her now,' he begged, as if Talbot had the power to make it possible. 'She wants to see me, she says so. Surely that is enough.'

'Perhaps.'

Setting the card back in pride of place on the mantelpiece, Hayward said, 'I shall get some holly, decorate the fire surround, light an open fire, make it special.'

Like a shrine. 'Frankie…' Two big brown eyes turned towards him. 'I can only do what I can do, as far as you meeting Lilly, and I shall do my best, you know that.'

'Yes, yes, I believe you will do your best.'

'Frankie, I *can't* promise anything.' Talbot raised his voice a little, drove the point home.

The fizz went out of Hayward and he lowered his head, then watched his feet as he walked towards the kitchen.

They sat in silence as they drank their tea, Talbot itching to ask so many questions that were blocked by Permissions, his own desires bumping into what he knew was the right thing to do. Correct procedure would have been to remove the Christmas card, analyse it for fingerprints, photocopy it, and file it away somewhere safe.

Talbot just didn't have the heart. Years Hayward had waited for this contact, the closest thing he might ever have to holding Lilly's hand, something she had touched. You couldn't deprive a man of something so special, so precious. He compromised and took some snaps with his phone, warned Hayward to keep it safe, and decided that he too would buy an expensive point-and-shoot camera like the one Yates had. After all, it was no good right now sitting in Yates's pocket when it was needed here.

'Frankie, are you free tonight?' he asked as he put his coat on ready to leave.

'I'm always free.'

'There's someone I would like you to meet, but I need to check whether it's okay with them first.'

Hayward tilted his head inquisitively. 'Do I need to dress up?'

Talbot shrugged. 'If they're happy about meeting you, I'll call and give you my address. Can't say what time yet.'

Opening the front door he could sense Hayward assessing him, his eyes flicking up trying to catch his gaze.

'Is she pretty?'

Hayward's question made him freeze. He didn't turn and look at him, but focused his attention on the guy across the street, who was standing on a very high ladder and overreaching while trying to hang up Christmas lights. Icicles, by the look of it.

'Was Lilly pretty, when she was young?'

'She was stunning.'

'Frankie, how does she know your name?' He held his breath in anticipation.

'I told her when I visited her.'

'Would she know Keith's name, too?'

'I think he mentioned it.'

Talbot heard Hayward fold his arms and knew not to push any further. Unwittingly, Hayward had just confirmed that Keith had also visited Lilly: how else could he have mentioned his name to her? Suddenly Hayward's basement and whatever the two teenage boys had got up to down there became a point of extreme interest.

'I'll call you,' Talbot said, glanced to the closed door on the opposite side of the stairs as he left, then marched across the road to lecture the guy up the ladder about health and safety.

14

Before going home Talbot returned to the station, not for any special reason, but from habit alone. Hayward's revelation had knocked him sideways, spun up a thousand more questions which he knew damned well weren't going to get answered without those Permissions. How the hell did Lillian Charteris know Frankie's name? Why would she have called him her 'mystical gypsy' if she didn't know what he looked like? How the hell had she seen him? Oh, Frankie just snuck through the etheric veil and whispered in her ear. Sure, and he was Father fucking Christmas.

He was sitting at his desk, staring into space, turning his pen from top to bottom with each new thought when Yates burst in with the ever-giggling Trudy. They skidded to a halt, two comedy mice who'd accidentally burst into the cat's lair.

'Evening, sir, thought you'd have knocked off by now,' Yates said, pushing Trudy behind him.

'What did Mr Fix-it have to say?' Talbot brought his pen to rest and stood up. 'Well?'

Yates shrugged. 'Not much. He reckoned he couldn't win against a man like Charteris, so didn't bother.'

'Uh-huh.' Talbot smiled, lifted his coat off the back of the chair and as he strolled past Yates, slung it over his shoulder, nearly clipping him in the eye. 'Don't work too late, kiddies,' he said and whistled as he sauntered off down the corridor.

As soon as he got home, he set up his laptop on the kitchen work surface, fired up the net, and did a search for Mr Fix-it, convinced he must have an online presence somewhere. Yep, there was his slogan, *Ready Fix — If You Need It Fixed We'll Fix It Quick.* Ah, so Mr Stevens was a one-man band, based in Farnham, a mobile number suggesting he could be contacted on the hoof.

Self-employed people were always quick to respond and Mr Stevens answered his call in a flash. He didn't sound like he was on foot, but in a moving vehicle.

'DI Talbot, we met at Mr Hayward's house. Can you concentrate on answering a few questions while driving?'

Stevens must have the phone pressed against his ear, because his breath rasped against the speaker.

'No problem. Be home in a jiffy. I'm on hands-free, guv.'

As if! Talbot could hear windscreen wipers, and indicators, so Stevens might already be pulling into his drive.

'I understand you spoke with Detective Sergeant Yates earlier today.'

'Nah, was I supposed to call him?' Mr Stevens paused for thought, or driving, or both. 'Did he leave a message for me to call?'

'I haven't caught up with him; he probably didn't get round to speaking with you today as he said he would.' Talbot kicked one of the bags of groceries he'd stopped off for at the supermarket, then swore under his breath as he realised that was the one with the eggs. He'd queued for over ten minutes to check out, and now he'd smashed the eggs. Why couldn't it have been the one with the spuds? He was supposed to be impressing Kate by making a Spanish omelette. He could strangle Yates, he really could. 'We were just wondering,' he said, crouching down to inspect the damage, 'why you never made an official complaint after Mr Charteris struck you.'

'I'd come across him before, mate, nasty piece of work.' A key clicked in a lock and something heavy was dumped on the floor. In a low whisper Stevens said, 'Important call, love,' and Talbot recognised the sound of him pecking someone on the cheek. He smiled.

'What happened when you locked horns with him before?'

Stevens chuckled. 'Nice turn of phrase, guv. My Mrs said we were like two old bulls head-butting each other.' Thud… pause… thud; yep, that was his work boots coming off and being dropped on… yeah, the kitchen floor, no carpet. 'I did a job up at the golf course for him, bit of plumbing, you know. Well, he didn't want to pay me, did he. Said my work was shoddy. Well, you've seen my work. You know I do a proper job, don't leave no mess or nothing. Well, he said if I wanted the money I could speak to his solicitor, take him to court. Well, I can't afford that kind of caper, so, well, I squared up to him, didn't threaten him or nothing, and the next thing… smack! I had a right shiner for weeks.'

'You didn't call the police?'

'No witness, guv. His word against mine. Whose word do you think the law would fall down on?'

'"Money speaks" is a fallacy,' Talbot said, and wished he meant it.

'Yeah, yeah. Well, it's history now.' Stevens whispered, 'Thanks, love,' and paused to slurp a drink.

While he had his attention, Talbot thought he might just as well dig a bit deeper. 'What did you make of Mr Hayward?'

'Nice kid.' Brief and evasive.

'Personable sort of chap, isn't he?'

'Yeah, he's a nice kid.' Stevens sighed, obviously uncomfortable about being pushed into a corner. 'Look, he seemed a bit simple to me, bit naïve-like.' Click, click, that was him lighting a cigarette, inhaling deeply. 'I don't want to get involved, guv. He's an okay guy, treated me and Sammy just fine. I don't know why Charteris was having a go at him, that ain't my business.'

'You protected him from Charteris, stood between them, defended him.'

'How d'you know that?' Stevens sounded rattled.

'Someone caught it on their mobile.'

'Blimey.' Stevens paused again, sucked on his cigarette. 'Look, I reckoned that if Charteris walloped the kid, he'd do him in. He packs a fair punch, you know.'

'So you were genuinely concerned for Mr Hayward's welfare.'

'Well… yeah.'

'I'd like a statement to that effect, Mr Stevens. I'll send DS Yates round to see you, this evening.' Talbot lowered his voice and whispered, 'Just go light on the squaring-up part.'

'Got your drift, guv.'

Still holding his phone, Talbot picked up the damaged carrier bag and dumped it in the sink. With his free hand he fished around in broken egg white trying to salvage what he could of the bread and squashed tomatoes. Everything was slimy and sticky and stank of… oh Christ, he'd burst one of the cans of beer. This is what came of relying on that lazy, lying, little sod, Yates. He could never depend on him. Never! His sergeant's constant fuck-ups made him angry, then he lost his temper and did stupid things like kicking the shit out of his own supper. Damn him! He flicked the tap on full pelt, stuck his fingers under it, dried them down his sweater, and phoned Yates.

'You fucking little shit!' he roared down the phone at him. 'What the hell were you and Trudy up to today? Shagging? Shopping? Or just cruising around having fun?'

'Jake, there's no need to swear!' Yates was definitely flustered, using the 'I'm offended' line of defence.

'I don't give a fuck how fucking upset you are at my fucking swearing, you shit.'

The only sound filling the silence was Trudy fidgeting in the background.

'I gave you a direct instruction to go and interview Stevens. You claimed that you were on your way to interview Stevens. That was this morning. Then, less than an hour ago, you had the audacity to lie to me and say that you'd interviewed Stevens.' Talbot smashed his fist down onto the sodden groceries. 'How dare you! I should report you to Bailey.'

'Sir, I didn't think there was any mileage in it, sir.'

'Thinking, Sergeant Yates, is not your brief!' Talbot paused for breath, tried to find spittle and not choke on his own rage. 'What the hell did you do instead?'

Yates cleared his throat.

'Right. Well, there may be no mileage in it for you, but there is for me, so now that you have spent all day wasting the taxpayers' money, you can make up for it by spending your evening interviewing Mr Stevens and taking his statement.'

'Yes, sir.'

'I've already spoken with him, he's expecting you, and I know what he'll say in his statement.' Talbot lit a cigarette, filled the kettle and yelled, 'Understand!'

'Yes, sir.'

'Oh, and if I get one whiff that Trudy has gone with you, I'll have your balls toasted on a skewer.'

'Yes, sir.'

Sinking into a chair Talbot clasped his head in his hands. It felt like it would burst. It was the same old crap he'd been through with Yates all through the Lasseter investigation. Snide little remarks, laziness in following through on the minute detail, overlooking the specks of dust that go to make up the mountain. While it was fresh and fun and had instant gratification, Yates was fine, just fine, the obvious appealing to his practical mind. If he couldn't see it, then it didn't exist. He should have stayed a beat copper. If this went on much longer Talbot was determined to go to Bailey and recommend precisely that. Shit, this is why he was so stretched and so bloody exhausted.

He'd intended to phone Kate and speak to her about Hayward before she came over, but it was too late now; she was due in fifteen minutes. Part of him knew he should make an effort to sort the groceries and clean the sink, but the other part of him was desperate for a cup of tea, a fag and five minutes to chill before she arrived. He needed to shower too; his armpits stank and a clean shirt was the least she deserved.

Who cared if she thought he was a slob? Better to have a calm man than a clean man. The tea won.

SHE WAS PROMPT, the sound of her car pulling into the drive coinciding with the big hand shifting round to the number six. Lasseter had made him paranoid about studying clocks. Time, what was the time? His flight had been at seven, he couldn't possibly have been there at 6.35. Time didn't exist, time went one way and then another, depending on which way round the world one flew. One could travel backwards in time. Hayward's spirit travelled backwards in time. Lilly grew old. Time collided, met itself coming the other way.

'Hi, I thought that maybe…' Kate stopped, a look of concern puckering her brow. 'Are you okay?'

'I'm fine, hectic day and all that.' Talbot smiled and held the door open for her.

She motioned towards her vehicle. 'I was wondering if you could help me get the painting out of the car; it was a dreadful muddle getting it in.'

'Sure.' He followed her out, pleased he'd opted for the tea and didn't have wet hair.

Lifting the boot on her hatchback, he wondered how she'd driven there at all, unless she'd balanced the monster on her head.

'You could do with a van,' he said without thinking, and she bristled, embarrassed. Instantly he kicked himself for forgetting how poor she was. This was not how the evening was supposed to go, with her hovering, waiting to see if she could help, and a cold wind chilling them to the core: while his backside stuck up in her face as he tried to shift the thing onto its side. The mounting had wedged itself into the corner at the back near the door frame, and if he pushed too hard it was likely to fly up and smash the windscreen. Eventually Kate nipped round and opened the side door and heaved from the other end, and between them they gradually slid it up and out.

'I hope it isn't damaged.' She trotted behind him, barely able to keep her end of the painting from dragging on the ground.

'How on earth did you get it in there in the first place?' He propped it up against the hallway wall and hurried to close the front door before they froze to death.

'Karl helped me.' She crouched to study it for damage.

Of course, Karl, the boyfriend, or live-in lover, or general man in her life.

'You shouldn't be lifting anything with that arm,' he said, totally ignoring Karl's existence. 'You'll set yourself back.'

'I do try and rest it.' She wriggled out of her coat and followed him into the kitchen.

There they stood for a moment, on opposite sides of the kitchen table, he admiring her brightly coloured sweater, thinking how it complimented her dark hair, and she? Well, she was facing him, but looking this way and that in search of any sign of food preparation. She rested her gaze on the empty mug and the half-full ashtray, noticed the bag of spuds on the floor and then… oops, she'd spotted the crash victims in the sink. Side-stepping the undamaged carrier, she carefully peeled back the soaking wet plastic and explored the mess that should have been supper, then said, 'Oh, dear.'

'Had an accident,' he said. 'I'll order a takeaway.'

'We can save some of this...'

'Rescue it, but don't cook it; I'm taking the easy option.' He joined her, plunged his hands into the cold water, and ended up convinced he sensed a thrill of shared desire when their fingers accidentally brushed against each other. Turning away from her to throw the carrier in the bin, he took a deep breath and said, 'Would you mind if someone else joins us for supper?'

'Of course not, it's your home.'

Her diplomatic response made him look round, and he saw that the sparkle had gone from her eyes.

'It's work.' He perched on the table and tried to smile. 'You see, those Christmas cards you sent for Lilly: well, one arrived... and...' Shit, how much of the truth could he tell her? 'Look, you don't have to...' Pushing away from the table he yanked open the drawer he'd stuffed the takeaway leaflets into. 'It's a bad idea, forget it.'

Without a word she lit two cigarettes and passed one over. 'I forget that you're a policeman,' she said at length. 'At dinner the other night it was police work covering for pleasure, and tonight it's—'

'Forget it.' He raised his hands for a truce.

'How can I when you look so worried?' She flicked ash across the table, missing the ashtray by a mile.

'Look. We don't know where Lilly is. We don't even know if she's still alive.'

Kate's eyes sprang wide open. 'You mean I might have been one of the last people to see her?'

He nodded. 'It would mean a lot to this person if he heard first-hand what happened.' Shit, what had Helen called it? Begging. 'No, no, it's wrong of me to involve you, goes against the rules.' And that was enticement.

'You win. Helping a policeman break the rules sounds like fun.' She smiled and gestured for the fast food flyers. 'As long as I get to choose which junk we shove down our throats.'

On impulse he kissed the top of her head. 'You're a gem. I'll call him.'

'What's his name?'

'Frankie Hayward.'

Kate threw her hand up to her mouth and cried, 'Not *the* Frankie Hayward! Not the guy who writes that really cool blog.'

'That's the one.' Talbot smiled even though his stomach knotted tight with envy. Frankie was a star, a celebrity in the hazy networks of the World Wide Web, and there was no competing with that.

'WHO IS IT YOU want me to meet?' Hayward asked after he'd already agreed to come over and stated that his preference was for Chinese food.

'You'll see. No, it isn't Lilly… but hopefully it'll be a pleasant surprise.'

He turned up looking dapper in a chunky burnt orange sweater and black corduroy jeans, a bottle of expensive wine in one hand and a large box of chocolates in the other. Over his shoulder Talbot spotted a top-of-the-range Mercedes, which flummoxed him, because he definitely hadn't seen that car parked in Hayward's road. Later he'd make an excuse to go out to his own car and get the registration number.

'Oh, you bought the painting,' Hayward said excitedly.

'Not quite.' Leading him into the kitchen he introduced Kate as the artist, and a wry smile crept across Hayward's lips as he recognised her. 'Kate works part-time as a care worker,' Talbot explained. 'She helped Lilly post her Christmas cards.'

'Thank you,' Hayward said with awe, and gazed at Kate in utter adoration. Placing the wine and chocolates on the table, he pushed them a little closer towards Kate, as if they were a gift especially for her, and a sign of his gratitude. 'Please,' he said quietly. 'Would you mind talking to me about Lilly? I'd like to know how she is, and… and what she looks like now.'

'Of course.' Kate smiled and invited him to sit down beside her.

'If you'll excuse me, I'll quickly nip upstairs and freshen up,' Talbot said, feeling out of place in a suit. 'When the food arrives it's all paid for.'

As he left the room he felt Kate watching him, only he couldn't see whether she was smiling or frowning. He knew he was breaking the rules and that it wasn't wise for two people involved in the same case to meet, but to hell with protocol, Hayward might never get to meet Lilly in the real world.

Over supper they chatted about art and antiques, Talbot sensing that Hayward was bursting to button-hole Kate again and bring the subject back to Lilly.

'Why don't you go in the sitting room and I'll bring some coffee through,' he said, ensuring Hayward was given the opportunity to pour his heart out. He opened a new packet of ground coffee, and the fresh smell burst out with a life of its own, exciting and inviting, reminding him of how his evening was supposed to have been. He liked to think that Kate had looked downhearted when he'd suggested inviting someone else along for the evening. It felt like he'd shot himself in the foot by involving Hayward, and he'd certainly lost the opportunity to spend quality time alone with Kate, getting over the victim-copper issue, and developing a friendship: but given the chance, would he go back and do it any differently? No, probably not. The evening hadn't turned out so bad. The sound of Kate and Hayward's banter drifting in from the other room was rewarding, the tearful joy in Hayward's voice making it all worthwhile. He could hear Kate putting a positive spin on how well Lilly was, and how good she looked for her age, the physical abuse issue played down so as not to upset.

At precisely 11.30 Hayward unexpectedly announced that he had to leave.

'I mustn't be late visiting Lilly.' He clasped Kate's hand in a firm handshake, looked terrified when she pecked his cheek, and hurried towards the door. 'You should buy the painting,' he said, as Talbot walked him to his car.

'I will.' Talbot glanced down at his registration and made a mental note. 'I'll be in touch.'

Sitting in the driver's seat, holding the steering wheel, Hayward looked straight ahead as he said, 'Thank you.... That meant so much to me.'

'I wish it could have been more.' Talbot closed the door, calling out, 'Drive carefully,' and waved him off.

As he turned to walk back in, he saw Kate standing in the doorway, shifting from foot to foot to keep warm, tears glistening.

'He's unwell, isn't he?' she said softly.

'I can't answer that.' Instinctively he put an arm around her shoulder to lead her indoors.

'Of course, you're a policeman, it's probably confidential.' Shrugging him off she faced away to wipe her cheeks. 'Poor love. Lilly probably put the wrong address on the card and Frankie's confused her with his fantasy woman.'

'That would be the one,' Talbot said, and hoped she'd stay for another coffee.

15

AT THREE A.M. TALBOT promised himself to stop typing... soon. By four he was on his third cup of coffee and had changed tack and decided to go for bust. If those Permissions bureaucrats wanted a full report, then they could have a full report, every tiny detail, except sensitive issues like Helen's name. He struggled not to pepper it with questions (such as how the hell did Lilly know Hayward's name?), and tried to simply state it as a fact. Fifteen more minutes, and he'd have to finish. He was down to his last few fags and refused to get back into the habit of driving to an all-night service station and paying top whack.

Pushing the keyboard away, he rubbed his eyes and lit one of the few. There was a positive slant on Kate deciding to leave shortly after Hayward; if she'd stayed, he'd never have been so productive and got all of this done. She'd said she was tired, and had found Frankie exhausting, her final comment making him believe it was the right decision.

When he'd helped her on with her coat, Kate had said, 'You don't have many paintings for a man who claims to like art.' She'd laughed. 'In fact, you don't have any at all.'

'She took them.'

That had put a real damper on things. He imagined that when she got home she would tell Karl all about the strange policeman, and the even stranger Frankie Hayward.

AT FIVE PAST FIVE he emailed a copy of the report to Bailey and backed it up onto a memory stick. Reading it through, he realised there were certain issues he could deal with while waiting to see if he received his Permissions, and he ought to get onto them first thing in the morning. Christ, he needed those Permissions.

At the station his office felt as frosty as the bleak winter's day unfolding outside. Yates crept around like a misty vapour, smothering the air in a chill atmosphere that wasn't warmed even when they each paused to make their own tea.

First, Talbot phoned Dr Weissman, got as far as his voicemail. He opted not to leave a message, but jotted down the time he'd made the call. Yates momentarily sat back and sucked the end of his pencil, pretending to ponder while sneaking a glance at what Talbot was up to. Once Yates settled back down to work it looked as though he was typing up his report, or Mr Fix-it's statement, or both, his fingers plodding across the keyboard and frequently reaching for the delete button.

After ten minutes searching, Talbot couldn't locate their copy of the local telephone directory, so he went along the corridor and stole someone else's. On seeing him walk back in with it, Yates produced a copy from a small shelf underneath his desk and plonked it down on the floor. Bastard, he should have kept it in full view. Methodically, Talbot went through every F. Hayward in the listings. Last night Kate had mentioned she gave Lilly a copy of the telephone directory, a fact that had never seemed relevant before, but now it was, because above all else, it proved that Lilly had made an effort to contact Frankie Hayward.

Not all of the people he called were in, and some admitted receiving a card from Lilly, but had already binned it, so he asked them, politely, to go through their rubbish and fish it out. No, it shouldn't be smelly, there was recycling now, and the card should be in the purple paper recycling bin, away from food. That was his afternoon taken care of: a drive around Surrey playing Santa Claus, collecting Christmas cards. There wasn't much to judge from them, except they were all in the same handwriting and all had the same postmark. But hey, it was evidence, of some description.

By Friday Yates was still acting the moody, hard-done-by victim, and by Sunday Farnham was ablaze with a startling array of Christmas lights. Saturday had been and gone and Hayward hadn't phoned as he'd promised. Someone must have got to him, threatened to lock him up if he said too much. Strolling through

Gostrey Meadow, the park opposite the police station, Talbot stopped to light a cigarette and admire the decorations. If someone had warned Hayward off again, that meant someone had read his report. Now was that good? Or bad?

First thing Monday morning he had his answer. The screen on his mobile said it was Dr Weissman calling. Odd, because he hadn't left a message asking him to phone back.

He answered the call, on guard, yet curious.

'Detective Inspector Talbot, this is Dr Weissman. I'd like to meet with you, just you. Can you be in my office in an hour?'

The building he was directed to was off Tunsgate Arch in Guildford, easy enough to locate, but a bitch to park close to, with streams of Christmas shoppers queuing for the car parks. A flurry of snow was whitening the pavements, putting people into a panic as they trotted beyond his beating wiper blades, heads down, ill-prepared for the sudden onslaught. Round and round the multi-storey he went, ticket shoved on the dash, searching for a free space. His palms grew sticky on the wheel. He was going to be late. Damn system, ticket to get in, had to pay to get out, so he was jolly well going to find the one and only space that someone had just vacated. Yep, it would have to be one of the few outside, wouldn't it?

With thoughts of having to dig his car free when he returned, and racking his brain to recall whether or not there was any de-icer in the boot, he scooted down the stairs and out across the street.

Reaching the door he straightened his tie and kicked the snow off his shoes. He pressed the buzzer and said breathlessly into the intercom, 'DI Talbot to see Dr Weissman.' The door opened into a hallway with various brass nameplates, and one directed him up the narrow flight of stairs.

As soon as she saw him, the receptionist motioned to a door on her left. 'Go straight in.' She glanced at her watch and logged his visit.

Now it would go down in history that he was late. Bugger.

To his surprise there was no Dr Weissman sitting behind the yard of wood set out with a note pad and pen. No computer screen either, no telephone, no heating and no houseplant. Instantly his pulse raced and his hackles rose. Was this a set up? The room was white and odourless, as if it had no life and was never used. A large window was behind the desk, the comfortable chair he was supposed to sit in facing it, so that to look at someone across the table would make them silhouetted and haloed, like a god. He chose to remain standing, drove his hands into his pockets, and waited.

It must have been ten minutes before the one and only door into the room opened and a man of about fifty came in carrying two mugs of tea. Bearded, he was one of those Guy Fawkes types, with rimless glasses and a brown corduroy jacket: stereotypical, as if he were play-acting the part.

'I hope tea's okay with you,' Dr Weissman said, and handed one over.

Talbot nodded and stared suspiciously into the brown liquid.

Placing his mug next to the pad, Weissman perched on the edge of the table and gestured that Talbot should sit down. Okay, so either he wasn't the only person who stuck his backside precariously against the edge of the furniture, or Weissman was playing mind games. Smiling, he sat down and cradled his mug in his lap. Well, it was that or put it on the floor, and he didn't fancy the idea of bending to pick it up again, and ending up even lower than the man who now loomed over him. 'Are you a good detective, Mr Talbot?' Weissman stared straight at him as he spoke, the eyes behind the glasses blue.

'I like to think so.'

'You've got quite a reputation now, after your success with Lasseter.'

That was deliberately barbed with mock praise, challenging him to react. Talbot kept his voice as flat as possible. 'It hasn't gone to court yet.'

'So, you're not counting your chickens.' Half laughing, Weissman swung round and picked up his tea. 'Did you know that a Talbot is an old English variety of pale-coloured dog with floppy ears, used for hunting and tracking?'

Yes, he did, and no, he wasn't going to answer that one.

'Are you as good as the dog, Mr Talbot?'

'Depends on the quarry.' He sipped his tea, discovered by the empty flavour that his hunch was right, and it was coloured with insubstantial half-fat milk. He set it aside on the floor. If they'd been checking up on his preferences, they hadn't done enough homework.

Moving round the desk, Weissman lifted the pad and produced a copy of Talbot's report from between its pages. He should have guessed it would be around somewhere. Instead of sitting,

Weissman took the report to the window and leant against the frame, as if needing the light to read by.

'Why did you choose to involve yourself with this case?'

'Curiosity.'

Weissman chuckled. 'Would you care to expand on that?'

'I couldn't understand why a man would go ballistic simply because someone wanted to visit his grandmother.' He stood up, hating to be lower down and cramped. 'It didn't make sense.'

Nodding, Weissman motioned that he should sit down again, but he pretended he hadn't noticed.

'What do you make of Frankie Hayward?' Weissman's face was down towards the report, but Talbot caught a glimpse of him looking sideways, wanting to see his reaction.

'His most significant trait is that he doesn't appear to have the ability to tell an outright lie. He fibs, but he doesn't lie.' Talbot smiled as Weissman raised his eyebrows. 'After the incident where Charteris broke his window, Hayward wrote it up on his blog. It was an accurate and factual account. I've read more embellished reports in police logs. Frankie said it as it was.'

'So, you believe all of this astral travel nonsense of his.' Weissman's statement was contemptuous.

'No. I think he's describing whatever he experiences as that, to cover up for something else.'

'Then he's lying.' Weissman grinned, as if he'd scored a point.

'No. He's protecting himself.'

'And that isn't lying?'

'No. He would tell the truth if he could. But he's frightened of being locked up.'

'That, Mr Talbot, is what we do with madmen.'

Talbot bristled. 'Then why haven't you and your people had him sectioned?'

Irritated, Weissman tossed the report onto the table and the pages splayed apart.

'You're already too personally involved, aren't you, Mr Talbot?'

'I'm keeping an open mind, Mr Weissman.' Well, if Weissman could drop his rank and title, then he could throw the same snide jibe back at him. Pompous oaf.

'If I order you to desist, will you?'

'Quite frankly, I don't see that you have any authority to issue such an order.' Talbot buttoned up his coat.

'Mr Talbot, sit down!'

A shot of adrenaline pumped through Talbot's veins and he stared at him. 'No, thank you.' He stepped towards the door. 'This is a human rights issue. If I'm pulled off the case, via the correct channels, I will continue to see Francis Hayward, socially. You're right, I like the man. He has yet to commit a crime, so I will not be associating with a felon.'

'What if I give you your Permissions?'

Talbot stopped and turned, his jaw tight as he met Weissman's gaze.

'You are a hound dog, Detective Inspector Talbot. Your report is extremely astute, and I cannot imagine you walking away from this case, not for one moment.' Gathering the spilt papers off the table, Weissman joined him at the door. 'It would be far better if you work with us, than against us. Shall we go through to my office?'

The adjoining room had far more of the paraphernalia Talbot expected to find in a psychiatrist's office. Comfy leather armchairs, desk well-equipped with a laptop and a desk-top, nice curtains, and a leafy houseplant. There was a hint of lemon air freshener about the place, and the radiator was pumping out a mellow heat that encouraged him to slip his coat off.

Speaking into an intercom, Weissman asked his secretary to bring through more tea, 'Full-fat milk for DI Talbot,' he added, sat behind his desk and gestured for Talbot to pull over a chair. In silence they waited until the interruption was over and the fresh tea was sitting on the desk, spirals of steam rising between them. Unexpectedly Weissman pushed a small ashtray towards him, inviting him to smoke.

'If you decide to continue with this, you'll be reporting to me,' Weissman said. 'Superintendent Bailey will be the only other officer you report to, and confide in. Yates is not to be informed of any further findings.' He sat back and took out a packet of cigarettes, didn't offer one over. 'You have a choice whether to go forwards or not, but you must make that decision before I divulge any highly confidential information.'

Talbot didn't move. He wanted to know the rules of play before making a final bid.

'It's been decided that you will take leave. According to your colleagues that is what you are doing: resting. You will, however, be given direct access to all files and information you require to proceed with your investigation.' He lit his cigarette, from a very expensive lighter. 'We will provide you with a laptop and a highly secure internet connection, and all necessary passwords.'

'Who's we? You're not a lone wolf, Mr Weissman. Who do you take instructions from? And why the secrecy?'

'I work in the psychiatric division of the MOD.' He half smiled. 'It's secret, because,' he pushed his glasses up the bridge of his nose, as if to better gauge Talbot's expression, 'we like to keep certain issues out of the public consciousness, Mr Talbot.'

'Sure, I get that, but why's the MOD interested in Hayward?'

'In time, you may get to find out… if you choose to join us.'

'And if I don't?'

Weissman gave the slightest of shrugs. 'We don't like people keeping certain secrets, and we like the people who uncover those secrets even less. High-security psychiatric units are full of such meddlers.'

Talbot lit a cigarette and sipped his tea, made out that he was fully at ease with the situation. Fuck, the guy had just threatened to lock him up and throw away the key. No, no, he still had a choice, join or back off completely. 'And it's been decided that I should work this case on my own?'

Weissman nodded. 'Are you prepared to become the maverick outsider, Mr Talbot? Are you able to cope with the strain of your colleagues whispering behind your back that you've lost it and been forced to take leave? Are you able to continue treading on people's toes, while officers like Yates tell you to shut up and shove off, because you're not supposed to be working?'

'Maybe.' Yates and Trudy's conversation reverberated in his head, stabbed him in the gut. Washed-up. Finished. Could he take even more of that?

Opening a small drawer on his side of the desk Weissman took out a police warrant card. He flipped it open and pointed to a shiny hologram logo embedded just below Talbot's photograph. Bloody hell, these people worked fast.

'That is your Permissions,' Weissman said. 'It will open doors you didn't even know existed.' He placed it squarely in the centre of the desk. 'Accept it and you're on your own. A hound without a pack.'

'With back up?'

A long worm of ash fell off Weissman's cigarette, and he blew it off the desk onto the floor. 'I'll be at the end of the phone.'

For a few dreadful moments there was a silence so loud that Talbot picked up the sound of a clock ticking far, far away. His heart was racing and his insides had knotted into a tight ball, like tangled wool, only he didn't have time to unravel the confused threads. An answer was expected. There was no going away and thinking about it, no discussion. Yes, or no.

Leaning across the table he fingered the warrant card. 'You'd best call me Jake,' he said, curled his fingers around it and slipped it into his pocket.

16

WEISSMAN BROUGHT A CHAIR ROUND, sat next to him and placed his laptop so that they could both see the screen.

With a few swift clicks he brought up a photograph of a youth with dark hair and dark eyes, smiling, laughing maybe.

'Do you know who that is?' he asked.

'Sure, it's Frankie Hayward, few years ago by the looks of it.'

'And this one?'

Talbot shifted his head to get a better view. The boy looked much the same age. Sandy haired, round faced, slightly freckled, sharp blue eyes, a pout on thick lips that made him appear sullen, moody, and awkward. Talbot folded his arms.

'Is that Keith McKenzie?'

A third photo slid onto the screen. 'And this?'

'That looks, to me, like a mock-up of McKenzie as he might be now.'

'What about this one?'

Oh, wow, was that Lilly? He wiped a hand round his face to cover the grin that was spreading uncontrollably across his lips. Taken way back in what he guessed might have been the early forties, or maybe late thirties, she had a smile that promised sweet treats and eyes that weren't afraid to look straight at you. Even in black and white she was stunning. Any and every man who wasn't made of ice would be fascinated by her.

'Lillian Charteris,' Weissman said. 'Née Lillian Baker, a very beautiful girl who was brought up in Farnham, daughter of a well-to-do couple who ran a haulage firm out of Alton.'

'I guessed it was Lilly.' Talbot couldn't take his eyes off her image. Christ, if she were young, free and single right now, he'd compete with Frankie for her.

'You'll be given a file containing her psychiatric reports.'

A shiver ran up Talbot's spine. He hadn't anticipated her having psychiatric reports, not at all.

'At age twenty she started hallucinating, seeing ghosts in her bedroom, on frequent occasions. She wasn't bothered by them, but she confided in her mother, who decided to seek medical help because she believed her daughter was somehow being possessed, or overly influenced by these spirits.'

'You said, spirits, plural.'

'On the ball, aren't you.' Weissman smiled. 'Study the report at leisure. With what we know now it makes remarkable reading.' He scrolled back to the photograph of the young McKenzie.

'Keith McKenzie, for years a next-door neighbour to young Frankie's grandmother, and for a while Frankie's best friend.' Weissman paused and lit a cigarette as if he needed one. 'Ten years ago Frankie walked into Farnham police station and said that his friend Keith had disappeared. Now, the police already had Frankie on file, because of his mother's peculiar aversion to him...'

'Why the police? She said psychiatrist to me.' Talbot studied Keith McKenzie's photograph. There was something about it that he found highly disconcerting.

'Frankie's mother accused him of theft, blackmail, and...'

'Blackmail?'

'All totally unfounded.' Irritated, Weissman stood up and started to pace the room. 'Because Frankie was known to us, nobody took him seriously, at first. This strange young man, not truly ill, yet not truly... normal, as we would call normal, either. '

'Where does he fall short of the normal zone?' Talbot had a few ideas but preferred to hear the professional version first.

'He finds it difficult to form close relationships, he's obsessive-compulsive, doesn't know how to play, smiles but doesn't appear to comprehend joy...'

Not obsessive-compulsive, Talbot thought; he counts his steps all of the time, sure, but he doesn't panic halfway down the road about whether or not he's locked the front door. Satisfactory relationships probably didn't come easily due to his mother's early attitude, and as for joy, well, Weissman obviously hadn't analysed Hayward in natural surroundings.

'You look doubtful.' Weissman stopped pacing.

'Let's just say I've seen a different side to him.' And no, he wouldn't mention Hayward's difficulty in accepting physical affection.

Perching on the desk, Weissman furrowed his brow. 'We won't get on well if you don't share your findings.'

'It's all in my report.' Talbot took out a cigarette, but didn't light it. 'If we're sharing information, then tell me why Frankie's mother hates him so much. Have you got to the bottom of that one?'

'To some degree. It wasn't young Frankie's intelligence she couldn't cope with; it was his early presentation of bizarre behavioural problems. Most mothers would have compassion for their child, but Dorothy Hayward felt deeply embarrassed and spared no words complaining about how he had ruined her life.' Weissman shifted, either because he was uncomfortable with the subject matter, or because balancing his backside on the desk was a strain. 'We never witnessed any of the specifics she described, certainly not the more outrageous accusations.'

'Which were?'

'That Frankie could lose control in a second, with no warning signs… at least none she noticed. He would never lash out at others, but would self-harm; and, apparently, see things which others could not. Her description was akin to certain behaviours that have been observed by individuals suffering from post-traumatic stress disorder.'

'And this was from birth?'

'So she claimed.' Weissman sat up a little straighter. 'Dorothy Hayward said that these aberrations did not diminish as he grew older; although she said he developed new ones: an ability to focus on something for hours without blinking, which truly unnerved her, and at other times, unexpected rapid blinking.'

'Perhaps those specific actions were only triggered by his mother.'

'I've experienced Frankie's hard stare.' He tapped the laptop screen where Keith McKenzie's picture was still showing. 'You don't like this boy, do you?'

Talbot shrugged.

'It was several days before anyone really listened to Frankie about Keith going missing, and then it was only because he refused to go away and stop pestering the police. Do you know what Frankie claimed? He claimed that he and Keith had been travelling back in time.'

'You mean physically? Not this astral travel malarkey?'

'Yes.'

Talbot laughed. How stupid. He should have seen that one coming. 'And were they?'

'We were unable to qualify that particular claim.'

'No time machine then.' Talbot shook his head, pushed himself out of the chair and went to stare at the white flakes falling outside the window.

'He had a device, a contraption, but it didn't appear to... well... work.'

'Did you confiscate it?' Pictures of Frankie's basement sprang to mind. Not sex after all, then.

'Of course, but it was nothing more than a computer with a programme that ran some swirly patterns akin to a screen saver.'

Now who was it who had said Hayward was a bright bastard? Ah yes. Mother.

'So how does this time travel work?'

'Frankie says that he doesn't really know. He says that he arrives out of body, and when he returns he's in his body.'

'Then he doesn't go physically,' Talbot corrected. 'He can't possibly. Most likely he nips off with Keith and when he comes back Keith's body isn't there.' Gazing down at the busy shoppers he popped a cigarette into his mouth, but hovered with the lighter. 'No body, no crime.'

'There was a full enquiry, Keith's parents following through with a murder allegation, but with no evidence, he got off.'

'Perhaps the kid came back early, before Frankie, and ran away from home.' Talbot tapped his teeth with the cigarette. 'Perhaps he got stuck in the past and dragged his body through some time portal to be with his soul.'

'You have a truly vivid imagination, Jake.' Weissman's attitude was condescending.

'You don't believe in the time travel part of it, do you?'

'Not in the slightest.'

Talbot chuckled. 'In most cases like this we discover that the kid's run away after some family bust-up.' Turning back to the window Talbot lit his cigarette. Oops, had he omitted to write in his report about how Hayward had gone back in time to stop Lilly dying in a plane crash? Surely they knew that already, the MOD and the psychiatrist and whoever else *they* were.

Weissman came and stood very close, just behind him, his proximity making Talbot bristle. 'Your brief is to find Keith McKenzie. Here, there, alive, a corpse—it doesn't matter.' Weissman breathed the last few words across his cheek, the smell and the implication making Talbot's insides curdle. 'Find Keith and we'll let Frankie visit Lilly. Now wouldn't you like to do that for him?'

17

Scapegoat, stooge, idiot, a thousand words spiralled through Talbot's head as he pushed the door open and inhaled a deep breath of freezing cold air. Freedom. Weissman's words made him want to spit. *'Find Keith and we'll let Frankie visit Lilly.'* Who the fuck gave that ruthless bastard the power to manipulate people's lives? He'd stolen Hayward's freedom of choice, his human rights, and that made Talbot want to punch him right between the eyes. Seeing his reflection in a shop window he shuddered at how menacing he looked. He unclenched his fist and tried to steady his thoughts.

There was no doubt Weissman wasn't being straight him with, no doubt at all. Turning his collar up, he strode down into town, the car and home and hassle with traffic beyond him right now, his feet needing to walk and his mind needing to burn off futile rage.

From today he was officially on leave. He'd been promised expenses, a fair wedge more on top of his normal wages; and a phone and a laptop, which would be delivered tomorrow. And Hayward's brother thought *he* was cheap at a couple of fags. It stank, tore his insides out, made him feel as if he'd sold his soul.

All around, lights were coming on as snow-laden clouds turned the sky grey and dusk crept in around the seams. It was bitterly cold, his toes freezing in smart leather shoes. Tomorrow he could wear boots and a hat and jeans, give up having to look respectable and official. Down towards the bottom of town he passed a café, and the aroma of fresh-brewed coffee tempted him to buy a large one, and risk frost bite sitting outside on a metal-rimmed chair so he could have a fag as well. Anything was better than Weissman's disgusting brew. Did Weissman really think he was that stupid? The second mug of tea had the same milk as the first. What was he playing at? Some psychological trick, where if he said it was full-fat milk it would taste like it? No, he didn't like that kind of mind game, not from someone who was supposed to be on the same team.

Notes, yes, he should make notes, before all of the mad ideas popping into his head were zapped off into outer space. Time machine, bloody hell, he'd be interviewing little green men next, and scanning the airways for flying saucers. Placing his notebook on the table he tapped his pen up and down. Just make marks on the paper, words, anything, don't think, write.

1)   *Frankie Hayward did not have a time machine... did he? Okay, so check it out. How? Good bloody question.*

He drew heavily on his cigarette and stared down the street at people hurrying about their business. A young woman nearly slipped on the snow and fell. Instinctively he stood, ready to assist. Haste. Now there was a good word to write down. He sat and scribbled.

2)   *Two people were in no hurry to do anything. Why didn't Keith's parents report him missing? Where were they in all of this before they cried 'murder!'?*

3)   *See if there are any early psychiatric reports on Frankie. Mother said there were, Weissman alluded to them. Perhaps they would come with the files Weissman had promised.*

4)   *How long has Lilly got to live? Stupid question, can't be answered. Not long.*

On better days he would have phoned Yates to run it past him. Suddenly there was only him, no sounding board, no second brain to fit the puzzle together. Closing his eyes, he smiled. So that was Weissman's game. Now the only confidante he would have was Frankie Hayward himself. Oh, how clever, single him out and throw them together. Shit, was Weissman expecting him to go the same way as Keith? Involuntarily he shivered and hugged his coat tighter around his chest. Images of the headline sprang before his eyes, '*Stressed copper on leave disappears, alien abduction suspected.*'

It was too cold to sit there any longer; his fingers were cramping and his ears aching. If he left town now he might just miss the worst of the rush hour crush. At the top of Tunsgate he doubled back to the camera shop. Why not? Weissman could pick up the tab on expenses. The manager served him with jovial expertise, happy to talk an idiot through a variety of functions on the latest point-and-shoots. Slim, lightweight, easy to slot into a pocket, clarity of image, instant results, one effortless sale and a satisfied customer. Buying a new toy should have made him smile, but it didn't.

Nor did Guildford's array of twinkling Christmas lights. As he pulled out of the car park, they spangled the sleeting snow and marred his vision past the wipers. He'd skipped lunch and was hungry, and his temper was frayed, yet his car had lost the way home and didn't bypass Farnham, but ducked down into the town and skirted round the one-way system before pulling up in front of the Victorian house.

Standing on the top step he dug his hands into his coat pockets and waited. There was a light on in the hallway, so he assumed Hayward was home, and pressed the doorbell again.

Suddenly the door opened. On seeing him, Hayward stared down at the floor and said quietly, 'You'd better come in.'

For a few awkward moments they stood in front of each other, Talbot with his hands still rammed in his pockets, Hayward staring at his feet.

'You've got your Permissions, haven't you?' Hayward's voice was no more than a whisper.

'Uh-huh.'

'Now you're going to ask me lots of horrid questions that you expect me to answer.' Hayward shifted from foot to foot.

'Uh-huh.'

'No doubt Dr Weissman will show you lots of terrible things they've written about me.'

'He's a git.'

Hayward didn't look up, but giggled. 'You can't say that about such an eminent man.'

'Too bad. He's a crap psychiatrist, or he's a liar.'

Slowly Hayward raised his head, the smile gone, his eyes scanning Talbot's face for the lie.

'I need you to answer one question for me,' Talbot said, and immediately Hayward looked back down at his feet. 'Frankie, did you kill Keith?' Hayward stood rock steady. 'No, Frankie, look at me, come on, look me in the face and give me an answer.'

When Hayward lifted his face, tears were glistening in the corners of his eyes. 'No, Detective Inspector Talbot, I did not kill Keith McKenzie.' He sniffed. 'Keith was my friend. He disappeared. I explained all of this years ago.'

Talbot raised his hands. 'That's okay, that's all I need to know for now.'

As he moved towards the door Hayward frowned. 'You going already?'

'I'm starving, I need to eat. I'll call you tomorrow.' Hayward's expression shifted from confused to crest-fallen. 'Would you like to go out and eat with me?' Talbot asked, knowing he'd prefer to be on his own, but a rare stab of guilt was twisting his gut.

'We could eat here.' Hayward smiled. 'We could get takeaway. It must be my turn to pay.'

Leaning against the door Talbot said, 'If we go out to a restaurant I'm less likely to ask you any of those horrid questions. Your choice.'

'I guess it'll have to be here.' Hayward spoke very quietly, his words quivering.

'Frankie!' Talbot threw his hands up in exasperation. 'Listen to me, for Christ's sake, the gloves are off! Do you understand that? Do you?'

'Yes.'

'Then for fuck's sake explain to me why you want to eat here? You do restaurants, you ate with me at the Maltings' coffee shop.'

Walking towards the kitchen, Hayward said softly, 'Perhaps I need to talk.'

Following on his heels, Talbot shouted, 'The only thing you need to talk about is Keith! Where is he, Frankie? Weissman's cut a shit deal. No Keith, no visiting Lilly.'

Turning to face him, Hayward stared, wide-eyed. 'I don't understand.'

Talbot took out a cigarette and chucked the packet onto the kitchen table. Lighting it, he said, 'I've been ordered to find Keith McKenzie, dead or alive. If I don't find him, then you don't get to visit Lilly.'

'But I don't know where he is!' Hayward stamped his foot.

'Then you'd better help me find him, hadn't you?'

WHILE WAITING FOR THE TAKEAWAY, they drank tea and Talbot twitched when the cat flap clacked backwards and forwards. Oh my, what a pretty little thing she was, Hayward springing up to lift the cat into his arms and soak up her comfort as she purred. So, he had told the truth, she had come home.

'Tell me about your time machine.' Talbot watched as Hayward fed the cat with an air of affection and excitement.

Still crouched down stroking the cat, Hayward muttered, 'It isn't a time machine.' He paused, then added, 'Jake, are we friends, or are you still a policeman?'

'I'm not sure. We're playing a ruse that I'm on leave while I'm investigating for Weissman.'

'If I tell you things, do you have to go and tell them to Dr Weissman?'

'Not necessarily.' That, Talbot thought, was the honest truth, after all; he hadn't been given a firm line of command, no instructions as to what type of reports were required, or when, or to whom.

The doorbell rang and Talbot flinched. Shit, he was getting jumpy.

'I didn't give them the real machine,' Hayward said as he trotted straight past Talbot to answer the front door.

The wily bugger, he *had* fobbed Weissman off with a dud machine. Wow, wow, Hayward just said it wasn't a time machine. Maybe there was no time machine at all, which is why he couldn't hand over a working model. So if Keith wasn't stuck in the past, where was he? Dead in a ditch, most likely.

Voices drifted into the kitchen, Hayward thanking the delivery boy, and the response being that he didn't have any change. Same old trick.

'Why did you do that?' Talbot asked, as they prised lids off leaking containers. 'Give Weissman a false device.'

'It's my technology,' Hayward said firmly. 'Why should the MOD get their hands on my invention for nothing? I went to them when I was fifteen, you know, told them I had the basic concept, and that a prototype was nearly perfected, but they didn't want to sponsor me, or employ me.'

Chuckling Talbot popped a prawn ball into his mouth. Mad kid creates time machine: yep, they would have mocked him, wanted to lock him up and throw away the key.

'Precisely what kind of machine did you offer them?' Talbot asked, sounding as serious as possible.

'It's a light-emitting astral projection portal. LEAPP for short. I tested the original model, LEAPP Mark1, when I was sixteen.' Hayward frowned, cleared some of the debris off the table and picked up a fork to jab and point with before sitting down. 'I never did find out quite what was wrong with the LEAPP Mark 1. It gave me the most dreadful headaches, and sometimes I was sick too.'

'Uh-huh.' Talbot tried to keep a straight face and make out he believed every word of it. Just having the conversation made his toes curl, it was so fantastical. 'Did it work, the LEAPP Mark 1?'

'Oh, yes, but the experience didn't last very long, couple of minutes at the most.' With meticulous precision Hayward filled his plate, each dish having its own designated area. 'Of course, I'm on the Mark 11 now, and do believe I could stay away for hours if I wanted to.'

'And you don't want to?'

Waving his fork round and round, Hayward spoke with his mouth half full, his accelerator pressed to the metal now that he was on his pet subject.

'Well, it's very difficult on one's own, to experiment, to keep oneself safe.' He stopped and almost dropped the fork. 'It was easier when Keith was assisting,' he said quietly.

'So explain the process,' Talbot said. 'How did Keith assist?'

Hayward shrugged. 'Just by being there, company…'

'Perhaps I could do that for you.'

Shaking his head, Hayward sucked his lips in and Talbot suspected he was biting the inside of his cheek to stop himself answering.

'Come on, Frankie, why not? Why not have me assist?' If he hadn't been so hungry, Talbot would have stopped eating there and then and shouted at him. Food went in on remote control, the complex flavours passing him by, all of his attention focused on how still Hayward was, and how his fork had stopped lifting to his mouth. 'You frightened I'll go the same way as Keith?'

'I don't know what happened to Keith.' His tone was flat, no emotion embedded in it.

Without asking, Talbot got up and poured himself a glass of water. The noodles were overly salted and his mouth was running uncommonly dry.

'You used to take Keith with you, didn't you?'

Hayward gave the smallest nod.

'So Keith met Lilly too, didn't he?' Talbot plonked the glass on the table, sat, and smacked his fork down hard. Hayward flinched, his eyes opening wide. 'Come on, Frankie, what went on? Did Keith want Lilly as well? Did you guys fight? Eh? Did you remove him out of jealousy? Was he muscling in on your girl?'

Hayward's eyes met his with a blank stare, the steadiness in them unnatural, the fact that they didn't blink unnerving.

'Is that why you won't let me assist? Are you worried that Lilly will turn her affection towards me?'

A tiny flicker shifted Hayward's eyelashes. Uh-huh, he'd rattled a nerve.

Almost inaudibly, Hayward said, 'You're not bad looking...'

'She loves you.' Talbot jabbed a finger at him. 'Real love stands up to tests, such as the introduction of new people.'

'You were very wary about introducing me to Kate,' Hayward threw back at him.

'That's different! I've only just met her. I haven't been courting her for ten years.' He reached out and picked up the dish of sweet and sour, determined to get more than his fair share. 'Lilly has stuck with you for decades. Her love for you has survived marriage to someone else, for Christ's sake.' Leaving one sweet and sour ball for Hayward, he mumbled, 'Anyway, Kate's got someone.'

'Has she?'

'Some guy called Karl.'

Hayward grinned. 'Oh, yes, she mentioned Karl.'

'See, you think my rival is funny, but as soon as you think I'm a threat to Lilly, it's all serious.' Shoving his plate away he lit a cigarette. 'Weissman's right, you don't have the full gamut of human emotion. You have no idea how to put yourself in someone else's place, to comprehend emotions from their perspective.'

The silly grin was still creasing Hayward's lips. 'Maybe you don't know me as well as you think, Detective Inspector Talbot.'

Talbot sighed and drew heavily on his cigarette. This was going to be the quality of his conversation for the next who knew how long. Fuck, it didn't bear thinking about!

'Go on then, make us a coffee, then you can give me a blow-by-blow account of what went on the night Keith disappeared.'

'What makes you think it was at night?' Hayward's cheeks had paled slightly.

'I'm the detective, you just said so. Remember?'

18

SETTLING DOWN IN FRONT of the old-fashioned roaring fire with his coffee, Talbot decided that the only way to listen to what Hayward had to say was with an open mind. He imagined that at one point this large room might have been two separate ones, because Hayward had drawn a wooden screen across to close off the office part and help contain the heat. With an element of flair he'd decorated the mantelpiece using long swathes of ivy and sprigs of holly, the robin on Lilly's Christmas card ready to jump down and eat the red berries. It didn't bother the cat; she purred and pawed at the carpet, eager to climb up onto Hayward's lap as soon as he sat cross-legged in front of the fire.

Listening to him made Talbot think of men of old telling tales around the camp fire, the smell of wood burning mellow and comforting as the soothsayer spoke of how he went into trance and brought back messages from distant ancestors. Hayward did use a computer programmed to produce a hypnotic image on the screen, much as Weissman had described. For a while the young genius banged on about alpha waves and brain pulses, and how the rhythm of the pattern encouraged deep relaxation and the transformation to the altered state that allowed for astral travel. At one point Talbot caught a hint that Hayward had other ideas along a similar vein, but to achieve various different unspecified outcomes.

'It's all based on the Fibonacci spiral,' he explained, and spent at least another half an hour talking about the golden section and complex mathematics that went way over Talbot's head. Even though he didn't understand, it was truly fascinating.

'You have to lie down and watch it,' Hayward said. 'I tried it standing up a few times, but that resulted in me passing out and hitting the floor.' He smiled and spoke to the cat. 'We've made it comfortable now, haven't we, Millie. Daddy's fixed the screen at the perfect angle, so no more stiff necks.' He sighed and stared into the fire. 'Keith and I used to hold hands, so that we went as one…'

'Say that again.' Talbot sat up straight.

Hayward laughed. 'Just so that we were one energy, nothing… you know.'

There was no easy way to put it, so Talbot came straight out with it. 'I didn't think you did so well with touching.'

Unexpectedly Hayward's cheeks flushed crimson. 'As a rule, no.'

Aha. That stupid git Weissman didn't understand Frankie at all. He'd never sussed where Frankie was at about touching someone else, and had refused to acknowledge that he *could* form close friendships. Was Weissman really that shit at his job, or was misinformation another one of his games?

'So, let me get this straight. You made an exception with Keith, and held his hand so that you could go as one.'

'Yes.'

Puzzled, Talbot rubbed his face, then chucked Hayward over a cigarette so that he didn't have to move and disturb Millie, or interrupt his train of thought to search for a fag.

'I have to ask these questions,' Talbot said, tossing his lighter over as well. 'Because I don't understand the process.'

Hayward nodded, lit up, and threw the lighter back. 'It's good that you're trying to understand.'

'So tell me, do you wear clothes? Do you turn up wearing clothes? Can you take things with you?'

'I wear clothes, I turn up wearing clothes. I take my clothes with me.'

'Uh-huh.' Now that was a literal answer if ever there was one. 'Weismann mentioned that your body stays behind.'

'Yes.' Hayward spoke with a hint of exasperation. 'I told you, it's a light-emitting astral projection portal, not a time machine. *I* don't travel anywhere. My astral body travels, not my physical body.'

'Can your astral body hold things, objects? Do you ever take anything with you? Can you leave things behind, or bring things back?'

'Oh, no, you mustn't do that!' Pushing the cat off, Hayward stood up, chucked his cigarette into the fire, and faced the mantelpiece. 'You mustn't change anything. You mustn't interfere.'

He was staring at the Christmas card, or maybe beyond it, to memories, his face puckering into a vicious snarl.

'You mustn't touch anything!' Hayward shouted at the wall above the hearth. 'I told you not to touch! Don't move it! Put it back!' He jabbed a finger towards the ground, commanding, insisting. 'Put it back!'

Within a second Talbot was on his feet, on guard, aware that Hayward wasn't quite with him and could be completely out of control at any moment.

'Put it down!' Hayward yelled, spun round, hands out, fingers grasping; he overreached, tripped and collided with the armchair. He bashed his knee and yelped, arms outstretched, his hands still reaching for something. 'No! Come back!' Sliding to the floor he knelt and doubled forwards, rocking, sobbing, the words tumbling out over and over again, 'Come back. Come back. Please, bring it back. Don't do this, please.'

Too wary to step up close and see if he could assist, Talbot moved backwards, a sudden spark flashing through his mind that Hayward needed a doctor and that he should phone Weissman. A shot of something to calm him down, that's what was needed. No, not medication, no medication. Never medication. His fingers were already searching for his phone, panicking, afraid of what he had triggered.

'I didn't do anything,' Hayward wailed. 'I couldn't stop him… but I didn't do anything.'

His fingers hesitated. Talbot's pulse was racing and he could feel a vein throbbing in his neck, the sight of Hayward, crumpled and distraught, distressing him beyond belief. Washed-up and personally involved. Shit.

Taking a step closer, he said softly, 'What did he take, Frankie?'

'I can't remember! I didn't see! I didn't see! I don't know!'

'It's okay, Frankie, it's okay.' Holding his hands out in a calming gesture, he stepped closer and crouched beside him. Instinct made him want to hold Frankie in his arms like a child, so that he could sob and wail and be comforted; only this was Frankie Hayward, and Frankie didn't accept human affection. Christ, he might lash out if he did that. 'Hey, Frankie, perhaps you could go back to before it happened, set things right.'

'I can't do that!' Hayward beat his fists on the floor, whack-whack, whack-whack; then he suddenly knelt more upright and beat his thighs, pummelling them so hard he was bound to leave bruises. 'I can't do that! I can't do that!'

Backing off a few inches Talbot raised his hands. 'Don't, Frankie, please, stop. Come on, let's leave it for now, eh?'

Tears were streaming down Hayward's face, his breath faltering as he choked and his words jammed. Snot dribbled from his nose and he stopped beating for a moment to smear it across his cheeks. Up close Talbot could smell his fear and feel the raw self-hatred exploding from every fibre of his being. If that angry self-loathing was turned outwards onto another human being it would be toxic. On and on it went, Hayward pummelling his thighs, then smacking his head and screaming, mad with pent-up rage. This was not a safe situation, and Talbot knew he had neither the training nor the experience to deal with this kind of behaviour. Behind Hayward was the fire and beside the fire were the fire tools, the tongs and poker, deadly weapons if he suddenly decided to turn round and grab one.

Talbot's mouth was dry, adrenaline buzzing through his veins and pumping his heart, making him wish he had some medical training. Is this what Hayward's mother had witnessed when he was young? Is that what had sent her over the edge? Moving as slowly as possible, he took out two cigarettes and lit them, held one at arm's length in the hope that Hayward would take it. He did. He stopped beating, and sobbed, the worst of his anger spent. Tears and snot wetted the end of the cigarette, Hayward wiping it away, his movements calm and precise. His forehead was covered in red marks where he'd smacked and hit; his hair was in disarray, perspiration making it frizz and curl and stick to his skin.

'Where's Millie?' Hayward's voice rose with concern.

'I'll find her.' Talbot stood and smiled. 'I'll put the kettle on as well, eh?'

Without waiting for consent, he went to the kitchen, stood over the kettle while it boiled, and beat back the desire to burst into tears and release his own distress. Shock, yes, that's what it was, shock. No, it was more than that. Normally he would have called for backup, or phoned Yates, or obtained medical assistance… Now there was no one, just him and his own judgement. This was one hell of scary place to be, alone in the desert.

Picking up the tea, he took a cursory glance towards the cat flap. Of course the ruddy cat had scarpered, who wouldn't, given half a chance?

'Millie's fine, she's out in the garden.' He hadn't seen her, but didn't want to risk setting off another eruption.

Hayward accepted the tea he was offered and mumbled, 'I'm sorry.'

'It's best that we leave it for tonight, talk about something else.'

Cupping his hands around the warm mug, Hayward nodded. 'I've been over that night so many times, over and over…' He sniffed and choked back tears. 'It haunts me.'

'We'll talk about it another time. Don't go upsetting yourself again tonight.'

'I can't undo what was done…' Tears welled again, great dewdrops in the corners of his eyes. 'I'm not smart enough—I'm too stupid.' He paused and sipped his tea. 'My machine has a flaw in it, Jake.'

Talbot gave a nod of encouragement. It took a lot for any man to admit failure.

'I can only go back exactly sixty years… to the day, no more, no less.'

Bloody hell, so he was now seeing Lilly when she was thirty, and if Keith was trapped back ten years earlier, then there was absolutely no way of reaching him.

On the drive home Talbot wondered if anyone caught in the past would grow older and keep pace with time moving forwards. He hadn't liked to provoke Hayward, to prod and poke about how he'd allegedly gone back and saved Lilly from getting on a plane destined to crash, which was an impossibility if he could only go back sixty years to the day. Unless, of course, he'd warned her well in advance of the event and hoped that she'd remember.

Oh, no, provocation might have resulted in another extreme display of abnormal behaviour, hence he'd left, promising to fathom how to get round the conundrum of Keith potentially being stuck in the past, siding with Hayward and hopefully making him feel that he, Talbot, was a man to be trusted. His head ached with it all. If Hayward was nuts, then it was all truly bizarre and far-fetched, and if Hayward was telling the truth, then he was nigh on a genius, and his mind far more complex than Talbot's little grey cells could keep up with. Wow, he needed a degree in mathematics, or quantum physics, or at the very least English literature, so that he would be well-versed in Asimov and other forward-thinking writers.

Turning the corner into his road his heart sank. That was Bailey's car parked at the kerb outside his house. What the hell was he doing here at nearly midnight? It was cold, and still snowing on and off; and his superior officer was huddled in a car waiting for him. Shit.

Bailey spotted him and was next to his car as soon as he pulled into the drive.

Climbing out, Talbot said casually, 'Evening, sir.'

'Evening, Jake. You've taken a long time to get home after leaving Weissman.'

'Didn't realise there was a curfew,' Talbot replied, his gaze resting on the goods in Bailey's hands. Ah, so he was the bearer of the laptop and phone. 'Better come in and get warm, sir.'

In the hallway Bailey stopped to admire Kate's painting. 'Bit large for here, isn't it. Can't really get a proper feel for the thing.'

'I might move it to the lounge.' Talbot gestured for Bailey to shed his coat and make himself comfortable.

'Is it one of Claire's?'

'No.' Gritting his teeth, Talbot prayed that Bailey would refuse a hot drink, knowing he was obliged to offer one.

'Coffee. Damn cold to be sitting out there for hours.' Bailey placed the laptop and phone on the kitchen table. 'So where have you been?'

'I have some… er… some occasional company.' Talbot grinned lasciviously to play up the lie. It wouldn't be polite to say fuck-buddy; but he hoped Bailey understood his innuendo.

'Well, that is good news, Jake. The rumour is that you're still mooning around over Claire, so it's good that you have… an arrangement. First step to moving on, excellent.'

'Nasty things rumours, aren't they, sir?'

'Don't like them myself.' Bailey sat down and pushed the laptop aside. 'What do you make of young Trudy that Yates is involved with? Not sure I much like the girl myself.'

'Why's that, sir?' Suddenly Talbot found himself glad that Bailey had come in for a chat. He was intrigued by his Super's outspoken comment.

'She's too… full of herself, arrogant.'

'She's very keen.'

Bailey chuckled. 'There's keen and there's downright irritating. It's insidious, almost as if she's going with Yates so that she can worm her way into more interesting cases—a user.' He leant close and jabbed his finger on the table to punctuate his words. 'At least the kind of arrangement you have is honest and open: you both know where you stand; but her type…' He pulled a face and shook his head, disgusted. 'Yates might have been allowed to work alongside you on this…' he drummed his fingers, 'but he's too immature, not thorough enough.' Leaning right back, Bailey scrutinised him, his brow puckering as he thought… Talbot feeling those thoughts prickle all the way down his spine. 'I don't always approve of your methods, Jake, but you're a damn fine detective.'

Talbot tried to smile. A reprimand followed by a compliment: quite good, from Bailey.

'Your report on the Hayward case was to be commended; Yates's was mushy, half-hearted.' He passed over a sheet of paper. 'Memorise all of those, then destroy the paper. You've got passwords, entry codes, and one emergency number you can call—but only in a true emergency; don't go crying wolf.'

'What do you class as a true emergency?' Talbot asked, thinking of Hayward's distressing behaviour.

'Life in danger.' Bailey smiled. 'And you must call it as soon as you find Keith McKenzie. We're not expecting you to apprehend him on your own.'

'Do you think he's a danger to me?'

'No point in taking any chances.'

Talbot nodded. 'And if he's dead you'll send men with spades to help dig him up.'

With a shrewd glance of 'no comment', Bailey lifted the lid on the laptop. 'Use this machine for our business, and only our business. In the notes you'll find details of an email account we've set up for you. Use your own machine for emailing Yates, and for Christ sake, don't let him get one sniff of this.'

For a few minutes Bailey ran through a set of unnecessary instructions, but if it made him feel useful that was fine.

'And no putting clever ring tones on this phone,' Bailey said, a jerk of his finger showing how adamant he was about sticking to the rules. 'Keep it blank and anonymous. Be like everyone else, read the screen to see who's calling.'

No more fun to be had there then.

When Bailey eventually asked if there were any more questions, Talbot jumped in with, 'I've been told that Hayward is a schizophrenic. What's the procedure if he presents with any behaviour that I believe requires medical attention?'

'Phone me, day or night.' Bailey said firmly, his authority not to be questioned.

'Not Weissman?'

'Jake.' Bailey lowered his tone to a conspiratorial whisper. 'You and I are police officers. This is a police issue, but others would make it more than that; try and take away our power to see justice done. We must stick together on this. Do you understand me?'

'I think so,' Talbot said, uncertain as to what was expected from him.

'What I'm saying is, if this proves to be a murder, then it's our business, not theirs.' Bailey's voice dropped to a mere breath of wind. 'Report to me as often as possible, keep me abreast of all new findings.'

'Yes, sir.'

As soon as he was gone Talbot breathed a sigh of relief and cracked open a beer. Christ, Bailey had as good as said that Keith was alive, and dangerous. No, no, he'd also implied it was murder. Perhaps Bailey knew nothing, making him read too much into it. Facts, that's what he needed, concrete evidence. Hayward's earlier outburst implied that Keith had broken the rules and taken something from the past. If Keith had brought something back, then it might be possible to find it. Now that would be evidence, wouldn't it?

19

HAVING FORCED HIMSELF TO go to bed and leave the laptop and all of its interesting information alone, Talbot stared up at the ceiling. He wasn't in the habit of lying to Bailey, but going over what had happened with Hayward would have been exhausting. Living it had been exhausting. Perhaps he should call Dorothy Hayward and ask how she'd dealt with Frankie's tendency to self-harm. It wasn't in Talbot's nature to deliberately hurt himself, and he tried to imagine being in Hayward's shoes. The closest he'd got to it of late was the feeling of sheer desperation he'd experienced after Claire had left, and the bottle of whisky he'd downed in less than half an hour. His head had ached for days afterwards, and his breath had stunk, adding to his feeling of wretchedness. That was self-loathing. That was torment. To experience that day in, day out, would be beyond human endurance.

His own spiral of torment started a little after five past nine in the morning when the *Dambusters* theme erupted from his old mobile.

'Hey, Jake, Bailey's put it around that you're on the sick.'

No 'how are you?' from Yates, more an attitude of having pulled rank by saying they worked together, so he'd be the best man to put the rumour to bed.

'Yeah, need some down time.' Keep it simple, no detail.

'Wow.' Yates paused, and Talbot's suspicious mind assumed Trudy was listening in. 'Bailey reckons you were taking the Hayward case too personally, started adding two and two together and making five.'

Talbot doubted Bailey would say that, but played along. 'Yeah, we had words, so I decided to back out and take some rest.' Ouch, that hurt.

'Probably for the best.' Yates paused again, then in a matey tone added, 'Well, you get your rest, eh. We'll catch up in a week or so, go for a beer, or grab a bite to eat, do the Christmas thing.'

'Sure, that'll be great.' Well, fuck you too! Talbot clenched his fist, convinced he could feel the vibe of Yates turning around and saying smugly to Trudy, 'Told you so.'

In such situations it was always best to focus the mind, so he settled down to a morning of exploring the laptop and its secret files. From the piece of paper Bailey had given him, it looked like there were only two main files, Frankie and Lilly, but once inside there were folders within folders, hiding sub folders, until eventually it descended to subterranean depths. Bloody hell, it would take months to read all of this. There was one vital piece of information he wanted to start with, and after half an hour and three fags, he found what he was hunting for: a character profile of Keith McKenzie. He knew there would be one somewhere.

Mostly it was a police report taken from interviews with Frankie and Keith's parents, but there was also a section written up by Weissman from having spoken with Frankie. He skipped through the visual description and concentrated on the man inside, jotting down notes as he went. Friendly, intelligent, outspoken, keen sportsman… competitive… aha!

The clock ticked round to twelve. He reached for his phone and suddenly it rang, making him jump with surprise.

'Jake, I'm so sorry to hear… if you'd needed to talk…' Helen's voice breezed down the phone, her concern barely masking her curiosity.

'I'm fine, really.'

'Is it this Hayward thing that tipped you over the edge? I heard that you were ordered to take some leave.'

Oh, weren't the tom-toms great. 'I just need some down time.' He glanced at the open laptop and gritted his teeth.

'Look, I've been pursuing this thing with Lilly, but if you'd rather I left it alone—'

'No, don't do that.' He knew he'd jumped down her throat and quickly softened his tone. 'You see, my superintendent was right, I became too personally involved. I do care whether the old girl is alright. So I'd really appreciate your help, just to set my mind to rest.'

'Oh, Jake, of course.' She paused, her voice coming back in a breathy whisper. 'Did you get any counselling, Jake? Did they offer any help?'

'Errr...'

'It's wrong, they should have given you some. What you witnessed in the Lasseter case was appalling.'

'I try not to think about it.'

'That's what causes stress.' She sighed. 'Look, why don't I come over this evening with a bottle of wine, make you a nice meal.'

'That's very sweet, but...' Yes, it really would be fun, but I'm working. 'I really do need to be on my own, for a while... to process stuff.' The laptop laughed at him and he gave it the bird.

'You will call me, when you're ready — for some company.'

'Of course I will.' He smiled. 'We'll get together before Christmas, promise.'

They left it on a high note, and by the time he settled back down again his mind had changed tack. What about Hayward's father? Where was he in all of this? There was no comment about him, at least not one that could be easily found. There was also precious little regarding Peter Charteris, which was odd; and, as yet, nothing about the plane crash that killed his parents. Joe Hayward had mentioned that his father worked in the city, so there was probably not much point in going up to visit until gone seven. So it was back to phoning Hayward and asking a few pertinent questions.

'Frankie, do you truly want to help me with this investigation?' He asked once the preamble was over, neither of them mentioning last night's upsetting scene.

'Yes, I do.' His tone was firm. 'I want to see Lilly. I have to, she's my whole life.'

'You do realise that if I find you guilty of murder —'

'I've been tried for that once already,' he said coldly. 'The judicial system took three prime years of my life, gave me huge stress and... and my grandmother died. She couldn't take the strain.'

'I'm sorry. I understand that you were very fond of her.' Talbot lit a cigarette. 'Look, I've been given some case files and I've got a million questions I need to ask you. Now, either I can phone every few minutes and ask them, or you could come over and work through some of this stuff with me.'

Very quietly Hayward said, 'I'd like to come over, if that's alright with you.'

It was best to work in the kitchen. Talbot gave Hayward his old laptop to play with, the one he'd upgraded from last year, so he could sit and surf the net, or update his blog in the spaces between questions.

'I can't believe they've written so much about me,' Hayward said in astonishment, as soon as he saw the folder upon folder of material Talbot had to wade through. 'Am I really so fascinating?'

'I've only skimmed, so I'll let you know once I've read it.'

Hayward laughed and Talbot shot round and gazed at him. That was a normal human reaction; in fact, that was a very self-confident reaction.

'Have I done something wrong?' Hayward asked.

'No, you're doing just fine.' Talbot smiled and pointed towards the kettle. 'Tell me about Keith. Tell me how you met and became friends.'

'He lived next door to my grandmother, next to the house I live in now.' Hayward filled the kettle and shrugged. 'He saw me one day in the garden, and spoke to me, and my grandmother asked if I'd like to invite my new friend round for tea.'

Normal stuff. 'Did you hit it off right from the start?'

'We seemed to.' Hayward stared down at his feet. 'I don't make friends easily, Jake, never have, so when Keith showed an interest in me…'

'You jumped at it.'

He nodded and placed tea bags in mugs, then carefully poured on the boiling water, intrigued, as if the entire process were alien to him.

'How often did Keith come round?'

'To start with maybe once a week, for Sunday tea, or sometimes after school.' He used a spoon to squeeze the tea bags, uncertain, as if copying it from an afternoon cookery programme. 'We went to different schools, so we didn't walk to school together or anything.'

'Did you ever go to his house?'

'Not often. I don't think his mother liked me.' He poured the milk in, stirring, watching as the colour changed. 'And my grandmother would have been lonely if I was always out.'

'You must miss her enormously.'

'She was good to me.' He lowered his head in that small reticent gesture Talbot had seen before, and his lips crumpled slightly. He sniffed and smoothed down his sweater, then proudly placed the tea on the table. 'We would read to each other, sometimes make up stories and write them down, or play cards.'

'Your brother said you didn't like cards.'

Hayward chuckled and sneaked his fingers towards the cigarettes, walking them across the table like a predatory mouse about to pounce. Two could play at that game, and Talbot edged them away, grinning and beckoning for an answer.

'Joe cheats.' Hayward eyed the packet, judging his moment. 'Joe always has to win. He changes the rules to suit himself, and if you do happen to be winning, he just thumps your arm, over and over again.'

Suddenly Talbot snatched the packet up, took one and swung it like a pendulum. 'Is this what Joe would do? Did he tease you?'

'All of the time.' Hayward sat back with practised nonchalance.

Tossing the cigarette over, Talbot asked, 'What about Keith?'

'He was okay to start with.' Hayward studied his cigarette. 'At first I wanted him to see what I was doing, to have a friend to share it with. Then he kept coming round more and more, asking if I'd made any progress, wanting to see what my machine would do.'

'Did you resent that?'

'I felt crowded.' He lit his cigarette, leant back and blew a long stream of smoke up to the ceiling. 'He made me feel… left out. As if our friendship only took place in my world.'

'How come?'

'He was a good friend, he did stick up for me,' Hayward said emphatically, and frowned.

'Come on, Frankie, how did he make you feel left out?'

'I didn't kill him.' Slowly he started to rock backwards and forwards.

Shit, he was going to go into one again. 'Frankie, do you understand what resentment is? Do you know what it feels like?'

He nodded. 'Resentment is active… bitterness. I ached, felt rejected. Not good enough.' On a forward swing he stopped rocking, placed his elbows on the table and clutched his head in his hands. 'Keith liked athletics. He competed in the area sports, and he wouldn't let me go and watch.'

'Why not?'

Looking up he said flatly, 'Because he didn't want to be ridiculed for having a nerdy friend.'

Talbot nodded and sipped his tea. So, Keith only wanted him as a private friend, was embarrassed to be seen with him in public, and probably slagged him off behind his back. Hmm, a bit like Yates, then.

'He won the eight hundred metres,' Hayward said quietly. 'He brought the medal round to show me.'

'Keith liked to win, didn't he?'

Unexpectedly Hayward's voice rose sharply and he cried, 'I like to win too!' He thumped the table. 'I like to be the best at what I do, but I don't like things where you have to elbow other people out of the way to get it. To... to bully people. To shove people. They can have it for all I care.'

'Except Lilly.'

'No! You're wrong!' Kicking his chair back, he stood up and pointed an accusing finger. 'If she wanted someone else I would back down, do what makes her happy.' He folded his arms tight across his chest. 'She didn't want Keith, she told me so, asked me to stop taking him with me.'

'But you were always with Keith. How could you speak to her in private?'

'I started going twice a day: once with Keith at eight o'clock, and then, after he'd gone home, I'd go again at midnight.'

And midnight was when he visited Lilly now. Of course, that's why he'd had to rush home from their supper party with Kate at 11.30.

'When did the split come, Frankie?' Talbot leapt to his feet and raised his arms. 'Jesus Christ! You told Keith he couldn't go any more, didn't you? On that last day. That's why the little shit took something, thinking he'd mess it up for you if he wasn't allowed to play the game.'

'I didn't think he'd do anything so stupid.' Hayward hung his head. 'I... I don't understand spiteful behaviour. That someone would want to break a toy if they can't have it.'

'I bet Joe did that too,' Talbot muttered and slammed the laptop shut. 'Let's go get a late lunch down the pub, I need some fresh air.'

IT WAS THE SAME pub he'd met Helen in, twenty minutes up the road and far enough to stretch his legs and make his ears burn with the cold. A hat was needed, and he could wear any kind of head gear he liked, now that he was officially unofficial. They ordered sandwiches and sat by the open fire, Talbot determined to keep the conversation on easy subjects so that Hayward didn't explode in public.

'Dr Weissman didn't put all of the pieces together, like you have.' Hayward lifted the bread and sniffed the ham in his sandwich.

Talbot smiled; he knew better than to go for cold meat in a place that didn't have a huge turnover, so had opted for cheese and pickle. 'I've only scratched the surface.' He shrugged, as if it were nothing. 'Frankie, do you think at some point I could see your machine?'

'You can't use it.'

'No, no, just to see it.'

For a moment Hayward thought, then he went over to the bar and waited ages for the girl to pass him some mustard. He came back and drowned the meat in it. 'Okay.'

'And sometime, after I've just seen it, do you think I could watch,' he nonchalantly inspected his own sandwich, 'while you go and visit Lilly?'

'Why would you want to do that?' Hayward looked genuinely flummoxed by the request—or by the flavour of his sandwich.

'Well, you said that your body stays behind.' Talbot paid further attention to his food, as if this was throw-away chit-chat and not worth concentrating on. 'I could keep an eye on it for you, keep you safe.'

'Oh, yes, I see.'

'I guess it would be interesting if we had a medic there too, someone who could measure your heart rate and other vital signs.'

Hayward placed his half-eaten sandwich back on the plate and ate the decoration of crisps. 'I don't want to be an experiment.'

'No, no, just someone to watch over you.' Talbot looked him in the eye. 'I really want to be there, to see what happens, but I'm worried in case my presence disturbs the balance.'

For a while they sat in silence, eating, looking around the bar, Talbot gazing into the fire and wondering if Hayward would take him up on his challenge. It was about time an outsider witnessed the phenomenon and was given an opportunity to study the machine in action, or at least analyse what happened to Hayward during the process.

'Okay,' Hayward said at last. 'Kate can come along; she's a trained nurse.'

Is she? 'No, Frankie, I can't involve a member of the public.'

'I'll employ her as my personal nurse, she needs work; she said so.'

'Frankie, no.' Talbot leant close and whispered, 'We can't let her in on this. The Permissions people will open a file on her, and who knows how that might affect her life.'

'It's her or nobody.'

Getting up, Talbot wished he had never mentioned it, thought about having a shot of something stronger put in his apple juice, but went outside and had a cigarette instead.

20

THEY SPENT THE REST of the afternoon sitting on opposite sides of the kitchen table at their laptops, Talbot occasionally throwing over the odd question, and Hayward giving some very odd replies.

'Why sixty years?' Talbot asked.

'It just happened.'

That was an evasive untruth, not quite a lie, but a fudge, the atmosphere between them not having been as easy-going since lunch. Thinking on it, Talbot wondered if Hayward wanted his blessing on the idea of involving Kate. Or was it simply that he hated being refused, or told not to do something? Right now was not a good time to probe, the tension building into a sense of friction, until Talbot experienced it as the child in Hayward wanting to be excused to go home, and not knowing how to ask. Yes, he was exuding an uncomfortable atmosphere, Talbot hating it so much he felt like getting up and clipping Hayward's ear.

Instead he made tea.

'Can you visit Lilly without your machine?'

'Never tried.'

Rummaging in the back of a cupboard, Talbot found an ancient packet of biscuits and emptied some onto a saucer. Tempt the child back with sweet treats. Back, yes, encourage him to return. It felt as if Hayward had disappeared and part of him wasn't there any more, a body without a soul.

'Sorry about the Kate thing,' Talbot said, and put the biscuits on the table. 'It's up to you.'

'I'll think on it.' Hayward smiled and chose the second biscuit down.

Woomph, he was back, the energy snapping into his body, Talbot sensing it rise up and embrace him with that warm smile.

Where the hell had he been? 'Surfed anything interesting?' Talbot tried not to glance over his shoulder to read the web page.

'I've been looking at some guy's theory on hypnotic mind pulse.' Hayward bit into his biscuit and shook his head, then spoke with his mouth full. 'It won't work. He's close, but his maths is all wrong.' He pointed at the screen and Talbot took the hint to lean close and read. 'See here, that formula isn't correct.' He laughed. 'He hasn't even got an accurate calculation for the equation; honestly, does he really think everyone is so stupid?'

'Most people are. To me it's all Chinese.' Perching on the corner of the table next to him, Talbot said, 'You were an ace student at school; why didn't you go on to university?'

'I couldn't concentrate on my A levels due to the court case.'

Shit, he should have realised that. 'It's not too late.'

'I was going to study aeronautical engineering, but my school decided it was best that I didn't go in while I was under investigation for murder.' He shrugged. 'The other students were bullying me, and the science tutor didn't like me anyway.'

'Why not?'

Hayward looked up, those two huge brown eyes begging for acceptance. 'Because I found flaws in his equations too.'

For a while longer they sat together, Talbot typing up notes and Hayward managing to stay connected with his body, making him feel like a real companion who was driven by human desires. Accessing his new email, Talbot found a message from Bailey asking how he was getting on, and wanting a return mail to show the system was working.

'Nasty rumour going around that you forced me to take leave,' Talbot wrote. 'Investigation going well. I require some vital information a.s.a.p. I need Keith McKenzie's school reports, a list of his classmates, and a list of pupils attending the same school for the two years above and below him. I also need newspaper articles about the area sports in which Keith won a gold medal. Oh, and any other sporting achievements.'

Within half an hour there was a response.

'Good God, you don't want much, do you, Jake! Going well? Excellent. Progress being made?'

All Talbot wrote back was, 'Lots more work to do. Couple of things slotted into place.'

At six o'clock Hayward made his excuses to leave, saying he needed to feed his cat. It was a pleasant goodbye, the earlier strain having disappeared along with the biscuits.

TALBOT WAS JUST ABOUT to climb into the car to go up and visit Hayward's father, George, when 'Run Rabbit Run' sprang from his phone. Enough time had passed for Hayward to have arrived home and contacted Kate, so Talbot answered it with an air of caution.

'You okay?' she asked.

'Yeah, sure, fine.' Don't say the rumour had spread to her as well. It was like a bloody virus.

'Sorry, I've caught you at a bad time.'

'No, no.' It was best to get into the car out of the cold and he tried to shut the car door as quietly as possible, so that she didn't think she'd interrupted him on his way out. 'I've been meaning to call you, about the painting.'

'No worries, I've been really busy.' She hesitated, then spoke her lines very quickly. 'Look, I know we don't really know each other, but I've suddenly been given a terrific opportunity to exhibit my work. It's a two-man show, but one of the people pulled out, and I've been offered the space. Terribly last minute, so it's all a huge rush. Karl's been working day and night to get the framing done for me.'

And he needed to know this, to hear how wonderful Karl was? 'Uh-huh.'

'Well, the private view is tomorrow evening, and… well, I thought you might like to come.'

'Sounds good.'

'I haven't had time to make up proper invites.' She sounded embarrassed. 'It's at the Maltings, seven o'clock.'

'I'll be there.' Ah well, at least he was on her client list. 'Look, Kate, I'm going to buy the painting; would it help if I brought round a cash deposit? Framing can be really expensive.'

'That's so sweet of you, but can we do that tomorrow?'

As in, you're busy with Karl this evening. 'No problem.'

'You can bring Frankie too if you'd like.'

Shit! 'Why don't you ask him yourself?' Shit, that was cutting, lighten up, be friendly. 'He'd like that.'

'Okay, I'll call him.'

By the time Talbot pulled up outside George Hayward's house, he'd stirred himself into a lather about Kate nursing Frankie and being sucked into some time warp never to be seen again. To hell with it. Kate was old enough to make her own choices. Kate was with Karl. Talbot was simply the copper who'd tried to get her some justice and failed. He was bottom of the pile.

Although it was next door to his ex-wife's, the house immediately conveyed a sense of grandeur. Maybe that had something to do with the brand-new Mercedes parked casually in the sweeping driveway, or the tidy borders, or the fine architecture of the early Victorian building. Two large garage blocks perfectly matched the older red brick, giving the impression they were traditional outbuildings and part of the integral layout. Welcoming light illuminated a peaked porch and the surrounding tubs were filled with bright winter pansies: very homely.

It wasn't George Hayward who answered the door, but Kirsty, the disappointed sigh on her down-turned lips a sure sign that she was expecting someone else. Today her pink hair was sticking out like a chrysanthemum.

'Dad! It's for you!' she yelled, leant against the wall in a 'guarding the gate' fashion, and fiddled with her mobile phone.

As he appeared from a side room, George Hayward's worried frown gave the impression that he was used to trouble calling at his door. On seeing Talbot's shiny new warrant card, he pulled out a twenty-pound note and shoved it into Kirsty's hand, saying, 'Take yourself down the pub.'

Without looking at it she pushed herself off the wall, threw Talbot a sneer, and then elbowed past him, not even bothering to put a coat on before walking off into the night. She smelt of fags and a hint of marijuana, her lack of gratitude betraying a self-indulgent nature.

Her father had the same wiry physique as his children, his suit hanging badly, as if it were a size too large. His dark hair was running to grey around the temples and his skin sagged slightly, but little else hinted that this was a mature man, and not a child dressed up in grown-up clothing. Nervous energy radiated from every fibre of his being, Talbot picking it up as a rush of anxiety, as if there were never any time to do anything.

'I need to talk to you about your son,' Talbot said, following him into the sitting room. Aha, so this was where the family antiques were stashed. Nice, very nice, and if he weren't mistaken, that was an original Cotman watercolour. It was hung correctly, away from the light, the dark-red walls offering a striking backdrop. In daylight the room might have appeared sombre, but with the lush brocade curtains drawn, it felt warm and cosy, even though the fire wasn't lit. Muted throws covered the downtrodden sofas, a lifetime's wear and tear sinking the cushions into lumpy masses. No TV, two cabinets full of knick-knacks, expensive knick-knacks, and the carpet threadbare in places showing that the furniture hadn't been rearranged for decades. Yep, this had been the family home.

'Which son? The bone-idle one or the bonkers one?' George asked, lifting a fine cut decanter and offering Talbot whisky.

'No, thanks.' Talbot shoved his hands into his pockets. 'Let's start with the bone-idle one.'

'Coffee then.'

The kitchen was as Talbot would have expected, modern farmhouse style, huge table topped by a slab of oak, flagstone floor, and various time saving gadgets; recently refurbished by the looks of it, George using a state-of-the-art espresso machine to make the coffee.

'I haven't done well with my children,' he said apologetically. 'Joe was trouble from the start.'

Ah, so now it was Joe who was difficult.

'Frankie might have had a better start in life if Joe hadn't always been on his case, bullying him, hitting him, lying about him.' He sniffed the milk before offering any up to the coffee. 'Right little tale teller.' Anger rankled as he added, 'Dorothy thinks the sun shines out of his backside.'

'And you don't?'

They returned to the sitting room with their coffees, Talbot wondering why he'd bothered with the milk, when he appeared to have shown it to the coffee rather than pouring any in. It tasted bitter, like his words.

Talbot stood by the hearth, because he liked to see what was in a room and how people lived.

'He's a lazy little sod.' George sat on one of the sofas and stared at the empty fireplace. 'Frankie's a bright bastard; Joe's cleverness lies in treachery and deceit.'

'Strong words.'

'Inspector Talbot...'

'Jake.'

He nodded his acceptance of first name terms. 'Do you have any children?'

Talbot shook his head.

'When two boys play together and one comes in saying the puppy's drowned in the river and his brother held the dog's head under, you go out and take a whip to the cruel child.' He leapt up and pulled a packet of cigarettes out of one of the cabinet drawers. 'Unless you're talking about Joe and Frankie.' He lit one and as an afterthought offered them over. 'Dorothy fell for it, I believed her...' He joined Talbot, leaning against the mantelpiece. 'It took me years to realise that Joe was the culprit—to many, many things. He always laid the blame for his actions at his brother's door, got his word in first, always left Frankie shouting innocent.' He rubbed his face, as if worn out by the whole issue. 'I was always at work. Night after night I arrived home to tales and arguments and being forced to take my wife's side.'

'So you split the boys up by sending Frankie up to your mother's.'

'I'm not that smart, Jake.' He dumped his half-smoked cigarette into the grate where it rested, along with several others, on top of the ash from last year's fires. 'My mother prised Frankie away. She was open about calling Joe wicked and refused to have him in her home.' He pointed at Talbot's half-empty cup and led the way back to the kitchen for more. 'I'm an only child, Jake. Do you have brothers and sisters?'

'A sister.'

'Get on well?'

It wasn't an avenue Talbot wanted to go down, so he nodded and said, 'Fair enough.'

'My mother adored Frankie, treated him like the other son she'd never had. Sure, I was a little envious, but she had different circumstances after my father died.' Inserting a new pre-packed capsule into the coffee machine, he flicked a button and watched as the dark liquid dripped into the cup.

Talbot wondered if he was counting, as Frankie would have done.

'My father was strict,' he said to the machine. 'After his death, my mother eased up and enjoyed life. Suddenly she had control of the money, and she and Frankie were very similar. She encouraged his experiments, backed him all the way.' With swift movements he swapped the cups around, ditched the empty capsule into the bin, and inserted another. Everything smelt strongly of coffee, and Talbot only wished it tasted as good as the smell promised.

'With Frankie away, Joe took to sucking up to his mother, and laid the foundation for constant bitterness.'

This time Talbot was invited to add his own milk. 'What was he like during Frankie's trial?'

Suddenly George's hand shook, and he clasped it tight with his other one. 'It was a very difficult time for us all. Frankie never trusted me again after…' He stopped mid flow, changed tack. 'Joe shouted guilty, drew Dorothy into his web, and my mother had a stroke from the strain. I sent Joe out to work; he doesn't really work, just comes up to the city with me and does a few odd jobs—useless specimen.'

'He seems to make enough to keep the family afloat.'

Picking up his coffee, George led them back to the sitting room. 'It's a front, Jake. I give Joe money, so that he can appear to be the strong bread-winner. We have an agreement. Dorothy creams me for every penny, and this way it looks like her precious Joe is supplementing their income.'

Even with more milk in it, the coffee tasted far too sour.

'Do you think that Frankie killed his friend Keith?'

George didn't flinch at the direct question, no shock, no dismay. 'Wouldn't have blamed him if he had; Keith McKenzie wasn't the nicest of people, arrogant sod.' There was no smile as he accepted one of Talbot's cigarettes.

'What about Frankie, do you believe he's mentally ill?'

'He's a strange one, that's for sure.' He knocked back his coffee and went in search of more. Bloody hell, no wonder he was so twitchy.

'And before you ask, I'm not sure about this time machine business of his.' Ah, so he knew about it. 'We were asked all of this during the murder enquiry, but I expect you've read the transcript.'

Not yet, but it would be top of his list for the morning. The espresso machine was gurgling again, pumping out its enticing aroma.

'Wait,' George said, 'I've got something I think you should see,' and trotted off upstairs.

Perching on the edge of the banqueting-sized piece of oak they classed as a kitchen table, Talbot let out a long, deep breath. Christ, this guy was agitated; too much time in his company and you'd soon get uptight. It made him wonder how Kirsty appeared so laid back. Probably the dope.

'Here, you can have them for a while,' George said, returning and handing over a pile of Polaroid photographs. 'Try not to let Frankie see them. He suspects I have them, and I did try offering them up during his trial, but your people didn't seem overly interested at the time.'

Bingo. A set of mottled images taken down in Hayward's basement. Aha, so this was the time machine… or light-emitting astral projection portal, as Hayward preferred to call it.

21

AFTER A BAD EXCUSE for a night's sleep, Talbot spent the following morning ploughing his way through the documents from the trial. Hayward hadn't contacted him to ask if he'd approached Kate regarding being his nurse, nor had he phoned to let him know if any arrangements had been made, and blowed if he was going be the one to initiate that particular conversation. Affidavits, statements, allegations, witness reports, it went on and on. Jotting down notes as he went he realised that the one thing that was obvious by its omission was the lack of any contact, whatsoever, with Lilly. Why not? Surely she was a part of this bizarre affair, yet the authorities had avoided speaking with her: intentionally, by the look of it.

He was reading through the court transcript where Hayward was under oath, and suddenly his mouth ran dry. His stomach knotted with such ferocity, it made him want to retch. Keep calm, he told himself, lit a cigarette, and read it through for a second time.

'When I went back and asked Lilly if Keith had returned to visit her on his own, she said no. She was very angry, and kept saying that Keith had taken her little green Bakelite box, the one she kept her hair grips in.'

The fucking bastard! Hurtling upstairs, Talbot yanked open the door to the spare bedroom and skidded to a halt. Come on, come on, where was it? Picking his way across a pile of magazines Claire had dumped on the floor, he reached across and drew back the curtains, letting in a smear of grey light. Bloody hell, it looked like a dump, and smelt fusty and rotten. Everything appeared brown, all of the bright colours stolen from his treasures by years of being shut away from the light, ignored and… oh what! No! Bitch! Crouching, he fingered the broken pieces of his majolica teapot, the crazy one the dealer had spent months tracking down. It had been a bit of a bet, the guy swearing there was a teapot with a monkey dressed up as a policeman, its tail forming the handle as it curled its arms around the orange pot. Maybe it was the police uniform that set her off. She'd smashed it on purpose, he knew she had; he'd seen enough crime scenes to recognise someone having had their head kicked in.

It was best to leave it alone, to get out of the room and sort it all out on another day, when he wasn't so busy. Shit, the silly bitch had made him forget why he'd gone upstairs in the first place. Over there, that was it, in one of the glass fronted cabinets. She hadn't broken the glass or stolen the key, but she had bent it in the lock and now it wouldn't turn; and his temper frayed, and he felt like smashing the glass to get at the stuff inside. Perspiration wetted his brow, and his pulse raced. Who was he angrier with? Claire for busting his key? Or Hayward, for shading the truth about Keith's thievery? He couldn't tell. Wriggling and jiggling the little key he eventually made it turn, swung the door back, and hesitated before taking out the green Bakelite box. His one had a small faux gold flower on the top, and Hayward had never mentioned that particular addition.

No more than three inches by two inches, and an inch and a half deep, they had been common in their day, women using them for pins, hair-grips, or mementos. Where the hell had he bought this one? The Maltings? That shop in Dorking? Or that antiques fair in Shere? What, about six years ago? It was junk then, but highly collectable now, something that had caught his eye as a snapshot of history, because... Carefully he lifted the lid and prised the top from the bottom; it still contained the two hair-grips left behind by its original owner. 'You're fucking mad,' Claire had screamed at him. 'That's disgusting.' No, the swirly pattern drawn into the brittle plastic was intriguing, and the golden flower a charming pretence that every girl could be a princess. Claire never could appreciate the history in anything, and right now those two 'disgusting' hair grips might prove to be tangible evidence.

Trotting back downstairs, he snatched up his new mobile and called Bailey.

'Humour me on this one,' he said. 'I want you to arrange a DNA test on something for me.'

'That's not a problem; I'll come and collect it this afternoon.'

'Immediately would be better, sir,' Talbot said firmly. 'I need to go out, as soon as possible.'

'Then I'm on my way.'

'You lying little shit!' Talbot hissed. He pushed past Hayward, slammed the front door, and leant against it. 'Why did you lie to me, Frankie?'

'I haven't lied to you.' Hayward's eyes opened wide, and he gaped.

'You told me that you didn't know what Keith stole from Lilly.' Talbot locked him in a radar stare, tracked his every movement.

'I never saw what he took.'

'Don't wind me up, Frankie!' Talbot hit the door with his fist. 'Under oath you say he took a green Bakelite box.'

'No, no, that's what Lilly said. I never saw it.'

'Don't be such a fucking pedant!'

'I never saw it.' Hayward clenched his fists by his sides. 'Lilly said Keith took it. She might have been lying…'

'Oh, give me strength! Now you're accusing your lover of making up stories.'

Pointing a finger right up in Talbot's face, Hayward said fiercely, 'She didn't like Keith, she didn't want him to visit again. When I said he'd gone missing, she was pleased, and then she mentioned the box.' He lowered his finger. 'To be honest, I'd never seen it, never knew she had it. She might never have owned one.'

'Come on, Frankie, why would she make something like that up?' Talbot headed for the kitchen, opened the back door, and stepped out into the cool air. His heart was racing and his head felt like it was going to explode.

Behind him Hayward said quietly, 'I don't know.'

Without asking permission, Talbot strode down the garden, his shoes quickly wetted by the soggy grass, his mind needing the influx of damp air to steady his senses. Barefoot, Hayward trotted after him.

'Why wasn't Lilly called to your trial?'

Unexpectedly, Hayward laughed. 'Because it had nothing to do with her. I'm mad, remember?'

Rounding on him, Talbot spat, 'Too bloody right.' He jabbed a finger at Hayward's chest. 'You're either seriously unhinged, or meddling in matters that should be left well alone.'

Hayward stepped back from the condemning finger. 'And they've chosen you to decide which, haven't they, Jake?'

Talbot half closed his eyes and grimaced. No, he had chosen to sneak, and landed himself in the muck all on his own. 'Look, Frankie, let's set some ground rules: next time I ask a direct question, try thinking round it, eh? Try filling in the detail, some background information. Help me out a bit. I've got a mountain of paper work to read through…' Hayward shrugged, and that slight, nonchalant motion was enough to light the blue touch paper. 'Well, fuck you!' Turning on his heel Talbot marched back towards the house. 'I don't give a shit whether you ever get to meet Lilly or not, that's not my problem.'

'I'll get to see her without your help!' Hayward yelled after him.

'No you won't!' Talbot spun round and shouted, 'I'll make sure you don't!'

Like a child Hayward ran up to him, eyes brimming with tears, his hands wide, pleading, his words tumbling out. 'Kate phoned me, invited me to her exhibition tonight. She was so sweet. I didn't ask her to be my nurse, Jake, I took your advice; I listened to you.'

'Good, then you won't risk going to trial for another murder.' He was halfway to the back door when Hayward tugged at his arm, the contact so unexpected that he raised his arm, ready to strike. 'Shit, don't creep up on me like that.'

'Can we go together?' Hayward was distraught, his eyes already reddened with unspilt tears. 'I never get invited anywhere. I'm not good at going to things like this on my own.'

'Then it's time you learnt.' Talbot sucked in his lips and stuck his hands in his pockets. 'I'll see you there, Frankie.'

'We could meet at the main entrance.'

'No. If I see you I'll speak to you, but I'm not holding your hand.'

22

Before getting ready to go out Talbot decided to put everything to bed for the night so that he could try and switch off. It was a long shot, phoning Bailey so late in the day, but he got lucky and his superintendent picked up instantly, as if the new phone was a hotline and might even be answered twenty-four seven.

'I need to interview Peter Charteris,' Talbot informed him. 'I need him to be co-operative. Any way you can… arrange something?'

'Well, Jake, I'm not a member of his golf club, if that's what you're implying.' Bailey paused. 'Leave it with me, Jake, I'll contact Weissman, have a word in his ear.'

'Thank you, sir, much appreciated.' Oh yes, the old boys' network was always a winner.

Taking his time, he showered and changed, choosing to go smart-casual in jeans, an open-necked shirt, and a black jacket, very much the Jeremy Clarkson look. While smoking a final cigarette before leaving, he studied the photographs that George Hayward had given him. They were laughable. The set designers on Star Trek would find them hilarious. Sure, there was the screen everyone kept mentioning, but the number of wires dangling down, Christ, Health and Safety would have a field day. One shot had captured the swirling pattern on the screen, but it was hazy with lines, the relay frequency at odds with the shutter speed. Another had young Frankie lying on a mattress on the floor, looking up at the screen, but it was switched off. Now hang on, hadn't George implied that Frankie only suspected these photos existed? Fetching a magnifying glass he strained to see the face of the young man lying on the floor. Bingo. That was Keith McKenzie.

He phoned Bailey back.

'Sir, is it possible to have access to some specialist photographic equipment?' He knew they had it, they'd used it extensively for the Lasseter case. 'I've got a photograph I need scanned and blown up, and enhanced.'

'You don't want much, do you, Jake.' Bailey let out a long whistle. 'Bit difficult to keep it hush-hush if we draw on too many resources.'

'Not to worry, sir, I'll purchase a scanner and some software.' Just went to show how much he usually depended on the expertise of others.

'That would be best.' A true hint of concern filled Bailey's voice as he added, 'Jake, don't overwork on this. You are taking some down time, aren't you?'

'Yes, sir. Just off out as a matter of fact.'

'Excellent.' Bailey chuckled. 'To see your… arrangement?'

'Not tonight, sir. Art exhibition, private view.'

'Keeps the balance, Jake, that's what I like to hear. Should have those school reports for you tomorrow.'

'Thank you, sir.'

Laughing, Talbot went to find his coat. Never before had he been so chummy-chummy with Bailey, and in a strange way he found it refreshing to be in agreement with the old duffer, and friendly rather than constantly snapping at each other's throats. It made for a most convivial exchange. He was still smiling when he reached Farnham, but then realised he'd have to use a car park like every other member of the public, the station being out of bounds while he was 'on leave'. The Maltings had its own car park, but that was chock-a-block, so he left his car up the small side road with the sign that insisted it was for residents only.

It was seven fifteen, Farnham was shrouded in a misty haze, the orange street lights sultry in the chill night air. Across the car park the people entering the Maltings were silhouetted against the harsh interior illumination. To the left of the entrance a tree was decked in blue Christmas lights, and somewhere in the distance, someone was burning autumn leaves, the smell invoking jacket potatoes baked in open fires and everyone muffled up to keep warm while having fun. For a few minutes Talbot stood and watched, enjoying the serenity and that magic hush of expectation that Christmas would soon be here.

Past the rows of parked cars he spied a solitary figure pacing up and down in front of the huge glass doors. Head down, counting his steps, hands by his side. Talbot smiled and shook his head. Poor little sod. As he approached, he saw that Hayward had dressed up in a black corduroy suit with a burnt orange roll-neck sweater underneath. Very arty.

'Hey, Frankie, you look great.' Talbot smiled and gestured that they should go in.

'You don't mind that I waited?'

''Course not.' Talbot led the way to the east wing gallery and Hayward chatted nervously as they trudged up the stairs. The gallery door was propped open and just inside, Talbot saw a sight that made his stomach churn. He stopped dead in his tracks. Turning around would be a very good idea, but, whoops, she'd seen him.

Painted nails flicked out as she descended. 'What the fuck are you doing here?' she demanded. 'You're not welcome, now piss off.'

Beside him Hayward looked horrified, the expression on his face one of stunned terror.

'And take your monkey with you.'

By Christ, her eyes were so cold, the blue like ice under that short fringe. She'd sharpened the spikes on her bobbed haircut too, the ends curling under her chin like claws, the only warmth the bright red of those lips that kept opening and closing as they spat out a string of vitriol.

'I have an invite,' Talbot said with the practised calm he used for interviewing suspected murderers. 'I'm Kate's guest.'

'Well, too bad, I'll tell her you couldn't make it.' She shut the red lips and puckered them into a nasty sucking creature that resembled a poisonous anemone.

Talbot swallowed the bile rising from his spleen. It tasted foul. 'I'll tell Kate myself.' Seeing her across the room he waved, and Hayward instantly took the hint, ducked past the demon, and raced towards Kate.

'You have no right being here, interfering with my life.' The nails jabbed downwards, probably to invoke a spell and have the ground open up and swallow him whole.

'Claire…'

'Don't you Claire me, you bastard.' She half raised her hand, ready to strike, and he twitched backwards, memories of the last time she'd tried that hurtling through his mind.

'If you can't be reasonable it's best that you step aside and cease having this puerile conversation.' He wanted to yell at her for breaking his teapot, but instead he said, 'You took your stuff. I paid you out. The end.'

Over her shoulder he saw Hayward ushering Kate away from admirers and towards their dispute. Heads were turning, curious, focusing the spotlight on him. Shit, how embarrassing. It wasn't going to impress Kate if he screwed up her show.

Kate looked fantastic, her flowing floral dress, heavy boots, and headscarf making her shine as all hippy and arty. He wouldn't get to compliment her, start the evening on a flirt. Her style put Claire's trim suit to shame. Business or art? How he could ever have fancied the uptight…

'Jake, how lovely you could make it.' All smiles, Kate breezed past Claire, pecked him on the cheek, took his hand and positively dragged him away. 'Let's find you a drink.'

'Don't make it too stiff!' Claire spat at their backs. 'He's a zero-tolerance freak.'

'What does she mean by that?' Hayward was laughing nervously and shaking, completely out of his depth with the situation, keeping close to Kate's side like a lost child.

'No alcohol when driving,' Talbot explained and chose a Coke from the makeshift bar.

'Have a drink, get a taxi.' Kate thrust a bottle of beer into his hand. 'I am so sorry, her behaviour was…'

'She's the ex.' Talbot put the beer back. 'It's my fault. If I'd known Claire was the other artist, I never would have come.'

Facing him, Kate took hold of both of his arms, looked him in the eye and said, 'Well, I'm glad you didn't know. I wanted you to come.'

'Then I'd best look round.' He knew Claire was staring at them, making the hairs on his neck prickle as Kate pecked his cheek and promised to catch up again later. It should have been a precious moment, but instead it felt like an ordeal by fire, a lump tightening his throat as he tried to swallow his pride.

'I'll have a Coke too.' Hayward swapped his drink. Now was that him trying to be part of the same tribe, or to gain respect? 'I like paintings,' Hayward said, his tone chirpy in an attempt to cheer Talbot up.

Together they walked round, standing for a few minutes in front of each painting, Claire shooting bad vibes at him every time he stood anywhere near one of hers. Talbot's heart was still racing, the adrenaline pumping, refusing to pipe down now that the spectacle was over. Price tags with big numbers on them floated in front of his eyes, the landscape from the hall that Claire had painted especially for him now commanding a healthy four-figure sum. Fuck her. A middle aged couple crowded them out and peered at it, waving a programme and saying how nice it might look in their sitting room. Muted sounds drummed on his ears, the clink of glasses and the burble of chatter. Everything fragmented, the noise grinding in and out, the overhead Christmas decorations reflecting false glory that floated before his eyes. He hated Christmas. Someone tugged on his sleeve. It was Hayward, his eyes all dewy as if they shared the same pain.

'Why don't you have that drink, Jake? I can drive you home.'

'Thanks, but I'll be okay.' No, he wouldn't, he'd stop off at the 'eight 'til late' on the way home and buy a bottle of whisky.

'Kate's paintings are much more... sunny. Aren't they?' Hayward smiled and steered him in the direction of two small landscapes with bold poppies swaying in the foreground. 'These might be better in your hall, with the large one in the sitting room.'

'Need a bigger lounge,' Talbot mumbled.

'The new shoe box was Claire's choice, wasn't it?' Hayward offered a sympathetic smile. 'With your love of antiques I'd expect you to choose something more like mine.'

'So would I,' Talbot agreed, and couldn't help but notice the handsome man who had made a beeline for Claire and was now all over her like a rash. That was him. *The* him who had stolen her away. The man she was shagging while sharing his bed. Christ, that was the guy from the gallery, the smarmy git she'd invited round to dinner. He sipped his Coke, trying to swap the bitterness for something sweeter. On his other flank Kate was linking arms with a sturdy thirty-something guy with

shaggy hair and a pleasant air about him. They appeared to be
closing a deal on one of her paintings with a well-off couple, the
wife grinning away as her husband shook Kate's hand. Someone
called out the name Karl, and the guy on her arm turned to see
who was after him. Even the Coke tasted sour. Kate was selling
well, she had 'Mr Nice Hunk' on her arm, and Claire was lobbing
icicles at him.

'Hold that a minute.' He smiled and gave Hayward his Coke.
'Got to go to the gents.'

Two minutes and he was outside, turning his collar up against
the frosty air, buttoning his coat. The night smelt good and clean.
He shoved his hands into his pockets and strode towards the car,
a guilty escapee, the cigarette his prize for making it over the wire.

THE WHISKY WAS WARM. It bit the back of his throat and promised
relief from barking demons. Taking the bottle as well as his glass, he
went down the hall and sat cross-legged in front of Kate's painting.
Hayward was right, her work was sunny and full of life. Right now
he wanted to be surrounded by that warmth and to forget Claire
and her cold, brown miseries. Drink was not the answer, but it
would do for now. It numbed the ache, made him realise that he
had chosen her when he was chilled to the core and dark inside,
Claire's brittle warmth all he could accept—and all he had wanted.
To have had more might have made him cry, and he hadn't had
time to cry. He shut his eyes. So close to the light, and yet the black
tunnel went on forever.

'Take some leave,' his superintendent had said. 'You can't simply
keep going, it'll catch up with you… sometime.'

Perhaps that time was upon him now. He lit another cigarette.
Transferring to Farnham, an easy patch, had seemed like the right
thing to do. Within months he'd met Claire, and the watery sun
shone, and everyone cheered him on. If only he'd known. Ironically
his new superintendent, Bailey, had been the one man to question
the ray of hope he took to be reality.

'Are you ready for a full-time commitment, Jake? Wouldn't a
little fun better fit the bill right now?' Bailey had leant close and
whispered, 'You can't replace what was lost. It takes time.'

'She makes me happy,' was his only response, but in retrospect it wasn't happiness at all, just a sticky plaster, which soon curled at the corners and should have been ripped off a long time ago.

Suddenly the doorbell rang and his heart leapt as if it had been gunfire. Who the hell… With a clack the letterbox flipped up and two dark eyes peered in at him.

'Go away, Frankie,' he called out.

Through the letterbox, Hayward blurted out, 'I need to speak with you. I have issues surrounding people disappearing, Dr Weissman says I should talk them through.'

Shit! You couldn't discuss that through a locked door. He hadn't even considered how Hayward might take it.

'You'd better come in.' Now it looked bad that he was swinging a whisky bottle to invite him in. Oh, crap.

Hayward stepped inside and barely gave him room to close the door. 'You ran away.' The poor sod was shaking, and looked like he'd been crying.

'I'm sorry. I was a coward. I won't do it to you again, I promise.' Talbot met his gaze and smiled. 'Shall I make us some coffee?'

'I don't mind if you have your whisky.' Hayward headed towards the kitchen, instantly taking control of making the coffee. 'You weren't a coward. Claire was hurling bad vibes at you and Kate was busy with Karl. It was a tactical retreat.'

'Uh-huh.'

'She wanted you to meet Karl.' Hayward turned around and smiled. 'I explained to Kate that you were upset. She said she'd call and invite us round for dinner, so that you can meet—'

'Yeah, yeah, the wonderful boyfriend Karl.'

'Jake.' Hayward hung his head. 'I should have told you before. Karl's her brother.'

'What!' Talbot swigged back his whisky. 'You bastard.'

Hayward nodded.

'Well, that makes us even, doesn't it?' Glaring at Hayward, his eyes followed the line of where he was looking. Shit, he'd left the photos that George had given him scattered across the kitchen table. Hurrying over, he scooped them up and shoved them in a drawer. 'Family snaps.'

'Will you be spending Christmas with them?' Hayward's tone was kind and genuinely interested.

'No.'

'Oh, don't you get on with them?' Now he sounded awkward at having enquired.

Yes, whisky would do it, just one more glass. 'They're gone.'

'All of them?'

'Oh, for Christ's sake, Frankie, leave it!' Talbot thumped the bottle down on the table. 'My father was killed by a drunk driver, at Christmas time. On Christmas Day my mother committed suicide. By New Year my sister was having a mental breakdown.' Snatching up the bottle he slopped more into the glass. 'She's in a home, being looked after… as good as gone.'

Aghast, Hayward gaped, unashamed to let the tears stream down his face. 'Jake, I'm so…' He wiped a finger under his nose. 'And she was so cruel to you for being zero-tolerance.'

'That's right, don't drink and drive, it fucks up lives.' Talbot knocked back his whisky, refilled the glass, and emptied the rest of the bottle down the sink. 'I hate the stuff.'

'Why drink it?'

'Come on, Frankie. Why do you thump your legs when you're upset? At the end of the day it's all self-harm.'

Hayward turned and started to make the coffees, slowly tipping the spoon as if counting the granules into the mugs. He said, almost inaudibly, 'I do it because I hate myself.' Suddenly looking at Talbot, he spoke emphatically. 'But there was nothing you could have done, about what happened to your family.'

'Oh, really? I could have spent more time with my mother, consoled her. I could have been there for my sister.'

Hayward shrugged. 'At least you didn't create the machine that made them go away.'

'Well, thanks, but that reassuring thought doesn't make me feel any better.' Staring into the glass he thought twice about whether to drink the stuff, but downed it all the same. 'I'll go and wash my face, come back in a better mood.'

In the bathroom he made sure he didn't look in the mirror, but splashed water onto his cheeks and the back of his neck, and brushed his teeth. He was already getting a thick head, the delightful mellowness short-lived. Swapping the shirt for a sweater made him feel slightly more human, and he tried to trot downstairs in a better frame of mind. The smell of coffee drifted towards him, and Hayward was sitting at the table studying a bunch of photographs. Shit!

'It's rude to take things from other people's drawers,' Talbot said firmly, going over and putting his hand out, expecting to be given them.

Instead Hayward warded him off. 'Where did you get these?'

'You know I can't divulge a source.' He snapped his fingers for them.

Wiping a hand across the photograph, as if to make the image clearer, Hayward frowned. 'That's Keith.'

'Yes, I thought it might be.'

Hayward glanced up, his face frozen into a blank, wide-eyed look, which Talbot had only ever seen on someone in extreme shock.

'Frankie?'

'He's alive.' Hayward suddenly came out of it and dug around in his pockets for cigarettes. 'That photograph was taken during the last year of the murder enquiry, three years after Keith went missing.' Tears streamed down his face. 'Whoever took it knew he was alive and didn't come forwards!' The tears turned to sobs, and he smacked the table.

'Here.' Talbot pushed a lit cigarette between his fingers. 'How do you know when it was taken, Frankie? How?'

Hayward's voice rose with indignation, and he spoke as if Talbot should have known. 'Because that's the LEAPP Mark 4! I didn't build the Mark 4 until then.'

23

'PLEASE TELL ME WHERE you got the photos, please.' Hayward was begging and sobbing and gulping back the wine Talbot had opened for him.

'Later, Frankie, later.' He drew heavily on his cigarette and regretted drinking so much whisky. It was confusing his head and making it impossible to concentrate on the right questions to ask. 'How did you find the…' He faltered, acutely aware that Hayward was choking on his sobs. 'Frankie. Listen to me.' Hayward met his gaze. 'As soon as I know more, I'll share as much as I can with you.'

Sniffing back his tears, Hayward nodded.

'So, tell me, how did you find the will power to build a new model during the enquiry?'

'I wanted to go back and put things right.' Hayward stood up, and started to pace the room. 'My old machine wouldn't do it, so I had to build a better one, to put things right, to get Keith back.' A plaintive wail escaped from his lips and he bit down hard on his hand. 'He's alive, all of this time he's been alive.'

'Not necessarily. He was alive then, but that doesn't mean he's alive now.'

'I didn't kill him!' Hayward screamed, slumped to the floor and started to hit his legs. 'I didn't take those photos, I haven't seen him.'

'Frankie, Frankie, please.' Talbot crouched down and looked him in the eye. 'He was alive. You didn't kill him.'

'But who took those photos?' Big brown eyes met his gaze, begging for an answer.

'I don't know, Frankie. I only know who gave them to me.'

'Now who's being the pedant!' Hayward shouted, curled up into a ball, and sobbed.

It felt right to let Hayward sleep on the sofa. He didn't deserve to be pushed out into the cold, alone and frightened, bundled into a taxi and told to deal with it on his own. Cruel people did things like that; but as soppy and drunk and he was feeling, it didn't stop Talbot from easing his desk across and blocking the bedroom door, just in case.

Earlier, wine-soaked, Hayward had wailed and screamed, and at one point tried to go out and get into his car.

'I have to visit Lilly. I have to visit Lilly,' he had yelled, Talbot grabbing him in a tight hold and bolting both arms to his sides while he thrashed and kicked. The neighbours had loved that, curtains twitching and lights going out so that he couldn't see their concerned expressions.

'It won't be safe, not when you've had so much to drink.' It was poor mediation and Hayward had used it against him.

'I don't care! I never want to come back!'

That was the point where Talbot had smacked him round the face, shouted to the invisible watchers, 'It's okay, I'm a police officer!' and dragged Hayward back indoors. From there it had been coffee and tears, a warm blanket and ordering him to go to bed, just as one would a petulant child. None of it had made for sleep, and Talbot spent the night in his own personal drunken stupor, listening out for footsteps on the stairs, or for the sound of Hayward lifting his car keys off the kitchen table.

They breakfasted in polite quietness, Hayward sulky and anxious, eating the food placed before him like a good boy and oozing that 'I want to go home now' vibe. When Talbot told him he'd have to take a taxi because he was still over the limit, Hayward gritted his teeth and said defiantly, 'Then I'll stand outside and wait for it,' which is exactly what he did. For over half an hour he stood in the murky rain, like a dark sentinel at the foot of Talbot's drive, the anger he exuded drifting back into the house like an evil black cloud.

At last he was gone. Never again. Personally involved. Never fucking again! In a whirl of temper Talbot rushed around cleansing the house of Hayward's life-sucking atmosphere. He threw windows open and let in a sharp rift of cold air. He hung the blanket out on the line, thinking the cold and the rain might wash out the lingering despair. He even cleaned up the breakfast things before making a cup of tea and settling down to do some work.

What he really needed to do was walk, give his lungs a blast of fresh air, only his head was pounding and his legs ached, his whole system dehydrated and complaining with all kinds of painful twinges that made the idea of a brisk walk unbearable. Water, that's what would help. He lined them up, tea, water, tea, water... and only five cigarettes left until he managed to take that walk. Didn't Hayward ever buy any of his own? Smoking one of them, he read through the list of files, trying to decide which one to dig into next.

Hayward's file was exhaustive; he could spend a year studying that one alone. Keith McKenzie, hmm, didn't much fancy it, but had a quick whizz through to glean some salient points. Bloody hell, his parents only relocated as far away as Dorking, not up north at all. They moved, no police involvement, no official getting them away from the madman and his machine next door; just up sticks and left. He sat back, drummed his fingers on the table and phoned round a few antique dealers he knew in Dorking.

An infrequent haunt, Relics, had been taken over by some well-bred woman who dealt in shabby-chic. Disappointing. Next up was The Cellar, and he had a very pleasant but unproductive chat with the proprietor, Steve. Last on his list was an old favourite, Just Antiques.

'Long shot, Sid, but a few years back, did you sell me a small green Bakelite box?'

'Well, Jake, if I saw more of your face around these parts, I might remember who you are.' Sid laughed, a wonderful, earthy sound. 'How are you doing? Glad to read that you didn't waste your time on that Lasseter scum and that he's going to trial.'

'Keep your fingers crossed.'

'I'd string him up myself if it was allowed.' Sid sighed. 'The gallows had a lot to be said for it. Now, green Bakelite box... that's right, you bought one with a gold rosette on top.'

'I don't suppose you can recall where you got it from?'

'Cor, now you're asking.' He paused and Talbot imagined he'd be scratching his head, as he often did when perplexed. 'You'll have to leave that one with me, Jake, give me some time to go through my purchase ledger.'

'Thanks, Sid, I'll make it worth your while—come in and buy something horribly expensive.'

Hearing Sid's voice cheered him up a bit, reconnected him with the normality of the human race and someone who liked to get on and do an honest day's work.

Next he dipped into Lilly's file, Weissman having placed that lush photograph of her on the first page. On a whim he fetched down his printer, plugged it into the laptop and printed it out. She was gorgeous. For now he could keep the photograph on the table, but later he would hide it away in his bedroom, just in case he ever let Hayward across his threshold again. Madness was one thing, but jealous rivalry, in the hands of Frankie Hayward: no doubt that would be highly toxic and dangerous.

At eleven o'clock Kate sent him a sweet text saying, 'Sorry didn't get to say goodbye. Hope you're okay.'

No, he wasn't okay, but texted back, 'It was rude of me to rush off, sorry. Perhaps we could do dinner soon and I can pay you for the painting.'

All she texted back was, 'That would be nice.'

Now with an answer like that, was he supposed to rush and book a date, or leave it until he knew he had free time? He chose to leave it and phone her once his head had stopped throbbing.

At twelve o'clock Bailey turned up at his front door, the smile migrating off his Super's face as soon as he clapped eyes on him.

'Christ, Jake, you look rough.'

'Mmmm.'

Walking through to the kitchen, Bailey plonked a folder down on the table, picked up the photo of Lilly and said, 'Smells like a brewery in here.'

'Yes, sir.'

'Well, I hope it was fun, because the joy ride's over.' Bailey dismissed the beauty in his hands without comment. 'This case is… troublesome.'

'You got time for a coffee, sir?' Talbot recognised the expression on Bailey's face as concern mixed with exasperation, and wanted to know more.

'I've been warned off, Jake.'

'Sir?'

'Had a phone call from that twit Weissman, about an hour ago.' He nodded in response to Talbot waving the coffee jar. 'He told me I was making too many waves, asking too many questions, helping you out too much.' He pressed his index finger firmly on the manila folder. 'Keith McKenzie's school reports that you requested.' His lips curled into a snarl. 'I won't be able to offer much more. Damn people.'

'May I ask who these damn people are, sir?' Talbot asked, hoping Bailey knew more than he'd gleaned from Weissman.

'All I know is that they're a psychiatric unit connected to the MOD, and have a lot more clout than I do.' He frowned, sat down and picked up Lilly's photo again. 'And all for a bit of skirt.' Opening his fingers, he let the picture float to the table. 'Putting you on this case, they've stolen one of my best resources… and then they expect me to back down and not offer assistance.'

'Why exactly is that, sir?' Talbot smiled, amused by Bailey referring to him as a top resource. He placed the drink in front of him.

'Digging. Christ, you're allowed to go digging, unofficially, but it appears that anything I do leaves a footprint they're not keen on shadowing.'

'Odd, isn't it.' Talbot nonchalantly lit a cigarette. 'Weissman was correct in his prediction that being a lone dog wouldn't be much fun…' He leant very close to Bailey, tried not to grin, and said in a hushed whisper, 'Of course, sir, you've been behind a desk a while now; I guess you wouldn't be much interested in offering a little covert assistance.'

'I never have liked your methods, Jake, never approved.' Bailey sipped his coffee. 'What did you have in mind?'

'Maybe you could be another pair of eyes and ears, someone to run things past, unofficially, while enjoying a social cup of coffee.' He peered at Bailey over the top of his mug, sipping it slowly. Bailey's eyes flickered with interest.

'Well, I don't see the harm in visiting a fellow officer who's on the sick, find out how he's rubbing along.' Bailey ran a finger around his mug. 'Maybe if I popped up once a week, in person, left off with the phone calls and emails.'

Talbot nodded. 'I'd appreciate that, sir.' He leant back and opened his arms, laughing. 'Like you said, I'm not coping well; looking pretty rough.'

'And taken to the booze. Most unlike you, not seen you do that
since…'

'I bumped into her.'

'Oh, dear.' Bailey sucked in his lips and nodded his sympathy.

'But out of the shite came a tiny nugget of gold.' Talbot said what
he had to say as flatly as possible. 'I have an uncorroborated piece
of evidence that Keith McKenzie was still alive while Hayward was
being questioned over his murder.'

'Good Lord, Jake, that's excellent progress.' Bailey leant forward,
beckoning him into a huddle. 'Have you informed Weissman?'

'No, sir, I thought it best kept to myself, until I have more facts.'

'Yes, Jake, I like that approach, very wise.' For a moment they
sat in silence, Bailey drinking his coffee and obviously thinking it
through. 'So your man's innocent.'

'Not necessarily.'

Bailey raised his eyebrows. 'Glad to hear you're keeping
objective.' He stood and brushed himself down, ready to leave.
'The DNA report you asked for is in there too, although God knows
what you'll be doing without someone to match it with.'

'And Charteris?'

'No introduction, I'm afraid.'

Bailey left on a sour note, scrutinising Hayward's abandoned
vehicle with due interest and muttering that he didn't like this case,
no, he most certainly did not.

24

ONCE BAILEY HAD DRIVEN AWAY, Talbot bundled up into warm clothes and went for the promised walk, out across the back fields and into a small stretch of woodland. It was so peaceful here, the cars and turmoil of life a mere background buzz, the damp trees and misty corridors of light a temporary haven. He walked and thought, and occasionally stopped to breathe in the cool air and watch the birds hop from branch to branch overhead. The earthy smell of mouldering leaves cleared his throbbing headache, acting like an aromatic tincture, some native remedy rising up from the ground to heal his wounds.

For a while he sat on a fallen tree and smoked and thought. He couldn't help it: the case, the facts, the unfinished jigsaw puzzle, wouldn't let him alone. His most prominent concern was George Hayward handing over that photograph in such an innocent manner. Had his new hologrammed warrant card truly been a signal for such a significant piece of evidence to be dusted off and forced into the light? Had George taken the photo? Had he acquired the photo from someone else? Or stolen it? He couldn't possibly have previously offered it up as evidence, surely not. In truth, Hayward's trial hadn't been a murder trial at all. It had been an enquiry into a missing person, a suspected abduction with an accusation of murder, and an entire army of people waiting in the wings to arrest and charge Hayward had murder been proven. It was a strange one, not the type of thing that should ever have gone to court in the first place. If George had possessed the photograph back then, surely he would have thrust it under the judge's nose and declared his son innocent. Nope, he couldn't have had it; not a fact, but a sure-fire certainty. So where had he acquired it?

The other big question was: how did the photographer get into Hayward's basement to take the photo in the first place. House key? Break in? Hayward himself had never questioned that. Everyone claimed that his grandmother had died within a year of the court case starting, so she hadn't been around to open the door and let someone in. So, what about key holders? Hmm, had Hayward ever given Keith McKenzie a house key?

It all came back to the alleged time machine, and how it worked, and what precisely it was meant to do. After all, Keith himself might have taken the picture using a self-timer. He might have zapped back from wherever, caught wind of the mayhem surrounding his disappearance, and decided to snap a memento before legging it.

Christ, he was so hooked up in Hayward's world he was beginning to believe all this mumbo-jumbo. Nope, it was more likely that Keith did a bunk to frighten Hayward after he refused to… refused to what? Visit Lilly? Too right. The woman in that photo was gorgeous, and he for one would feel pretty pissed off if Hayward suddenly declared she was out of bounds. Bloody hell, even thinking like that was nuts!

No… It was more likely that Hayward had refused to let him continue playing at building a pretend time machine down in his basement. Yes, that had to be it. But then Keith had caught wind of the enquiry and taken a Polaroid to… to do what with? Prove he was alive? Shit, his head ached with it all.

Time to visit Hayward and ask a few choice questions.

Driving was out of the question, so he took a taxi, Hayward opening the front door just in time to see it pull away.

'What do you want?' he asked abruptly, holding the door half-open and using it as a shield.

'I came up to see if you were okay.'

'Why pay for a taxi all the way up here when you could have phoned.' It was a cold, accusing statement, his face gripped in teeth-clenching anger.

'You don't want me here.'

'I just want you to leave me alone!' Hayward smacked the side of the door with his fist.

Jerking backwards, Talbot raised his hands. 'I'm sorry that you missed visiting Lilly. It was unavoidable.'

'Go away!' Hayward clenched his fist. 'I don't want to speak to you.'

'Then why open the door, Frankie? Why not simply ignore me?' Talbot nodded as he twigged what was going on. 'Who's warned you off?'

'Dr Weissman says I have a codependency issue.' Hayward spoke quickly, as if reciting lines. 'It isn't good for me to spend so much time with you.'

'Well, that's too bad.' Talbot took the final step, eased the door aside a fraction more, and stepped inside. Hayward glared at him, big brown eyes wide open. 'When did you last speak with Dr Weissman, Frankie?'

'That's none of your business.'

'Well, I'll tell you then.' Talbot drove his hands into his pockets. 'It was between ten and 10.30 this morning.'

'How do you know that!' Hayward clutched the edge of the door for support.

'I'm a detective, and that's what I've detected.' He gave a wan smile. Good old Bailey, thank God he'd mentioned it was an hour before his arrival when Weissman had called and told him to shove off. 'I need to ask you some questions, and then I'll leave you alone, for a while.'

'I… I mustn't spend too long with you.' Hayward stared down at his feet. Yep, he would walk in a minute, he was getting ready to count.

'Of course not. Weissman's frightened by you spending so much time with me; he'd hate for you to say too much and give the game away. To let me work out what really happened. That's why he phoned and told you not to see me.' Talbot laughed. 'He's going to ensure you never see Lilly.'

'That's not true!' Hayward's face shot up and he met Talbot's gaze with fierce conviction. 'I'm codependent. I rely on others too much. I must learn to be self-sufficient and individuate.'

'Bollocks. Everyone needs friends, people they interact with. It stops the "*lone*-liness", the sense of isolation that we all experience. Once we're out of the womb we're on our own, and we all want to climb back in, only that isn't possible, so we climb into others, through friendship, through sex, through sharing a meal together.'

Hayward frowned questioningly.

'I told you, I have a sister who is mentally unwell.' Talbot took out his cigarettes. 'I've listened to a lot of psychobabble.' He lit a cigarette but didn't offer one to Hayward, wanting to see his reaction. 'You're codependent with Lilly. Doesn't Weissman insist that you drop her too?'

He shrugged, eyes locked on the smoke curling upwards.

'You live alone, Frankie. You have no friends. First comes the individuation and then comes the desire to bond.' Talbot leant against the wall, watching Hayward intently. That little twitch in his eye, the way his lips half parted, ready to speak, the way his sweater moved, showing his heart was racing. 'Dr Weissman told me that you don't understand human emotion, that you have no empathy.'

Hayward nodded.

'Last night you exhibited a huge amount of empathy.' Hayward looked him in the eye and Talbot nodded. 'But last night you were amongst people, not sitting home alone with only your thoughts and a lover whom you can't even touch.'

'I do want to touch her.' Hayward hung his head.

'Quite frankly, you won't be able to when you get to it unless you start waking up to the real world, and stop flinching when a pretty girl gives you a peck on the cheek.' Easing off the wall, Talbot held out his hand, inviting Hayward to shake it. 'Who's it to be, Frankie? Dr Weissman or me?' Hayward stared at the hand, his expression frozen, his eyes unmoving. 'You remember that deal we made. I promised that if you tell me the truth, the absolute truth, that I'd help you visit Lilly.' Talbot took a step closer. 'Come on, Hayward, take it, bond with me. Help me find Keith and you'll get to see Lilly.'

IT MUST HAVE BEEN the quickest, guiltiest handshake in history, Hayward barely letting their fingers touch before he was flying off towards the kitchen and putting the kettle on.

'How did it all start, Frankie?' Talbot asked, stepping outside to sip his tea. It was dark now, but the air smelt good and stopped the headache creeping in again around the seams. 'Why astral travel? Where did the desire come from to go back in time?'

'When I was little my grandmother used to talk to me about it.' He came over with a plate of biscuits and held them out as a peace offering. Chocolate digestives. Very nice. 'She said as a young woman she'd seen a handsome man, like a ghost in her bedroom, and believed he came from the future.'

Bloody hell, that was how Lilly had described the experience too, it said so in her file. Had the two women known each other, shared secrets?

'We'd make up stories.' Hayward laughed and sat down at the kitchen table with his back to Talbot.

If that was how he felt comfortable talking, then Talbot was happy to continue staring up the garden.

'I always had the impression that my grandmother was infatuated with her ghostly visitor, because they were such romantic stories. So I decided to build a machine and see if it was possible to project oneself back in time.' Hayward got up and took some cigarettes from a drawer, offered one over. 'She believed… no, we decided, that everyone has a soul mate, only that one's true love might not be living at the same time as you… if you go along with the theory of reincarnation. So we called it our love machine.' Meeting Talbot's gaze, he sighed. 'You think I'm mad.'

'No, no, go on.'

'Well, we needed to find a focus, some object of love to desire. My grandmother was a hoarder, and loved her antiques, and had loads of old copies of the *Tatler* magazine, you know, the one about the glossy lifestyle of the upper classes. Anyway, I chose a woman I thought was beautiful in one of those and she became my focus.'

'And that was Lilly?'

Hayward grinned. 'She's much more beautiful in real life: crystal blue eyes, and lush auburn hair. Her soul is so sweet.'

Uh-huh, he'd seen the beauty, but wasn't going to share that particular piece of information. 'Have you still got the magazine? The original picture?'

'No, it disappeared.' Hayward's mouth suddenly dropped open. 'Jake! It vanished at the same time Keith disappeared. How stupid, I'd never put the two together before.'

'Perhaps he took it.'

'I don't know.' He started to pace up and down the kitchen. 'You see, once I'd met Lilly the photo wasn't so important.'

Tossing his cigarette end out onto the damp grass, Talbot closed the back door and shivered. 'Can you remember the date on the magazine?'

'I think it was June 1940, but I can't be certain.'

Somewhere, Talbot thought, someone would have an archive, so with any luck it would be traceable. It was beginning to make sense, why Hayward could only go back sixty years, because Lilly was his focus, and the photo he had initially put all of that attention onto was sixty years old at the time. 'What would happen if I chose a focus image? Would I go back to a different time and place?'

'I guess so.' Hayward traced a finger round his lips, a tiny gesture Talbot read as fear of saying something. 'I… I don't think I'd like to experiment, if that was what you were thinking.'

'No, no, just trying to get an idea, of the process.' Yep, there was every possibility he could end up going the same way as Keith if they started tinkering around. 'What about when you're there, with Lilly. I mean, do you just stand there, or can you go for a walk together?'

'Mostly we stay in her room and talk, but we used to go for walks.' Millie came in, rubbing around Hayward's legs, hunting for attention, so he reached down and picked her up. She purred and he smiled.

'Why did you stop going for walks?'

Hayward laughed. 'Because it was so difficult to talk. When we tried it, everyone would stare at Lilly, and she didn't like that.'

'Hang on, hang on, are you telling me that other people, out in the street, couldn't see you?' Talbot sat down and drummed his fingers on the table. 'Only Lilly could see you?'

'Yes, of course.'

'No, Frankie, there's no of course about it.' Talbot spread his arms in exasperation. 'You have to tell me these things. I don't know these things, because I haven't experienced them.' He sat back and folded his arms. 'Why can't they see you?'

'I don't know.' Frankie let Millie jump down to the floor, and opened a pouch of food for her. 'Is it important?'

Talbot shrugged. Whatever Hayward's machine did or didn't do, it sounded like it only created a one-to-one journey, like plugging into someone's psyche. Bloody hell, get your head round that one.

'Hey, Frankie, why don't you show me your machine?' He stared at the table, fiddled with his cigarette lighter. 'We keep talking about it, but I need a visual here.'

'No. I mean, yes, but not tonight.' Out of the corner of his eye Talbot saw that the fear was back on Hayward's face.

'Oh, come on, Frankie, be a sport.' Fiddle, fiddle with the lighter, show disinterest, as if the issue were neither here nor there.

'Tonight isn't good.'

Laughing, Talbot stopped fiddling and met his gaze. 'Why? Because I'd get to see the real machine and you won't have time to swap it for a dud?'

Hayward gritted his teeth.

'You really would cheat me, wouldn't you, Frankie?' Slipping his lighter into his pocket, Talbot stood up and jabbed a finger at him. 'Don't fuck with me. If I want to see your machine, I shall get to see your machine, whether you like it or not. I shall go to the top, and get a search warrant, and strip this house down to its bare bones.'

'They won't give you a search warrant.' Hayward stepped back, away from the finger, his eyes wide and his hand reaching out to grab something for support.

'Oh yes they will. Especially when the only piece of evidence showing Keith McKenzie alive was taken down in your basement, next to your machine.'

Talbot headed along the hallway to the front door, calling over his shoulder, 'They'll give me a warrant, Frankie, mark my words, they will. I shall tell them that Keith's body is most likely buried in your basement!'

25

THERE WAS PLENTY TO do that didn't involve Hayward. The little shit had sneaked round in the night and driven his car away, disconnected them from each other. He could stew in his own terror a while for all Talbot cared. Fuck him.

With a clearer head now that the hangover had worn off, Talbot spent Friday morning loitering around Peter Charteris's home, seeing what he could see. By lunch time he'd taken a few snaps around the place with his new point-and-shoot, but there had been zero activity in and out of those palatial gates, and his feet were frozen, and there was snow in the air; so he gave up and headed for the 3Gs golf club instead. There were only so many trees you could photograph before getting bored with playing hunt the human.

By contrast the clubhouse of the 3Gs was bustling with activity. Undeterred by the freezing weather, the happy golfers had made it as far as the bar, if not the fairway. It was a mixed crowd, mainly men, with a few wives thrown in, and a small group of lady golfers all smartly turned out in slacks and criss-cross patterned sweaters. Over in the dining area several groups were settling down to enjoy their Christmas lunch alongside fellow competitors, and the atmosphere was festive and convivial. He knew that in a couple of hours the noise level would be deafening once this lot had a few drinks inside them, and that all of those expensive crackers would have been pulled, and the waitresses would have sore feet. A fine Christmas tree acted as a foil between the bar and the toilets, and its abundant pink and blue themed decorations smacked of no expense spared, and a fair amount of taste. Perhaps they'd employed a professional service to set it up.

Enticing smells drifted over from the dining area, and as much as he might have enjoyed their 'winter warmer', a bowl of hot soup with crusty bread, Talbot decided not to risk it. He was pretty sure it was members only, so went and introduced himself to the receptionist to talk about joining. Smiling and efficient, she handed him all of the relevant paperwork. Club rules, a list of fees, including day membership, and a glossy pamphlet outlining the club's history and achievements.

'You're welcome to use the bar while you peruse them,' she said, in a pleasant, tempting manner. 'We have an extensive bar menu if you'd care to lunch, but the restaurant is reserved for members.'

Excellent, he could eat, warm up, and watch the comings and goings for a while. The 'winter warmer' it was then.

He chose a table tucked away in a corner with a clear view of the room, sipped his apple juice, and read up on the club's history, the most interesting point being that six years ago Peter Charteris had initiated the creation of three new bunkers which had to be dug out and sanded up. One was depicted in glorious colour, the golfer taking a keen swing out of it. He was mulling the height of that ridge, and the fact that it was wide enough to bury a body under, when the waitress brought his soup over. Without glancing up, he thanked her.

'Inspector Talbot?'

Christ, that was Melanie Charteris. Instantly he stood up and offered his hand. 'Miss Charteris.'

'Melanie, please.' Her slender hand slipped into his, all long nails and hand cream. Up close she looked pinched and gaunt, her long hair fairer than he recalled, although she might have dyed it. 'I thought I recognised you from over there. Do you mind if I join you?'

'Not at all.' So, she'd played waitress to get a closer look. Now he was going to eat lumpy, slurpy, splashy soup in front of an elegant woman. Better be best table manners then, push the spoon away and not towards you.

'Are you here in an official capacity, Inspector?' She was soft-spoken and had a hint of the delicate flower about her.

'The name's Jake; we don't want to frighten your customers away.' He smiled and she nodded her understanding. 'As a matter of fact I'm on extended leave, and thought a spot of golf might do me good.'

'We offer police officers a special rate.' She smiled and pushed the plate with his roll and butter nearer, encouraging him to eat.

'Ah, yes, I'm sure PC Oliver mentioned that to me a while back.' Nothing wrong with a bit of artful fishing.

'He comes along quite regularly, with his colleague PC Reynolds.' She leant closer and whispered, 'They don't play particularly well.'

'Now, why am I not surprised to hear that?' Good hook, right catch. Corrupt bastards.

For a moment she paused, then said thoughtfully, 'I read about you and that awful Lasseter case. Is that why you're taking leave?'

'Something like that.'

'I'm so sorry, I've embarrassed you.'

He waved her worry away.

Looking like she was about to go, she said, 'So, you're off work?'

'I *am* still an acting police officer.' He smiled past his spoon, then dabbed his lips with his napkin. 'I'm sure there's nothing in particular you wanted to say to me, but I shall be Christmas shopping in Farnham tomorrow…'

'Not Saturday,' she said in a low whisper. 'For all of Peter's grand ideas, this place doesn't run itself. Monday, Elphicks Department Store, tea room, one o'clock.'

'Then we'll lunch.'

MONDAY WAS A LONG way away and he wondered how he was going to stop thinking about what Melanie might want to say. His ever-hopeful side told him she was going to reveal Lilly's whereabouts, but his pragmatic side kept butting in and telling him to grow up.

On Saturday he drove over to Dorking and pitched camp a short distance from the McKenzie home, a moderate semi-detached in a quiet backwater. He wanted to watch their comings and goings, only that was difficult given the neatly trimmed privet hedge which cut out the choice view of the front door and windows. At ten o'clock they left together and he guessed they'd gone Christmas shopping. Now who did people without children go Christmas shopping for? Each other? Nieces, nephews… the dog? He would have to go shopping and buy something for his sister, not that Anna had reacted to anything for years, but he still visited her twice a year, once on her birthday and then again at Christmas. 'You should come more often,' they said, but seeing her broke his heart and took weeks to get over, so he stayed away.

At first she had screamed on discovering her mother lying motionless on the bed, an empty bottle of pills on the dresser; or so the neighbours had reported. The paramedics had sedated her, and from there it had been a downhill spiral. Talbot lit a cigarette. He tried not to blame them, or resent their hasty use of medication, but it was difficult not to want to thump somebody. Oh, Jesus Christ, you and your bloody birthday celebrations bring it all back; time and time again, year in, year out; there was no getting away from it. Christmas Day, blue lights flashing in the night, the ones on his car mingling with the array on the emergency services vehicles, and the dancing Santa across the street.

'I'm her brother!' he'd shouted. 'Let me through.'

Anna's hand had reached out to his and she'd mouthed his name, 'Jake'… and hadn't spoken a word of sense since. Catatonic stupor they called it, and other fancy names, but all he knew was that the bright young thing had gone, and no amount of shouting, screaming, praying, or talking could bring her back.

'It's a type of post-traumatic stress,' one doctor had said. 'She could pop back at any moment.'

As yet she hadn't popped back, she wasn't even slipping back gradually under cover. Perhaps she preferred it wherever she was, away, off with the fairies that lived in the wall she stared at day in, day out. Maybe on Tuesday he'd visit her. Maybe on Tuesday she'd respond, and smile.

Into his maudlin thoughts came the theme tune to the *Antiques Roadshow* and he laughed.

'Sid, you must be psychic: I'm near Dorking and was thinking of dropping in.' Little point in saying he was only a couple of streets away.

'I'll get the kettle on. I've remembered where I got that Bakelite box.'

'Describe her again.' Talbot leant against the open back door and smoked while Sid brewed the tea.

'Young, teenager, skinny, like a bird.' Sid scratched his head, Talbot convinced the habit had created that ever growing bald patch on top. 'You know, you stirred the old grey cells by asking about that box.' He swiped a hand gently across his open purchase ledger. 'She was such an unlikely sort to be bringing in such gear.'

'What else did she have to offer?' Talbot ditched the cigarette and went to read over Sid's shoulder. 'Wow, Capo Di Monte figurines.'

'Yeah, she had a dozen of them, worth a fair bob or two, and look…' Sid pointed to a row of writing. 'Now where's a slip of a thing like that get handfuls of expensive jewellery? Mind you, a lot of it was costume jewellery, but still collectable and sought after.'

'Where did she say she got it from?'

'Well, she said her gran had passed away, and it had been left to her.' Closing the ledger he opened a drawer, fished out some papers and handed Talbot photocopies of the relevant pages. 'Got me well-trained, haven't you.' He poured milk into the tea. Nice bone china mugs, very smart. 'I ran it past your boys at the time, but they hadn't got any stolen property that matched; however…' He flicked through an old receipt book, chuckled and gave Talbot another photocopy. 'Her address is there, but I don't know if you can make out the name on that signature, it's such a scribble.'

It was faint, the imprint hardly having gone through the carbon on the receipt book. 'Oh yes,' Talbot said. If you made out the address, the name came into sharp focus, because you knew what you were looking for. 'It says Kirsty Hayward,' he explained, tucked the papers away, and went to browse in the shop to find something horribly pricey to set against expenses.

It was tempting to phone Hayward and ask him how many antiques and knick-knacks had gone missing from his house around the time of his court case, but Talbot thought he already knew the answer to that, what with the grand array at George Hayward's home. Nasty, thieving sods. He was in two minds as to whether Kirsty was the true perpetrator or merely the clock-work toy wound up and told to go in and sell stuff off. But for whom? For George? For Joe? What about Dorothy? Talbot wasn't fond of the word conspiracy, but it kept drifting into his thoughts, along with the hunch that there was more than one person involved in Keith McKenzie's disappearance.

Getting back to the car with a very sexy art deco bronze of an Egyptian dancing lady in a highly risqué pose, he settled down to watch the McKenzie's front door again. Momentarily he wondered if Lilly was as exciting as this tantalising piece of art, but quickly chided himself for letting his mind drift onto such a question. But hey, if that photo was anything to go by... The image of it in his head made him smile.

He would put Miss Egypt next to the TV when he got home. He could exhibit his own taste at last, stop living in a morbid shoebox. Ah well, it had only taken the best part of a year to start making the space his own.

After sitting in the car for an hour in the cold and dark, with only a Quick-to-Go beaker of coffee to keep him warm, he saw Mrs McKenzie return, apparently on her own. After a moment he spied her husband walk round a corner, and assumed he'd been off parking the car, or was simply lagging behind. Laden with shopping, he struggled to get out his key and let himself in, so Talbot gave them ten minutes to sort themselves out before ringing the doorbell.

26

FLIPPING OPEN HIS WARRANT CARD he said, 'Detective Inspector Talbot. May I have a word, please?'

It was Mrs McKenzie who answered the door, stout, fiftyish, and well-kept in dress and style if not in the face. From behind her Mr McKenzie appeared, drowning out her voice as she began to speak.

'If this is about Keith,' he said in a harsh Scots accent, moving his wife aside and barring Talbot's path, 'there's nothing more we can say.' Two watery blue eyes met Talbot's. Yes, he was older than his wife, by a fair few years from the looks of it. 'We've had all the upset we can take, Inspector, now please, leave us alone.'

'Some new evidence has come to light.' Talbot spoke evenly, but firmly. 'And I do need to ask you a few questions.'

'Let him in, let him in,' Mrs McKenzie begged. 'What new evidence? Hamish, please, I have to know.'

Reluctantly he stepped aside. 'You'd best come through to the sitting room.'

The room he was shown into was tasteful but ordinary, a happy snap from your average furniture catalogue, the sofa looking like it was replaced every three years when its MOT was due. Paintings decorated the walls, all clever reproductions.

'Well, what do you need to ask?' Mr McKenzie signalled that his wife was not to go and make tea, when she looked like she might.

'A document has come to light that implies your son Keith was alive during Francis Hayward's trial.' He waited for the eruptions.

Mrs McKenzie gasped, as Mr McKenzie scowled and yelled, 'That simply isn't possible!'

His wife looked horrified. 'Hamish, how can you be so certain?'

'Because... because we both know that weirdo Frankie bloody Hayward did away with him.'

'Do we?' She grabbed his arm and spun him round to face her. 'We went to court for three years, spent all of our savings, and never got to the truth. How dare you sound so certain that my boy is dead.'

'Because I know he is.' Mr McKenzie thumped his chest. 'In here, Maggie, I feel it in here.'

'Well, I haven't given up hope,' she spat, and turned her back on him. 'What is it you need to know, Inspector?'

Suddenly her husband rushed round and stood in front of her. 'No, no, don't answer any more of their bloody questions.'

'Out of my way, Hamish.' Her jaw set firm and she glared at him. 'You're the one who raised the issue. You're the one who started spending money we didn't have on solicitors and barristers, so don't tell me now that you don't want to get to the truth.' With a flick of an index finger she motioned Talbot to follow her through to the kitchen, throwing a final barrage over her shoulder at her husband. 'You never thought ahead, did you? It never crossed your mind that the police would interview us and that we would become suspects. Not once, Hamish, not once did you consider what it might drag up.'

Oh yes, that would make excellent reading on Sunday, their interviews and court statements.

'What is it you'd like to know?' She filled the kettle and swept aside a pile of groceries that had been unpacked but not yet put away.

'I realise that you've explained all of this before...' Well, he assumed so, even though he hadn't read it yet. 'I'd like you to run through what happened on the last day you saw Keith.'

'Well, I didn't see him at all on the day he disappeared, but you know that from my statement.'

'Uh-huh.'

She sighed, and shrugged off Talbot's offer of help as she strained to reach up and fetch down two mugs, the height of the cupboard more suitable to a taller person. So why hadn't the husband lowered them? A glance around the room told him that everything about her home, and her, was ordinary. Flat walking shoes, pleated skirt, hair dyed light brown, pearl stud earrings, an old fashioned style that showed her age, unlike Helen, who reeked of vibrancy and sexuality, even though they must have been much the same age.

'I'd been staying over with my sister in Guildford. She wasn't very well, and Hamish said he and Keith could manage on their own for a day or so.' She sighed again, a sure sign of depression. 'The first I heard was when Hamish phoned and told me to rush home because Keith was missing.'

'What did you think at that point? Were you worried?'

'Of course, but not overly so.' While filling the mugs, she jerked her head backwards and Talbot followed her lead to glimpse her husband hovering behind the half-open door. He felt like informing her that he was interviewing frightened sisters and troubled wives in Farnham on Monday, away from their aggressors. 'You might as well come through, Hamish,' she called out.

He sidled in, bold in his contempt, his hands shoved deep into the pockets of his sports jacket. Hmm, was that the type of thing you wore for golf?

'You see, my husband didn't inform me on the actual night of Keith's disappearance, did you?' Her words were accusatory. 'Tell him, Hamish, tell him how you only flew into a panic once that idiot Frankie had wound you up by saying he'd been to the police.'

'I didn't think it was any of his business, going tittle-tattling to the police.' He folded his arms. 'It was then that I knew he'd done away with him, making a big scene and all… ranting about his pathetic leap machine.'

'Uh-huh, and what about before he went to the police? What did you make of it then?' Talbot nodded his thanks for his tea and helped himself, Mrs McKenzie being far more intent on her domestic argument. He wondered whether this was their usual bickering, or if his arrival had given her the opportunity to air grievances she'd kept bottled up for years. He suspected the latter.

'Boys,' Mr McKenzie barked, 'will be boys. They play silly pranks on each other, and hide-and-seek is a very popular game.'

'They were far too old for such childish pursuits.' Astounded, Mrs McKenzie picked up a tea towel and slapped it back down in temper. 'If you thought Keith was playing some silly practical joke, why didn't you help Frankie hunt for him? You knew the poor boy was short of a sixpence.'

'Because I thought Keith would come home.' Throwing his hands up in the air, he spun on his heel and stormed away.

Her face contorted in anguish, Mrs McKenzie leant heavily on the work surface and stared out of the window to the night-blackened garden, her reflection leaping out as she moved. 'As God is my witness, I wish I had never gone away,' she said. 'To not say goodbye to someone is the hardest thing, Inspector, the hardest thing.'

'Yes. It is.' He paused give her a moment to compose herself. 'Did you speak to Frankie after he'd reported Keith missing?'

'I went round, spoke with him and his grandmother. She was in the most dreadful state, had a cut on her lip and her face was all bruised.'

Shocked, Talbot nodded. 'Did she mention how it happened?'

'Oh, aye, she said she'd walked into a door.' She started putting the shopping away. 'Isn't that what all women who've been beaten up at home say?'

Hayward would never have hit her, but it was wiser not to express such an opinion. 'What did Frankie have to say on it?'

'He claimed it happened while he was down at the police station.' She sighed, lobbed a packet of tea onto a high shelf, and stopped. 'He took me aside, you know, poor lost soul.' Pulling out a tissue, she dabbed her eyes. 'I didn't listen.' She met Talbot's gaze. 'I should have done, the poor child was so… frightened. You see, he accused my Keith of having hit her, and as a mother I wasn't accepting that, now was I? Frankie said he thought Keith was hiding in the house or roundabouts, and that his grandmother must have come across him.'

'But she said it was a door.'

Mrs McKenzie nodded. 'Oooh, she was frightened too, mark my word on that, the way they clung to each other, like the babes in the wood.'

Images of someone leaping out in the dark and thumping poor Frankie's grandmother filled his head. She probably hadn't seen her assailant's face and didn't know who it was, but Keith was the most likely suspect, although Talbot preferred the idea of a separate intruder or an accomplice.

'Did you help Frankie in his hunt for Keith, Mrs McKenzie?'

'Of course I did!' The tissue rose to her eyes again. 'For days, weeks. I even went down to his creepy basement.' Suddenly she pointed an accusing finger at Talbot. 'Your people told me I was interfering with their enquiry, messing up a potential crime scene.

All I wanted was my son, and that Dr Weissman was so rude, and arrogant.' She lowered the finger and scrunched the tissue up so tight it completely disappeared in her hand. 'Dr Weissman took Frankie over, told him whom he could speak to and whom he couldn't, like a puppet. Oh, the lad and I had never got on that well, but to be forbidden to speak with me, to be told that he couldn't even talk to his own grandmother.'

'I understood he nursed her when she was ill.'

'Oh yes, but a stroke, she was a vegetable by then, Inspector Talbot, no use to anyone.'

There was a natural lull and Talbot placed his empty cup on the drainer. 'And you've never seen Keith again?'

'No.' She gave up with the tissue and wiped her tears with her hand. 'And now you say you have evidence that he was alive.' The flood gates opened and she sobbed, clutched the work surface and bowed her head. 'If he was alive, why didn't he show his face? Why didn't he come and see me to let me know he was safe?'

'Perhaps he wasn't able to,' Talbot said quietly, patted her hand, and said he'd let himself out.

27

ON THE WAY HOME Talbot popped into PC World and brought a scanner and some photographic software, so that he could copy the photo of Keith; and all day Sunday worked on the case and read files until his eyes ached.

He started on Keith McKenzie. What had he been like? Bit of a shit by all accounts. Excelled at sports, fast on his feet, not an A grade student, that was for sure; bit of a bully and liked to throw his weight about. The hard copy files Bailey had brought over proved Talbot's hunch to be a fact. Keith had attended the same school as Peter Charteris. Now wasn't that interesting.

It was also deeply fascinating that Mr McKenzie had been so adamant that his son was dead… as if he knew it to be a fact.

The legal documents and court transcripts went on forever. Neither Hayward nor Keith's mother had mentioned any hint of an intruder or Hayward's grandmother's bruised face. Why not?

On one thing Bailey had been correct: without a comparison the DNA report was useless, and the only vague hope of getting a sample of Lilly's DNA was the envelope she'd licked when she sent Hayward's Christmas card. Assuming she'd licked all the envelopes herself and Kate hadn't helped her out. Yes, yes, he still owed Kate for the painting and he would get round to it, when he had time for a quiet dinner.

Lillian Charteris's psychiatric case notes made fascinating reading, especially in light of Frankie's claims about the LEAPP machine. She had been visited, night after night, by a ghost named Frankie; and even gave a fair description of him. At one time there had been two boys visiting, and it was some time after the disappearance of one of the boys, along with her green Bakelite box, that she had mentioned these visitations to her mother. In fact, it was because her mother asked after the box that Lilly confided in her. A ghost stole it.

Leaning back Talbot stretched and yawned. He had the TV on in the background with the sound off, and it kept silently screaming that there were only five more shopping days until Christmas. Online shopping it was then, or he'd never get any groceries in. Miss Egypt's tantalising spread of thigh made him momentarily consider that he might be feeling horny and it could be worth giving Helen a call. With any luck, she'd be up for it, and they could have some fun.

Tempting, but far too much of a distraction to be dealing with right now.

What he wanted most of all was to see Hayward's alleged time machine and the much talked-about basement. Barging in and demanding it was one thing, but after their last explosive encounter over the damned thing, he'd much rather play the softly, softly approach and lure Hayward round to inviting him to share his secret. A tame target was always preferable, and he had no intention of being fobbed off with a dud machine as Weissman had been.

ON MONDAY HE WENT into Farnham early, so that he could hunt down a suitable Christmas present for Anna before meeting up with Melanie Charteris. It was bitterly cold and the buzz in the overheated shops was that it was going to be a white Christmas. Assistants thrust pretty scarves under his nose, and perfume and jewellery, when in response to their questions, he said he was looking for a gift for his sister. What was the point? What was the fucking point? She couldn't enjoy any of these things, and most likely wouldn't understand them either.

As a last resort he mooched around Elphicks, the department store he was to meet Melanie in, because it had a little bit of everything. Last year he'd bought Anna a sweater, but the home she was in was centrally heated, and he doubted they ever dressed her in it. Upstairs, near the coffee shop, he idled away fifteen minutes in the toy department. Perhaps a drum so that she could beat out her frustration, or a pop gun so that she could enact shooting the drunk who'd killed their father. Then he saw the soft toys. Now there was an idea. Anna had always been a tactile person, like he was, the two of them always being told not to touch everything in sight by their parents. Touchy-feely, yes, they liked to stroke and caress and get to know something through their fingertips.

A blue elephant, about a foot high with big floppy ears and perpetually sitting down, grabbed his attention. Wow, that was soft. The stupid expression on its face made him smile, and he was busy making silly faces back and wobbling it from side to side when Melanie crept up beside him.

'Having fun?' she asked.

He laughed, his heart racing from the unexpected voice in his ear. 'I'll just go and pay for this and we can lunch.'

'Oh, you're buying it?'

'Uh-huh.' She was waiting for an explanation, so he lied. 'For my neighbour's daughter, nice kid.'

She frowned, as if she didn't comprehend the notion of bonding with people one lived alongside, but didn't comment. Today she was wearing tight white jeans and a body-hugging white leather jacket, which couldn't possibly have been warm enough and was obviously a chic fashion statement, along with the straightened, slightly unkempt hair. She stank of the same overpowering perfume he remembered from before, a toxic odour that tainted the atmosphere. Choosing food from the 'push-along-your-tray' serving area, she made no small talk, and it struck Talbot that she had far fewer natural communication skills than Hayward. They ate in silence, she appearing at ease, while he experienced rising discomfort and a sense of apprehension he couldn't explain.

'What did you want to talk to me about?' he asked over coffee.

'I'm worried.' She peered out of the window at the shoppers passing far below. 'My brother's behaviour is becoming more and more irrational—and he's obsessed with Frankie Hayward.'

'In what way?'

'Peter keeps saying that he'll get him, and make him pay for ruining our lives.'

'And how, exactly, has Frankie Hayward ruined your lives?' Talbot watched her face, caught the strange way she pursed her lips as if chewing inside her top lip.

'His obsession with our grandmother.'

'But Frankie has only ever approached her twice. That's hardly excessive.'

Turning to face him Melanie unexpectedly curled slim fingers around his hand, her touch cool, the long nails painted to perfection. It made him shudder.

'Can I speak with you in the utmost confidence?'

'Of course, you have my word.' Until she said something incriminating.

'Ever since I was a child my grandmother has said Frankie's name. Frankie Hayward, her Frankie, her dream man.' She gripped his hand tighter. 'You can't imagine what this has done to us as a family.'

'How did your grandfather take it?'

'Do you really want to know?'

'Uh-huh.'

She leant horribly close, pulled him in, refused to let go of his hand; and then whispered, 'Poor Grandpa knew she didn't love him, that she had this fantasy, this imaginary lover. He told me that he knew it was a marriage of convenience, a trade-off. She was nuts, but her family were wealthy, and he could do okay out of it. Plus, she was beautiful, and he said that if such a beautiful woman wanted to make love to him, even if she was thinking about someone else, then that was fine by him. He reckoned that her passion for Frankie made for great sex, so he wasn't complaining.'

Talbot tried very hard to suppress a grin. He'd seen from the photo how beautiful Lilly was when she was young, and damn it, he'd have snapped up a deal like that. Good old Grandpa, he knew which side his bread was buttered.

'I'm very broad-minded, Jake, so it never bothered me; and it never worried Dad either, but somehow it has always upset Peter. The fact that his father was conceived under pretence. It's always made him feel less of a man.'

'But your parents, they loved each other?'

She let go of his hand, shrugged and flicked her hair over her shoulders.

'So, you and Peter have heard the name Frankie Hayward all of your lives.'

'Oh yes, Peter calls it the devil's name.' She sipped her coffee. 'When we were younger he used to shout at Gran to shut up about him.' Pushing the cup aside, she stared out of the window again. 'He might never have known there was a real Frankie Hayward if not for that awful court case in which his friend went missing.'

'How did he react?'

'Angry, unpredictable… oh I don't know. Strange.' Abruptly she stood up. 'I need a cigarette.'

They walked round to St Andrew's churchyard at the back of the shops, where they couldn't be seen from the street, and then lit up. Picking his way between the gravestones, Talbot turned his collar up against the biting wind, pulled the earflaps down on his hat and hugged the blue elephant. Melanie didn't appear to feel the cold at all, which he found unnatural.

'Father made Peter a full partner in the business when he was eighteen, which was the same time that boy went missing,' she said, drawing lightly on her low-tar cigarette. 'Peter's first act as a shareholder was totally irresponsible, and Father was furious with him.' Halting by a bench, she looked Talbot in the eye. 'Peter withdrew a large sum of money against company funds and refused to explain what he'd done with it. Things were never the same. It created a huge rift between them.'

'How much is a huge sum, Melanie?'

'£350,000.'

'Bloody hell!' A house, an income if invested well, plenty to last a fair old while. 'Do you think that this money and the boy's disappearance might be connected?'

'I didn't,' she said, grinding her dog-end out on the cobbled walkway. 'Until recently.' She shivered and started to walk on down towards the alleyway that led to the river. 'Peter rants. He gets all het up and shouts, and goes on and on. Recently he's been drinking too much and ranting about how much Frankie Hayward has cost him, and that he thought he'd dealt with that once already.'

'Do you really think he was referring to money?'

'Oh yes.'

The alleyway was dark, graffiti splashed across the wooden fencing, the narrow space unsavoury and unclean next to Melanie's bright white outfit. Talbot sensed her distaste as she turned around to walk back.

'My brother spoke to someone on the phone about it, shouted that he wasn't going to spend any more money on getting rid of Frankie.'

'Do you know who he was speaking to?'

Shaking her head, she glanced down at her watch and quickly made excuses to leave.

His heart raced and he leapt in with, 'Before you go, Melanie, do you know where your grandmother is at the moment?'

'Of course I do.'

'Where is she?'

'Mellow Acres nursing home.' Flustered, she looked at her watch again.

'And you've seen her recently?'

'Not for a month or so.'

'I'd like to speak with her.' He stepped into pace beside her as she headed back towards town.

'That's up to Peter,' she said. 'I don't interfere where Gran is concerned.'

'Perhaps you could have a word with him.'

Melanie halted abruptly, glanced up and around, then said, 'I really must be going.'

'Look, let me take your number.' He pulled out his phone, ready to tap it in.

'I'd rather not. Peter snoops.'

With that he let her go, gave her thirty seconds head start, then shadowed her up the high street.

IT WAS ALL WELL and good, having such a dynamic piece of information land in his lap, but as much as he wanted to believe it, Talbot had trouble trusting it. The implication that Peter Charteris might have paid Keith a large sum to disappear was huge. She'd never once mentioned that Peter and Keith had attended the same school, oh no, she'd cleverly skirted round that one. So was it all false information? Melanie Charteris stood to gain control of an enormous fortune if her brother was convicted of foul play. A quick search of the public records at Companies House showed her and Peter to be equal partners in all business concerns, but there was no information regarding shareholders. Why would she suddenly want to come forwards with such incriminating evidence? It certainly made him suspicious; he had never been one to believe in Santa Claus making your wishes come true at Christmas. Only, he had glimpsed whom Melanie had met up with after leaving him, so perhaps there was a Father Christmas after all.

THE FOLLOWING DAY TALBOT changed his clothes four times before settling on what to wear. Jeans, white shirt and a dark blue sweater, boring, but practical. If Anna could see him she'd think he'd grown old before his time. He'd phoned ahead to warn of his visit, he always did, and he always hoped that it didn't make any difference, and that they always dressed her up smart, and washed and brushed her hair. Closing his eyes he took a deep breath to steady his nerve. If he ever found out that they didn't, that they left her in a soiled bed, or without any blankets... Trust, he had to trust. It was a good private nursing home, over in Haslemere, with fine views of the very ground that Tennyson had walked on, and specialist staff that understood and could help with her needs. Thank Christ she'd had adequate medical insurance, that he'd persuaded her to spend the few quid every month, because he could never have afforded the expense, even with the little bit Mum and Dad had left them.

After Melanie had gone to her car and the surveillance was over, he'd spent another hour or so wandering around the shops and eventually chosen a Christmas card for Anna, one with birds in the snow and no promise of baby Jesus offering redemption. He'd bought wrapping paper to match and Blue Elephant was now tucked away inside; and he wished that Anna's face would light up when she opened it, and that she'd tell him that he was stupid and she was no longer a kid.

Having collected his stuff, he opened the front door, and there was Frankie Hayward striding up the driveway towards him. Bugger.

'Not now, Frankie.'

'I need to speak with you, Jake.' Hayward stood right in front of him, arms by his side, submissive yet determined to be heard.

Motioning him aside, Talbot said, 'Not now, Frankie, I'm taking a day off.'

'You can't do that!'

'Well, I can, and I am, now step aside.' Talbot glared at him, and Hayward's eyes drifted down to the bright wrapping paper.

'You've got a present. You're going to visit your sister, aren't you?'

'Fuck off, Frankie.' Talbot took a step to the right and Hayward danced across, nearly tripped him up.

'I could come with you.'

'No, you fucking well can't, now piss off.' Sweeping round him Talbot made a dash for the car, but as soon as he popped the locks Hayward had leapt into the passenger seat. 'How dare you! Get out!'

'I need to talk to you.' Hayward folded his arms and stared straight ahead. 'You'll be late if you don't get going.'

The clock on the dash flipped round to ten past twelve precisely and he'd arranged to be there at one. He could afford to waste five minutes. An hour, he was going to spend an hour with her; which was just about as much as he could take, and not too short to make them think he was shirking his duties. Gripping the steering wheel he watched condensation build on the windscreen.

'Frankie, this is personal and private. Please leave me alone.'

'You think I don't understand!' Hayward shouted. 'You think I don't feel things like you feel things. Everyone thinks I don't feel pain or compassion…'

'Yes, you do, Frankie, you do, I know you do.' Oh shit, now he had to deal with Hayward's emotional turmoil and give warmth to someone else when he needed it himself.

'I nursed my grandmother, alone, for a whole year before she died.'

'After her stroke, yes.' Talbot fired up the engine to put the blowers on and clear the screen; the policeman in him overrode the sad human being, and he swung round and faced his passenger. 'Do you think that punch in the face was what triggered her stroke? Or was it a door she walked into, I can't quite recall.'

All of the colour drained from Hayward's cheeks and for a moment Talbot thought he might do a runner, so he slammed the car into reverse and pulled off the drive.

'Put your seat belt on, Frankie, we can talk while I drive.'

28

'THE POLICE WOULDN'T BELIEVE ME,' Hayward said, checking all of his pockets for cigarettes. 'First I say Keith's missing and then I say he's hiding in the house and has hit my grandmother, and she keeps rambling on about it being a door. But, Jake, I knew it wasn't a door.'

Without permission, Hayward tried the glove compartment, pulled out Talbot's emergency fags, and lit two.

'Within two weeks my grandmother had a stroke. A stroke!' Hayward clenched his jaw as he passed over a cigarette. 'I wanted to change the alpha wave pattern on the LEAPP machine. If it can take me into a state of unconscious awareness, then I should be able to adjust the sequence to make it realign someone's brain function. I wanted to heal her.' He took a long drag, sucked in the nicotine. 'I wasn't even able to run the preliminary tests to make sure I could keep her safe, because Weissman kept snooping. He'd call round without a moment's notice, at all times of the day and night, asking questions and constantly looking over my shoulder. There was never any warning, and I was obliged to let him in.'

'What did he make of her injury? Did he question whether you'd done it?'

'Of course he did.' Hayward glanced pleadingly at him. 'I never harmed her, Jake, I swear I didn't.'

'I know.' Talbot nodded. 'Do you think Keith *was* in the house?'

'Someone was.'

'How can you be so sure?'

'A presence. I kept thinking Keith was hiding because I felt a presence, you know, the hairs on your neck bristle and you call out, "Is anybody there?"'

'Did Keith have a key to your house?'

'No. Gran had one, I had one, and Dad had one.'

Caught at traffic lights, Talbot drummed his fingers on the steering wheel. He could see that it was all snarled up along the Tilford Road and wished he'd chosen a different route. If he was going to be late he ought to phone them. They'd have told Anna and she'd be expecting him and he didn't want her to worry. They said that she didn't comprehend such emotions any more, but what did they know? Wasn't it the worry about Dad not coming home that had started all of this?

'Jake, are you okay?' Hayward asked, his tone soft and concerned.

'Not really.' He pulled away and joined the queue of traffic waiting for the railway barrier to go up. Everyone was spilling out of the station, purposeful in their need to struggle home with logoed carrier bags full of well-intentioned gifts. A vendor had set up a stall selling roast chestnuts and mince pies, but Talbot couldn't smell them, not even when he wound down the window and tossed out his cigarette. Little point in smoking when anxiety had stolen the flavour.

'Do you mind if I talk?' Hayward asked.

'Look, Frankie, you're here now, I'm a trapped audience, just get on with it.'

Hayward smiled, back in his own world and what was important to him. 'I've been thinking, a lot, about this idea of you monitoring what happens when I go and visit Lilly, and I'd like to set it up… under your guidance.'

Bloody hell. He'd won Hayward's confidence at last, and been invited to take the lead. 'Would you like Dr Weissman to be there?'

'No.'

Yep, he thought he'd say that. 'So you're still thinking it should be Kate?'

'Unless you can come up with someone else we can trust.'

At last the barrier went up. Pulling away, Talbot thought of how fascinating it would be to go and visit the lush woman in the photograph, to have a glimpse of what she truly looked like when she was soft and supple, perhaps smell her essence.

'Can you smell things at the other end?' he asked.

'Oh yes.'

Mmm, tempting.

'Don't you remember how I told you that the wave pattern on the LEAPP machine encourages deep relaxation and the transformation to an altered state that allows for astral travel?'

It sounded vaguely familiar, not that he'd understood a word when he'd first heard it. 'Meaning?'

'That the soul travels while the body remains behind. The soul experiences everything, therefore one retains the ability to smell.' Hayward maintained a fixed gaze. 'I believe that the technique can be modified for other purposes. I mean, if I can currently use this sequence of pulses to achieve astral travel, then I'm sure it can be adjusted to generate various other altered states of consciousness.'

Talbot chuckled. 'I should leave well alone, if I were you. One machine's got you into enough trouble to last a lifetime.'

'Maybe.' Hayward shrugged, but Talbot glimpsed a tiny smile twitch his lips. 'As you're going to be monitoring me, I thought we could try an experiment,' he said enthusiastically. 'I was thinking that we could try a different focus.'

Talbot laughed. 'Let's sort one mess out before we create another.'

For a few seconds Hayward went ominously quiet, then launched his rocket. 'If we could go back… we might be able to stop your father being killed in that accident.'

'Whoa, hang on a minute!' Cars were moving everywhere and Talbot didn't dare take his eyes off the road to look at him. 'You said you did that with Lilly's plane crash, you said so on your blog…'

'But it worked, Jake.'

'How? How did it work? You said you could only go back exactly sixty years…'

'I told you. I warned Lilly not to get on the plane. I reminded her every few months of the date and time. She wrote it down.'

'Uh-huh.'

'But it worked, Jake. I changed the outcome, stopped her being killed.'

'Didn't she think to warn her son and daughter-in-law?'

Hayward grinned. 'Do you think they would have listened? To someone they thought was mad?' Leaning closer, he half whispered, 'I can help you in the same way, Jake…'

'Whoa! Whoa! Don't help me, help yourself!' Talbot smacked the steering wheel. 'Why not go back and stop this bloody mess with Keith ever happening?'

'As you say, I can only go back sixty years.' Hayward chewed his lip. 'I tried. I went back and saw myself…'

'You did what!' Talbot jerked backwards.

'It didn't work. Going back and visiting myself made me ill, really ill, for months. It was too dangerous. I thought of attempting it again, trying to change that time with Keith… but I didn't know if I'd survive it.' For a moment he paused, then leapt back with, 'Don't you see, Jake, it's different, changing your time line is easy. If your father doesn't die, then your mother doesn't kill herself and your sister isn't unwell…'

Furious, Talbot swung down a side road and slammed on the brakes. 'And we never met, so we're not parked here on this road together! No, Frankie, no.'

'Why not? Don't you want your family back?' Hayward tilted his head to one side and met his gaze full on, oozing a persuasion that was pure temptation.

'Of course I would like them back.'

'Then let me help you.' It was sugar-coated and dark.

'No, Frankie.'

'Why not?'

Talbot clutched his forehead and stared at anything but Hayward and those mesmeric eyes. 'Because what is… just is… it happened, I live with it…'

'But you don't have to.'

Cigarette, yes, he needed a cigarette. Lighting one up, he stared out of the window at the leaves blowing along the pleasant suburban road, ephemeral and soon to decay. Why not change the past? Bloody hell, what an offer. If they hadn't died, he wouldn't have transferred to Farnham, and he'd never have met Claire, and he would be saved that pain and bitterness, too. How bloody tempting. Hayward was staring at him, watching his every move, climbing inside his head with that penetrating gaze and... fuck, it felt like they were merging, Frankie taking him over. He wound down the window and let in a blast of cold air.

Think straight, stay focused. No Farnham, no nasty criminals banged up. No Lasseter soon to be on trial. No abused children given justice. No, no, there were other coppers who could have dealt with that case as efficiently as he had. Only, the force had been after Lasseter for years, and everyone else had failed. Hey, it might have landed on his desk anyway. No, he wouldn't have climbed the ranks so fast, been so determined, sank himself into his work so much.

There'd be no here and now, this precise moment, with all of the acts that had led up to it... and he wouldn't be wanting to visit Lilly.

'Too much would change,' he said.

'What are you frightened of, Jake?'

'The consequences,' he replied, shoved the car into first, and began to understand why Peter Charteris had called Hayward the devil.

'YOU ARE NOT TO MENTION any of this within earshot of Anna,' Talbot said, as they pulled up outside Tennyson Way Nursing Home.

He took Hayward's nod to be a promise, raced up the front steps, and smiled as he shook hands with Mrs Shipley, his sister's personal nurse.

'Jake, Merry Christmas, Anna will be so pleased to see you.'

It was the usual lie, a pleasantry. An impossibility.

'How lovely, you've brought a friend with you.' She glanced down at the bunch of flowers across Hayward's arms, unaware of the rumpus created to get them, Hayward insisting that they stop at a petrol station because he hated visiting anyone without taking a gift.

'You're not visiting anyone!' Talbot had yelled.

'But I'd like to meet your sister,' Hayward had pleaded, and eventually Talbot had caved, through duress, through fear of being late, and through his own discomfort of sitting alone with his sister for a full hour. Claire had never visited Anna, never accepted his invitation to share his sadness. For once it would be good to have a companion, any companion.

'Frankie,' Talbot said, and watched Hayward shake Mrs Shipley's hand and smile with polite efficiency. He definitely performed better away from situations he found stressful.

Today Anna was sitting staring out of the window at the wintry Surrey countryside, bleak in the dismal grey of cloud and drizzle. It was a wide bay window, her comfy chair at an angle to the bed, the stage prepared so that he might sit on the bed and face her. She didn't turn her head on hearing the door open, but Talbot no longer expected her to, although the disappointment never diminished. Dressed in last year's Christmas sweater, with contrasting slacks and her hair swept back over her shoulders, she appeared more serene than lost.

Going up and cradling her head close to his chest, he kissed her crown and murmured, 'Hello, my sweetheart.' She smelt good, as only family could. On his own he might have wept, but Frankie was there, behind him, patiently waiting for attention. Perching on the edge of the bed and taking hold of her hand, he looked Anna in the eyes and smiled. She didn't even blink. He swallowed the grief welling to a lump in his throat.

'This is Frankie,' he said, forcing a happy tone. 'It'll soon be Christmas and we've brought you presents, look.' He shook the brightly coloured package.

'May I take her other hand?' Hayward asked.

Share her! She was *his* sister. His family. Shaking off his defensive reaction, he tried to think about how the psychiatrists kept telling him that a variety of experiences were good for Anna. To share Anna was to share his own pain, and nobody had ever wanted to do that before.

Finally Talbot said, 'Yes, of course,' and momentarily flipped back into work mode, intrigued by Hayward's desire to touch when usually he avoided physical contact.

Gently Hayward lifted her hand and stroked it against his cheek. 'Hello, Anna, would you like to open your card first?'

He took forever over it, talking, showing her how to do it, and then placing the card on the window sill, so that if the window were opened the birds might fly free. Talbot would have set it on the bedside cabinet, given her a reminder of him when she went to bed. When the elephant burst forth, at least Hayward displayed all of the childish glee Talbot had wanted from Anna.

'Look, Anna,' Hayward demanded, and stuck the fluffy blue thing right in front of her face, his dark eyes peering at her from in between two floppy ears. For one dreadful moment Talbot thought he might be going to hypnotise her with it.

'What are you doing?' He stood, ready to snatch it away.

A raised hand halted him. 'Sit down, Jake, Anna's enjoying her elephant.' Hayward stroked the soft fur down her cheeks and encouraged her fingers to explore the deep blue pile. Tucking it into the crook of her arm, he maintained eye contact and said, 'Stroke the baby, Anna. Here, like this. Elephant's softer than my cat Millie, and she's very soft.' He talked incessantly, a driving repetition in his words, a bizarre rhythm rising up as he lifted her hand and stroked it across the elephant time and time again. 'Look, feel, touch, see, look, feel, touch, see.' The mantra went on and on.

At three o'clock Mrs Shipley came in to close the curtains against the gathering gloom and to invite them to indulge in afternoon tea.

'We have bicycle sheds if you need to hide away and smoke,' she said to Talbot, and smiled adoringly at Hayward, as if he were the genius who had brought the elephant. Jealousy was such a cruel affliction.

'Do you have a pen and paper I could use, please,' Hayward asked, and while Talbot smoked a sly one out of a half-open window, he filled up several pages of A4 notepaper with mathematical hieroglyphs.

'Come and kiss Anna goodbye,' Hayward suddenly said. 'We need to talk and I don't want to say certain things in front of her.'

When Talbot kissed the top of her head, he looked down to where her fingers were embedded in the soft blue fur. He waited for them to slide off, as they always did when she was given something to grasp, only they didn't. Imagination made him see them move, just a fraction, but he knew that was hope and stupidity, and Hayward's weird influence.

Outside they lit up and walked around the grounds, Talbot relieved to be in the biting cold that brought a sense of aliveness and reality. It was dark, the big cypress tree uplit with a blue light at its base, making it appear ethereal and special as, deep in thought, Hayward counted, and Talbot waited.

'I can do it,' Hayward declared. He stopped and faced Talbot, gesturing with his hands as he spoke. 'I've had it all wrong, Jake. I've been far too influenced by my grandmother. Going back to the past was her idea, her need to reconnect with her lost love. If I turn my knowledge to the now...' He paused. 'Jake, I think I can heal Anna.'

Instantly Talbot raised his hands to ward him off. 'Frankie, don't...'

'Hear me out, Jake, please.' He shook the pieces of A4 paper. 'Sitting with Anna, I could feel her vibration, pick up the rhythm inside her head.'

'No, you couldn't!'

'I felt it with my grandmother, too. I could feel the sluggishness inside her. Look, if I create another machine, a different type of vibrational machine, I can program it to adjust the alpha wave pattern...'

'Just... don't.' He turned away.

'I know you're frightened, I can understand that, but look, I've calculated the formula, worked out the exact wave pattern I need to create.' Frankie held the computations up to his face. 'It'll stimulate Anna's brain and help bring her back.'

'Frankie, please; don't give me false hope!' Desperate to believe him, Talbot hit the tree in sheer frustration. 'I'm not convinced. It isn't possible.' He hit the tree again. 'And if you *can* build such a machine, what if it goes wrong? What if she goes further away, closes her eyes, falls asleep and never wakes?'

'These are all risks, Jake, but I can get it right, I know I can.'

'It's too... dangerous.'

'No! It isn't.' Hayward folded his pieces of paper and tucked them away. 'It's drug-free, it's pain-free, it's non-invasive...'

Talbot leant a shoulder against the tree and stared up at the starlit sky, a black piece of paper with thousands of pin pricks and some mysterious light shining through from the other side. Who truly understood how the universe worked? Or why it worked? Or if it worked?

'Let's go and get something to eat,' Hayward whispered and placed a hand gently on his arm.

CONVERSATION OVER SUPPER was punctuated with possibilities, Talbot roller-coastering between excessive elation, disbelief, and outright fear that he might lose her completely. Every word that Hayward said sounded plausible, invited him to dream of a new future full of fun and laughter—full of Anna. What was he thinking? He hadn't even seen the current bloody machine. Personally involved. Shit, it should never have got this far. He should never have got so close so that he could be personally... tempted.

'If you work on a new type of machine, will you stop visiting Lilly?' Talbot asked.

'Now that is a silly question,' Hayward replied, and they laughed, and drove home in the silence of true friendship, where each man is allowed to have his own thoughts without being considered sullen.

A heavy frost was settling and Talbot marvelled at its beauty as they wound down quiet country roads. He wanted to be on his own, to contemplate life and its mysteries and a man who claimed he understood the complex patterns that sustained and controlled it. He didn't pull straight into his drive, but hovered with the engine running, so that Hayward would take the hint.

Facing him, Hayward smiled, his fingers resting on the door handle. His attention caught on something beyond Talbot, and his brow puckered. 'Jake, did you leave your front door open?'

'What?' Talbot swung round and stared at the front door. He'd shut it, locked it, and now it was half-open. Shit. 'Stay put,' he ordered, leapt out of the car and ran across the garden.

Ducking down under the hall window, he reached round, pressed his fingertips against the door and eased it open a fraction wider. A sound from inside, a flicker of torch light shimmering up the wall, searching. His heart lurched. Wrong move. He swallowed hard, crouched down and pressed his back against the wall. Running was the only option. Not yet. Listen. A boot scrunched on broken glass. It stopped, shifted in the dark. One person? Two? The narrow beam of light drifted out as far as the front door step. Talbot held his breath. A voice, low, masculine, whispering. Time to run.

He did no more than lift his head and the shot whizzed past, cut the air with a single phut before bouncing off his near-side front tyre. He froze. Stared at the car. Holding his breath he covered his mouth, tried not to let white vapour escape. The night went deathly quiet. Hayward had cut the car engine. Behind him, Talbot felt the house let out a sigh of relief. Glass scrunched; were they were back about their business? Careless, the light skimmed past the front door and he heard footsteps hurrying up the stairs. Up, then straight back down, and out the front door? Shit. A rush of adrenaline shot through his veins and thundered into his ears, roared like the sea. Run, now, but where to? Perspiration wetted his brow, cooled rapidly, chilled him to the core.

Down by the car a shape moved, crept silently through the flare of the sulphur street light and emerged like a dark fog to sit behind a wheel. Hayward had swapped cars, climbed into his Mercedes. Talbot crouched low, ready to sprint. Lights, engine, acceleration. Now! Rear door, back seat, no time to run round the car. Get in, just get in. Tyres screeched, engine kicked back a beat and dragged them away.

'Drive, Frankie!' he yelled, glanced back at the house and glimpsed a dark shape standing at an upstairs window.

'Where to?' Hayward asked, his voice hoarse with fear.

'Round the block. Turn right here, cut back round and down.' Phone, phone, where was the bloody phone? Christ, his hand was shaking, he could hardly push the buttons. Come on, Bailey, pick up, answer the bloody phone.

'Jake, I thought we'd agreed...'

'Sir, my house is being burgled, ransacked. Intruder shot at us. Request permission to dial 999. Or am I supposed to contact Weissman? Please advise. Repeat, please advise.'

'No, no, I'll deal with it. Jake, are you okay? Where are you?'

'Running away from the scene, sir. Circling round to see if I can ID their vehicle.'

'I'm onto it, Jake, immediately. I'll call you back.' Click.

Hayward was driving like the clappers, reckless, fear confusing his judgement.

'Slow up, Frankie. Pull over, I'll get in the front.'

Somewhere near where they had started, under a street light, Hayward came to a halt. Going round and climbing in beside him, Talbot suddenly smelt the rich leather upholstery, his senses kick-started, now that the adrenaline was abating. So, this was what it felt like to be inside a top-of-the-range Mercedes.

'You okay, Frankie?'

Hayward nodded, hands gripped tight on the wheel, eyes wide and staring.

'Well done, that was quick thinking.'

'We were having such fun,' Hayward said, his voice sad and quiet.

'This is fun, too,' Talbot said flippantly. 'It's a good game. Spot the burglar.'

'We don't need to spot them.' Hayward lit two cigarettes and passed one over. 'That black Mercedes, down there, the one that's pulling away, that's my brother Joe's car.'

No, surely that was the same one that had been parked outside George Hayward's home, Talbot only catching half of the registration before blue lights swung round the corner and blinded him. Shit. His phone erupted into life and they both jumped, Talbot's hand shaking as he lifted it to his ear.

'Sir.'

'Some anonymous caller dialled 999. You're on your own, Jake, you'll have to wing it.'

And we were spotted driving away from the scene. Talbot thumped the dash in exasperation.

'I'm coming up myself,' Bailey went on. 'I'll have to treat you like an idiot, Jake, no choice. I was arranging to get Weissman's boys in, but the 999 call was flagged up and it was a no-go.'

'I'll do my best, sir.'

'We need to debrief on this as soon as possible.'

'Yes sir, as soon as I have some idea of what they've nicked.'
Clutching his head in his hands he growled, shook away his anger,
then turned up his collar and said to Hayward, 'We're in the shit,
Frankie. Just follow my lead, stay close, and don't speak unless
spoken to.'

29

'You can't go in there.'

Talbot flicked his warrant card up into the PC's face. 'Detective Inspector Jake Talbot. I live here.'

There was a second's hesitation while blue light strobed across the officer's face as he looked towards the house. Beyond him Talbot saw two patrol cars and one unmarked vehicle he recognised. Of course.

'Jake!' It was Yates, calling him over from the doorway, beckoning as soon as he turned. Talbot took a moment to light a cigarette before sauntering over. 'Jake, you have been done over, big time, mate.'

'Clever sods,' Talbot said jerking his thumb up towards his alarm system. 'Took that out rather neatly, didn't they.'

'Must have been a crap system.' Yates drew close, manoeuvred him to stand on the doorstep, huddled so that he couldn't go in and see the damage. He spoke in a hushed whisper. 'The 999 caller got the car reg as they drove away. It was Frankie Hayward, Jake.'

'Did you get the caller's number? It was the burglar who called.'

'Don't be daft.' Yates drew back an inch, let out a shocked gasp, and suddenly gripped Talbot's arm so hard he nearly yelled. 'What the fuck are you doing with him?'

'Frankie and I were out together...'

'Out? Jake, have you lost your senses?'

Yates dragged him inside and shoved him into the narrow space behind the door, out of sight. They hadn't put the lights on and it was dark, eerie beams of torchlight creeping up the walls like ghostly intruders and blue lights flashing through the window behind him. Wine, Talbot could smell wine, Claire's best red uncorked and floating free. There was perfume too. No question as to the perpetrators, none at all.

'Don't stand there like a plank, Jake.' Yates shook his arm. 'Don't go all quiet, then tell me you're thinking.'

'I came home to find my house being burgled…' He drew on his cigarette, flicked ash onto the carpet.

'Then you should have phoned 999, just like anyone else.' Someone called out, a woman, Trudy, asking if they could switch the lights on now; and Yates yelled back for her to get on with it. 'I know you're on leave, Jake. We all know you're stressed and that this time of year is never good for you, but that doesn't give you the right to go flaunting the rules. Driving away from the scene…'

'Someone shot at me—'

'Don't give me that crap.' Yates pointed a finger right up into his face and Talbot was tempted to bite it. 'No one reported hearing gun fire.' Woomph, the lights came on, silhouetted Yates. 'And running around with Frankie Hayward… how stupid is that. You can't go getting chummy-chummy with known felons…'

'He isn't a felon.'

'Jake, you're not listening to me, the man is trouble. You shouldn't be associating with him.' Yates stepped back and stuck his hands on his hips. 'Bailey is going to hang you out to dry.'

'I was shot at. My near-side tyre was hit.'

'Jake, it's still standing.' Yates pushed past him and peered out of the window. 'Nothing wrong with that tyre at all.'

'Why don't you take a closer look?'

'Because I have enough to be getting on with in here.' Yates sneered. 'It's my investigation, Jake, just stay put and answer questions.' He shook his head. 'Christ, you have some explaining to do.'

'I'll walk round and let you know what's missing.' Not caring, he ground his spent cigarette out under his heel.

'For pity's sake, Jake! You're contaminating a crime scene.' Yates bent down and picked it up. 'Don't do that again! And don't touch anything, either. It's my investigation, Jake. You're the victim.' He pulled a face towards Hayward. 'And keep your astral traveller under control. Weirdo.'

Hayward was standing on the doorstep, in the freezing cold, staring at his feet, no, staring at his hands, typing a text message. Who the hell was he—? Talbot's phone ping-pinged, and Hayward tilted his head sideways and smiled.

The message read, 'Joe has air pistol. Look for pellet, it'll be squashed, on the ground.'

Talbot nodded and patted his leg for Hayward to come to heel and stay close.

Hayward caught the signal and joined him, pinging another text as he did so. 'Woof-woof.'

Very funny. He texted back, 'Good boy.'

Hayward met his eye and gave an almost imperceptible nod, as if to say he'd do anything he asked of him right now. Talbot looked away. He had to hold it together.

As he surveyed the trash that had once been his possessions, bitterness rose. Why the destruction? A knife had been scored straight up through Kate's painting. Ruined. He bit back a sudden rush of emotion. Bugger, he'd have to lie to the insurers, claim it was his property. Beside him Hayward stood very still, his eyes glistening. In the kitchen everything breakable had been broken, mugs, plates; they must have been at it for ages before he turned up and interrupted their fun. Pasta shells were soaking up the wine, inflated coracles sailing across the floor. The table was overturned. The back door was wide open, footprints of wine marching out of the door into a flurry of snow. Had the perpetrators opened the door? No way out of the back garden. Shit! He swallowed hard.

From the darkness an officer stepped back inside. 'Freezing cold, and nothing out there,' he muttered to himself, blowing on his fingers before pulling out his pocket notebook.

Talbot moved round the table to speak with him, advise him to go back outside with a torch and make a more thorough investigation.

'Don't walk in it, Talbot!' Trudy's voice, sharp and scolding, halting his progress across the sea of wine. 'What's he doing in here?'

'Mr Hayward's a witness.' Talbot avoided eye contact, patted his leg and herded Hayward into the sitting room.

Two uniformed officers were inspecting the mess, sterile gloves leaving no imprint on the coffee table and TV. Claire's half-dead plant had been hurled to the floor, the pot smashed, clumps of dry mud already trodden into the carpet. Bloody hell, that would have taken some effort to break. Unless it was shot at. Crouching down Talbot started to pick through the pieces.

'Don't touch anything, sir.'

Talbot smiled up at the uniform. On standing he noticed that Miss Egypt was intact, perfect. Not your usual marauding burglars, but he already knew that. On his way back through to the kitchen he sent a text message to Hayward.

'Which one of your family most loves antiques?'

'Joe.'

Hmm, thought so.

Someone had had the savvy to switch off the blue swirling lights and stop upsetting the neighbours. It was very still without them, as if a giant bird had stopped beating its wings. Halfway up the stairs he heard the hush of intrusion and rape. He'd never be able to sleep easy here again, he knew that from the moment he saw his bedding strewn across the floor and his underwear hacked to pieces. Hayward touched his arm and he flinched, swallowed down the wail erupting from deep inside.

Across the hall he caught a snippet of Trudy laughing, sniggering. 'Who wears that kind of underwear these days?' He lit another cigarette, stared at the shreds of blue-tack where Lilly's photo had been ripped off the wall. Why steal her? Did they know who she was? It wouldn't have been difficult to guess. Trudy's voice drifted over, disparaging and cutting. 'What a load of junk.'

'Waste of money if you ask me, when it's all shoved in here.' That was Yates. 'He lives in the past, looks back to better times, but I suppose you would if you were him. He should have quit ages ago, gone and done some simple job.'

'Well, it's caught up with him now.' Trudy giggled and he heard china break as it hit something hard. Bitch!

Striding across the hall, Talbot stood in the doorway and blocked their exit. 'You've broken my Clarice Cliffe vase.'

'Worth something, was it?' Trudy asked.

'Uh-huh.' About seven hundred pounds, but he wasn't going to give her the satisfaction.

'I'm sure your insurers will cough up.' She made to move past him and he stood his ground, clenched his fist. 'You are insured, aren't you?'

He wanted to spit in her face, smack her, beat her to a pulp. Yates was behind her, worry creasing his brow.

'That's all they broke, Jake.' Yates emphasised the word *they*, edged past Trudy, and stood as guardian. 'You must have disturbed them when they got to this room. You got off lightly in here.'

Talbot might have responded by thumping him in the face, but a voice called up the stairs, 'Yates! Bremmer!'

It was Bailey's distinctive command, the way Trudy stiffened a sure indication that she was Bremmer.

'We're up here, sir.'

Talbot let Yates past, but Bailey was already halfway up the stairs. 'Go and organise your men, find out how these bastards broke in. Now!' Obediently Yates and Trudy thundered past. 'As for you, Talbot, what the hell are you playing at driving away from the scene?' Bailey spoke loud enough for Trudy to snigger, and as soon as the coast was clear he ushered them into Talbot's bedroom and asked in a whisper. 'Who's this?'

'Frankie Hayward, sir.'

Offering his hand, Bailey said, 'Superintendent Bailey.'

Hayward smiled and shook.

'This is a bloody mess.' Bailey scanned the room. 'Apart from the laptop and confidential data, what were they after, Jake?'

'A photograph, I suspect, although I haven't been permitted freedom to roam and check if it's still there.'

Bailey nodded. 'Any idea who?'

'Yes, sir.'

'Keep that to yourself, Jake.' He smiled at Hayward. 'Mr Hayward, please do not speak to any officer unless asked a direct question. Least said the better.'

'Yes, sir.'

Bailey chuckled. 'Good lad.'

'Before you yell at me, sir, get them to check out my near-side front tyre. I was shot at. It may have been with an air pistol. Look for a flattened pellet on the ground nearby.'

'Good Lord, are you serious, Jake?'

'Uh-huh.'

'Right.' Bailey opened the bedroom door wide and said very loudly, 'I don't like your methods, Talbot! Never have! It won't wash, you know, not with me. Now leave my men to carry out their investigation. Do you understand!'

'Yes, sir!'

Trotting down the stairs Bailey ranted to anyone who would care to listen, 'Well, have you got any answers? Come on, come on, he may be on the sick, but let's play ball. He's a member of the public who claims he's been shot at. Has anyone checked out that tyre? Eh?'

Talbot stepped out into the hall and lit another cigarette from the one he was smoking. It was going to be a long night.

'Should we stay up here?' Frankie asked.

'Uh-huh.' He offered over a cigarette, took up a vantage point on top of the stairs and watched the proceedings below. It was no longer his home, but a crime scene, the men in overalls dusting this and that. Voices mumbled about motive and set the blame firmly at Lasseter's door. Only a nutter would wreak such havoc. Only a man in shock would stand and stare, speechless. He could feel Hayward sucking him in, wanting to psychically paw away at his insides and heal his wounds. Not now, not when it was so raw and painful.

It was over half an hour before a uniform cried eureka on discovering a single mangled pellet on the ground near his tyre. There wouldn't be any ballistics, not on an air pellet. The calibre, maybe, but nothing much else. Car keys, they wanted his car keys, to get to the jack to steal his wheel… the entire bloody wheel. Why? The tyre held no evidence. Would he have done the same? Shit, it hurt. He folded his arms.

AFTER A FULL HOUR Bailey shouted up the stairs, 'Talbot, get down here and take a bloody interest.'

Robotically he did as he was told, gave a full statement as to what had occurred, and provided a rough description of what he could easily spot had been stolen.

Standing in the kitchen amidst the sea of red wine and pasta boats, he noted that some unthinking idiot had shut the back door to keep a bit of warmth in; but was clueless as to whether the door had been left open by the thieves, or if that officer had opened it just to poke his head outside and test the weather. Several sets of footprints had been clear before getting churned up by one officer or another, and were now melting into the sea of wine.

Sod them. He'd check outside for himself tomorrow. Do their job for them. Stop being the victim.

Eventually the men in protective overalls collected their tools and disappeared, followed shortly afterwards by the uniforms.

'You'll need to get this place made secure,' Yates told him, as if he didn't know the procedure.

'Uh-huh.'

'Make a list of anything you find is missing.' From habit Yates passed over his card.

'Don't be stupid, he knows your number,' Trudy said, and snatched it away before Talbot could take it. 'Let's go.'

With a sniff of disdain Yates followed, out to the car and a final huddle on the doorstep with Bailey, who was saying he was going to stay on and give Talbot a good dressing down in private.

'Coffee would be good,' Bailey said, coming back in and slapping his hands against his arms to get warm. 'Damn, all of your crockery's broken.'

'I've got a rather nice Spode tea service upstairs, sir, we'll make do with that.'

Hayward was spying out of the window, making sure they were gone, phone in his hand waiting for someone to pick up his call.

'Frankie, who the hell...'

'Mr Stevens, the fix-it man. I'm sure he'll come out if we pay him a bit extra.'

Talbot nodded. It took him a while to find the tea service, his eyes blurring as he leant against the door of the spare room and blocked out the world. We, Hayward had said we, and of all things, that one word somehow made him feel just a little bit better.

30

SITTING ON TOP OF the kitchen table, to keep his leather shoes out of the red sea, Bailey sipped his coffee and watched Hayward chat away to Mr Stevens, who was fixing the front door. They were laughing at the noisy drill, giggling and joking about needing to be quiet or someone might call the cops and have them arrested for disturbing the peace.

'He's different than I imagined,' Bailey admitted.

'Misunderstood genius.' Talbot slammed the drawer shut and grunted in utter frustration. 'Yep, they took the photograph.'

'Well, that's a bugger. No proof it ever existed.'

'I took the precaution of scanning it onto the laptop, sir.'

Bailey sighed. 'Perhaps you are overworked, Jake. Has it escaped your notice that they took the laptop?'

'No, sir.' He stared at Bailey's backside, positioned approximately where he had last seen the laptop, then grinned. 'I emailed it to myself. To several web based accounts.'

'You crafty sod.'

'Uh-huh.' Oh my, didn't coffee taste so much better out of bone china. 'They shouldn't be able to access anything on the new laptop.'

'I wish.' Bailey shook his head. 'Codes can be cracked, Jake, it's never a secure system.'

'I encoded the laptop for fingerprint recognition, sir.' He waggled his fingers. 'The only thing that will open it is my fingerprint, and they failed to steal one of my hands.'

'You wily…'

'Of course, they could remove the hard drive and rig it up elsewhere.'

Bailey laughed. 'Come on, Jake, fill me in. You must be getting close to something, or this would never have happened.'

'I have hunches, no facts.'

Sliding down from the table, Bailey signalled that they should go into the sitting room, which was off the kitchen and a little bit further away from the men at the front door. There was no sitting on the sofa, not when it was slashed and torn and held the echo of someone's hatred.

'The missing photograph proved that Keith McKenzie was still alive during the final year of Hayward's trial. Frankie's father, George Hayward, gave it to me, but I believe he stole it from someone else.'

Bailey nodded. 'Go on.'

'Most of this is supposition,' Talbot warned. 'Peter Charteris and his sister Melanie had heard their grandmother, Lilly, speak about Frankie Hayward all of their lives. Now, that is a fact.' He lit a cigarette, thought as he watched the flame flicker. 'Peter Charteris and Keith McKenzie went to the same school, which is probably how Peter got wind that a real Frankie Hayward existed. A Frankie Hayward who had become obsessed with some woman from the past named Lilly. I believe that Peter Charteris, or he and his sister Melanie, paid McKenzie to disappear.'

'So he's still alive, in hiding.' Bailey rubbed his chin and nodded, apparently liking the idea.

'No, sir. I believe that McKenzie got greedy, demanded more money, and they did away with him.'

'Well, how do you get from there to there, Jake?'

'McKenzie's father is convinced that his son is dead. He obviously knows more than he's letting on, and was probably in on the original scheme.'

'But they took Hayward to court! It cost them a fortune.'

'Ah, well, I don't think that Mrs McKenzie was in on it; they kept her out of the loop so that she could genuinely play the distraught mother. I think the idea was to discredit Frankie and have him locked up. Only it backfired. As you say, the court case cost a mint, and the money ran out. I reckon Peter Charteris was footing the bills and ultimately he didn't feel like spending any more.' Talbot chuckled. 'It would have been somewhat difficult, and no doubt costly, for McKenzie's father to do a U-turn and admit that he knew his son was alive. He'd have been done for wasting the court's time and banged up for perjury. So he was left to drain his own funds. I think someone took the photo of Keith as an insurance policy, to prove to Mr McKenzie that his son was still alive… keep him playing the game.'

Bailey paced round and round, sneaked a look down the hall to see how the front door was getting on, and motioned for Talbot to hurry up with his explanations.

'The Charterises had an accomplice in Frankie's brother Joe. They probably had to include him because he could get access to a house key, or he found out and they had to include him. Very sly is brother Joe.'

'This is all well and good, but why, why would they do this?'

'Money, sir, and lots of it.' Talbot dropped the spent cigarette to the carpet and stamped it out. 'And revenge.'

'For what?'

'Ruined childhoods.'

Absent-mindedly Bailey ran his fingers down Miss Egypt's lush curves. 'There's a long way to go yet, Jake. We need the how, and we need the body… or the man, if he isn't already a corpse.' Suddenly he turned and jabbed his finger at the ground. 'And if McKenzie is maggot feed, then you have to prove that your man didn't kill him… or he won't get to see Lilly.'

'Oh no, that was never part of the deal.' Talbot drove his hands into his pockets. 'I find McKenzie and Frankie gets to see Lilly.'

'Not if he killed McKenzie, he doesn't.' Bailey buttoned up his coat ready to leave. 'Weissman's department will make up any shortfall that your insurers won't pay on. You'll be set right, Jake.'

Like a child, Hayward burst in, the grin on his face crumpling as he collided with the atmosphere. Instinctively he raised his hands to ward it off, then sank back into the corner, folded his arms and stared at his feet.

'All done!' Mr Stevens called out and popped his head round the door. On seeing Hayward his jaw dropped. 'You alright, mate?'

'We're all over-tired and upset,' Talbot said. He ignored Bailey's departure and went to inspect Mr Steven's handiwork.

In a hushed whisper Mr Steven's said, 'It was a professional job, guv. Very clever, only ever seen it once before.'

'Where was that?'

Mr Stevens laughed. 'Now that's the copper in you asking, isn't it?'

'Uh-huh.'

'Up Frensham way. The guy reckoned he'd locked himself out of his own house and had to break in, but bust his alarm system and the lock in the process.' Mr Steven's turned his lips down in disgust. 'I wouldn't touch it, told him so, more than my job's worth. Told him to get the alarm company in.'

'And you'd have the address on record.' Talbot smiled. A test run, it had to be. 'Let me know the details and I'm sure we could arrange a little extra something for Christmas.' Talbot took out his wallet.

He was shooed away. 'Mr Hayward's already paid.'

'Then have a tenner on account. For when I employ you to come and clean this mess up.'

'I don't feel comfortable with this,' Talbot admitted. Two inches of snow lay at his feet, he was hungry, he was frozen, and yet he still couldn't bring himself to cross the threshold and accept Hayward's hospitality.

'I'll not have you stay in a hotel,' Hayward said for the hundredth time. 'Now, come in before all of the heat goes out.'

It was only a small step, but a huge boundary to cross. 'Just for tonight.'

'For as long as you need somewhere to stay.' Hayward closed the front door, smiled and headed for the kitchen. 'I'll make us some tea, and we'll light a proper fire, and I've got some tins of soup; the bread's stale but we can toast it.'

Millie came trotting out of the sitting room and nuzzled up round Talbot's legs, purring like the clappers, demanding attention. He bent and picked her up. Soft, affectionate, warm… Christ, he wanted to cry, to sit on the bottom stair and howl.

He imagined he heard Hayward call out from the kitchen, 'It's okay to cry,' but dismissed it as shock-induced hysteria. There were things to be done, calls to be made, action to be taken.

'I'd best phone my insurers,' he said, placing Millie down next to her food. 'I'll probably only get a recorded message, but I have to start the ball rolling.'

After pressing the right number options, he got through to a human being and ran through details, while Hayward served hot mugs of tea and heated up tins of mushroom soup. Eleven o'clock tomorrow morning, yes, he could be at home to meet an assessment officer at eleven o'clock. His car insurers weren't so available, and weren't interested unless he'd been in a road traffic accident, or had broken down.

'I need the fucking courtesy car!' he shouted as he hung up. 'It's what I pay for.'

Edging a bowl of hot soup across the table towards him, Hayward said, 'I can help you, Jake. Tomorrow I can help you make calls, or take you to pick up a hire car.'

'That's really good of you, Frankie, thank you.' He swallowed the lump in his throat and wished his eyes would stop smarting. A spoon, Hayward was pressing a spoon into his hand. The soup tasted of nothing. He didn't even like that house, so why take it so badly? He was tired, he'd been shot at, he was overwrought… No, his entire life had been violated, and it felt like a stampede of wild horses had kicked him in the gut. From the end of a hollow tunnel, he heard a clock tick as the hand moved round. Half past one in the morning. Shit. 'I'm sorry,' he said quietly. 'You've missed visiting Lilly.'

'I might go anyway,' Hayward said. 'To cheer myself up.'

'Won't she be asleep?'

Hayward smiled, his dark eyes gleaming with roguish playfulness. 'Then I'll watch her sleep.'

Talbot understood that one, the fascination with watching a lover sleep, the ecstasy one could experience when the object of one's desire wasn't nagging or bitching at you. To love and be loved: it was all one ever needed.

For a while Hayward left him sitting alone at the kitchen table while he scurried about building up the fire in the sitting room. Twirling an unlit cigarette round and round, Talbot stared at it. Don't think of the destruction, think of the crime. Yes, they wanted the photo. That meant that they had known he had it. Who had George Hayward stolen it from? The perfume, yes, that was the same scent that Melanie Charteris wore. The back door open. What had they dumped in his garden? The air pistol most likely. Why the total destruction? Two spoilt and unhappy children on the rampage. Joe had killed their puppy and blamed it on Frankie.

Shit, it was just the two of them. Peter was the fall guy.

A sound behind him made him flinch and turn, his pulses racing at the sudden noise. Hayward stared wide eyed, as if he'd read his mind and knew which way his thoughts were going.

'You've worked it out,' he mouthed.

'Uh-huh.'

He could see Hayward swallowing hard, controlling his anxiety. 'I thought I'd make some coffee and we could sit by the fire and get warm.'

'I'd like that.'

They didn't say much as they sipped and smoked, the rush of warmth making Talbot ease up and start to feel sleepy. What a day.

At precisely three in the morning, Hayward said, 'I'm going to go and visit Lilly.'

'You enjoy your love,' Talbot said. 'It's precious.'

Getting up and placing a hand gently on his shoulder, Hayward said, 'I'd like you to come and watch. To come down and see my machine.'

Bloody hell! What a time for him to ask. When he felt so drained and exhausted. A ploy? No, a gift, Hayward was trying to give him something to cheer him up. A rush of adrenaline swept through him, triggering tingles of excitement. Hayward thought Talbot was going just to watch, but Hayward was wrong. Talbot was going to visit Lilly. Don't show too much enthusiasm, don't smile, play it cool.

'I won't interfere,' Talbot promised, stretched and yawned, and followed him down to the basement.

31

Access to the basement was through the locked door to the right of the staircase. No surprise there, but the contents of the room it led into made him chuckle. He should have guessed. How could you build a LEAPP machine, any machine, without electronic equipment and metal casing and mother-boards? Now he could smell the soldering wire. Several workbenches were jam-packed with ancient computers, their guts spewing out like multi-coloured spaghetti. Cables were everywhere, the far wall white with a bank of sockets, the heartbeat giving life to the plugs attached to cables that were channelled in down the wall and under the floorboards. Bloody hell, this was mega… no, hang on.

Hayward wasn't the type to tolerate something this messy. It had to be a smokescreen; surely all of those cables and wires were too much of a bodge job to run a complex machine without risking an electrical meltdown. Somewhere, probably disguised as something innocuous, would be the real hub.

Opening a door in the corner of the room, which Talbot judged would lead under the main staircase, Hayward switched on a small torch.

'Follow close,' he said. 'The stairs are steep and there's no light.'

Why not put one in? He was perfectly capable. To make intruders trip? The old-fashioned steps were slatted, more like a ladder, very tricky. At the bottom Hayward flicked a switch and mellow light seeped into the black walls. No, they weren't black, not quite, more black with a hint of purply blue. It was a large room, a king-sized mattress topped with soft bedding lying centre stage, with plenty of space to walk right around it. On the far wall, rigged up from the ceiling and tilted at an angle, was a huge plasma screen. It would be extremely high quality. He couldn't imagine Hayward using anything but the best.

'I need to settle down,' Hayward said, almost apologetically, and lay on the bed.

'You do what you need to do,' Talbot replied. 'I'll just be over here, out of your way.'

He leant against the farthest wall, at an angle to the bed, so that he was looking down on the pillows, but standing slightly behind Hayward. Talbot judged he would be well out of sight here. Whatever happened, he didn't want to be a distraction—or let Hayward glimpse the equipment he'd smuggled in. Claiming he might get cold, he'd brought his coat along and when bending down to place it on the floor, had sneaked out his point-and-shoot. A quick twist of the dial set the camera to high ISO and no flash, so it would do the job. Hayward had laughed at the coat, said it was roastie-toastie in the basement, but let him bring it anyway. In fact it was rather warm, snug and soporific. To keep his nerves on edge Talbot stripped off his sweater and made do with just his shirt, a clean white shirt that glared against the funereal background.

The place reminded him of a seventies smoking den, the atmosphere holding the illusion of a fug, and a faint hint of incense. Fully clothed, Hayward had covered himself with a burgundy-coloured duvet, then spent ages plumping up the pillows and fidgeting around, getting comfortable. Eventually he settled down.

'Ready?' he called over. 'I'm going to switch the light off now.'

'Okay.' Talbot swallowed hard and ran his tongue over suddenly parched lips. His heart was already racing as Hayward lifted a small remote control. Slowly the overhead light grew dimmer and dimmer until there was pitch blackness. Out of that darkness a cool glow filtered into the room from the screen. Hayward had already given him a prep talk, laid down a set of rules, trusted Talbot not to break them; so he knew to be exceptionally quiet during this initial phase. No photographs now; wait until the main feature.

Colours drifted across the TV screen, faint streaks of pale pink and turquoise. Pretty. Blue followed, sky blue and violet, a muted palette, the hues perfect and clear. It was like a colourful sea lapping idly against the shore. Suddenly yellow appeared, the explosion of vivid light making Talbot gasp. Tears filled his eyes and he swallowed down a lump in his throat. Such beauty. Such an overwhelming sense of unity and love. Such a desire to run forwards and throw himself into the ocean. Gradually the waves built up speed as they intertwined and dragged in new colours, indigo and orange, silver and gold. He thought of Lilly. He couldn't help it. That lush smile, those soft lips that promised to fulfil his every desire. Don't go yet, not just yet, stay one more moment to lift the camera and push the shutter.

There she was, sitting at her dressing table, her back to him, momentarily looking over her shoulder, smiling, her long dark hair tumbling down over porcelain skin. With her head tilted to one side, she started slowly brushing it, daydreaming, hardly gazing in the mirror at all. Oh my god, he could see her reflection in the mirror. Stunned, he held his breath. She was beautiful. His heart started racing, pounding against his chest, quickening his breath, making it impossible not to want to cry out. He sucked in his lips and stared. Was she naked? No, no, there was a tiny strap to her negligee, a thin line over her shoulder. Silk, yes, it was silk. His eyes scanned down her body, halting at the curve of thigh sculpted in cool cream fabric. He could smell her essence, a slight hint of perspiration mingling with a delicate perfume. Oh wow, that was so sexy.

She stopped brushing. Was she listening? Looking? Yes, she was peering in the mirror. Unexpectedly she giggled.

'Are you Father Christmas?'

'No…' He faltered, overcome like a nervous schoolboy given permission to speak with the girl he had a crush on. He couldn't speak to her. She was a dream, a fantasy, something to be adored from afar.

Turning around, she smiled and asked, 'Then what are you doing in my room, boy?'

'Visiting.'

She laughed. 'Were you at the party? I didn't see you at the party.' She lowered her head and peered up through tumbling hair, those two brown eyes flirting with him. 'I'm sure I would have remembered such a handsome man.'

Everything about her made him tingle from head to toe, and now she was flirting with him. It just didn't get any better.

He smiled. 'I'm not really meant to be here.'

Covering her mouth to hide the cheeky grin, she said, 'I know that. A man should never enter a woman's bedroom without permission.'

'I thought you'd be asleep.'

'Did you come to harm me?' Her tone dropped to a hushed whisper.

'No, no. Don't be afraid. I'm visiting, from the future.'

'The future?' She laughed and picked up her brush, pretended to smack him. 'Naughty boy, that's the best excuse I've ever heard.'

'I should go.'

'Oh, please, don't go, not yet.' She whirled round to face him. 'Stay awhile and talk with me. The party was such fun and I'm still buzzing from all the excitement. I shall never sleep, you know.'

'Was it a Christmas party?'

'Of course. Daddy throws the best parties ever.' She sighed. 'Why didn't you come? Didn't you get an invitation?'

He shook his head. 'Another time, maybe.'

'Next year,' she promised, then frowned and pouted. 'You will visit, in-between, won't you?'

'I don't think that will be possible. I really do come from your future…'

'Don't be silly…' She bit her finger, her eyes dewy with emotion. 'That's a cruel game.'

'I'm truly sorry, I really am.' His throat was so tight with emotion he could hardly speak. Now he'd hurt her and he hated hurting people he loved. 'Perhaps, perhaps we'll meet again… many years from now.'

'I don't want to wait that long,' she murmured, stood up, and gripped the back of the chair for support. Beyond her, on the dressing table, he spied a familiar Bakelite box with a gold motif. He smiled. She'd never know how happy it made him to own that box.

'You are… a beautiful woman.' He spoke softly, the words hardly his own. 'No…'

'Not beautiful?' Her eyes opened wide and she touched her cheek.

'Beauty goes beyond the body,' he said. 'It comes from deep within the soul, and… I can feel…'

'I can feel your soul, too.' She gasped. Held out her hand for him to take.

Such a small step. He couldn't resist. He had to see if it was possible. To touch, to embrace. A kiss, just one kiss.

SOMEONE WAS SOBBING. Rolling onto his side Talbot groaned and attempted to lift a hand up to the back of his head. Shit, that hurt.

'Jake! Jake, you're alive.' It was Hayward, his voice frantic with worry.

'Aw, fuck, did you hit me, Frankie?' Talbot winced, gave up and rolled onto his back again; it was easier.

'You fell, you hit your head.' Hayward gripped his upper arms, and shook him so hard Talbot's head wobbled.

'Stop, stop.' Talbot's brain was swimming, aching, a dreadful thump-thump hammering away inside.

'Jake, open your eyes, look at me,' Hayward demanded. 'Open your eyes, Jake, come back. You have to open your eyes.'

Open them? No. To open them would destroy the image floating in amongst the debris of pain. He'd seen her. He'd actually visited Lilly, travelled back in time and… no, it had to be a dream, an illusion. Inwardly he smiled. Real or not, this is what Frankie experienced night after night, and it was delicious. He'd touched her cheek… felt her warm flesh, just for a moment.

'Oh my God, I touched her cheek.'

Smack. A hand struck his face, swung his head sideways, stung. Fuck, that hurt.

'Don't hit me, Frankie.' He tried to move. He was pinned down. Now was the time to open his eyes, only they wouldn't budge. 'I need a hand free to rub my eyes, they're stuck together.'

'Idiot!' Hayward's fury chiselled into Talbot's pounding head.

He felt the grip release on his right arm. Lifting his hand was like levering up a dead weight. It fell heavily against his face, the fingers loath to take commands from the brain. That's it, just the one eye to start with. He blinked and the crusty gunk gluing them shut started to shift. All he had to do now was focus. Ah yes, there was Hayward's face, gazing down at him, his eyes red-rimmed, his skin pale. He blinked again, and frowned. 'Have you been crying?'

'I thought you were dead!' Smack. Pain careered up the side of Talbot's face. Now what had he done to deserve that?

'I wasn't dead.' A smile spread across his lips. 'I was visiting Lilly.'

'No, you weren't, don't lie to me!'

He closed his eyes again and a vivid picture of Lilly filled the darkness. 'She was gorgeous,' he murmured. 'Divine.'

Hayward shook him and yelled, 'Don't mess with me, Jake. You did not visit Lilly. I visited Lilly… and you weren't there.'

Talbot laughed. 'Perhaps we were seconds behind each other.' Opening his eyes, he saw that Hayward was sitting astride him, body weight pressing on his groin, pinning down his left arm. So that's why he couldn't move. 'Come on, Frankie, give over, let me shift a bit.'

'Not until you explain what happened.' His lips pursed with fierce determination.

With a sigh, Talbot relaxed. He could hardly feel Hayward's weight, a weird sensation, just a feeling that he couldn't move and that something was trapping him, pulling him into the floor more than pushing down from above. If he let go of any desire to move and fought past the pain in his head, he discovered an overwhelming euphoria. Bliss.

'I was sucked in,' Talbot said quietly. 'And there she was, sitting at her dressing table, brushing her hair. Such gorgeous dark brown hair…'

'You didn't see her, you read about it, in a report, didn't you. Jake, stop—stop!'

Laughing, Talbot tried to swing his arm sideways to release Hayward's grip. Nope. He was too exhausted and Hayward was stronger than he looked.

'I didn't read it, I visited Lilly. She was getting ready to go to bed after a Christmas party…'

Whack. Shit. That was harder. He giggled, he couldn't help it.

'Stop it, Jake, stop it. Please, don't do this to me, please.'

'I can't help it, Frankie.' Another wave of euphoria flooded over him, his lips forming words that were beyond any conscious control. 'I'm in love… our souls met… and I touched her cheek. I actually touched her cheek.'

'You're lying, you're lying!' More slaps, harder this time.

Enough. Hayward was hitting, not holding. Mustering his strength, Talbot brought up his right hand and swiped hard, punched Hayward in the face, knocked him off balance, and caught his wrist.

'I said, pack it in!'

They stared at each other. Hayward seethed with pent-up hostility. Anger. Not jealousy? No, Talbot couldn't feel jealousy. He tried to work out why his head hurt so much and what he had done that was so atrocious. An attempt to nudge Hayward aside failed; he refused to budge.

'She loves me, not you,' Talbot said, recalling how she'd held out her hand, encouraged his kiss. 'Love's a tough game, and I've won.'

'You didn't visit Lilly!' Hayward screamed. 'You weren't there. Lilly was asleep. I was only away a few minutes and when I returned you were… gone.' He burst into tears. 'You were on the floor, cold and motionless. I couldn't find a pulse. I thought you were dead.' He choked back his sobs, determined to talk. 'I didn't know what to do. You'd fallen down, hit your head… I could see blood. I turned off the machine and dragged you up here…'

Talbot gazed around. Shit, they were in the workshop. How did Frankie manage to get him up the stairs?

'Didn't you think to call an ambulance?' That was the copper in him talking. Automatic pilot had kicked in. So his brain still functioned, remembered who he was.

'No, I bloody well didn't,' Hayward said vehemently. 'And you know damned well why not.'

'You swore.' Talbot laughed, and couldn't stop smiling. He'd never heard Hayward swear before. 'Come on, Frankie, let's go and have a coffee and talk this through.'

'First, describe Lilly.'

'Dark hair, slim, curves in all the right places… wonderful thighs.'

'Lilly has auburn hair.'

'No, it was dark, almost black.'

'How did you have her as a focus?' Hayward wiped a hand under his dribbling nose, calmer now. 'The truth.'

'Dr Weissman gave me a scanned photograph of her on the laptop.'

'That would be from the original I gave him,' Hayward said quietly. 'The one of my grandmother.'

32

Stunned, Talbot stared at Hayward, saw his expression change from shock to horror.

'Jake, you idiot!' Hayward's voice rose in despair, and he covered his face with his hands. 'How could you…' He stood, revealing an expression of utter torment, lips quivering and tears starting to fall.

Before Talbot could get to his feet, Hayward bolted from the room and left him to his own devices. The sound of Hayward's heart-wrenching sobs echoed back through the house like the howl of a wounded beast wailing at the moon. Talbot thought he understood his anguish, but the full meaning behind it eluded him. So far the pieces hadn't all slotted into place, and as Hayward's sobbing calmed down, he knew he needed sleep and fresh air to bring clarity. Right now finding upright was difficult, so he sat first, and held his head in his hands for a minute or two, waiting for the man with the hammer and chisel to stop trying to break into his skull. Bastard.

From there he rolled onto his side and groped around a bit, wondering if he might do best to crawl along on all fours. That would be undignified. He had to stand. Eyeing the clothes next to him with curiosity it occurred to him that, after helping him from the basement, Hayward must have abandoned him for a moment or two, and rushed down to collect his coat and sweater and… ah yes, the camera. Shit, he'd seen it. Sitting again, Talbot picked it up to see if any image had been recorded when he'd pressed the shutter. He blinked. He rubbed his eyes. It couldn't be.

'Frankie.'

'Jake?' The sound of Hayward blowing his nose jarred his nerves.

'Frankie!'

'Jake? Jake!' Rushing in Hayward skidded to a halt next to him. 'I'm sorry, I should be helping you; you must be feeling dreadful. I can remember how bad it was on the times when I passed out—'

'Take a look.' Talbot passed him the camera. Would Hayward see what he saw? The screen, the swirling milky pattern, and a ghostly shape clearly formed in it.

'That's my grandmother.' Hayward crouched down beside him. 'You've captured her image.' His eyes sprung open wide. 'Jake, I've experimented with photographing the experience, but I've never captured a face... never.'

'I pushed the shutter as I went,' Talbot said, allowing in a rush of acceptance. He had travelled back in time, his soul, or whatever it was, had left his body, and passed through a mysterious portal to a different time and place. A week ago he wouldn't have believed it possible: but there on the point-and-shoot was the evidence.

'Let's go and download it onto my PC, have a closer look.' Hayward stood and held out his hand to help pull Talbot up. 'The coffee's nearly ready.'

Taking Hayward's hand, Talbot said, 'You know, this entire episode proves one thing. You dragged me up those stairs while I was still... visiting, yet when I came round my... my...'

'Astral body,' Hayward helpfully filled in.

'Yes, my... astral body—' shit, was he really using those words? '—reconnected with my physical body, even though it wasn't in the same place as when I started my journey. It proves that someone could have moved Keith's body while he was...' he snapped his fingers at Hayward, 'what do you call it?'

'Travelling.'

'Yes, so while Keith was travelling someone moved his body, and on returning, his astral body found his physical body, regardless of where it was.'

'You've cracked it, you really have.' Hayward spoke with pure admiration.

'Yeah, sure, my head.' Talbot said with a chuckle, and leant heavily on Hayward's arm, his feet uncertain of where the ground was.

THE FIRE WAS HOT, the coffee was bitter, the thoughts in Talbot's head bungling along; the see-saw tipping up and down until in the end it was euphoria that fell off, leaving a sense of loss. He rubbed his brow and hid his tears.

'Did I hear you right, did you say that I...' he swallowed hard, coughed to disguise the sudden gasp of emotion, '... that I visited your grandmother?'

'Yes, Jake.'

'How the hell did Weissman get her photo in the first place?'

'Jake, I told you, I gave it to him.'

'Why the fuck did you do that?' Talbot sniffed back his grief. 'Where are the cigarettes?'

'Here.' Hayward passed them over. 'I'm so sorry, Jake... really I am.' He started to cry again. 'I gave it to him because I only had the little one from the magazine; and that disappeared with Keith. I never even looked for it at the time. I hated the idea of Weissman ogling Lilly, so I substituted a photo of my grandmother. I didn't know he was going to give it to anyone.' He smacked the arm of the chair and shouted, 'You should have told me you had a photo, you should have shown it to me! Trusted me.'

'Don't you dare fucking well blame me for this... this time loop, this fucking mess.' Talbot lit his cigarette, watched as his hands trembled and the flame shuddered. 'Now you're trying to push the blame onto me for the entire... everything!'

'Oh, Jake, this is awful, absolutely awful.' Hayward let out a wail and continued to sob. 'You're the ghost my grandmother saw. Look at you, white shirt, jeans, belt with a brass buckle... exactly as she described him.' He folded his arms and started to rock. 'She... she told me it was after the Christmas party... She was... so sad that you never visited again. Grief-stricken.'

'Well, how the fuck do you think I feel!' Talbot leant forwards and buried his head in his hands. 'At least you've got a chance of seeing Lilly... but your grandmother... Oh God, Frankie, she's dead, I'll never get to see her... never.' Wiping his eyes, he drew heavily on his cigarette, then sat up straight and sipped his coffee. 'You could at least tell me her name.'

'Frances.'

Talbot nodded. 'So you were named after her.'

'Yes.'

There was a pause in which Talbot heard the fire crackle and a clock tick round to 4:30 a.m. Time: it stole your life while you weren't looking. He could still smell her perfume and the powder on her cheek. Soon they would be gone forever, faded memories. The rich colours would turn sepia, the silk would rot, the gravestone would endure until it too tumbled. A stab of despair hit his gut and his mind jolted across a detail. Someone had struck her in the dark, brought on her stroke, killed her.

Now it was personal.

'I need another coffee,' he said, and held out his mug.

Standing to take it from him, Hayward said, 'We've been set up, Jake. Weissman knew what my grandmother looked like. He met her.'

'Then we both have someone to blame.'

OVER THE SECOND COFFEE, they huddled round the computer at the far end of the room and printed out the photograph. Twice. A copy each was only fair.

'The photograph Weissman gave me was on the laptop,' Talbot said. 'The burglars stole the printout I had in my bedroom.'

'You mean you had a photo of my grandmother on your bedroom wall?'

'I genuinely believed it to be Lilly.'

Hayward chuckled. 'Jake, I should be disgusted. You've been perving over my grandmother, lusting after her...' He turned and scowled at him. 'I'm more upset that you wanted to steal Lilly away from me.'

'I know.'

Hayward sat back, stared at the printout and sighed. 'You're right about it being a time loop. Chicken and egg, which came first?'

'She's beautiful.' Tenderly, Talbot ran his fingers across the ethereal image. The way she turned and smiled was as if she had heard him arrive, or was expecting him. If only…

'I could let you… you could go and visit her again… I wouldn't mind.'

Talbot sighed. 'Thanks, Frankie, but no. We've created enough damage as it is. She saw me once, let's leave it as a sweet memory.' He grinned and nudged Hayward's arm. 'If I went back you might not exist. She might never have married your grandfather, then you'd never build the machine… and where would I be then?'

'Stuck.'

'Maybe Keith got stuck, too. That day they took the Polaroid of him, perhaps they used your machine, sent him back in time and changed history.'

'You're crazy for even thinking that,' Hayward said, lit a cigarette and furrowed his brow.

MORNING SHOULD NEVER HAVE arrived so early. Talbot could have sworn he'd set his phone alarm for 9.30, to give him time to get up and over to his house by eleven for the guy from the insurers. He groped around for his mobile, managed to press the correct button, and when it stopped ringing, it squeaked at him.

He lifted it to his face and grunted.

'Jake? Jake, are you okay?'

'Helen?' Shit, what time was it? He rubbed his eyes, groaned, and winced as his back shifted in the chair. He was getting too old to sleep in chairs… even one of Hayward's comfy old things.

'Jake, I am so sorry to hear what happened. You poor darling, you must feel absolutely gutted. If there's anything I can do, anything, just let me know.'

'Uh-huh.' How the hell had the tom-toms already drummed out a message to her?

'I've woken you, haven't I?' She sounded contrite.

'Yeah, no worries.' He peeled his aching body out of the chair and heaved himself to his feet. Instinctively a hand went to the back of his head. Christ, that hurt.

'Look, I know this is bad timing, what with your house being burgled, but I have to see you, today, this morning.'

He stifled a groan. 'Helen, can't it wait?'

'No, I'm afraid not. I've set up an important meeting with someone for you, at ten o'clock.'

Stubble rasped under his fingers. Everything was sore, or ached, or throbbed, or just plain hurt. In front of the fire, Hayward was curled up with Millie snuggled in the crook of his arm. He stepped over them and made his way to the kitchen, pressing his fingers into the base of his spine as he went.

'Can't it be put off?' he asked.

'I don't wish to sound churlish, but it's taken a lot of effort…'

'Okay, okay, but I must be at my house by eleven.'

The kitchen clock shrieked half past eight at him. Less than two hours kip. It was inhuman, impossible to function. Running the tap, he splashed cold water up into his face, jerking his phone away at the last minute.

'I've heard you're without a vehicle. I'll come and pick you up, say around 9.30.'

'No, no…' He slurped water from his hand, cold and guaranteed to shock the system into overdrive. 'I'm not at home. I'll meet you somewhere.'

'Where are you staying? I'll come and collect you.'

'I'll meet you in town, coffee shop under the walkway in East Street.' He scowled at the clock. 'Nine fifteen, we'll do breakfast.'

'Don't be late.'

Leaning heavily on the sink, he stared at the plug-hole wondering if he could escape down it, never to be seen again.

A purr manoeuvred around his feet and then Hayward's voice said quietly, 'I'll make us some tea while you have a shower. I've got a clean towel and a spare throw-away razor.'

Talbot turned round and smiled. 'Don't suppose you could stretch to a shirt as well.'

ONE DAY HAYWARD WOULD make someone a very good mother. Weissman had got him so wrong, so very wrong. It wasn't that Hayward didn't feel emotion, it was simply that he expressed it in a different way. His time spent looking after his grandmother had made him a very efficient carer, and Talbot felt like a boy starting a new school when Hayward packed him off out of the front door and into the waiting taxi, clean, shaved and refreshed.

The amount of caked-in blood that had washed out of Talbot's hair had frightened him. Hayward had said that he'd fallen heavily against the end wall, enough to split his head open and knock him out. Perhaps he should go and get it checked. Later. Whilst shaving he'd discovered a couple of choice bruises rising up beneath his left eye. Those he attributed to Hayward's heavy-handed assault, but under the circumstances, he guessed he deserved it, Hayward's anger justifiably spilling over once he'd sussed that it was his grandmother and not Lilly who had been visited. His aching back he blamed on Hayward dragging him up the stairs. Bloody hell, the guy must have had adrenaline pumping like crazy, giving him the strength of a cart horse.

When the taxi dropped Talbot off, he spied Helen, muffled up against the cold, hovering around the café, and he darted across the road and into the newsagents to stock up on fags before they became involved in conversation. Snow had settled overnight and the pavements were churned into two inches of slippery slush. He was picking his way through the grey muck when she waved and smiled.

'Jake, you look dreadful,' she said, pecking him on the cheek.

Huh, she should have seen him half an hour ago. Lighting a cigarette and sending her in to order his bacon sarnie, he sat down on one of the cold steel chairs and wished he'd spent more time drying his hair.

'Who are we seeing?' he asked, when she returned with the tea.

'I'm not, you are.' She half reached out to touch his swollen cheek, shook her head at the state of him and fiddled with her spoon. 'I've tracked down Lillian Charteris's lawyer. He's agreed to speak with you, and only you.'

'Helen, you are a gem.' He folded his hand over hers and squeezed.

She flushed and smiled and sat back as the waitress set down his sandwich. 'Eat your breakfast.'

33

THE OFFICES OF WILLIAMS & POTTER, Solicitors, were up the far end of Farnham in one of the fine Georgian town houses that fronted West Street. Inside it was the usual pale green walls and cream wainscoting echoing the period, maintaining an air of quality with wooden desks and discreet technology. It was Potter who greeted him, a stout man in his late fifties with a good firm handshake that Talbot approved of. A slight wince and a moment too long staring at his face showed that Potter had noticed his bruises, but was far too polite to mention them. That was the joy of excellent manners; they saved on lengthy explanations.

Out of habit Talbot flicked open his warrant card.

'Very interesting ID you have there, Detective Inspector Talbot,' Potter said, and smiled; and Talbot glanced down at the winking hologram. So, this was one of the doors it opened. Gesturing for him to sit down in one of the comfy chairs, Potter positioned himself on the business side of his desk. 'Coffee?'

'Thank you, sir, but only if it's quick, I have another appointment at eleven.'

'Then we'll get on while my secretary makes it.' Potter spoke into an intercom, sat back and opened a drawer. From it he took a large manila folder. 'We both know that you're here to discuss Lillian Charteris.'

'Yes, sir.' It felt right to call him sir, his suit and old school tie demanding respect.

'Many years ago,' Potter said, 'a very sweet woman named Lillian Charteris called upon me to draw up her last will and testament. I thought it a strange request because, back then, she was still a relatively young woman. What she instructed me to write, I found even stranger.' He opened the manila folder and drew out a document. 'At the time, I did advise Lillian that this was not a particularly wise bequest to make, but people can do what they wish with their money and possessions. I am merely the scribe, and the executor.' He ran a finger across the document, skimming through until he found the detail he was after. 'Blah, blah, name, etc.… do leave all of my worldly wealth and possessions to one Frankie Hayward, whom I believe resides in Farnham…'

Talbot laughed and shook his head; excellent, absolutely brilliant. 'Sorry.' He sucked in his lips and tried not to smile.

Potter masked a chuckle by clearing his throat before reading on. 'I believe that Frankie is a real, living person. There may be more than one Frankie Hayward residing in Farnham, but you will know him by asking him to tell you the pet name I call him…'

'My mystical gypsy.'

'Good Lord! You know it.'

'Uh-huh. Poor girl, she's goofed on that one. She sent out a whole batch of Christmas cards to every F. Hayward in the telephone directory.' Talbot sighed, the fun was gone. 'She wrote, "I am so looking forward to seeing you, my mystical gypsy", so they'll all know by now and come clamouring.'

'She does include many other details,' Potter said, 'but the nub is, Inspector Talbot, that events have surpassed her testimony, and we now know of her association with Frankie Hayward, don't we?'

'We do indeed, sir.' The smile was back on Talbot's lips.

There was a brief interruption while the secretary brought in coffee, beautifully served in cups with saucers, alongside a dish of biscuits.

'What you may not be aware of,' Potter said as he stirred his coffee, 'is that Lillian Charteris owns everything.'

'Everything?'

It was Potter's turn to grin. 'Her grandchildren merely run the estate, and are partners in a business. Yes, they can draw a wage and use reasonable funds, but she owns it all, outright.'

'The golf course? The hotels? That big house?'

'Everything.'

The monumental implications took time to sink in. Sensibly, Potter gave him a few seconds for his mind to stop somersaulting. It came to rest on one succinct statement. Bloody hell.

'Frankie has the power to pull the rug right out from under their feet,' Talbot said.

'Precisely.' Potter stood and took his coffee over to the window, gazed out at the fluttering snow.

'Are Peter and Melanie aware of the terms of her will?'

'Possibly. Several years ago this office had a break in, and Lillian's will was one of the documents exposed to prying eyes.'

Now why didn't that surprise him?

'The more recent bit of disconcerting news is that on Monday I had an impromptu visit from Melanie Charteris…'

'And friend.'

Potter nearly dropped his cup and saucer. 'How do you know that?'

'I'm a detective, sir.' Talbot smiled and helped himself to a biscuit. 'So, what was Miss Charteris after?'

'She wanted me to give her power of attorney, claimed her grandmother is senile and can no longer run her affairs.'

Talbot frowned. 'Capable or not, Lilly isn't allowed to.' He decided to join Potter at the window. 'Peter Charteris wouldn't even let her write Christmas cards, let alone sign any cheques.'

'I don't know about that.' Apparently uncertain of Talbot's response, he raised a hand. 'But I do know that even *I* can't consent to any legal action without due process through the proper authorities, the proper advice from doctors and carers. It's a lengthy procedure, Talbot, it doesn't just happen overnight." He pondered for a moment, smoothing down his tie as if it helped him align his thoughts. 'Peter Charteris isn't an unreasonable man. I'll have a word with him; discuss how best we can get the ball rolling on having Lillian assessed.'

'I doubt that Peter will cooperate.'

'Why on earth should you think that?' Potter wrinkled his brow. 'Melanie won't, that's for certain.' Thoughtfully, he stirred his coffee again. 'I've always judged Peter to be a sensible sort of fellow, hard-working, astute, as fair-minded as the next man. More so than most, I'd say.'

Talbot met Potter's gaze, unable to hide his scepticism.

'Mind you, I've noticed a change in him over the past few years, seen him drink too much.'

'Any idea why he's drinking so heavily?'

'I play golf over at their club, the 3Gs, and happened to overhear Melanie bullying him. She was picking a fight with Peter about nothing in particular, completely stressing him out. I saw him down a few after that.' He rubbed his bottom lip. 'He won't like the fact that Melanie's gone behind his back to try and obtain power of attorney over their grandmother. No doubt another of her bullying tactics.'

'Do you think she holds some kind of power over him?' Talbot's mind was tripping over a hundred possibilities.

'Money,' Potter stated. 'Years ago Peter withdrew a huge sum from company funds, to cover his debts or something. She's never let him forget it.' He shook his head. 'I'm not one to pass comment, but Melanie has always struck me as self-serving and fairly ruthless.' He gestured that they should move away from the window, suddenly seeming uncomfortable as people walked past outside. 'The other day when she came in, I didn't like the man who was with her, not one little bit. Two of a kind, if you ask me.'

'That was Frankie's brother, Joe.'

'Was it!' Potter went extremely pale. 'He introduced himself as Hemmings, kept backing Melanie up, and insisting that Frankie Hayward was a figment of Lillian's deranged mind.' He leant heavily on the table as he sat. 'And now you claim it was Frankie's brother.'

'Yes, sir.'

Pulling a clean white handkerchief from his pocket, Potter dabbed at his brow. 'He was the most dreadful man. Never before have I been spoken to like that, and in my own office. I addressed myself to Melanie, of course, he having nothing to do with the situation. I requested to visit Lillian, to judge for myself how the land might lie.'

'Did you get to see her?' Talbot met his gaze, anxiety rising and tightening his chest.

'Last Tuesday.' He paused. 'She's in a nursing home, Mellow Acres over in Guildford…'

'I understood she'd been moved from there.'

'Briefly, but she's back now. The conditions are appalling, so I've made arrangements to relocate her. As her legal representative I can draw on funds to pay for a much better home.'

'Is that where social services and Helen came in?'

Potter nodded.

'I'll have a word with her, discuss the details.' Glancing at the clock, Talbot paced his final few questions so that he could be out of there in under five minutes. 'How was Lilly? Was she in good health?'

'Good spirits, Talbot. She's frail, weak, but hopefully better care will encourage more robust health.'

It wasn't what Talbot wanted to hear. He wanted her rosy cheeked and strong, strong enough to stay alive long enough to see Hayward and hold his hand.

'Will you do something for me, please, sir,' Talbot said, and heard the same begging tone in his voice that Helen had derided.

'It all depends.'

'I'd like you to apply for a court order to keep her grandchildren away from her.'

Potter laughed and showed questioning palms. 'On what grounds?'

'Mental, emotional, and physical abuse. I can pass over a witness statement from someone who saw Peter Charteris throw something at her and cut her cheek, if that would help.'

The laughter left Potter's face. Nodding, he steepled his fingers in front of his lips. 'I'm sure it can be arranged.'

WHEN HELEN PULLED UP outside his house, Talbot said, 'It would be best if you don't come in.' His heart was racing, adrenaline pumping at the thought of going inside. Would the dread be any less if he were on his own? Would he feel less anxious if he wasn't so ashamed of having her see the total destruction?

'I'll keep you company until your man from the insurers turns up,' she said, and took her keys out of the ignition.

Following her from the car, he unlocked his front door and stepped into the house first, then stood back and let her choose whether or not to enter.

'Oh my God.' She breathed the words, her cheeks instantly losing their colour. 'This is worse than...' She walked into the kitchen, her gaze on the smashed crockery. Stopping, she stared down at the pooled wine on the floor spoiling her shoes, then turned, her eyes brimming.

'Come on, I'll see you to your car,' he said, and held out his hand for her to take.

Her fingers were cold, her touch making him shiver.

Clasping him to her, she whispered, 'Stay safe, Jake, please.'

For a moment he buried his head in her hair, desperate for her warmth, confused as to why her sweet smell had been so quickly stolen by the stench of blood and stale red wine. Her tenderness threatened to destroy his composure at any moment. Feeling fragile, he pulled away, embarrassed to think he might still reek of blood.

'I'll be in touch,' she promised, 'about what we discussed on the way over,' and drove off, leaving him alone with her trail of red footprints marring the pristine white snow.

He didn't go back inside, but chose to stand outside and smoke while waiting for the insurance man, who was late by well over five minutes.

'AND YOU A POLICEMAN and all,' the man said, jotting down notes as he walked around. 'Do you think this break-in might be connected to your work?'

'No idea.'

'This painting,' he said, jerking a thumb at Kate's landscape. 'Estimated value?'

'Fifteen hundred.' It was more than Kate was asking, but worth chancing his luck.

In the bedroom the man frowned and screwed his eyes up to better examine the damage. 'Why on earth would anyone want to shred your underwear?'

'No idea.' Because I was lusting after his grandmother, ogling the photo that he ripped off the wall; but you don't need to know that. Or that I now have a photo from when I visited Frances, which I've transferred to my phone. It's private, my love for her, something I'll have to keep secret forever. Talbot folded his arms.

Left with a stack of paperwork to fill in and instructions to send it off as soon as possible, he stood clutching the documents. Where the fuck was he going to file them?

Coffee was what was required, if the milk hadn't gone off. Dumping the papers on the kitchen table he filled the kettle. A knock came at the front door and he spun round, on guard and terrified. He'd deliberately left it open, afraid to be locked in with the aftershock of personal violation and hatred.

'Mr Talbot?' The man on the doorstep smiled, a clip-board tucked in the crook of his arm.

'And you are?' Talbot strode towards him, keen that he shouldn't step inside.

Glancing down at his paperwork, the man said, 'Hire car, arranged by one Mr Francis Hayward. I just need you to fill in a few formalities.'

'With pleasure.' To prove identification he showed his warrant card and the man grinned, took his signature and passed over the keys to a top-of-the-range Mercedes. 'You haven't taken down the number off my credit card,' Talbot pointed out.

'All paid for, sir,' the man said, and walked away, stroking his hand across the gleaming black paint-work as he passed the car.

Taking the insurance documents, Talbot stowed them away in the glove compartment, caressed the supple leather upholstery, and phoned Hayward.

'Frankie, you are brilliant, thank you.'

Hayward giggled. 'Nice model, that one, isn't it?'

'Superb. Let me know how much and I'll pay you back.'

'No, no, my treat.'

'Nice gesture, Frankie, but I can shove it against expenses.' Talbot heard the disappointment in his little sigh. 'Look, I shouldn't say anything, can't say anything really, but I've had word today that Lilly is alive and well.'

For a moment there was silence, then a faint gasp. 'Thank you, Jake. You don't know how much that means to me. Where is she?' Emotion filled Hayward's voice and Talbot knew he was crying.

'I'm sorry, I can't say at the moment. I'll call you later.'

No sooner had he hung up than a text came in from Kate.

'I've heard how bad this time of year is for you so thought it better if we get together after Christmas. Thinking of you, Kate.'

Bollocks. Talbot laughed. Hell, he didn't have time to meet up with her anyway. He texted back, 'Send address and I'll pop cheque in the post for painting.'

Resentment brewed. Claire must have taken her aside and rammed in the knife. You don't want to get involved with him. He's always screwed up at this time of year. Cold fish. More trouble than he's worth. The bitch.

Taking his misery into the kitchen, he made a coffee, lit a cigarette and went out to look at the back garden. Last night that door had been open, swinging wide, his intruders having gone out there for some purpose or other. Today everything was swathed in two inches of crisp white snow, virgin and twinkling in a burst of sunshine. A pocket handkerchief was how he thought of it, a twenty foot square of grass surrounded by two foot borders planted with easy care shrubs. Same as the house, really, a modern excuse for good living. Now it was a starched handkerchief, any traces of last night's grime hidden under Mother Nature's frosty gown.

He walked as far as the centre, turned around and studied the line of his footprints leading out from the back door. On the right the bird feeder swung empty and chirpless, a short-lived fad. On the left some shrub he could never remember the name of drooped under the weight of fluffy white pom-poms. Below it an ornamental statue sat round and white, the perfect base for a miniature snowman. Perhaps he should play and build one, avoid going in and dealing with the atmosphere inside. Perhaps, if he weren't in such a state, he'd be able to recall Claire buying it and putting it there. Damned if he could.

Stepping up to it, he crouched down and swept the snow away. It tumbled sideways, stared up at him. A rush of adrenaline jerked him backwards and his stomach somersaulted. He froze. Don't touch it. Walk slowly back to the house. He couldn't move. He swallowed the lump in his throat. Unable to take his eyes of it, he stared, and Keith McKenzie stared right back at him.

34

THE SOUND OF COLD WATER drumming against the kitchen sink pummelled in Talbot's head. The sick swirled round and round, the big bits refusing to go down the plug-hole. Orange and brown and everything tasting of puke, and probably more to spew out if he couldn't keep it down. Perverts he could deal with. Nutters he could deal with. Fresh hacked heads he obviously couldn't. He should be grateful that it had been kept on ice and didn't stink. Shit, the guy would have been a walking, talking human being this time yesterday. It didn't bear thinking about.

Hayward took forever to answer his phone, and when he did Talbot said, 'Frankie, listen to me and do exactly as I say,' his voice hoarse from retching and vomiting.

'Jake, are you okay?'

'I want you to lock yourself in the house, as soon as we finish speaking. You are then to go over every inch of the house to make sure that you are the only person inside it. You are then to search all over again. Check every cupboard, every tiny space where someone might hide…'

'Jake, something dreadful's happened, hasn't it?'

'Don't interrupt me!' Talbot yelled. 'Don't think, listen.'

Hayward whimpered.

'Every room that locks, you are to lock. Do not go and visit Lilly, stay with your body. You are to lock the cat flap and keep Millie indoors with you. You are not, I repeat, *not* to open the door to anyone, anyone at all—'

'Jake, what if I know them?'

'I don't care!' Talbot hollered down the phone. 'The only person you are to open the front door, back door, any door to, is me.' He punctuated his words by jabbing a finger down at the floor over and over again. 'Do you understand?'

'Yes, yes, but you're frightening me.'

'Good, that's how I want you to be, safe and terrified, on guard and doing precisely as I say.'

Through his tears, Hayward said, 'I've ordered groceries.'

Speaking firmly but more calmly, Talbot said, 'They'll keep on the front-doorstep; they won't go off in this weather. Talk to the guy through the letterbox, eh?'

'And if I have someone here at the moment?'

Shit. Family? 'Who's with you, Frankie?'

'A friend.' Talbot heard Hayward stamp his foot. 'It was meant to be a surprise.'

'Then finish your tea, and say goodbye, nicely.' Talbot bit his finger. 'I have to go. If anything happens, call me. If anything bad happens, dial 999. Don't hesitate, don't think twice, just do it.'

His hands were shaking as he lit a cigarette before calling Bailey.

'Jake, I thought we agreed—'

'I am going to string Yates up to a lamp-post by his balls!' Talbot drew heavily on his cigarette, and cut across Bailey as he tried to speak. 'The fucking idiot didn't do his job properly. He didn't pay enough attention to what went on last night…'

'I know you're upset…'

'That, sir, is an understatement. I've found Keith McKenzie. His head is playing ornaments in my back garden. It should have been discovered last night, date-stamped and tagged, not left for me to come home and find leering at me. If it wasn't for the fucking snow, it would look like I'd put it there.'

'Good Lord, Jake, how do you know it's McKenzie?' Bailey sounded dumbfounded.

'Oh, just a little something to do with the freckles, and the sandy hair, and the six inch nail sticking out of his forehead.' Talbot lit a second cigarette from the one he'd just finished.

'This is dire; you were seen driving away from the scene.'

'Well, fuck you! Sir. That head was planted in my garden…' He thumped the table and growled his frustration. What a crass thing to say. 'I have been set up.' He hit the wall. 'I did not kill Keith McKenzie.' He kicked the chair. 'I want forensics round here, I want a pathologist round here, I want a full and thorough investigation. I want police protection on Frankie Hayward twenty-four seven—'

'Surely he isn't in any danger?'

'I am not prepared to take that risk.'

A whoosh rushed down the phone that Talbot recognised as the sound of Bailey's pen pot spewing its contents across his desk. Good, he was panicking too. Tugging at his key ring, Talbot removed his house key. 'I am going to leave my front door key under a flower pot outside. Nobody'll have nicked it if you get your men here quickly. Preferably not Yates, as he's too stupid to see what's right under his nose. Closing fucking doors so that he keeps warm.'

'You should have been more hands-on last night, Jake.'

'Don't shove this on me. I was told to keep out of it. I was told, in no uncertain terms by Yates, that it was his investigation and I was the victim. Well, you know what, sir, I don't feel like being a victim, not today… not for murder.' He stopped and drew in a deep breath, tried to steady his nerves, stop his insides from trembling. 'I am going to leave my front door key under a flower pot outside,' he repeated, went out and placed it there. 'The one to the right of the front door on entering.'

'Oh no, you don't,' Bailey said. 'Jake, stay at the house. For Christ sake's man, don't make this worse on yourself.'

'I am not going to hang around playing "let's arrest the cop on suspicion" while the perpetrators decide who else to carve up for Christmas.' Getting in the car he fired it up, shoved the phone onto speaker and drove away. There was no plan, only an overwhelming desire to be free.

'Jake, what car are you using?' Bailey came across as gently inquisitive, the pleasant tone of a friend who was concerned.

'Hired myself a hack, cheap little run-around, silver hatchback.' Go chase that and leave me alone, he mouthed.

'Where are you headed?'

'To go and sit and work out who the fuck did this.' He knew who'd sliced Keith's head off; it was the proving it that was the hard part.

'There's no need, it's an official murder enquiry now. Weissman and his department can't possibly overrule me on this. I won't let them.'

'Oh no, this is my case, my assignment,' Talbot shouted towards the phone. 'You told me that Hayward wasn't in the clear until I'd proved he didn't do anything to Keith McKenzie. So you know what? I'm going to go and catch the bad guys. I'm going to prove that Frankie Hayward had absolutely nothing to do with any of this, and then, whether Weissman likes it or not, I'm going to take him to visit Lilly.'

'Jake, just leave it. Go back to the house, help my men with their enquiries. The team can deal with it from here on.'

'Sorry, sir, no can do, I don't like their lack of method.' Reaching across he pressed the end-call button, and while held up at the next set of traffic lights, switched it over to silent.

Left with just the burble of the engine, he lit a cigarette, stared out at the gathering darkness, and felt very alone.

PARKING UP IN HASLEMERE, he gritted his teeth and called Weissman. No, he wasn't going to tell him everything, or shout at him about tricking him over the photograph. It felt like making a pact with the devil, but it was the only tactic he could think of to try and get some clout behind the situation and overrule Bailey.

After listening intently to a brief resume of the most pertinent facts, Weissman said, 'Bailey's out of his depth; this is no longer a police matter. I told him last night we're taking over from here. I'll call you back in five minutes.'

Unclenching his fist, Talbot slotted the phone into the in-car charger, focused on the shoppers struggling to heave over-laden trolleys through the supermarket exit, and waited. For a moment he closed his eyes and took in a deep breath, needing the intoxicating smell of the leather upholstery to give him a sense of reality. Images of Keith's severed head flashed through his mind, the tiny detail, the sandy hair stuck to his temples, the rusty nail protruding from the centre of his forehead, the way a wedge of snow had fallen away from his right eye as it had slumped sideways. Wham and he was alive, the blue eye staring, as if he'd been startled at being disturbed. Talbot's stomach lurched, this time everything dragging down to his bowels instead of up to his mouth. Keep it in, just keep control, or they've won.

All around, lights danced against the falling snow. Street lights. Christmas lights. Car lights. Heart-stopping blue lights. Fuck, he was on the other side, on the run, the suspect. Everything spangled on the windscreen, surreal, while people hurried here and there, as if preparing for a siege.

Head cut off first or nail through forehead first? What type of twisted mind was he up against? He shivered and folded his arms. Some primitive instinct told him it was nail first. A picture evolved of Keith being held down and tortured, told that he had become too much of a liability, and was more useful dead than alive. Wallop, down came the hammer. He could hear it driving in the nail, crunching the bone.

Talbot's mouth was parched, dry from too many cigarettes. The longer he sat with the engine off, getting colder and colder, the more his head ached. Not his hair reeking of blood after all. Keith's blood mixed in with spilt wine, red wine, most likely why they'd poured the stuff everywhere: to mask the smell and hide any drips of blood. Oh Christ, was Keith murdered in his house? Surely not. Where was the rest of him?

The phone rang and his hands jerked out to fend off the blow. Shit, he was jumpy.

'What's your next move?' Weissman asked.

'To prove who murdered Keith.'

'Any ideas?'

'Uh-huh.'

'Don't confront your suspect, Jake. As soon as there's any sniff of trouble, follow instructions: phone the emergency number on the mobile we gave you. It will come straight through to my department. You'll have backup within five minutes.'

'Yes, sir,' he said, clutched his head in his hands, and wished the dreadful sense of being alone would go away.

WITH AT LEAST AN HOUR to spare before he could make his move, Talbot went in search of food. A pub up the road was offering an early bird special, so he sat and ate and thought, and tried not to dwell on the snowman's head bouncing around in his garden. Freckles. Fair-haired people usually had more prominent freckles in summer, in sunshine. Shit, that was where Keith McKenzie had been hiding: overseas. Probably Europe, travelling to France first on a yacht with private moorings, most likely dodging passport checks. It had to be. So why the hell had they called him back now? When, precisely, had he returned?

The food was making him sleepy, slowing down his thinking, reminding him of how little kip he'd had. When the waitress cleared his plate, he ordered a pot of coffee, told her he'd be outside having a smoke.

Pushing past a group of rowdy Christmas revellers, Talbot made his way out to the pub garden and the patio heaters. He smoked and sipped his coffee, ran through every minute detail of the case, until his mind rested on one conclusion. Keith had been called back immediately after Hayward had attempted to visit Lilly at the care home. That's why Peter Charteris was drinking so heavily. He must have caught wind of Keith's return. Yes, that would be it. Melanie had cracked and couldn't stand her grandmother's obsession ruling their lives anymore. So they'd decided to murder Keith and set Hayward up for the crime. Properly this time, with no mistakes. Only Hayward had acquired a new friend, a policeman, no less, so wouldn't it be fun to make them both look guilty.

SNOW WAS A PROBLEM, not because it was slippery and icy and bloody cold, but because it left footprints, and tyre tracks, and recorded your every move. Not such an issue on the roads, but a menace once he'd parked some distance away from George Hayward's house and was walking back up towards it. He fiddled around in his pockets doing a mental check. Both mobile phones, set to silent. Car keys, safe. Fags and lighter. Dictaphone, always in the top pocket. Warrant card, easy access. There were no street lights here, the residents of rural Frensham preferring the dark and the stars, and being equipped with a barrage of well-charged torches to choose from. Here and there, orange squares glowed on distant houses, their windows cats' eyes watching him in the dark, silent creatures waiting to pounce. Talbot shivered and pulled his collar higher, tried to protect himself from the chill wind that sliced across his neck.

Halting outside George Hayward's property, he looked down the sweeping driveway. The light was on in the peaked porch, throwing out an arc of yellow that bathed mysterious mounds on one side only, their dark sides in sharp relief against more mysterious yellow and black monuments. Those were the tubs of winter pansies. What was that? A small shrub? A bag? A head? He swallowed hard and fought the urge to clear his throat. Silent running was best. Snow had drifted into the porch-way, or been walked there, the tiled base covered in a churned-up mess, several sets of footprints walking in or out. Tyre tracks swept round and disappeared into one of the garage blocks, one set of footprints showing that someone had hopped out before the car was driven in, the other exiting from the garage. Two people. So where was George's car? Shit, he'd probably quit work early for Christmas and been tucked away indoors all day, his car stored before the snow fell. Or there was an office party and he wasn't home yet. No, no, there would be tyre tracks if he'd left early that morning.

Talbot pulled out his mobile and checked the time. Precisely 7.15 and three missed calls from Hayward. Listening to them would have to wait. The well-trained copper in him kept shouting that this was the point where you called for backup, for assistance, and did not go in alone. He exhaled and listened, the strokes of his heartbeat pulsing in his ears. There was no backup, no one to judge the moment except himself, only a number to ring if he proved his suspects guilty. One light was on in an upstairs room, which did nothing to convince him of their location within the building. Front door was best, after a quick circuit of the house.

He was about to make his move when a car came screaming up the road, full beam glaring in his face, blinding him. Instinctively he shielded his eyes, expecting the vehicle to drive on past, but at the last minute it swung towards him, as if to go up the drive. Black ice caught the speeding driver off guard and the car skidded out of control, came straight at him. Talbot's gut lurched and he dived sideways, threw himself into a hedge, spun round in time to see the vehicle slew across the road. Wheels spun and the engine roared. Slip, slide, wallop, it buried its nose into the hedgerow opposite, the sharp sound of breaking glass suggesting it had made impact with something tougher than hawthorn. Shit. Racing towards it, Talbot could make out a man slumped onto an inflated airbag. Bright white lights lit up the hedgerow's snowy branches and the single tree marking a boundary, the one now embedded in the car's bonnet.

Yanking the driver's door open, Talbot jerked back as a waft of whisky hit him full square. Rage overtook him and he raised a fist.

'Die, you drunken bastard!' he shouted.

In response the driver slowly lifted his head and groaned. 'I must get to my sister.' He sat upright, and ran a hand around his neck.

Backing down and unclenching his fist didn't come easy for Talbot, painful memories momentarily playing havoc with his judgment. Taking a deep breath, he pulled himself together, reached across and switched off the ignition, flicked off the lights, gritted his teeth and said, 'You and I need to talk, Mr Charteris.'

35

THE INTERIOR LIGHT ILLUMINATED Peter Charteris's face as he stared up and frowned.

'You're that copper.'

'Yes, sir, and you're drunk.' Talbot fiddled around in his top pocket, as if looking for something, and turned on his Dictaphone.

'Been drinking, but not drunk,' Charteris said, grappling past the air bag to undo his seat belt. 'I'd only just sat down with a glass of whisky. I wasn't expecting to get called away.'

'Called away to where, precisely?' Talbot asked, casting a glance over his shoulder at George's house. No new lights, but that didn't mean they hadn't heard the crash.

'My sister, Melanie, she's not feeling well.'

'I'm sorry to hear that, sir. Where is she? Perhaps I can assist.'

'She's over at…' Charteris sucked in the rest of his words, took his keys from the ignition, motioned Talbot aside, and heaved himself out of the car. 'She's in that house over there,' he said, and pointed.

'Have you been there before, sir?'

'As a matter of fact, no, I haven't.' Trapped between Talbot and the open car door, Charteris stretched his arm over the top of the vehicle, as if prepared to stand there all night.

'Who's she visiting, Mr Charteris?'

'Her boyfriend.'

'And do you know the name of her boyfriend?'

Charteris drummed his fingers on the roof of the car. 'Joe.'

'Uh-huh, and would that be Mr Joe Hayward, Frankie Hayward's brother?'

The fingers kept drumming, the look on Charteris's face blank, only his tight lips giving the game away.

'Well, Mr Charteris, you can answer my questions, right here and now, or I can charge you with obstruction.'

'You wouldn't dare.' Charteris's eyes popped open wide and his jaw line quivered.

Packed a hefty punch, Mr Fix-it had claimed. Talbot resisted clenching his fist in readiness, or stepping away.

'I have to see my sister; she isn't well.' Charteris thumped the roof of the car, then swept his hand down and tried to push Talbot aside. 'Out of my way.'

Talbot stood his ground, pinned him in by resting a hand against the side of the roof, leant close and spoke right into his face.

'You can't protect Melanie from this, not any longer. It's over.'

'I don't know what you're talking about.'

Smiling, Talbot moved away and swept a hand towards the house, inviting him to take flight. 'Your choice, Charteris. Right now you might get off lightly with aiding and abetting, or simply withholding evidence. But once inside that door...' he paused, gave Charteris time to think, or panic, or both, 'you're a party to murder.'

Charteris's mouth dropped open. He gaped, tried to speak, his voice breaking. 'She hasn't...?'

'Hasn't what?' Talbot demanded.

'She said she wouldn't harm him, she promised.'

'Harm who?'

Charteris met his gaze. 'You said murder. Who's dead?'

'Your friend—'

'Oh my god, she's killed Keith.'

There was no need for Talbot to say any more, the way Charteris trembled with shock as he reached into the car to fetch his coat being clear enough.

'Too bloody cold to be standing around.' Charteris pulled his coat on and wrapped a scarf around his neck. 'Let's walk.'

THEY STRODE TOWARDS TALBOT'S CAR, Charteris having the common sense to keep a torch on board, neither of them saying a word until they were sitting in the vehicle with the engine on and the heater running.

Out of habit Talbot flashed his warrant card. 'Just in case you forget who you're talking to. This is on the record...'

Unexpectedly, Charteris snatched the card from his fingers, flicked on the interior light and snorted back a chuckle. 'I was warned about this, years ago. So you're the Lone bloody Ranger.'

'Uh-huh.' Nice one, Weissman, warn Charteris in advance that a man will come riding in with a twinkling warrant card, and then it's game over.

Placing it back in his pocket, Talbot exchanged it for a cigarette, Charteris scowling as he lit up.

'You have ten minutes,' Talbot warned. 'Then I am going to make a house call. Alone.'

'Then you're a bloody fool. You don't know how spiteful Melanie can be once she gets going.'

'Oh, I think I do.' Nail first, then cut off the head. Oh yes, Melanie and Joe made a very nasty pair. 'Let's start with the money you gave Melanie to pack Keith McKenzie off overseas.'

'I was over a barrel...' Leaning his elbow on the window sill, he stared out into the dark, his fingers tracing around his lips as if he were afraid to speak the words. 'Through my mate Keith... we did sports together... she tracked down Joe Hayward, became... involved. I warned her off, I swear I bloody well did.' His voice quivered and he bit down across his hand. 'Jesus Christ, I didn't even know there was a real Frankie Hayward until Melanie started ranting about it. She became obsessed, as mad as Gran, banging on and on about him, shouting about how she had to get him away from Gran, to get him to leave the old girl alone, to stop possessing her.' He paused and sniffed loudly. 'Then she came home one day and said she'd worked out a good way of ridding us of Frankie Hayward, to stop him ever turning up on our doorstep. She and Joe had devised a plan. I thought the idea was that Keith was simply going to take off...'

'Where did they initially hide him?'

'One of our outbuildings. He'd been there six months before I stumbled across him. Bored, smoking, unfit... not the guy I knew, the friendship lost.' Clutching his head, he said vehemently, 'I didn't want anything to do with it. I told Melanie to get him out of the country. Christ, by that time everyone was shouting murder.' He glanced across as Talbot flicked ash onto the floor. 'Good Lord, you've got a right shiner.'

'Walked into a door.'

Charteris didn't react, which near enough proved that he hadn't been the one who'd struck Hayward's grandmother, Frances, in the dark, and triggered her stroke. No, that would have been Joe; her own grandson. Talbot flicked more ash into the foot well, aware that he'd been poised, ready to strike, if Peter had been at all involved. 'And once Keith had disappeared?'

'They asked me for a large sum of money…'

'They?'

'Melanie and Joe. Thousands, hundreds of thousands…' He blew out a long, deep breath and clenched his fist. 'I didn't have access to such a large sum, not personally, so I borrowed company funds. Oh, she set it up sweet, created such a rift between my father and me…'

'Why didn't you come forwards, inform the authorities that McKenzie was still alive? You put poor Frankie through hell.'

'Fear, anxiety… call it what you like.' He wiped his face and drew his bottom lip down. 'I was a total coward. Afraid, yes, afraid of what the two of them had set in motion. Melanie was only a kid, but Joe… oh, he was the grown-up, the master planner.'

'Have you ever spoken with Frankie's mother?'

'No, never.'

Talbot chuckled. Joe was a sly bastard, you certainly had to give him that, making out it was his mother who was in cahoots with Charteris.

Looking away, back into the dark, Charteris said, 'I had contact with Keith's father though, via Joe. Hamish McKenzie had his hand out all of the time, demanding more and more money to keep his mouth shut…'

'Blackmail?'

'Yes, his wife had forced him to accuse Frankie of murder and —'

'No, not his wife. I suspect that was Melanie's doing.'

'Shit.' Charteris folded his arms. 'Hamish caught a glimpse of Keith one day, out with Melanie. That's when they decided to pack him off abroad.'

'No, they took a photograph and showed it to Hamish McKenzie.'

'You have got to be…' The side of Charteris's hand went back in his mouth, an unconscious substitute for the glass he was used to sipping from, his comforter.

'Melanie convinced you that as long as McKenzie's son was alive, you had to pay him not to blow the whistle; to avoid the truth coming out that Melanie and Joe had set Frankie up, and wasted everyone's time and money. And destroyed a young man's life. You just kept on protecting her. Only, the McKenzies never saw the money. You paid it to them through Melanie, didn't you?'

Charteris nodded.

'Well, she kept it, all for herself.'

'No...'

'The photograph they showed Hamish McKenzie was of his son lying in front of Frankie's machine, so Hamish was convinced his son was dead, sent off to some other time and place and stuck in the past forever.' Talbot laughed, wound down the window, let in a blast of freezing air and chucked his dog-end out. 'Melanie and Joe have laid a wicked trail, come forward with information, and paved a road firmly to your door.'

Charteris wiped his lips. 'Christ, I could do with a drink.'

'Stress does that to you.' Talbot glanced at the clock on the dash. Almost eight o'clock. 'It would have been a lot easier if you'd simply let Frankie visit Lilly.'

'I wasn't going to invite him,' Charteris said harshly. 'By the time he turned up in Kent he'd already been in court. That was the first I ever saw of him.' He shook his head. 'It had already gone too far.'

'When did you first speak with Dr Weissman?' Talbot switched the engine off and removed the car keys.

'He took me aside during Frankie's court case. Warned me that if I was at all involved in Keith's disappearance, how everything would blow up in my face. He said that he would swear blind that Frankie was mad and that there was no such thing as a time machine, and that I was to keep my grandmother away from him, at all costs.'

'And that's why you thumped Frankie in Kent and assaulted Kate.'

'Kate?'

'The female carer at Mellow Acres who helped Lilly with her Christmas cards.'

'Oh... her.'

'Yes, her.' Talbot jabbed a finger at Charteris, ordered him to stay put, and opened the car door.

Scowling, Charteris snapped his fingers for the keys. 'Come on, I'll sit tight.'

'Maybe, but you have been drinking, Mr Charteris, so I'd rather not take the risk.'

IT WAS CRUEL, ordering Charteris to hand over his mobile, but Talbot didn't feel like gambling. For someone in desperate need of her brother's help, Melanie was suspiciously quiet, so he had to assume they'd witnessed the car crash. When waiting for someone to turn up on a snowy evening, he would have phoned if they didn't arrive within a reasonable time; that was human nature, and the rules one must adhere to, even if one was play-acting. There were no real surprises in Charteris's statement, just confirmation. Bloody hell, Charteris was edgy and drawn out so taut he was fit to burst. Just being in the car with him rattled Talbot, the cold bite outside a blessed relief. Now Charteris was a well-primed cannon ready to blow, sitting, waiting, getting cold… and wanting a drink. With Bailey determined to question Talbot on suspicion, taking Charteris in to the station was out of the question. There was risk, and then there was downright stupidity.

The only astonishing piece of information was that Weissman was so heavily involved. Bastard, he was using Hayward's machine as a glorious experiment, making sure that everyone blocked Frankie from getting close to Lilly in order to keep the LEAPP machine alive, and see which way the dice might fall. Talbot kicked himself for being an unwitting participant in this complex game. The temptation of love and sweet treats had tumbled him straight into the trap of going to visit the woman he believed to be Lilly.

WALKING STRAIGHT UP TO George Hayward's front door felt like asking for trouble, so Talbot skirted round down by the hedge, scuttled across the lawn, and came up by the rear windows, thinking to peer in and gain some idea of where everyone was in the house before knocking on the door. Glancing back he saw the hoppity tracks he'd left, like a snow rabbit, a faint light from an upstairs window throwing them into sharp relief. His feet were still frozen and had never quite thawed out in the car. Standing created a dull ache that rose up to his knees and competed for attention with the rapid pulse of his heart. At least he could no longer feel the thump-thump in his head; the cold was seeing to that. Breathing on his fingertips to warm them, he listened at the window. Nope, couldn't hear a thing from inside.

Further along were some patio doors, a chink of light shining through where the drapes didn't quite meet in the middle. It was too narrow to make out much, except that someone was sitting in an armchair with his back to the windows. Dark haired: it could have been George or Joe. Melanie had called Peter over to embroil him in some scheme, maybe even to set him up for Keith's murder, if the blame ended up at the burglars' door. But if that was Joe sitting in the armchair, then where was George? How innocent or involved was he?

The French windows were old-fashioned, wooden-framed, the door handle the usual type, and not one of those new security locks. Placing his hand over the freezing metal, Talbot eased it down, thinking the figure in the chair might turn at the sound and he'd see who it was. He held his breath and listened as the bolt shifted, his mouth dry and a lump lodging in his throat when he tried to swallow. Keeping his hand firmly on the handle he stood stock still. The figure didn't budge. Dead, or playing dead? The silence was eerie, too quiet, the snow damping every sound, so that all that was left was a terrible hush. A shiver ran down his spine. Something was different. Unexpected. Come on, come on, what was it? Something in the air. Dust? Ash? Cooking? No, surely that was the faint odour of a log fire burning. Last time he was here, George hadn't given the impression that he bothered with open fires, the grate being filled with old ash and cigarette ends. So why build one now?

An unnerving thought crossed his mind, and the hairs on the back of his neck stood on end. Automatically he turned his collar up against the cold. A pale shadow glanced across the snow behind him. Uh-huh, was that someone sneaking a look from an upstairs window? Keeping close to the wall he crept round to the front of the building, leaving the patio doors leaking the ominous odour. Controlling his breathing, he pressed the doorbell, scuffed snow off his boots, and smoothed back his hair.

From the rear of the house he heard raised voices, a high-pitched one complaining that they should have got on with the job quicker, and be finished with it. Now was the time to phone for back up, whilst the suspects argued amongst themselves. Nasty, head-hacking suspects, who probably had a trick or two in mind for him. Nail first? Shit. He slid his hand into his pocket, closed trembling fingers around the mobile with Weissman's emergency number. The man had cheated him, used him, hurt Frankie. He swapped it for the one with Bailey's number, stared at the screen. Hayward had to be proved innocent or he wouldn't get to visit Lilly.

Fuck 'em. Evidence first, then phone.

At least two minutes passed before anyone came to the door, by which time he was breathing more easily and could manage a show of normality. Joe didn't look at all pleased to see him, his mouth quivering with rage, his eyes sparking with hatred. Wearing a long coat, he was overdressed for a warm house, making Talbot wonder if Joe was thinking of going out, or leaving altogether; if that was indeed a packed suitcase he glimpsed tucked in around the corner.

'Hi, Joe, is your Dad in?' Talbot asked, smiled, and took the liberty of stepping inside. Bloody hell, were they cooking Christmas dinner early? Was that what he'd smelt outside? Chicken? Pork? Cook them now, and have them as cold meats for the feast.

'No, he's popped out.'

'You won't mind if I wait, will you.' He spoke it as a statement, one of those closed comments impermissible in court. 'Just need to run through a few things with him.'

'Anything I can help you with, Inspector?' The charm was back in Joe's voice, a smarminess belied by his lack of human interest in Talbot's black eye. No curiosity at all as he hurried Talbot through to the kitchen, the sitting room door shut firmly against prying eyes.

Following him, Talbot decided it was best not to point out that Joe was in the house of a man he claimed never to speak to. It was Christmas, it was an exception: that would be his excuse. The kitchen was stone cold. Nothing cooking in here, yet it really did smell like pork. Recalling that burning human flesh was supposed to smell like pork, Talbot twitched and once again the hairs on his neck stood to attention. Oh shit, were they really burning Keith's remains on the hearth in the family sitting room? Choice cut human chops or random limbs slowly roasting? Hiding his abhorrence, he perched on the edge of the sink unit and watched as Joe fumbled with the coffee machine, lacking his father's dexterity and adeptness for gadgets. Perhaps he was fumbling under scrutiny, losing his cool, sensing that Talbot had smelt their guilt crisping in the grate. When he turned and placed two mugs on the huge wooden banqueting table, Talbot noticed a subtle difference. Something dark had seeped into the grain, blood most likely, and there were deep score lines, as if someone had been using it as a butcher's block. Trying not to focus on that particular detail, Talbot pushed away from the sink and smiled as Joe offered milk. Where the hell was George? Christ, was that his blood on the table as well as Keith's? Were they both sliced up and stacked on the fire?

A clock ticked round to 8:45, and Joe said, 'Well, how can I help you, Inspector?'

'Your father gave me a photograph, an old faded Polaroid…'

Joe didn't blink as he shrugged; the wind slammed an upstairs door shut and Talbot smelt a familiar perfume waft in from behind him.

36

'Kirsty home?' Talbot asked, perching back on the sink unit, so that he could see most of the kitchen. Where the fuck was Melanie hiding?

'Out, doing the Christmas thing,' Joe explained, and stripped off his coat. Shit, that was an ugly sweater.

'Well, if you don't know anything about the photo, I'd best wait and speak with your father.'

'Do you always work so late, Inspector?' Joe sugared his words, no doubt attempting to sound sympathetic. His eyes darted towards a door that looked like it led down to a cellar or larder. 'I can always take a message and get him to phone you later.'

'Where's he popped out to?' Talbot sipped his coffee.

'Supermarket.'

'Just my luck.' Talbot shook his head. 'I bet he's stuck in a queue.'

'Yes, probably.' Joe shrugged, as if there were nothing to be done.

'Tell you what, why don't you give him a call for me, ask how long he'll be.' Talbot smiled encouragement.

'Is that really necessary?'

'I wanted him to have a look at this photo.' Talbot tapped his breast pocket. 'It was taken down in Frankie's basement. There's a lad lying on the floor, but I can't make out who it is.'

Joe's cheeks turned ashen. He was going to pick up his coffee, but changed his mind. Instead he folded his arms. 'It must be Frankie.'

'No, the lad's got fair hair.' Easing away from the sink, Talbot sighed. 'I guess it could be Keith McKenzie, but I don't have any photos from when he was alive.' He pushed his fingers down into his breast pocket. 'However, I do have this one, of when he was dead...' Talbot sighed and shook his head, watched every change on Joe's face as his eyes widened and his pupils dilated. 'Can't really, confidential evidence.' Talbot grinned. 'But we know who killed him.'

'Do you?' Joe picked up a half-full mug, his hand trembling. He faced away and busied himself.

'Oh yes, I saw them driving away... in your car.'

'Oh, really, Inspector Talbot!' Joe spun round, waving his hand, spilling slops of coffee as he shook the mug. 'That is an absurd allegation. I was nowhere near your house last night.'

Laughing, Talbot spread his hands. 'Did I mention my house?'

Now was the time to call for backup. *Wait.* Get him to admit it, just a few words more. The cellar door handle rattled, loud and uncompromising. Joe's gaze darted towards it. Talbot's heart lurched.

'You implied it,' Joe blurted out. 'You said that you saw, so I assumed you were at home.'

'Uh-huh. So was your car out of your possession, or stolen, last night?'

The cellar door was moving, nudged open bit by bit, a cool draught whipping around Talbot's neck as the gap grew larger. Fear tightened his chest.

'I lent it to someone.' Joe strode round the table and slammed the door shut. 'Damn thing, catch is broken.' He pressed firmly against it.

'Who did you lend your car to, Joe?' Talbot casually followed him round the table, pulled out his cigarettes, and offered one over. Better to be nearer the hall door and a quick exit, not have the enemy block his path.

'My girlfriend.' Across the lighter's flame, Joe met his gaze.

'And her name is?'

Joe drew heavily on his cigarette and smiled. 'Melanie.'

'And her surname is?' Talbot smelt her perfume. Listening to the silence, he could almost hear Melanie holding her breath behind the cellar door. Joe might have answered. He just might have betrayed her had the front door not banged open. It whacked back against a radiator, the sound so sudden and unexpected that Talbot flinched and his heart somersaulted. The door slammed shut. Joe dropped his cigarette, scrunched it out with his foot, looked towards the kitchen door.

Kirsty's voice rang out down the hallway. 'Dad? You in?' Within seconds, she'd opened the sitting room door. She screamed, and screamed, and screamed, the shrill pitch expressing a terror such as Talbot had never heard before.

Adrenaline shot through his veins, chilling him to the core. Shit, she'd found the burning pork: roast Keith, and possibly roast father too. For a split second no one moved, then Joe leapt towards the work surface, hand outstretched towards a block of knives.

'I'm not going down for this! I'll kill you first, you meddling…'

The cellar door burst open, and Melanie flew out, brandishing a gun, wild with hatred. Shit, that looked real. He dodged sideways, dived towards her legs, felled her to the floor. The pistol discharged, sound exploding in the air. She went down hard, face first, let out a cry as her head cracked against the flagstones, fingers still clutching the gun. Talbot grabbed her wrist and slammed it onto the floor, forced her to let go. The gun skidded off under the table.

'Do something, Joe!' Melanie shouted, and Talbot pressed his knee into her spine, stopping her from crawling away.

He had her pinned down, trying to get her hands together. Fuck, fuck, no cuffs. He should have brought bloody handcuffs.

Kirsty's scream was going on and on, filling the air with such tension that Talbot almost didn't notice Joe running towards him. At the last moment, he glimpsed a flash of steel, and dragged Melanie round. Couldn't let her go, or both would attack. Inevitably her body shielded him. As the knife drove straight down he felt the spray of blood. Melanie screamed. Her convulsion juddered through him. The handle of the knife rose up by her ear, stuck in the muscle behind her collarbone. A carving knife. Oh, shit.

Joe was backing away. Running, escaping, grabbing at the back door handle.

Shouting, bashing, a commotion coming from the front door. Talbot pushed Melanie away and threw himself at Joe. Melanie wailed, Joe swore, Talbot punched. Dead square, up across Joe's cheek and into his eye.

A fist came up and Talbot caught Joe's wrist in full swing, spun him round and yanked his arm right up behind his back. Thrusting his knee into Joe's spine, Talbot fought to maintain a hold, force him to the ground. Joe kicked out, desperate to break free. A final twist of the arm, an ominous crack, and he caved, buckled to the floor.

'You fucking bastard, you can't pin anything on me!'

'We'll start with assaulting a police officer.'

Astride his back, Talbot pulled Joe's hands together. Fuck, no fucking cuffs! Perspiration wetted his brow. Melanie was lying half under the table, groaning. He glanced towards her, saw the red stain spreading across her white leather jacket. Gun a few feet away, slim chance of her reaching it. Noise, what was all that fucking noise? Wood splintering, men shouting, feet thundering up the hallway. Kirsty still screaming.

'Get her seen to!'

'Upstairs, check upstairs.'

The kitchen door burst open, kicked in, wood cleaving, a voice yelling out, 'Armed police, drop your weapons!'

'Call an ambulance!' Talbot shouted, 'And get me some cuffs!'

Out of the pandemonium rose a familiar voice. 'Will these do?'

'Yates? What the fuck are you doing here?'

'Nice to see you too, sir.' Yates crouched down beside him, flicked the cuffs open, snapped them around Joe's wrists, and smiled. 'How about I take charge of the prisoner from here?'

Slowly Talbot stood up. Shell-shocked, he surveyed the scene. His heart wouldn't slow down. Thump, thump, his head reeling, his hands starting to shake. He clutched the work-surface, felt his knees begin to cave. Slumping to the floor would not be dignified. Keep standing, whatever happens, keep upright.

'You alright, sir?' an officer called over.

Bewildered, Talbot stared at him.

'Blood, sir, on your face.'

'Fine, fine, thank you.' He looked down at Melanie, two officers in attendance, waiting for medics. She was so very pale. Shit, they should have thought, brought an ambulance, just in case. 'It's hers,' he said, lifting his fingers to smear the blood. Moving round the table, he started to bark out orders. 'Gun, down there! Bag it. Kitchen table, don't touch it. I want it sent to forensics. Blood match with the head in my garden. Pull this place to pieces. Find the murder weapon. Every knife, every tool in the outbuildings…'

'Jake, Jake.' Yates spoke quietly into his ear. 'It's okay, we've got a good team, we'll take over from here.'

Looking him in the eye, Talbot said, 'Are you up to the job?'

'Yes, sir.' Placing an arm gently behind Talbot's back, Yates guided him out of the kitchen. 'Bailey gave me a right dressing down.'

'That's always fun,' Talbot said, and halted at the sitting room door. Leaning against the doorframe, he lit a cigarette. Several officers were gazing open-mouthed as a photographer recorded the scene. A peculiar layer of smoke hung in the air, creepy in its wispiness, choking where it tangled together in thick clumps. There was no fresh air amidst the acrid smell of burning flesh and vomit. Limbs lay on a black sheet of polythene in front of the open fire. An arm, part of a leg, a foot, a hand, choice chops, neatly cut, pink and red and exuding a strange aroma as they basked in front of the flames. Char-grilled remains filled the grate. 'Poor Kirsty. Poor kid.'

'She's being looked after,' Yates assured him.

Talbot nodded. Perhaps she'd go the same way as Anna, her mind pushed into far-off places that were safer than reality.

On the edge of the hearth he spied a familiar shade of green.

'What's that? Down there?' He motioned the nearest officer towards it.

'Looks like half melted plastic, sir.'

'Bag it. Make a note. I want a DNA sample taken from it.'

'Sir?' The officer frowned, perplexed.

'It was a Bakelite box. Ladies used to keep their hair grips in them.'

'Bit of a long shot, sir.'

'It's the most important piece of evidence in this room,' Talbot said firmly, and wondered what Keith had set in motion by bringing it back.

FROM UPSTAIRS AN OFFICER called down, 'Is that ambulance here yet? This guy's in shock.'

'I can see it pulling in now,' Talbot shouted up. Thank Christ, they'd found George.

Leaving Yates to do his job, Talbot stepped into the freezing night air. Bloody hell, they must have cut all leave and roused the entire force. Officers were everywhere, radios buzzing; voices loud against the cold still air. Torches blazed, lights flashed, gunmetal winked. Cars filled the driveway, bumper to bumper, the lane outside choked with vehicles of every description. Wiping his face, Talbot forced his emotion back. He ditched his cigarette, pulled up his collar, and strode towards the end of the drive.

Up ahead he could see Bailey, patiently waiting at a distance while everyone got on with their jobs. Across from him a slight figure was being held at bay by two officers.

'Frankie!' he yelled, and sprinted towards him.

On seeing Talbot, the officers let him go. 'Jake! Jake! Bailey forced me,' Hayward cried.

Without caring what anyone thought, Talbot swung an arm across Hayward's shoulder and pulled him close. 'Thank God you're safe.'

'Bailey forced me,' Hayward repeated. 'I tried to ring and warn you. Bailey phoned, and phoned, and then he came round and threatened to arrest me if I didn't tell him who we'd seen driving away from your house last night.'

'It's okay, Frankie. Honestly, it is.'

'Let's go home, Jake. I can make us tea while you freshen up, and I'll build a fire…'

'Just don't cook anything on it,' Talbot murmured.

Haloed in blue light, Bailey stepped forward and offered his hand. 'Well done, Jake, excellent job.'

Talbot shook his hand and nodded, then fished his Dictaphone out of his pocket. 'Inadmissible as evidence, sir, but should make for an interesting bedtime story.'

'Gives us a head start with the questioning, Jake, well done.' Walking up the road with them, Bailey added, 'We've got Peter Charteris.'

Together they looked towards the car, where two officers guarded him. In the half-light Talbot read the anxiety etched across his face.

'You'd better let him know about Melanie.'

'We'll see to all of that,' Bailey assured him, snapped his fingers for Talbot's car keys and handed them over to Hayward. 'He's in no fit state to drive. You keep him safe, my lad. I'm trusting you with my finest resource.'

37

IN SILENCE THEY WALKED back to the car, Talbot sensing everyone's eyes upon him as he slid into the passenger seat. He shivered when a lingering hint of Peter Charteris's subtle aftershave caught in his throat. Bailey had put off his debrief until tomorrow, so for now Talbot could go home, to be looked after. Hayward fired the engine and Talbot flinched and clutched his head in his hands. That was a mistake. The stench of Melanie's blood on his fingers, around his face and staining his clothes brought the contents of his stomach lurching into his throat. He swallowed it down, sat back, and accepted the lit cigarette, hardly knowing what to do with it.

In slow motion the car ground its way across the snow and up onto the main road to Farnham, leaving behind it a stream of blue lights and bullet-vested, armed police. Fuck, he was alive. He wanted to speak, or cry, or scream; but nothing came. Adrenaline had wound him up, and then it burnt him out. He was numb.

The journey took five minutes, ten minutes; he had no way of knowing, only that it ended; and when it ended, the adrenaline discovered hidden resources and surged again. Suddenly he was awake, alert, the sight of Hayward's open front door stirring up an anger that was almost beyond his control. From the doorway a stream of yellow light stained the snow. An unmarked white van sat at the kerb, its rear doors wide open. Grey shadows cut into the yellow, and men in white boiler suits emerged carrying large cardboard boxes. Out of the door they came, like automatons, robotically following orders to search and destroy; to dismantle and remove; to not ask questions.

'Stay put,' Talbot ordered, jabbed his finger down, yanked open the car door, and ran towards the house, leaping the steps up to the front door and slamming to a halt next to a familiar figure, silhouetted in the doorway.

'You fucking bastard!' he shouted, and hit Dr Weissman square on the chin.

Reeling backwards from the blow, Weissman raised his hands to protect his face.

Talbot grabbed one of his wrists and twisted his hand aside. 'Look me in the eye, you little shit.'

Behind his rimless spectacles, Weissman's eyes watered. 'It's over.' Slowly he lowered his other hand and prised Talbot's fingers off his wrist. 'We're confiscating Hayward's LEAPP machine, and there's nothing you can do about it.'

'You can't just break into a man's home and steal his life's work, his unique technology, without recompense.'

'We can. And we are.' Now free, Weissman stepped back a pace. 'If we deem it a threat to national security.'

'Bollocks!' Instinctively, Talbot flicked out his warrant card.

'Unfortunately, for you, Detective Inspector, my authority outweighs yours. Put it away before you embarrass yourself any further.'

Belligerently, Talbot stood his ground, knowing full well they were blocking the doorway and holding up the automatons. 'Well, I've shown you mine, now you show me yours. Where's your fucking authority?'

Like wraiths unfurling from the ground, two men in full military uniform stepped out of the shadows, complete with loaded machine guns and grim expressions.

'The MOD is always top dog, Mr Talbot. You should have realised that by now.' Weissman smiled, tilted his head and motioned for his subordinates to continue their ant-like procession.

Warrant card still gripped between his fingers, Talbot watched, powerless to protect; unable to halt what his natural instinct knew was official theft. Bastards.

When two white clad men emerged from the basement struggling to man-handle Hayward's expensive plasma screen, Talbot opened his arms wide and tried to bar their path.

'For Christ's sake, that's just a fucking TV!'

'Is it?' Weissman eased Talbot aside, and hurried his men along.

From behind them a voice called out, 'Let them have it. Let them take it all!'

Talbot spun round to see Hayward standing at the bottom of the steps, fists clenched.

'It won't work for you, Weissman!' Hayward yelled. 'It only works for good people.' Suddenly he unclenched his fists, pointed and shouted, 'It's a love machine! You're full of hatred. It'll never work for you!'

'Have you tampered with it?' Weissman demanded, and before he could storm down the steps and reach Hayward, Talbot had grabbed his arm and tugged him backwards, tumbling him to the floor in a sprawling heap.

Standing over him, Talbot smiled. 'Now, how the fuck could he do that, when he had no warning of your little visit tonight?' Giving him space to stand up, Talbot jerked a thumb towards his men. 'Get your storm troopers to hurry up, get your henchmen out, and fuck off—before I wring your bloody neck.'

'We're nearly done,' Weissman said, brushed himself down, leant uncomfortably close and whispered, 'One more outburst from you and your boy won't get to see Lilly. I have the power to give, and trust me, Talbot, I have enough power in my little finger to make her disappear… forever.'

'You wouldn't dare.'

'Stand quietly, over there, and he gets to see her. Now, do as you're told.'

'There should be a law against people like you,' Talbot hissed, stepped back, and drove his hands deep into his trouser pockets.

Within ten minutes, Weissman followed the last man out into the cold night air and a fresh fall of snow that promised to cover his tracks forever.

CLOSING THE FRONT DOOR behind them, Hayward sighed heavily as he leant on it, a symbolic yet futile attempt to bar any bid for re-entry, should Weissman's henchmen wish to call again.

'I have to see if Millie's okay,' he said, and looked towards the kitchen.

'Wait,' Talbot ordered, and held his hand out. 'Give.'

Hayward giggled. 'Jake, really, you are so suspicious.' Digging into his trouser pocket, he fished out a small electronic component and placed it lovingly in Talbot's open palm. 'I suspected Weissman would try and do something as soon as Bailey started to bully me into saying who we'd seen burgling your house. I guessed then that Keith was dead.'

'Joe and Melanie killed him.' Talbot closed his fingers around the component. 'I'll keep it safe,' he promised, and smiled.

38

Leaning back, Talbot stretched and burped. 'Frankie, that is the best Christmas dinner I have ever had.'

Hayward giggled. 'You're just saying that.'

'Nope, definitely the best.' He poured Hayward more wine and helped himself to another beer. The clock on the mantelpiece ticked round to 2:15 p.m. precisely. Shit, time was pressing on.

'I've got you a present,' Hayward said joyfully, and like a child, dashed away from the table to go and fetch it.

'Frankie, you shouldn't have,' Talbot called after him. 'I haven't had time to get you anything.'

'It doesn't matter, really it doesn't.' Hayward hurried back in, struggling to carry two large flat objects beautifully wrapped in shiny red paper.

Talbot laughed and pulled himself to his feet, grinning. 'Frankie, you didn't? Kate's paintings?' Ripping the paper off, he chuckled, and grinned, and laughed. They were glorious. Stunning. Red poppies swayed in the breeze, promising sunshine and happiness forever. For a moment Talbot closed his eyes. They smelt of Kate: linseed oil and lavender.

'She was round here when you phoned,' Hayward said, his tone excited and eager to explain, now that it wouldn't give away the surprise.

'Ah, so Kate was the mysterious friend.'

'She was so frightened for me after what you said.' Hayward grinned mischievously and helped prop the canvases against the far wall, so that they could admire them. 'She wanted to take me home with her.'

'Lucky you.'

'I've invited her and Karl over tomorrow, for drinks and nibbles.'

'Frankie, that's brilliant.' Talbot sat on the sofa and lit a cigarette. They'd moved the kitchen table into the sitting room, so they could be in front of the fire; and with crackers, and Millie excited with her toys, it really did feel like Christmas. 'You've made friends,' Talbot said quietly. 'Frankie, I really am so pleased for you.'

'Oh, they're your friends, too,' Hayward insisted. With a happy sigh, he sat down, and playfully snapped his fingers for a cigarette.

The clock ticked slowly round to 2:25. Come on, come on. Yes! Talbot's phone rang out with the tune to *Mission Impossible*. He stood to answer his call, faced away as Hayward said, 'Who's *Mission Impossible*?'

Talbot raised a hand for silence. 'Uh-huh, uh-huh. Okay. Yep. Will do.'

Keeping a straight face, he tucked his phone away and said, as flatly as possible, 'I thought we'd go up and visit Anna.'

'Oh, Jake, you didn't warn me.' Hayward scowled and jumped up, filled with anxiety. 'I haven't got anything to take for her.'

'Don't fret about that.' A smile escaped from Talbot's lips. 'Come on, let's get you washed and smartened up.'

Black corduroys, chestnut roll-neck sweater, black corduroy jacket, leather shoes. Very smart. Comb hair or leave it shaggy? Shaggy was good.

'You're such a silly.' Hayward flicked Talbot's hand away. 'Stop fussing. We can't get there, anyway. You've been drinking, and so have I.'

The clock ticked round to three p.m. precisely. The doorbell rang. Bingo.

'I've arranged transport.'

Laughing and racing him to the door, Hayward gasped with delight on seeing who was there. 'Mr Stevens. Happy Christmas!'

'Merry Christmas, Frankie. You ready then, lad?' Behind Hayward's back he gave Talbot the thumbs-up, and they clambered into the cab of his van. Hayward got centre seat, being the smallest, and he grinned and laughed as they headed off down the snow-laden roads.

'I've never been in one of these before.'

'On top of the world up here,' Mr Stevens declared. 'King of the road. Here, put some music on, I've got the best Christmas CD ever.'

Slade was banging out foot-stomping, hand-clapping merriment as they pulled up outside Anna's care home in Haslemere. Talbot's heart was pounding, anxiety making his palms sweat. Dropping down onto the snow, he lit a cigarette, sent Hayward off to knock on the door, and had a quiet word with Stevens before going in.

'Give me a buzz when you're ready,' Stevens said in a hushed whisper.

Discreetly, Talbot pressed a bundle of notes into his hand.

'No rush,' Stevens assured him. 'One Christmas without a bevy won't kill me.'

'Thanks, I'll get you a case of your favourite.'

Ditching the fag, Talbot went and joined Hayward. 'You look terrific,' he said and Hayward laughed, abashed.

In the lobby two nurses were waiting for them, all smiles and silly Santa earrings. Out of a room on the right, Helen appeared, looking festive in a maroon and cream suit, her hand outstretched to greet Hayward.

'My friend Helen,' Talbot said, and nearly died as Hayward cringed under her embrace. He wasn't going to make it. He just wasn't going to cope. Talbot swallowed hard.

From the wings, two nurses appeared, laden with goodies.

'I knew you wouldn't be happy without bringing a gift,' Talbot said, and helped load him up with a bouquet of flowers, a box of chocolates, and a bottle of champagne.

Trembling, Hayward met Talbot's gaze. 'A dozen red roses. And where did you find a heart-shaped box of chocolates?'

'Father Christmas.'

'I'm not going to visit Anna, am I?' Hayward's voice trembled.

'No, Frankie. We'll see her later.' Placing his hands gently on Hayward's shoulders, he turned him to face the door opposite. On cue one of the nurses went over and opened it. Inside, lights sparkled on a Christmas tree, and an old lady stood by a chair, her arms open wide, inviting Hayward to run to her.

Looping her hand under his elbow, Helen said softly, 'Come on, Frankie. Let's go and visit Lilly.'

About the Author

Novelist Toni Allen was born in London and brought up under the sound of jumbo jets in Bedfont, and later, Ashford, Middlesex. Even though she learned to read at an early age, she was never keen to sit still with a book, much preferring to walk along the river bank at the end of her garden and make up stories in her head. At junior school, her teacher read the classics out loud, a chapter a day, as an end-of-day story. Heroes, as in *The Three Musketeers,* and troubled souls, such as Scrooge, fired Toni's imagination, and furthered her lifelong interest in storytelling.

Now, having been a professional Tarot reader and astrologer for thirty years, Toni brings personal awareness of the paranormal to her debut mystery novel, *Visiting Lilly.*

She is frequently invited to be an after-dinner speaker and radio performer. Her stories grab people's attention: the fascinating facts of what she sees in practice, from ghostly visitations, to stunned reactions when predictions come true. This wealth of knowledge, from both the believer and non-believer's point of view, is subtly woven into her fiction.

Toni is also the author of two non-fiction books, *The System of Symbols: A New Way to Look at Tarot*, and *Sex & Tarot. The System of Symbols* is published in Italy by *Spazio Interiore* as *Il Sistema dei Simboli.* In addition, she has had numerous non-fiction articles published, and has won awards for short fiction and poetry.

When she isn't working, writing, or presenting workshops on astrology and Tarot, Toni enjoys walking in the beautiful Surrey countryside, taking photographs of the local wildlife.

www.ToniAllenBooks.com

Coming in 2015

SAVING ANNA

MORE GREAT READS
FROM BOOKTROPE

No Shelter from Darkness by **Mark D. Evans** (Paranormal) In the post-Blitz East End of London, orphaned teenager Beth Wade is bullied for looking different. But it goes far deeper than looks. With a growing thirst for blood and the arrival of a man who could kill her just as easily as help her, Beth must fight for control of her life... and of herself.

Outside the Spotlight by **Sophie Weeks** (Fiction) In a world created by human ingenuity and dreams, Isabella has lived in Christmas for over four hundred years. But when she seeks a vacation and visits the foreign genre of Mystery, she discovers that the world of ideas is more dangerous than it seems. If an idea is murdered, does it bleed?

The Stories We Don't Tell by **Melissa Thayer** (Fiction) When fate gives Nick an existence he can barely recognize, he searches for meaning in the future he wishes existed, and attempts to escape a past that cannot be told save for in the pages of a faded memory.

What Echoes Render by **Tamsen Schultz** (Romantic Suspense) There's a killer in Windsor intent on making Jesse Baker burn for the sins of others. But arson investigator David Hathaway isn't about to let that happen. As the past echoes through their lives, will they remember that history, like fire, can give life just as easily as it can destroy it?

Discover more books and learn about our
new approach to publishing at **www.booktrope.com**.

Lightning Source UK Ltd.
Milton Keynes UK
UKOW03f1401191014

240301UK00002B/32/P